Praise for Lexi Blake and Masters and Mercenaries...

"I can always trust Lexi Blake's Dominants to leave me breathless...and in love. If you want sensual, exciting BDSM wrapped in an awesome love story, then look for a Lexi Blake book."

~Cherise Sinclair USA Today Bestselling author

"Lexi Blake's MASTERS AND MERCENARIES series is beautifully written and deliciously hot. She's got a real way with both action and sex. I also love the way Blake writes her gorgeous Dom heroes--they make me want to do bad, bad things. Her heroines are intelligent and gutsy ladies whose taste for submission definitely does not make them dish rags. Can't wait for the next book!"

~Angela Knight, New York Times bestselling author

"A Dom is Forever is action packed, both in the bedroom and out. Expect agents, spies, guns, killing and lots of kink as Liam goes after the mysterious Mr. Black and finds his past and his future… The action and espionage keep this story moving along quickly while the sex and kink provides a totally different type of interest. Everything is very well balanced and flows together wonderfully."

~A Night Owl "Top Pick", Terri, Night Owl Erotica

"A Dom Is Forever is everything that is good in erotic romance. The story was fast-paced and suspenseful, the characters were flawed but made me root for them every step of the way, and the hotness factor was off the charts mostly due to a bad boy Dom with a penchant for dirty talk."

~Rho, The Romance Reviews

"A good read that kept me on my toes, guessing until the big reveal, and thinking survival skills should be a must for all men."

~Chris, Night Owl Reviews

"I can't get enough of the Masters and Mercenaries Series! Love and Let Die is Lexi Blake at her best! She writes erotic romantic suspense like no other, and I am always extremely excited when she has something new for us! Intense, heart pounding, and erotically fulfilling, I could not put this book down."

~ Shayna Renee, Shayna Renee's Spicy Reads

"Certain authors and series are on my auto-buy list. Lexi Blake and her Masters & Mercenaries series is at the top of that list... this book offered everything I love about a Masters & Mercenaries book – alpha men, hot sex and sweet loving… As long as Ms. Blake continues to offer such high quality books, I'll be right there, ready to read."

~ Robin, Sizzling Hot Books

"I have absolutely fallen in love with this series. Spies, espionage, and intrigue all packaged up in a hot dominant male package. All the men at McKay-Taggart are smoking hot and the women are amazingly strong sexy submissives."

~Kelley, Smut Book Junkie Book Reviews

A View to a Thrill

Other Books by Lexi Blake

EROTIC ROMANCE

Masters And Mercenaries
The Dom Who Loved Me
The Men With The Golden Cuffs
A Dom Is Forever
On Her Master's Secret Service
Sanctum: A Masters and Mercenaries Novella
Love and Let Die
Unconditional: A Masters and Mercenaries Novella
Dungeon Royale
Dungeon Games: A Masters and Mercenaries Novella
A View to a Thrill
Cherished: A Masters and Mercenaries Novella, *Coming October 28, 2014*
You Only Love Twice, *Coming February 17, 2015*

Masters Of Ménage (by Shayla Black and Lexi Blake)
Their Virgin Captive
Their Virgin's Secret
Their Virgin Concubine
Their Virgin Princess
Their Virgin Hostage
Their Virgin Secretary
Their Virgin Mistress, *Coming April 14, 2015*

CONTEMPORARY WESTERN ROMANCE

Wild Western Nights
Leaving Camelot, *Coming Soon*

URBAN FANTASY

Thieves
Steal the Light
Steal the Day
Steal the Moon
Steal the Sun
Steal the Night
Ripper, A Thieves Novel, *Coming January 20, 2015*

A View to a Thrill

Masters and Mercenaries
Book 7

Lexi Blake

A View to a Thrill
Masters and Mercenaries, Book 7
Lexi Blake

Published by DLZ Entertainment LLC

Edited by Chloe Vale
eBook ISBN: 978-1-937608-29-3

McKay-Taggart logo design by Charity Hendry

Acknowledgements

Thanks to my team—editor Chloe Vale, beta readers Riane Holt and Stormy Pate and the wonderful Liz Berry and Fiona Archer for all the help in getting this book ready to go. I also thank my husband and kids and the amazing Top Griz for his service to our country and for sharing his knowledge with writers.

Prologue

The village of Norsely, England
Thirty-one years ago

Simon opened the door from the garden. The light of day seemed to fade away as he moved into the house. Quiet. It seemed too quiet, but then he had to be quiet when the tours came through. Every now and then his mother would walk through the hallways with a group of people he didn't know, telling them all about the house, though she always neglected to show them the best parts. She showed the people the grand parlor, but never the football goals their father had set up for him and Clive. She didn't even show them the smashing new game room with toys and a table where he could play tennis with his brother.

Though Clive was always tired now.

He ran through the halls, his feet pounding against the wood floors as he moved from light to shadow with each window. His brother used to play a game with him. They would try to jump from the patches of light the big windows made just before afternoon turned to dusk. They would leap over the shadows in between and most often one of them would fall and laughter would ensue, and their father would sometimes join them calling them little monkeys and tickling them until they couldn't breathe.

"Simon?"

He stopped at the sound of his mother's voice. He turned and she was standing in front of the hall that led to the family rooms. She never took people down that hallway. It was for them, she said. The rest of the house could be for history, but that wing was their home.

"Mummy." He raced toward her. She'd been gone all day. They'd all been gone. "Where's Dad and Clive?"

She got to one knee, and he could suddenly see the lines on her face. She always looked pretty, but there were little black streaks around her eyes now and her mouth had a grim turn. "They're upstairs. Clive is resting, but your father is packing."

"Where are we going?"

She shook her head. "You're staying here, love. You start school in a few weeks. I'll try to come back to help get you settled, but if I can't, then Nanny Deborah will make sure you get to school."

"Where are you going?"

"To London. We're taking your brother there. Clive is very sick, Simon."

Sick? Clive always seemed sick. He wasn't sure how going to London would help, but it was all right with him. He just didn't want to be left behind. "I can go to London, too. I can help."

She sniffled and then stood up. "I'm sorry. I think it's best you stay here, love. It will be very boring in London. When school starts you'll be busy, so busy you won't have time to worry. That's what I want for you. Normalcy. You need normalcy." She squared her shoulders. "We'll be back in a few weeks so we should see you at the next holiday."

Holiday? But that was months away.

"But I want to go with you," he said. He suddenly felt very small. Like he wasn't really there at all.

His mother shook her head. "It's decided. You have to be strong. Your father and I want what's best for you and that isn't living in some hospital for months at a time. Your brother loves you. He wants you to have a normal life. None of us wants you affected by this."

By cancer. He'd heard the word. Clive had cancer and cancer was a bad thing. But it was affecting him because he was being left behind.

He nodded though because crying wasn't the Weston way. Westons stuck together. That was what his father said.

Except he seemed to be the only Weston not sticking together.

His mum kissed his forehead and turned down the hall, her heels clicking as she walked toward the place where his father was likely packing up for the trip.

Simon sat on the bench in front of the big windows and watched as the light faded. It didn't matter that he was five. He had to be brave. He had to be strong.

Because he suddenly understood that he was alone.

* * * *

North Carolina coast, USA
Seventeen Years Ago

Chelsea ran, her bare feet sinking into the sand. It was hot, but she was used to it. She was a beach baby, as her momma said. She'd lived her whole life close to the ocean.

"Chelsea!"

She turned and saw her sister. Charlotte's hair whipped behind her as she ran to catch up. She had sneakers in her hand, her feet still wet from splashing through the waves.

"Hi. Were you with your boyfriend?" She used a little

singsong voice, absolutely sure to make her sister crazy.

Charlotte's nose wrinkled up. "Ewww, gross. Bobby is not my boyfriend."

"He looks like your boyfriend."

"Does not."

"Does, too." Charlotte spent entirely too much time with the pimply faced kid. And his feet smelled.

"He's just a friend. Trust me. When I get married someday I'm going to marry a man who treats me like a princess."

Chelsea smiled. This was one of their favorite games. Someday. Someday Charlotte would be a lawyer or doctor or actress, depending on the day. Chelsea knew what she wanted to be. A teacher. She wanted to be just like her mom and teach little kids all about how to read. She wasn't sure she needed to get married. Her mom didn't need a man.

Still, sometimes she thought it would be nice. Sometimes she thought Momma was lonely. She caught her every now and then reading a book of poetry and crying.

It's just because it's so lovely, dear. The poems remind me how much I love you.

Someday she was going to read those poems.

But now it was just fun to tease her sister. "I don't think Bobby is a prince."

They started walking toward the little cottage on the beach that had been their home for as long as Chelsea could remember.

"Someday, I'm going to marry a handsome man who is polite to everyone around him." She turned around, her arms out as she made a full circle before starting to walk again. "And everyone will love him. He'll be the sweetest guy in the world."

Charlotte would find that man. Her sister was the sweetest girl in the world, and she deserved the best guy possible. A man who would love her and treat her gently.

If she ever got married, Chelsea wanted someone smart and kind and who would never, ever hurt her.

"Whose car is that?" Charlotte stopped, her hand going up over her eyes, shielding them from the sun.

Chelsea looked up and there was a big black SUV parked next to their clunky station wagon. A man stood at the front, his face turned toward their little cottage. She caught the glint of metal at his waist, but she wasn't sure what the sun was catching. His belt maybe.

Charlotte reached for her hand. "I don't know. He looks scary. Maybe we should go to the Johnsons."

Chelsea slipped out of her sister's grasp because there was a roll in her gut. Something was wrong. Her mother only had female friends and none of their husbands drove ominous black SUVs. She started to run, the sand dragging her down, but she knew she had to get to her mother.

"Chelsea," Charlotte said beside her. "Chelsea, Momma told me to hide if we ever thought strange men were after us."

Men with accents. Her mother had told her the same thing, but these men didn't seem to be after her and her sister. They were in the house with Momma. Chelsea had to know. She couldn't run and hide when her mother was there. She didn't think, simply acted, running toward the house she'd known her whole life, the place where she'd been safe.

She was almost up the hill when the door opened and a man stepped outside, casually wiping something off his hands. He was a big man, maybe the largest Chelsea had ever seen. He had hair like Charlotte's, blonde threaded with streaks of red, but unlike her sister, he wasn't smiling. There was a grimness that made Chelsea stop in her tracks.

Charlotte stopped beside her.

"Is that blood?" her sister whispered.

Chelsea couldn't take her eyes off the handkerchief in the man's hand. Bright-red blood marred the white fabric. Blood.

Why was he bleeding? He didn't look hurt. He was standing tall, his shoulders perfectly straight. He looked out over the beach as though searching for something. He spoke then, and Chelsea shivered at the sound.

"Найти ее."

Charlotte pulled on her hand and this time Chelsea didn't fight, but when they turned they found the way blocked.

And the sun. The massive man in front of them blocked out the sun, casting a long shadow over Chelsea and her sister. Charlotte's hand squeezed hers so tight that Chelsea's eyes filled with tears for two reasons. There was pain, but the only reason her sister would ever cause her that pain was out of fear.

Something bad was going to happen. Something very bad.

"Charlotte?" a deep voice asked.

Charlotte turned, pulling Chelsea with her. "Where's my mom?"

The big man with the accent shrugged negligently. "She's suffered an accident. I'm afraid she's gone, but I'm your father and I'm here to take you home."

Gone? Gone where? Her mother never left for long. She went to work, but someone always watched them and it wouldn't be a scary man with blood on his hands. Where had her mother gone?

She wouldn't leave them. Momma wouldn't leave.

Unless…

Chelsea saw the world through blurry eyes as the truth hit her. Gone. It was a word that adults used. She'd learned that adults had lots of words that meant more than one thing. Gone was adult speak for the truth.

Dead. Gone was dead. It was a stupid word because gone meant leaving for something, but dead was just dead. Dead was a useless word and her mom wasn't useless. Her mom couldn't be dead.

Charlotte started to struggle beside her as the big man picked her up. Their hands came undone, and Chelsea had the horrible fear that Charlotte would be gone and she wasn't sure in what way.

Charlotte kicked and screamed out Chelsea's name. She pleaded with the man taking her as Chelsea stood, her feet planted to the ground because she wasn't sure what else to do.

She closed her eyes. When a dream got bad, she had to remind herself that it was only a nightmare and that she could wake herself up. She was going to wake up. Tears squeezed from her eyes, dripping down her cheeks like warm rain.

Let me wake up. Wake up. Wake up.

When she woke up, Momma would be there making breakfast and Charlotte would say she didn't like Bobby even though Chelsea was sure she did. The screaming would stop when she woke up. The crying would stop.

"Bring the other girl. She could prove useful," a dark voice said.

A hand wrapped around her arm, and Chelsea opened her eyes. A man with a huge scar running down his face frowned down at her as she heard a car door slam.

"I'm sorry, little one. If it were up to me I would reunite you with your mother quickly. It looks like fate has other plans. Come along." He started to walk, seeming not to mind when she stumbled.

Her feet hit the concrete, skin tearing in little streaks of pain and blood. She tried to keep up, tried to make her legs move faster, but it was useless.

She was shoved into the car. Immediately her sister was there, arms going around Chelsea.

She huddled in the car with Charlotte as it took off. She looked back, the little cottage fading into the distance, and wondered if she would ever see it again.

Chapter One

"Someone's trying to kill me."

Simon Weston tried to let the words settle on his brain, closing the door as Chelsea walked through. Chelsea Dennis, otherwise known as Denisovitch, the daughter of former Russian mobster Vladimir Denisovitch and niece to the recently deceased head of the Denisovitch Syndicate. Recently deceased because Simon's boss, Ian Taggart, had taken care of the fucker. Simon often wished he'd been the one to stick a blade in the bastard's heart.

He turned and couldn't help but stare. Chelsea wasn't the most beautiful woman he'd ever met and yet she stopped him in his tracks. He'd escorted some of the world's great beauties on red carpets and to royal events, but it was a little criminal mastermind who got his cock hard just by walking in a room. She wasn't exactly plain, either. With chestnut-brown hair and a petite figure, she was actually quite pretty until one noticed her hips and ass. Those catapulted her into goddess territory. Anything she lacked in the tit department was more than made up for with that healthy ass and curvy hips a man could hang on to while he fucked deep inside.

If he could stop wanting her, he would, but he hadn't managed that trick yet. From the moment he'd seen her all those months ago, he'd been utterly fascinated. She was a mystery to him. Closed off, with more barricades around her than he could count, she still pulled him in the minute she walked in a room. And every time he got close to her, she smacked him with a *No Trespassing* sign right upside his head.

Unfortunately, he was a man who liked a challenge and he was definitely a man who never, ever learned his lesson. She was in his home without her sister to hide behind. She seemed to need him for something. The very idea made his dick hard. His stupid bloody cock was nothing but a puppy ready to play around her.

He closed the door behind her. "What exactly do you mean?"

He had to ask. Sometimes when she talked she spoke in an odd geek speak he didn't always understand. She could mean something entirely different, something innocuous.

God, he hoped this was a joke.

She turned, though her eyes went to anywhere but him. She looked around, seemingly curious about her surroundings. Given her wariness around him, it wasn't surprising she'd never been in his condo. He'd been in hers the day they'd met. He'd dragged her out of it. It might not have been the most auspicious of beginnings. "I mean that I got a little bomb sent to my apartment."

"What?" He managed not to shout.

She finally caught his eyes. "Don't worry about it. I defused the sucker. I just thought maybe I should find someplace safer to sleep tonight. Whoever it is, he knows where I live. What's your Internet like? Please tell me you have wireless."

She was awfully calm for a woman who had just escaped being blown up. His heart, on the other hand, was thundering in his chest, his blood pressure ticking up ominously. "You need to repeat that for me and this time I would like the story in much greater detail."

She turned those big green eyes on him, her bottom lip disappearing behind her teeth. It was a nervous habit. She was full of them. He'd catalogued every single one, from the way her good leg bounced when she was anxious to how often she braided and unbraided her hair when she was bored. “Simon, I know this seems weird, but I don’t have anywhere else to go. I can’t go to Charlotte’s. Ian would be up my ass in no time, and I don’t have anything to tell him yet. It would make Charlotte freak out, and I don’t need her to get any more overly protective. I can’t go to the others. They all have kids or they’re trying to have kids, except Jesse, who freaks me out a little.”

So he was her absolute rock-bottom last choice besides Jesse Murdoch, who sometimes became a raging lunatic ball of murder. That wasn’t so surprising. She turned away from him every chance she could. He hated the fact that every time she did it, it felt like a kick in his gut. “So you came here because you can’t go to Ian and I’m sure you want to avoid the police. Otherwise it would have been smarter to call them when you got a bloody bomb sent to your condo.”

“Oh, I didn’t have time to call,” she explained. “It was on a thirty-second timer. The minute I opened it, the timer began. Luckily it was a fairly simple setup. Still, I got pretty nervous when that sucker hit five seconds.”

She was going to give him a heart attack. “Where is the bomb?”

“I left it behind. I kind of just picked up my bug-out bag and came here.” She hefted the backpack off her shoulder and set it on the floor. It made her breasts move against her T-shirt. They were small, graceful and delicate. They would likely be very sensitive. He lay in bed at night and wondered if he could make her come just by sucking on her nipples.

He forced his brain off her tits. The fact that she even had a bug-out bag should scare the shit out of him. “Where’s your car?”

If someone had followed her, he needed to know about it. She likely hadn’t had time to check for locator devices.

Her eyes slid away from his. “I didn’t bring it with me. I hopped on a train and then I walked.”

She didn’t walk many places. Her leg gave her hell and she’d never done the work to strengthen it. A nasty suspicion took root in his gut. “Why?”

Her eyes slid away. “It seemed like the right thing to do.”

A lie. He couldn't afford to put up with that. She was in trouble, and if she'd come to him then she was likely in serious trouble. He had no illusions that she would attempt to take control, and if he allowed her to, she would treat him like an employee. He had no intention of being her lackey. If she wanted his protection, she would accept that he was in charge. Of bloody everything.

He moved into her space, watching her every movement. He wondered if this wasn't why he was so fascinated with her. He'd never watched a woman, taken such utter care in knowing how she reacted, the way he did with Chelsea. He'd spent hours simply studying her face, the expressions, the little lines she got when she was angry or sad. She tried to pretend nothing ever got to her, to pretend she wasn't hurt or upset, but Simon knew what to look for and she was scared. It was there in the little tremble in her fingers.

"Chelsea, was there a bomb on your car?"

"Yeah," she said, muttering under her breath. "I ran a mirror under it. It's a force of habit. I spotted it and left it where it was. Hopefully whoever it is thinks I'm still at my place."

He cursed and turned away because that wasn't the likeliest scenario. "They were probably watching you. Chelsea, they very likely followed you here."

Her eyes flared, her little chin coming up in a stubborn pout. "I was careful. I know how to get rid of a tail. They didn't follow me. It's not a big deal, Weston. If you don't want me here, I can go find a motel. I have a couple of cards that shouldn't be traceable."

Because she always kept a few extra identities on her just in case she had to run on a moment's notice, whether from the authorities or from her unsavory connections.

"This is because you lied to all of us and haven't gotten out of the business." Information brokering. It was how Chelsea had made her money for years.

"That's not true. I haven't done anything Satan didn't ask me to do."

Ian. When they'd been in Europe, he'd discovered Ian had requested that Chelsea keep up some of her connections on the

Deep Web so he could find information. He and Ian were going to have a talk. It likely wouldn't go well. The fact that he didn't really have any right to complain nagged at him. Chelsea wasn't his. By all rights, Ian had more right to protect her since she was his sister-in-law. "I want to know everyone you've talked to in the last six months. I want access to every record you have."

Whoever it was, they'd taken no chances. They'd had a backup plan. Someone really wanted her in pieces.

She turned her chin up, a stubborn look settling in her eyes. "This was a mistake. Just tell my sister I'll call her when I figure this shit out."

"You're not going anywhere."

The tears that suddenly sheened her eyes damn near killed him. "I didn't know where else to go. I really don't have another place here in Texas. I've never been on my own before. I can pay you."

Oh, he could come up with a hundred different ways she could pay him, none of them having a thing to do with money. "We'll talk about that later. You look pale. Have you eaten?"

"No. I found the stupid bomb this morning when I got home from the airport. I've been running all over Dallas ever since. I rode the train for hours. I actually went to Fort Worth and came back here to make sure I wasn't being followed," she said as she turned and started to walk into his living room. Bloody hell. His cousins were still here. The minute she'd shown up, he'd forgotten all about them.

They'd shown up this afternoon because he hadn't been out to see them in months, and now he had to find a way to get rid of them.

"Hello, pretty lady," a low voice said. Damn it. JT pretty much hit on anything with breasts. Chelsea could take flirting poorly. She'd been physically abused by her father, and from what her sister had told him, she was afraid of men. His cousin could be a bit over the top.

He hurried behind her in an attempt to put himself between the two.

"Hi." Chelsea's voice came out a little breathy.

"I'm JT, Simon's cousin, and this is my far less attractive

brother, Michael." JT was on his feet, his hand held out.

Chelsea giggled. She actually giggled. She never, ever giggled. Laughed at him from time to time, but this was a girlish, flirty sound he'd never heard from her before. She stepped up and placed her hand in JT's. "He looks like he's your twin."

"I'm definitely the prettier one." Brooding Michael was on his feet, too, giving Chelsea a charming smile.

Chelsea turned and shook Michael's hand as well. If she was scared because there were two massive walls of masculine flesh surrounding her, he couldn't tell. She simply flashed a gorgeous smile and looked between the two of them. "Uhm, identical, much? Sure I see that JT has longer hair, but I think that's because he was smart enough to avoid the Special Forces."

Michael chuckled, absolutely unperturbed. "Hey, I can't help that I'm a military man. Big brother there was always too fond of cow shit to leave the ranch."

"That's no way to talk about the future CEO of Malone Oil," Chelsea chided.

JT's grin faded. "How did you know that?"

Michael shot his brother a superior look. "Because she has way more in common with me, brother. She does her homework. It's nice to meet you, Chelsea Denisovitch. Or do you prefer Dennis? Or The Broker?"

Simon stepped in. "Do you want to explain how you even know that term has any correlation to her, Michael?"

Chelsea had stiffened a bit, and Simon was deeply satisfied with the way she stepped back toward him. "I think I was right about the Special Forces, but it looks like your cousin is involved with the Agency, too."

JT tilted his head, obviously not following the conversation. "I'm a little confused."

Because he was the smart one who hadn't gone into the intelligence field. Michael had mentioned earlier in the evening that the CIA was sniffing around him, but if he knew who "The Broker" was, it was more than a quick sniff. "You've been working for Tennessee Smith. He wouldn't have talked to you about her if you hadn't already said yes to him. He's the devil, you know."

Maybe that was laying it on a bit thick, but he didn't like the fact that Ten was still thinking about Chelsea, still wondering if she or Charlotte had been the powerful information broker who had been responsible for taking down numerous arms dealers and human traffickers. Charlotte had attempted to take all the credit, but Simon knew it had always been Chelsea. Tennessee Smith was what the Agency liked to call "a handler." He was the man who recruited and sent agents out into the field. He'd been Ian Taggart's handler, and roughly six months before he'd made an attempt to bring Chelsea into the fold.

If Chelsea went into government intelligence, she would be lost forever. She was an addict. She craved the power she got the minute she touched a computer. If she got a whiff of the kind of power Ten could offer her, she would be lost to a world Simon wouldn't be able to rescue her from.

Michael stepped back, crossing his arms over his chest in a show of defensiveness that came right out of their childhood. Michael had never taken well to having his actions questioned. "Just because it didn't work out for you with MI6 doesn't mean I have to sit on the sidelines, cousin. You can keep your opinions about my career to yourself."

And there it was. He was a fuckup. He screwed up everything. He'd mishandled an operation and that was why he no longer worked intelligence.

"Didn't work out with MI6?" Chelsea looked up at him. "What is he talking about?"

Michael seemed to understand he'd stepped over a line. "Nothing. I didn't mean a thing."

"He's referring to the fact that I mishandled a case and got myself reprimanded. I chose to quit rather than wait for Damon to fire me. Luckily Tag needed someone with British connections." Cold. He needed to remain utterly cold. His cousin was right. It wasn't his business and no one wanted his counsel.

Chelsea turned on Michael. "Are you trying to imply that Simon did something wrong on the United One Fund case? Because you're wrong. I've read that case and he did everything he could. How the hell was he supposed to know Charlotte faked her death? All he had was the fact that Ian Taggart's wife had died and there was a massive cover-up around it. If you had that information, wouldn't you act on it? It's damn easy for a green agent to question the actions of a superior one, but you better back down because Damon Knight would never have fired him. He's not a stupid man. Your cousin, on the other hand, can be a bit of a drama queen."

Simon frowned. She'd read the reports about the UOF case? And she was defending him? And what the hell did she mean by drama queen?

JT grinned as he sank back into his chair. "I would watch it, Mike. She looks like she's ready to take you down. I wouldn't insult Simon there when he's got such a fierce protector."

Michael's arms came down, his shoulders relaxing. "I'm sorry. To both of you. And I'm really not totally a hundred percent sure about working with Ten. I shouldn't even be talking about the job."

JT stared at his brother. "Those friends of yours who are out at the ranch, do they have anything to do with the Agency?"

Michael shook his head. "Like I said, I'm not going to talk about this."

JT turned to Simon as though he could do anything about it. "He's got a couple of Navy buddies out at the ranch this week. He's using the guesthouse and I'm supposed to give them space or some shit. I thought he was just partying. Soldiers work damn hard and they play hard, too. I stayed away so he could blow off some steam with his friends. Now I'm wondering if he's not meeting with the Agency. I don't know that I like that happening on my land."

Michael's eyes narrowed. "The last time I checked, the Circle M still belonged to our father. You want to take it up with him? Like I said, stay out of my business, big brother, and I'll stay out of yours."

Chelsea frowned as she turned his way. "They're pleasant."

"They're leaving." He needed to get his cousins out of here. He couldn't do a damn thing to figure out what was going on with Chelsea until they were alone.

The doorbell rang.

Chelsea stiffened, her eyes going for the door.

Shit. It was probably his food, but he couldn't take that chance now. And he couldn't hide it from his cousins. In this case, he definitely preferred Michael to JT. "Are you carrying?"

Michael's whole face slid from angry to blank in a second. He reached around and pulled a SIG Sauer out of its holster at the small of his back. "Trouble?"

"Probably not. It's probably Kung Pao chicken and two egg rolls, but it's a rough neighborhood." It was an upscale neighborhood. They wouldn't buy it, but he had to let them know he wasn't going to discuss it.

JT's eyes had gone wide. "Why the hell are you carrying a gun?"

Chelsea had pulled her Ruger and was expertly checking the clip. "Why the hell aren't you carrying a gun?" She looked up at Simon. "I'll stay here with the cowboy."

At least she wasn't going to fight him. Simon nodded to the door and Michael moved across the floor on utterly silent feet. He got behind the door, ready to take care of whatever was on the opposite side.

Simon couldn't risk looking through the peephole. He opened the door with a quick motion and prayed Michael followed his lead.

He didn't need to be worried. A thin young man who couldn't be more than nineteen stood in the hallway, holding out a paper bag. "You ordered the beef and broccoli?"

Nothing was going right with his day. "Sure."

* * * *

"Should I call the police?" JT Malone kept his voice down but there was no way to miss the worry there. He was a future CEO. Chelsea was sure his day was made up of reports and checking the company stock. He very likely had never had anyone send him a bomb. His green eyes were tight with tension. He was what her sister would undoubtedly call smoking hot. With thick black hair and a lean body, there was no doubt Jackson Tyrell ranked heavy on the delicious scale, but somehow he couldn't compete with Simon's urbane good looks. JT fit the all-American cowboy mode, but Simon was a mystery. There was a dirty Dom under all that metro finery. It made her want to strip him down and figure out just what made him tick.

"I think Simon can handle it." She could hear him talking, asking how much he owed. Her stomach rumbled at the thought of food. She hadn't eaten on the plane and then she'd pretty much run around Dallas for hours hoping no one murdered her. No time for tacos.

She lowered her gun. It didn't look like she would need it.

What was she doing here? God, she should have just taken off the minute she realized someone was after her. Why was she here?

You know why you're here. When that stupid bomb was about to blow up, all you could think about was him. You're here because you don't want to die without knowing what it feels like to be with him just once. You've been looking for any reason to hop into bed with him even though you know it's a terrible idea.

"I don't like this at all. This is wrong." JT moved in front of her. "You should be the one standing back. I should protect you."

So he was a women-and-children-first kind of guy. It didn't surprise her. It kind of went with the cowboy motif. If he was anything like his cousin, he was a heroic, self-sacrificing guy—the kind that she'd been sure didn't exist anymore and maybe never had. They'd been a myth until she'd found McKay-Taggart and their band of Dommy men. Unfortunately, she couldn't indulge JT.

"I'm the one with the firearm and the knowledge of its use," Chelsea explained. "Have you ever shot anyone?"

"Hell, no, but that doesn't mean I don't know how to use a gun. I've lived on a ranch all my life. I don't go out without a shotgun."

Naïve. "There's more to shooting a man than knowing how to fire. It's different than killing a coyote. There's a certain coldness that comes with pulling the trigger on another human being."

She'd felt it several times before. She'd felt that cold seep over her when her father's man came for her that night. She'd felt it again when she'd buried the man's body and cleaned up the blood. Sometimes, she could still see the blood on her hands. So dark against the color of her skin.

"You just went white." Simon was suddenly in her space. "What the hell did you do?"

She glanced up, and he wasn't looking at her. His angry question had been directed at his cousin.

JT Malone shook his head, his hands held up. "Nothing. I did absolutely nothing and that's the problem. I told her I should be the one protecting her, not the other way around. She should have given me the gun and stayed down, though I'm not sure why she needed protecting from the delivery guy. Is she allergic to MSG?"

Simon's eyes narrowed. "Perhaps I overreacted. But she's not giving up that gun to anyone. Is that understood? Now, I believe Chelsea's come to speak to me on rather urgent business. I have to cut our chat short. I'll call you in a couple of days."

"I don't think that's a good idea. I think we should stay." JT looked at his cousin. "I don't know what the hell is going on, but I don't like a minute of it. I think we should call someone in. If you're so worried you won't answer the door without backup, something has to be done about it. We'll call in the police or the feds. I've got contacts."

Michael groaned. "This is Simon's gig. You can't play the CEO card with him."

"He's my family," JT replied with a stubborn look. "You watch me. I know you two think I'm the soft one, but I can be a ruthless bastard when I want to be. I will protect this family with everything I have."

Simon softened slightly. "I'm asking you to let me handle my own business, JT. This is my territory. If I need help, I will ask you."

"Come on, brother. I think he can handle it. He's not the same skinny kid who showed up at the house thirty years ago. You don't have to protect him anymore. The same goes for me." Michael put a hand on his brother's shoulder. "Let's go get a beer and we'll talk."

With obvious reluctance, JT Malone allowed himself to be hustled out the door.

She'd known Simon had cousins here in Texas, but seeing them, being in a room with them, made it more real. So often he was some sort of god in her head. Cool, calm, collected. Infinitely sexy. He was damn perfect in her mind.

And he'd been a skinny little kid who needed protecting. She'd needed protecting, too. She remembered clinging to her sister's hand during the flight from North Carolina to Moscow. They'd watched their father kill their mother and then they'd only had each other.

"I'm sorry about that." Simon moved to the big bar in his kitchen and started unloading the bag he'd set there. "My family can be a bit overbearing at times."

"They love you." That was obvious. She'd made a study of Simon, but the truth wasn't always in data. It was the frustrating thing about life. Data, information, numbers were her specialty, but while she'd known about Simon's ties to Malone Oil, she hadn't counted on the fact that Jackson Tyrell Malone, billionaire heir to what amounted to an American kingdom, would truly love and want to protect his family. Or that his family would buck and fight against the constraints of that protection.

"Of course they do. They're my family." He brought down a plate and began to spoon food onto it.

That was easy for him to say. Family hadn't been so easy for her. Just thinking about her "family" made her leg ache. Of course the damn thing ached all the time, and running around the Metroplex for eight hours hadn't improved the condition. She needed a distraction, and work was her drug of choice. "What's your wireless password?"

She needed to get on the web and continue her investigation. Whoever was pissed at her likely had blabbed to someone else. There were always tracks. Always hints and clues there for a smart girl to connect.

"Eat."

"That's a terrible password." They had to work on his security. A password should be something utterly random. At least seven characters long, and with a myriad of numbers, letters, and symbols. Too many people made the mistake of choosing something meaningful to them like "ilovedan" or "cutekitty." Yeah, those suckers got hacked and fast.

She dragged out her computer. It was a lightweight laptop she'd had custom made and kitted out to do things ninety-nine percent of computers couldn't. She had a hotspot, too, but it was almost out of charge. She'd run through her backup battery. Where to set up? She was going to be up all night, so she might as well make herself comfy. If she was smart, she could figure the whole damn thing out by morning and Charlotte never had to know how her baby sister had fucked up again.

A shadow fell across her screen. She glanced up, hating the way her breath hitched. He loomed over her. Simon, in all his suited up and very British glory. He'd ditched the coat, but his tie was still in place. The white dress shirt he was wearing couldn't hide the lean, muscular lines of his body. She was alone with Simon. Simon, with his sandy hair and deep blue eyes and shoulders that seemed to go on for days.

"Put the computer away and come and eat."

"I can eat while I work." It damn near hurt to look at him so she let her gaze drift back to her screen.

A big hand came out and flipped the screen down. "You will sit down like a civilized person and eat until I'm satisfied and then we'll have a chat about how this is going to work."

Damn him. He was using his Dom voice on her, the dark, rich commanding tone he used on the subs at Sanctum. The one he'd used on her when they'd played together in The Garden. Play. It was a stupid word to describe what had happened between them. It hadn't felt like play. It felt real and powerful and serious, and that was why she shouldn't be here.

Do you know how I could make you feel?

She still heard him growling the words at her, offering to take her to an aftercare room. He'd asked her to give over to him, but she couldn't. Not that way. She did know exactly how he could make her feel. Vulnerable. Lost. Aching.

"Simon, I've thought about this and I just need a place to stay for the night. Maybe two, tops. Just let me do a little digging and I'll get out of your hair." Now that she was here with him, she remembered how dangerous he could be to her peace of mind. "You don't have to concern yourself too much with it."

He nodded shortly and turned away from her.

Well, at least that had been easy.

He strode to the bar and picked up his cell phone. After a single push against the screen, he placed the phone to his ear. "Hello, Tag. I'm sorry to bother you."

Fuck. Fuck. Mother fuck. She stood up and shook her head, keeping her voice down. "Don't you dare."

"Yes, it was a long flight. Hang on a moment." He pushed the mute button. "I can tell him I'm not coming into work tomorrow or I can hand you over and let him deal with you. It's your choice."

"That is not fair."

"I don't care about fair. You'll deal with him or me. Make your decision. If you're going to deal with me, you will go sit down at the table and eat dinner. If not, get your bag together because I have the feeling Ian will move very quickly."

He was a son of a bitch.

And you're stupid if you lie to yourself. You're here because you knew damn well he wouldn't leave you alone. You're here because you can't handle him the way you do everyone else.

He wouldn't back down. He wouldn't compromise. If she didn't want to end up at Ian and Charlotte's, giving the entire investigation over to Ian, she better move.

She stood up, leaving her computer behind because apparently it wasn't welcome at Simon's civilized dinner table. She very quietly sat down in front of the plate Simon had made for her. Naturally his small dining area was immaculately kept and the presentation even of take-out Chinese food was lovely. She microwaved things or ate her take-out straight from the bag. She had the place Charlotte had bought, but her sister had selected everything in it. She rarely used the dishes and wasn't sure just how long it had been since she sat down for dinner. Chelsea pointedly picked up a spoon and started in on the wonton soup.

"I need a few days. Yes, something's come up with my cousins. No. I don't think we need to bring the team in. I'll take Jesse with me and we'll see if my cousin is being paranoid." He stared at her as he spoke, never taking his eyes off her. "Yes, once I get out there, my aunt won't let me leave for a day or two. Excellent. Thank you. Yes, I'll check in."

He put the phone down.

"You're a son of a bitch."

He shrugged a little and picked up his own plate. "My mother is actually quite lovely. My cousins, on the other hand, can be a bit rough around the edges. Did they frighten you? I know you don't like to be around men you don't know."

Because even the men she'd known as a teen had been violent and aggressive. Because her own father had beaten her so badly she still couldn't walk straight. "I wasn't afraid of them."

"Why? They can be aggressive around a woman."

"I wasn't afraid because you were here." The words were out of her mouth before she could think to call them back.

In a graceful move, he seated himself and pulled a napkin over his lap. His blue eyes looked infinitely warm as he glanced her way. "They would never hurt you. My cousins are good men. They're solid. But you should know I wouldn't let anyone hurt you. Anyone."

Except himself. He wouldn't mean to hurt her, but there was no way a man as beautiful and blessed as Simon Weston stayed with someone as cursed as Chelsea for long. He liked to play the white knight. Once he realized she wasn't worth saving, he would move on to the next wounded girl he found. She couldn't live in his world. He was the second son of a duke. She was still wanted by several governments and numerous criminal organizations.

It was better to keep focused on work. "Let's talk about how you can help me. You bought me a couple of days. I appreciate that. I just need to keep a low profile."

He shook his head shortly. "No. We don't have anything to talk about until we agree upon your contract. We can discuss it after dinner. You're a bit shaky. I won't go into it until you've got your strength back."

She didn't need her strength to find out how much he was going to charge her. "Don't you mean your contract? Let's have it. How much do you charge by the hour?" It couldn't be too much more than what Ian charged. After all, she was only getting

Simon and Ian would bring an entire team with him. He would also bring his own personality, which included assholiness and more sarcasm than she could handle in a single day. And Charlotte. Ian would bring Charlotte. A few months into standing on her own two feet for the first time and Chelsea was in serious trouble. If she wasn't careful she would find herself living with Ian and Charlotte, and both she and Satan wanted to avoid that at all costs.

"No, I was talking about the BDSM contract we're going to sign." Simon dropped the words casually, and for the second time that day, Chelsea felt like she had a bomb in her lap just waiting to go off.

She nearly lost her spoon. "What?"

He was perfectly calm. "That's my requirement for protecting you. I don't want money. You'll sign a contract making me your Master or I can call your brother-in-law back. How is the broccoli beef? I've never tried it before. Would you like some wine?"

She nodded numbly. She was going to need it.

Chapter Two

Simon looked down at the contract and wished he'd had a bit more time. He'd been forced to start with a standard contract and write in just some of his own language. He didn't like using a standard with her. Chelsea was different, but if he gave her any time at all she would find a way to wiggle off the hook he'd caught her on. He could still hear his Uncle David teaching him to fish.

When you catch the right one, you reel that sucker in and fast, son.

His uncle would likely have preached caution and patience. His uncle was a good man, but he'd never had to deal with Chelsea Dennis.

He'd written in their personal portions of the documents after they'd eaten dinner and then given it to her to read. He'd tried giving her some privacy, but when he'd come out of the bedroom, she'd been staring at her computer screen instead of the contract.

"Should we go over hard and soft limits?"

She rolled those beautiful eyes of hers. She was the very picture of petulance, sitting on his sofa, her arms crossed over her chest and a sulky frown turning her lips down. What would it take to get her to smile? When he ate her pussy until she screamed, would she smile afterward? "My hard limits are everything. Simon, this is stupid. Why are we doing this? I'm looking for a bodyguard, not a play partner. Besides, didn't you learn anything in London? I'm not submissive. I just use it for pain management."

Yes, he knew that was what she told herself. "I learned that you're incredibly stubborn and you like to lie even to yourself. As to why we're doing this, it's because I always have a plan *B*."

"How is this plan *B*?"

She was incredibly smart when it came to computers, but she wasn't much of a forward thinker. "From the moment you walked in and announced your problem, I've been running possible scenarios through my head. I think I've come up with the way this is most likely to end and I'm planning around it."

She snorted a little. He really shouldn't find the sound so charming. "You planning my funeral?"

He had to work on her pessimism. "No. I wasn't talking about your eventual death. I have no intention of allowing that to happen. I'm talking about the likelihood that Ian discovers what's been happening and takes over."

"That can't happen. I might rather die than have that happen. Maybe I should just run."

"He would find you." Only if Simon didn't find her first, but he didn't say that out loud.

"How does the fact that I let you smack my ass protect me from Satan?"

He also needed to work on politeness. "He cares about you, you know. Anything he would do would be to protect you."

"I am willing to admit that he loves Charlotte. If he would do anything for me it would be out of duty." She groaned a little and let her head fall back. "I love my sister. That's why I don't want her involved in any of this. She's gone all baby crazy. She deserves to focus on having Satan's child and being the happy goddess of the underworld. She doesn't need the stress of watching after me."

A very good sign. Since she'd walked into his life—technically since he'd dragged her kicking and screaming into his life—she'd clung to Charlotte like a co-dependent life raft.

He simply needed to let her know that she could depend on more than Charlotte. If she needed to cling, it was damn well going to be to him. "That's what this contract is going to ensure."

"How?"

He sighed. She was going to question him every inch of the way. "Think about it for two seconds. Ian Taggart doesn't live in the modern world. Much like my cousin, he believes himself to be the king of the castle and the protector of those considered to be his family. If you're in trouble, he will take the responsibility for protecting you and that includes making all the decisions for you until such time he decides you're safe."

"That sounds horrible." She shivered a little.

"You know it's the truth." He glanced back down at the checklist. "Let's talk about impact play."

"How is a flogging going to save me, Simon?"

Had she not heard a word he said? "There is one thing in the world Ian Taggart respects fully."

Her eyes widened. "BDSM. You think if I sign a contract and become your sub then Satan will leave me alone."

"First of all, you will cease calling the man Satan. It's rude."

"He calls me the bitch from hell."

"Yes, I intend to talk to him about that." He didn't like it. Ian might say things like that in jest, but Chelsea needed affection. She didn't need more reasons to put walls up. Once she signed the contract, he would protect her from everything, including her brother-in-law's smart mouth.

"You realize how dumb this is, right? It's just a contract. I can walk away. You can't hold me to it. Despite what Ian thinks, this is still the twenty-first century and you can't own a woman."

"I'm not trying to own you. I'm trying to start a relationship with you that comes with well-defined boundaries intended to make both parties feel secure in their duties and responsibilities to each other."

She frowned. "I never thought about it like that. Huh. Put like that it sounds better than dating."

Now that he'd been in the lifestyle for a while, the idea of dating made him shudder. It wasn't that he didn't want to go to dinner with Chelsea. He wanted to spend time with her, but in the vanilla world he couldn't just come out and say what he needed. When he'd played it vanilla, he'd spent most of his time trying to read his partner's mind. "I understand that you can walk away at any moment. I'm not naïve, Chelsea. I can only promise you that I will honor the terms of this contract. I won't walk away."

Her arms fell away and she finally sat forward. "I don't love being tied down."

"You let me do it in London." He could still feel her skin under his hands as he worked the rope over her. Silky smooth. She was so soft under that rough exterior.

"It scares me."

He gave her a moment, trying to leave an opening for her to talk. Silence fell between them. He nodded shortly and marked bondage as a hard limit.

She shook her head, her voice going low. "No. Don't make it hard. Soft. It's a soft limit with you."

Ah, the second time of the night she'd taken him out of the cesspool she seemed to place all men in. When she'd turned to him and claimed that she wasn't afraid of his cousins because he'd been there, he'd known this could work. By making rope bondage a soft limit, it gave them room to experiment. A hard limit would have meant absolutely none. "All right. It's a soft limit. We'll play a bit with it."

She trusted him. Under all that swagger, there was a spark between them and he intended to fan that flame.

"When we're not defusing bombs, you mean." She groaned a little and stood up. "I don't know when we're going to find time to play, Weston. If you would let me get to work, I could probably figure this thing out and then we wouldn't need a contract."

"Have you thought about the fact that this contract can simply be in place? It doesn't have to end when we figure out who's trying to kill you. You need a play partner."

"You don't. You play with everyone."

So the little brat was jealous? "I wouldn't need to if I could play with you."

That was about as bold as he was going to put it.

"What about sex?" She said the word like it was distasteful.

He tapped the contract to get her attention back where it needed to be. "We haven't gotten to that part of the contract. We'll cover it."

"That wasn't what I meant, Weston. I meant you will probably want sex from your play partner."

"I don't always get what I want." God knew that was true. This whole thing was a big gamble with her. He could end up signing a contract with a woman who would never have sex with him. He didn't think so. It was a bet he was willing to make.

"I have a hard time believing that."

"Chelsea, you seem to think I'm someone I'm not. I appreciate your earlier defense of me, but the truth is I did leave MI6 before Damon could fire me. I made a mistake." He'd made several. He'd followed some information he'd received down a rabbit hole that had almost led to the deaths of Liam O'Donnell and his now wife, Avery.

"You didn't. You did what you should have done with the information you had."

"Information supplied to me by the enemy." It still stung. He'd gone over and over it. He'd been damn lucky Tag was a forgiving sort. Or perhaps Tag understood that a man who made that kind of mistake tried his damnedest not to do it again.

"You couldn't know that. Damon should have trusted his agent. He could have told you he was bringing in McKay-Taggart. It's Damon's fault."

She was huffing at the end of her declaration, her passion obvious. And that was why he was willing to gamble a few months of celibacy. It wasn't like he was living it up as it was. He only wanted one woman. He had since the moment he'd seen her. His brother thought he was a playboy with no sense of responsibility and his cousins still saw him as a kid who needed protecting. He was a man and he wanted something beyond his useless existence. He wanted to see if it could work with her. Maybe he was a masochist at heart, but he wanted her.

"How about we leave the question of sex open? The Dominant and submissive can have sex at a mutually agreed upon time in the future if they so choose." He flipped to the part of the contract mentioned and wrote in the lines needed. He had to wonder about her experience. She was twenty-seven years old, but he would bet she hadn't had many boyfriends. There was an odd innocence about her that constantly battled with the blanket of weariness she wore. She was a study in contradictions.

"All right. I can handle that." She stood up and started to pace. "Can you just skip all the bodily functions stuff?"

He gave her a little smile. He'd wondered how she would handle going over the more extreme fetishes. "I believe so."

"It's good to know you're not into the seriously twisted stuff. I don't think I can even watch blood play."

"I'm a very staid and traditional pervert."

The smile that lit her face made his cock tighten. "I like that." She turned her face to the windows and stared out over the lights of Dallas at night. "It's a weird world, but there are some things I like about it."

"I would like for you to not be murdered by a sniper. Please come away from the window."

She looked up as though shocked. "I…" She stepped back. "Damn it. I don't make those mistakes. I'm not stupid. This isn't exactly the first time this has happened."

"It isn't the first time someone's tried to kill you?" He didn't like to think about the years she'd been on the run.

"Nah. A couple of people figured out Charlotte and I were working them and they got a little pissed. A cartel. A jihadist group. You know, the usual suspects. And then dear old dad's syndicate was always in play."

Yes, there was a reason he didn't like to think about it. "So the list of people trying to kill you is long."

"Yes." She sat back on the couch, well out of range of the windows. "You should think about that before you ask me to sign a contract."

He sat back and watched as her arms crossed again, her walls coming up the minute she mentioned her father. "What have you found out about this particular attempt? I can't imagine you haven't already been out on the Internet searching."

She had a hotspot device that went with her everywhere. If she'd had to ask him about his access, it was likely she'd already drained the battery, which meant she'd been searching.

Her gaze trailed to her computer. "I put some feelers out. I know you don't believe me, but I really have been trying to be good. Ian gives me a lot of work. Most of it's mindless, but it keeps me busy. He got me on with the Dallas PD as a consultant so I had a lot of fun a couple of weeks back busting kiddie porn sites."

Because she was like an addict. She didn't have anything else to focus on so Ian had given her a little methadone to keep her away from the hard stuff. She'd become addicted to being powerful on the web because she felt like she had so little power in real life.

"And none of these feelers have come back?"

She shook her head. "No, but these people I sent messages to have multiple addresses and they don't necessarily check every day. It could be a while. I also set up some searches that could take a couple of hours."

"All right. Can I discreetly call Adam in?" Adam Miles was McKay-Taggart's resident communications specialist, and by communications they meant hacker.

Her eyes rolled. "There's nothing Adam can do that I can't and he'll tell Ian."

"I doubt that. I'm bringing Jesse in. I can assure you he won't talk if I ask him not to." Jesse Murdoch was loyal to the team, but Simon felt like he could trust him implicitly. "I don't care what you say, we do need backup."

"All right." Her eyes came up, staring straight at him. "You know my limits, Simon. We don't need to do a one by one listing of them. You're avoiding getting to the bad stuff. Why don't you tell me what you require?"

Well, she'd summed him up pretty well. He did know her limits. She didn't like to be naked in public, but he'd managed to push that limit while they were in London. He intended to get her used to being nude in private, used to being intimate with him. He knew what she liked when it came to sensation play. He also knew she wasn't going to like his list of must haves. "Fine. I require obedience in the field."

She nodded as though she'd known that one was coming.

"Not when we're alone?"

"Anything having to do with this case and your protection fall under my purview and you will obey me. I'll take your lead on all the Internet stuff, but if I feel it's dangerous to you, I'll shut it down. If we're intimate then I'm in charge, though you should always know you can stop me. I'm going to ask you to give it a chance. If I ask you to be still, I'm doing it to enhance your pleasure. Do you understand?"

"Sort of. Is that all?"

"No. If I'm your Master, you're going to join me in daily exercise. I'm going to tailor a program to suit you."

Her face screwed up in a mask of distaste. "Why? Are you trying to say I'm pudgy?"

"No. You're quite slender but I fear that's from poor dietary habits and not anything healthy. I'm going to make you strong. You can handle a gun, but a gun can be taken away from you. You need to be strong mentally and physically."

"Simon, I think you're forgetting about the fact that I have a bum leg. Or do you want to see the cripple try to exercise?"

He set his pen down and allowed the moment to sit between them as he gathered every bit of patience he had.

She fidgeted under his glare. After a moment of uncomfortable silence, she obviously couldn't take it anymore. "What?"

"You should be very glad you haven't signed this contract yet or you would find yourself with those pants down and over my knee. If I ever hear you use that word to describe yourself again, there will be punishment and it won't be erotic. If I'm your Master I intend to protect you from everyone, and that includes that part of yourself that can't help but stick the knife in. Are we understood?"

"I'm just honest with myself. I have a limited capacity. Running is difficult. My muscles were affected by the breaks. They never really healed properly."

"And you've done physical therapy?" He knew the answer to that question, but he was interested to see if she would lie to him.

"No. Oddly enough my dad wasn't big on fixing the things

he broke. I was lucky that he needed something from Charlotte at the time or he likely would have let me die. I was the useless one in his eyes. Charlotte was the one he trained."

Simon got to his feet and joined her on the couch. "You're not useless. You're one of the most competent women I've ever met."

She laughed, a bitter sound. "Now who's got rose-colored glasses on, Weston? I'm good at one thing and one thing only."

"Because you don't try anything else. It's not too late to get the mobility back in your leg. We'll start with yoga in the morning and then I want to work on building up the muscles around your knees to protect them. So, to sum up, all I'm asking for is obedience in the field and that you give me a shot at making you stronger."

"And that I bottom for you."

Yes, that was part of his plan. He needed time to show her it wouldn't be so bad. Giving herself over to him could actually be quite pleasurable. He enjoyed taking care of a woman and she was in need. Charlotte had done her best, but Chelsea had never had a man watch out for her, never had a man who was dedicated to her pleasure in and out of bed. "Like you said, we probably won't have much time for play."

She laughed again, but there was a nervousness about the huffing sound that let Simon know she was very much aware of him physically, and not in a bad way. "Yeah, we'll be too busy dodging bullets and stuff."

He was close to her, a mere inch away from their thighs touching, but even that was far too distant for him. It was time to push those boundaries just a bit. He pulled her into his lap in one quick move. She gasped a little, but her arms came up and around his neck. "I do have one more request. Kiss me, Chelsea. Nothing more."

Her breath was shaky and she wiggled a little on his lap, making his cock lengthen almost painfully. "You want me to kiss you? Why?"

"Because we might have to make Ian believe it. Come on, love. I want a kiss. I'm not going to attack you. I'm going to sit here and be satisfied that we're close." He let his arms go securely around her waist, settling her in. He stroked down her back. "It's just a kiss."

She nodded and stared at his lips for a moment. Patience. She required a man with a patient hand. Though his every instinct was to take over, he intended to give his little sub what she needed.

After a long moment, her hands came up as though she'd decided he wouldn't let her fall and she could explore. She placed her palms against the sides of his face, brushing over his whiskers. He should have shaved but between the flight and getting home to find his cousins on his doorstep, he hadn't had time. She didn't seem to mind. She took her time, running her fingers over his cheeks and the bridge of his nose. She skimmed his eyebrows and stroked his chin. Finally she got to his mouth, her thumb running along his bottom lip.

"You know it should be a crime," she murmured. "Most women would kill to have lips like yours. They're really beautiful when you look at them closely."

"Is that what you're doing? Are you studying me?" While she took her time with him, it gave him another chance to watch her. He took in the way she ran her tongue along her lips to wet them, how the pulse jumped in the delicate vein of her neck, how her breathing had picked up. She was becoming aroused and all he had to do was get close to her.

"Sometimes when you look at a piece of code it's just numbers on a screen and that's all most people see. I like to study it. Those numbers mean something. They're not just random. They make up a piece of the coder. I don't look at people the same way, but your face says something about you. I don't know what yet."

"You don't have to," he replied. "You only have to know that you're safe with me. Kiss me."

She took a deep breath, seeming to steel herself, and then she leaned forward, bumping her nose lightly against his before meeting his lips. A quick brush and she pulled away. "There."

Oh, she didn't know him at all if she thought he would let her get away with that. "Now it's my turn."

She stiffened in his arms. "Your turn?"

"Now I'm going to kiss you." He didn't give her time to think, simply cupped the nape of her neck and gently brought her down so his lips met hers. Warmth sparked against his skin and the need to get her on her back was almost overwhelming. He could prove to her that she belonged underneath him. He could spread her wide and by the time he let her up, she would know she was his woman.

Or she would think he was her assailant. No. He molded his lips to hers ever so gently, giving her time to relax. He would play this her way for now and that meant not giving in to his very Neanderthal need to drag her away somewhere and brand her with his cock.

Very slowly she relaxed, her hands coming up to cup his shoulders as she started to respond. When her mouth flowered open, he took advantage, letting his tongue rub against hers in a slow slide.

Her chest met his, and there was no way to miss how her breasts felt, how that gorgeous ass of hers wriggled around on his lap. She moved and then she was rubbing his erection in all the right ways.

Her eyes flew open and she scrambled off his lap. Her voice was shaky, her lips a nice pink from their session. "I think that's enough for now. I'm really tired and some of the searches I need to do could last all night. Do you think I could grab a shower and a nap?"

He would certainly be taking a very cold shower. "Of course. It's back through the main hall. The last door at the end of the hallway."

Maybe he'd gone too fast. He had no way of knowing if her father had kept his abuse to the physical. God, he wanted to kill the man. It was really too bad the bugger was already dead.

Chelsea stopped and turned back. Without saying a word, she picked up her bag and stopped at the table Simon had been sitting behind. She picked up the pen and quickly signed her name on the bottom line. "You've got a deal, Weston."

He was smiling as he watched her walk away. Yes, he finally had her where he wanted her. He just had to find a way to keep her alive.

Chapter Three

Chelsea couldn't stop thinking about it. About him. She was thinking about Simon. She wasn't thinking about his penis. Nope. She wasn't thinking about his big old man part at all. She wasn't thinking about how that thing had felt against her backside.

She sighed and stared at the screen. It wasn't like staring at it would make someone respond faster. Her friends were careful. They were all underground hackers who tried to ensure no one could locate them, so they would all think about what they would and wouldn't say. There was no surety that they would contact her at all. If they decided it would hurt them, they would stay silent.

Because at the end of the day, they weren't necessarily really friends. She'd just had such a shitastic life that she believed a loose group of acquaintances—only a few of whom she'd actually met in person—formed her circle of friends. She'd learned that wasn't true. Real friends became family, and real family bled and died for each other like the McKay-Taggart group did. If she had been relying on them for information she would have had it in seconds. They wouldn't have left her staring at a screen and praying.

She sighed in frustration. She couldn't concentrate and it

wasn't about how much anxiety she'd dealt with during the day. It was all about the man lying not ten feet away from her.

After she'd taken her shower, she'd walked out to find him drying his hair from using the guest bath for a shower of his own. He'd been dressed in nothing but a pair of pajama bottoms that somehow managed to cling to his hips right above that place on his body that she was trying hard not to think about. Hard. He looked hard everywhere. From his sculpted shoulders to those abs she wanted to touch because they couldn't possibly be real. He'd told her to take the left side of his enormous bed and he hadn't liked it when she argued. She'd narrowly avoided a spanking.

Now he was sleeping and she was…

Why was she waiting? What the hell was she doing? She was twenty-seven freaking years old and if she didn't do something about it, she was going to die a virgin, and didn't that just sound pathetic?

Years had passed since that day she'd almost lost her innocence to violence. Years of fear and worry and confusion, and finally a sad acceptance that she wasn't meant to have that kind of intimacy. Now she wondered if she shouldn't at least try. Just to say she'd done it.

It wouldn't work with Simon. Not in the long run, but she did feel safe with him. He might rip her heart out, but he'd be polite about it and there wouldn't be any awkward run-ins at work and family functions. No, never for the duke's son. After he was done with her, he would likely try to convince her that he wanted to be her friend. He would never cause a scene. He would smooth everything over and wait the exact right amount of time before introducing a new girlfriend to the group. Chelsea would get to watch him find a girl he could really love and she would be alone but he would never try to push her out of their shared social circle.

Simon moving on would happen one way or another. Would it really be so much easier to watch him with his perfect girl if she'd never slept with him? Or would she always regret not taking the chance?

She glanced over to where his still form lay on the bed.

It wasn't like she was making love with the dude. She was merely scratching an itch she hadn't even known she had before Simon Weston showed up in her life. She could get the whole deflowering thing over with and he probably wouldn't even know if she brazened her way through it.

God, she wanted to talk to Charlotte. She glanced down at her cell but decided against it. It was two o'clock in the morning. She would wake Satan up and he was a surprisingly gossipy demon. He would want to know what was going on and then everyone in the world would know her business.

But she really wanted to ask her sister's advice.

"You should come to bed, Chelsea. It's very late and we've got a long day ahead of us." Simon's deep voice rumbled through the room.

How could just the sound of his voice make her heart pound? This was stupid. She was not going to get up and go to him.

Her feet weren't listening to her head. She stood up. How to handle this? It was best to just get it over with. She was a "rip the bandage off" kind of girl. It was best to take the hit and get the thing done quickly.

Surely sex wouldn't be so bad. She'd liked kissing him. She'd kind of loved kissing him right until the moment she'd felt his cock and then she'd shut down, her mind going to all kinds of bad places.

She couldn't live like that. She had to let it go or she would end up an old lady with a houseful of computers watching cat videos because she couldn't even bond with a real one. Simon was safe. She could use him to get over her fear and then maybe she could find a more suitable man. A nice nerd who wouldn't make her exercise. What was that about?

Focus. She needed to be focused.

"Do you need something?" He sat up. The room was dark, lit only by light from his alarm clock and what was streaming out from under the bathroom door. She could still see his chiseled features but maybe he wouldn't be able to see her scars. Was there any way to have sex without taking her pants off?

"Yes." She tried her best to sound somewhat seductive. Her

hands were shaking. She didn't want to be afraid anymore. She needed to know that she could do this. She needed to not be such a flipping freak show. Maybe if she fucked Simon, everyone would get off her back about being pathetic. "I think I know what we both need."

He turned his body so he was facing her, swinging his feet around until they touched the carpet in front of her. "A throat lozenge? You sound a bit hoarse, love. Are you coming down with a cold?"

So she wasn't good with the sexy voice it seemed. Maybe he preferred forward women. "Look, Weston, here's the deal. You're here. I'm here. We signed the contract. I've thought about it. What's the point in waiting?"

He ran a hand through his hair and yawned a little. "Waiting? Is your leg bothering you? You want a session at this time of night?"

Oh, he was slow on the uptake. "Sex, Simon. I want sex."

And then he wasn't slow. She gasped as she found herself flat on her back on the bed before she had time to say another word.

He loomed above her, his body pressing against hers. He weighed roughly two hundred pounds, all of it muscle. It should have made her feel pinned down, but in that moment she just loved being close to him.

"You want sex?" He didn't have the same problem she had in the sexy voice department. His voice was like warm honey sliding across her skin.

"Yes." She breathed him in. He smelled like soap. She had the strangest urge to run her nose over his skin so she could memorize his scent the way she'd memorized the feel of his face, the way his whiskers felt under the pads of her fingers, how silky his lips had been.

His hips moved against hers. "You want my cock?"

"Yeah." She hoped he would stop talking soon and just take her. Get it over with so she could know it was done and then maybe he would hold her. That was what she really wanted. She wanted to be in his arms. The sex stuff probably wouldn't work for her, but she'd liked kissing him and she thought she would like cuddling. She liked it when he touched her.

He stared down at her. “Tell me how you like it.”

“Like what?”

It was his turn to sound a little impatient. “Sex, Chelsea.”

She had no idea. She kind of thought she didn’t, but she couldn’t be sure. It seemed like a thing to get through to get to what she did want. She’d seen enough movies to at least have the lingo down. From what she understood about dudes, they didn’t want to take their time. She was cool with that. It would get her to the good stuff faster. “Hard and fast, buddy.”

Rip the bandage off. Yep, that was the way to go.

His face loomed over hers and she was almost certain he would kiss her again. “Chelsea? How many lovers have you had?”

God, when did he turn into chatty Cathy? “A bunch. Come on. Let’s go.”

His hand went to the waistband of her pants. “You’re ready? You’ve had a ton of lovers and you’re ready for me to just shove my cock in and start thrusting.”

She was pretty sure that was some kind of trap, but she was committed at this point. “Yes. I know what I want.”

His hand started to snake under her pants, moving quickly to get under her panties. She squirmed, trying to get away. For the first time, she felt some nervousness set in. She’d said she wanted fast, but he was moving at quantum speed.

“Stay still. How am I supposed to fuck you if you don’t let me in? This is called getting into someone’s knickers where I’m from. You want a quick tumble? A little in and out?” His tone had gone hard and she could feel his erection against her hip. God, he was big. Maybe this was a horrible mistake.

His fingers slid over her mound and she couldn’t help but try to move away. It was too intimate, too much, and it didn’t feel anywhere close to good. But she couldn’t get away because he was so heavy on top of her. He pinned her down and now it felt different. She struggled to breathe. He was so big and heavy. He could do anything he wanted to her.

Why had she put herself here? Panic threatened to take over.

“I’m just another cock, right?” The question came out on a

hard grind. "You've had a hundred and one more won't matter."

She nearly screamed as his fingers parted her labia. Tears blurred her eyes.

Simon cursed and rolled off her.

Chelsea could breathe again.

"You're not even wet. You want me to rape you? Is that what you want? You want me to prove what a bastard I am?" He was on his back, his chest moving up and down with the force of his breaths.

Chelsea practically jumped off the bed. "You are a bastard, Weston. I don't need empirical evidence. I just know."

He sat up, running a hand over his head. "Did you even know you're supposed to be wet, Chelsea? How did you expect to take a cock when you're not even aroused?"

She understood the process. She'd had a couple of horrifically embarrassing incidents all involving him. "I guess I don't want you after all."

"You're such a little liar." His head turned her way and she felt pinned again. "How many lovers, Chelsea. The truth this time."

She didn't want him to know the truth. What would he think of her? "Fine. Not many. I'm selective."

He stood up and stalked her way, his body all lean and predatory lines. It took everything she had to hold her ground when what she wanted to do was retreat. "How many? I would like a number. I'll give you an example. I've slept with sixteen women over the years. I started fucking at the tender age of fifteen, but despite what the British tabloids and my brother will tell you, I generally prefer to be in some form of relationship with the women in my bed. I don't like one-night stands, though I have had a few. If you want to add in the number of women I've played with in some way, either oral or hand jobs, the number does swell a bit and I'll admit to a few nights at Oxford where I'm not sure what I did. I'm disease free and I haven't had sex in six months. Well, unless you count my right hand. Really it's been my longest-term lover. Your turn."

"Five." That sounded like a good number. Why was he putting her in a corner?

"Names."

"What?" Her skin heated, embarrassment flooding her system. Why was he doing this to her? Did he want to check them all out for STDs? Somehow she'd thought he'd just take whatever she offered.

"If there were only five, then you should remember their names. Another example. Christina was my first lover. She was at the girls' school about a mile from my boarding school. We had sex in the girls' change room one night at a school dance. She told me I was quite terrible, by the way. I've thought about looking her up again to show her I've improved. Alicia came after that, and then the two Dianas…need I go on?"

He was taking up all the air. She couldn't breathe, couldn't think. She didn't want him to know. She tried to think of some names. Just throw out some names and maybe he would stop. "Alex."

His eyes narrowed as he stared her down. "Alex McKay? You slept with Alex McKay?"

Damn it. It had been the first name to come to mind. "No. It was a different Alex. Alex Jones. And then there was Harold."

"You slept with a man named Harold? How bloody old was he?"

"Damn it, it's none of your business. Why are you being such a shit?"

He crowded her, obviously using his height advantage for maximum intimidation. "It is my business. You told me you wanted sex. You told me you had many lovers. You lied on both counts because your pussy had zero interest in me, and if you've had more than one or two hurried encounters I'll be shocked. So I want the truth. How many and why? Why did you crawl into bed with me when you didn't want a fuck?"

Every word felt like a little bullet peppered on her skin. She'd wanted some affection, but like all things in her life, it had gone utterly wrong. She'd been stupid to try and she just didn't care anymore. He could think whatever he liked because he was an asshole. "None, okay. I haven't had any lovers. Is that what you want to hear?"

He growled and turned away and then somehow his fist was

going through the drywall.

The room got utterly silent and the moment seemed to linger. Chelsea stared, unsure of what to do. There had been more emotion in that single action of placing his fist through the wall than she'd ever seen from him. The trouble was she was pretty sure that emotion was pure rage. "Simon?"

He pulled his fist out, cursing as he opened the door to the bathroom and strode through, leaving her behind.

What the hell had just happened? Simon was always in control, always a gentleman. She'd never seen him less than perfectly courteous before she'd pushed him tonight.

Not always. Sometimes he was a Dom, and he'd brought her as close to pleasure as she'd ever been in her life.

"Go to sleep, Chelsea. I'll spend the rest of the night in the guest room." His voice floated out from the bathroom, a flat monotone, nothing like his usual lyrical tones.

Why had he turned on her like that? Shouldn't men want to have sex? He claimed he hadn't had sex in six months. Shouldn't he have been all over her?

Maybe everyone was wrong. They'd told her Simon wanted her. Jesse joked about it all the time, but she'd offered herself to him and he'd turned her down in a deeply brutal fashion. What had he meant by asking her for a kiss?

Maybe he wasn't as nice as she'd thought. Maybe he was just like all the rest. He was just better at hiding it.

He walked out of the bathroom, heading straight for the bedroom door, and she couldn't stop. The voice in her head was telling her to let the man go. She could go to sleep and come up with a new plan in the morning. She could leave before he was awake. Hell, she could just accept the inevitable, head to her sister's place and let Ian take over. Anything was better than picking a fight with Weston, who had just proven he was wishy-washy in the best case, a liar in the worst.

So why did she follow him out? Why did she march right behind him as he strode into the kitchen and opened the freezer?

He didn't bother to look back at her. "I told you to go to bed, Chelsea. It's late and I don't want another fight."

He might not want one, but she was primed to start one.

"What's up, Weston? Does the mighty Brit not like sad little virgins?"

He stopped for a moment, his head hanging down. "The bloody Brit doesn't want to hurt a woman who has no idea what she's asking for."

So that was what he thought of her. "Really? You think I don't understand the mechanics of sex. Wow. You do think I'm an idiot."

He pulled out a handful of ice and quickly deposited it on a kitchen towel. "I never said anything like that. Though you're naïve if you think that wouldn't have hurt. Don't try that on the next bloke. He'll take you up on the offer and you won't like it. You can't tell a man you want him to take you hard and fast and expect to not get hurt."

The next bloke. Not him. He was done with her. Somehow that hurt her deep. So damn deep. She hadn't been aware that she could ever ache like that again. She'd been sure she'd buried that part of herself so deep she wouldn't see it again, but Simon brought it out of her. He was her kryptonite, her weakness. Something nasty welled inside her. She wasn't going to let him see her hurt. She'd done that when she was a child and it had only made her tormentors happy. She wasn't going there again. "Maybe the next bloke will be able to get it up around me."

She turned, but didn't get more than a step away from him before he was whirling her around, her wrist caught in his hand.

Arctic blue eyes stared down at her and his jaw was as hard as granite. "I would suggest you tread very carefully for the next few moments. I'm a bit on the edge, love, and you're acting like a righteous bitch. You're rewriting history so I come out as badly as possible. Let's not forget. You came on to me."

"I won't again. Trust me. I learned my lesson. You can be quite mean when you want to be."

He dropped her hand and sighed, turning away. "I wish you would figure out which box to fit me in. It gets exhausting. One minute I'm pure evil and the next I'm some sort of neutered brother figure. This isn't going to work, is it? I'm being a bloody fool again."

Her anger deflated like she'd released a valve, and all the

bad shit slowly leaked out in the face of his slumped shoulders. When she looked at it without the filter of her embarrassment, she really had been hard on him. It wasn't his fault that he didn't want her. It wasn't exactly hers either. She'd always known he didn't really want her. He had a hero complex and there was nothing wrong with that. "I'm sorry. I thought I could see what it felt like. I really didn't mean to piss you off."

"You don't understand me at all." He slumped into the kitchen table chair.

Probably not. She wasn't good with people. It was why she should never have even tried. She'd spent most of her life hiding from people. Still, she couldn't walk away. She picked up the discarded cloth and sat down across from him. His hand looked all right, just a few scrapes. "I don't understand much of anything, Weston. Can I see your hand?"

He sighed and let her take his hand in hers.

She put the ice over it. "I know you're not evil." She'd seen pure evil and he didn't even come close. "And I certainly don't think of you as my brother."

A long moment passed. He allowed her to hold the ice to his hand. His eyes finally found hers and she saw a deep weariness there. "Why the heavy pass, love? I wasn't pushing you."

Because he didn't really want her. She'd misunderstood him. "It's not your fault so don't blame yourself. I guess I just got sick of being the virgin."

His mouth turned down in a fierce frown. "Ah, so you're curious."

Only when it came to him. She was pretty sure she'd go back into her shell now. It was better than the alternative, which was finding anyone other than Simon. She didn't want anyone but him and that might be her downfall. She latched on to anything but her humiliation. "Why did you go all berserker on the wall?"

He chuckled but it was a frustrated sound. "I think we can blame that on my unruly cock."

So he wanted her, but he didn't want to want her? Or he hated that he wanted her? She was confused about everything. It had all been one massive mistake. "I'm sorry."

"Why are you a virgin?"

Oh, she so didn't want to go into that with him. "I was busy with my amazing career of being the world's information broker. Not a lot of time to hook up."

He sighed. "Why can't you ever be honest with me?"

"I am." Partially. "The only person I trusted was Charlotte. Charlotte spent five years pining over Sat..Ian. There weren't a ton of double dates. We kept to ourselves. I was on the run for most of my adult life. Charlotte and I were always on the move. We never stayed in any one place for more than a couple of months."

His face softened as he continued to look at her. Something about the way he never looked away made her feel like the center of the damn planet. "Has settling down been hard?"

Something released inside her as his voice went back to normal. He was letting it go for now, thank god. She felt the weight of his hand in hers. She wished she didn't like it so much. "It's easier than I thought it would be. It's the little things that make it nice. I thought I would miss seeing new places and the thrill of the exotic, but the truth is I spent most of my time in front of my computer so I didn't take advantage of it. Dallas is good. It's hot, but I kind of enjoy it. I was born in North Carolina. I like to think the heat is my birthright. I was always so cold in Russia." She bit back the need to shiver at the way she'd been torn from her mother. She forced herself to turn to pleasanter thoughts. "I like my place. It's nice. I like this taco stand across from my building. I have no idea what kind of sauce they use but the beef tacos are like heaven. Weird people. Seriously weird. Like I heard them talking about trolls one day, but even that's kind of cool. I like knowing I can always walk over there and grab one. That sounds stupid, but I like knowing I don't have to find a new taco place."

She pulled the ice away and looked at his hand. It was only a little red. Even his damn hand was big and masculine, and she shivered at the thought of the way he'd touched her when he'd kissed her.

"Don't worry about it. It's fine now." He flexed it, only wincing a bit. "Just a little bruised, but I assure you I can still handle a gun. I'll be perfectly fine by the morning."

From her right, her cell trilled. She turned toward the sound.

"Who the hell would call you at this time of night?" Simon stood up.

She was kind of a night owl. Pretty much anyone who knew her and needed something would call her at all hours. "I have people I know all over the globe, though usually they get me on the computer. A couple of people have my cell."

He got to the phone first, picking it up and looking down at the screen. "Who is The Mixer? What does that even mean?"

She laughed a little. It was only reasonable that Al was the one who got back to her. He'd always been chatty. He almost never had great info, but he was incredibly smart. "His real name is Albert Krum. He's a sweetheart. He's also a hell of a hacker. He's known for code mash-ups. He's made some super-fun viruses. He's also one of the people I asked to look around for me so I should probably talk to him."

Simon handed her the phone. "Put him on speaker."

She slid her thumb over the screen and then engaged the speaker. "Hey, Al. Thanks for getting back to me so quickly, though you should know it's the middle of the night here. I moved to Dallas. Where the hell are you? Did you finally buy an Asian bride off Silk Road and move to Thailand? I told you that would get you in trouble."

His voice came over the line, the sound harsh in her ears. "Chelsea, I am so sorry."

Her whole body went cold because she could hear him breathing. He was panting as if he'd just run a long way.

Or as if he was scared for his life.

Simon's whole body had gone stiff. He'd obviously heard the same thing she had.

"Al? What's going on?" Chelsea asked.

His voice came out in stuttery pants. "I didn't know. You have to understand, Chelsea. I didn't know. I'm a rebel, not a killer. They just wanted me to write some code and then hack into a server. It was so much money. I thought they were just idiots. When I figured it out it was too late."

"What are you talking about? You had a job go bad?" It

wouldn't be the first time. They'd all gotten into trouble at one time or another. The plan was always to run and hide and find a new identity. There was a whole team of hackers Chelsea had befriended. They helped each other when the heat got bad. "Who were you working for? Mob? Cartel? I told you to stay away from the Yakuza. It's not like anime. How much do you need and where should I send it?"

He would need cash to run. She certainly owed it to him. He'd helped her and Charlotte more than once. Al had been one of the only people she could actually count on.

A sniffle came over the line. "Won't work. Money won't change anything. Nothing's going to work, Chels. Nothing but you. Hey, you remember the fun we had in Europe? When we spent that weekend there? That was a good time."

They'd met the once. Why was he reminiscing when he obviously needed help? "Yeah, it was a blast. Have you called Jim and gotten a new passport? You need to move and fast. I'm in the same boat quite frankly, as evidenced by my earlier message."

"Chelsea, I sent you a package."

She shrugged as Simon stared at her. "A package, why?"

Another sniffle from Al. "I needed someone to know."

Where is the package? Simon mouthed the question.

"Where did you send this package? What addy did you use?" She had a dozen different e-mail addresses. She used them for different reasons and with different people, but Al could figure out all of them. He was that good.

"I didn't do digital."

Now the room really went cold. Fuck. He was serious if he'd sent a hard copy. "To my home location?"

Had he sent her the damn bomb? What the hell? Or was the package the reason she'd gotten the bomb?

Simon was suddenly behind her. She could feel his heat and she knew she wasn't alone. Somehow she resisted the urge to lean back into him, to beg him to put his arms around her. It was right there, always there. The minute she'd met him, she'd felt that instant connection that seemed to be more about her girl parts than her brain. There was this weird part of her that truly believed that Simon would take care of her.

There was the sound of sniffling and a hard cry before his voice came back on the line. “I’m so sorry. I couldn’t think of anyone else who would do it. I shouldn’t have given them your name. I should have just done what they said.”

Tension ran along her spine. What was he trying to tell her? “Who, Al? What are you talking about? Who were you working for? The Russians?”

It made her halfway sick, but the Russian mob was pretty much into everything these days. She had to hope it wasn’t her father’s syndicate. Her cousin’s syndicate. Her father and uncle were dead and Dusan led the syndicate now. Dusan, who had oddly helped her. She could remember when everyone was looking for the man who had almost raped her and Dusan had looked back at her and Charlotte and given them a solemn nod before turning back to their father and claiming that he knew where the man had gone. Dusan had claimed her almost rapist was a drug addict and he’d gotten lost in the scene. Strangely, she rather thought Dusan would let her be. If it was Russians, at the very least it wasn’t her blood. It gave her an odd sense of courage.

“Worse. So much worse. Not mob. Not Yakuza. They’re everywhere.” She heard a hiccupping sound. “I’m so sorry, Chelsea. I wish I’d kissed you that day. You remember the time we spent together in Europe. Sometimes I still feel the wind in my hair and the sun on my face. I really do. That was a beautiful day.”

She’d met him once in Italy. They’d had pizza and talked incessantly about the craft of coding. Not once had he seemed like he wanted to kiss her. Actually, she’d kind of gotten the feeling he played for the other team. She’d been very comfortable around him. Al had been the kind of guy she could actually talk to. Of all the people she’d met through her hacking and bargaining, she’d probably been closest to Al.

The voice changed abruptly. “As you can tell, Miss Dennis, he’s very apologetic. How long he remains that way is up to you.”

There was not breathy panting to this voice. Smooth. Calm

and collected. The professional had arrived. It made her go cold.

"Who the hell are you?" She couldn't imagine who had found Al.

No hesitation at the question. He simply moved forward. "I represent a group of men interested in maintaining a certain level of balance in the world. What Mr. Krum has done threatens that balance. He took a very reasonable work order and chose to misuse his power. You wouldn't want to be a part of that, would you?"

"Hang up the phone, Chelsea," Simon ordered.

"Oh, my. That sounds like a British accent." The voice over the line came through so much clearer than Al's had. "Might you be with Simon Weston? That is helpful information."

Simon's hand came around, but she was faster. She moved away. She couldn't let him hang up the phone. Al obviously needed her, and she wasn't going to let him hang. "Who are you?"

"I'm the man who is going to kill Albert Krum if you don't tell me where you are. I need your physical location. You're obviously not at home. I've sent people there. Are you with Weston?"

"Hang up that bloody phone, Chelsea." Simon didn't keep his voice down this time.

But she couldn't listen to him. Al needed her. "Don't hurt him." Albert Krum wasn't violent. He could be a bit mercenary but then he'd helped her take down some nasty organizations, too. He'd helped her move money from some big corporations to orphans in the Sudan. He'd played pranks on dumbass CEOs and he sent her links to YouTube videos where dogs did cute things. Al was her friend. Her real friend. She couldn't let him hang.

"I don't want to, but one does what one must, Miss Dennis. It's my job and I'll do it if you don't tell me where the information is. He sent you a file folder. I can't tell if he did it by mail or in virtual form. His lie detection was inconclusive. I only know that he sent the information to you and he truly cares for you. He believes you two are friends. I have a gun to his head right now. Is he your friend? Do you want me to pull the trigger? He won't tell me where he sent it except to you."

"Don't." She couldn't be the reason he died. She just didn't know the information this guy needed. "Maybe he sent it to my home. I've been gone for a couple of weeks. I didn't get all of my mail. I'll go and look."

She'd already looked and someone had sent her a damn bomb. In two different ways. It wasn't at her place. But in that moment, she would promise him anything to make sure Al lived.

That smooth as silk voice didn't hesitate. "No. Your home has already been thoroughly searched. It's not there. Where else would he have sent it in order to reach you? I'm not foolish, Miss Dennis. I know who you are. You're The Broker. You have more than one address. Tell me now or I'll put a slug through your friend's brain."

If Al wouldn't tell them then he was serious about it. "I don't know, but I can find out. I do have more than one place he could have sent it to. You have to give me time. I can't just hop on the net and find out. Some of those places require a personal visit. Give me time."

Simon practically jumped on her. She felt his body slam into hers and then he was reaching for her phone. He easily wrestled the phone away. He hung up with a flick of his thumb.

"Simon!"

He stepped back, his eyes on the phone. "You were on the line for long enough for them to trace you. That's why they let him call you in the first place. Damn it. You have five minutes. We're leaving in three hundred seconds. If it isn't in your hands or on your body, it's staying here."

He took the phone and tossed it on the table and then started to walk away.

"How could you hang up like that?" She felt like her feet were glued to the floor. He'd just ruined everything.

When Simon turned, all of their prior intimacy was gone and there was nothing left but the cold-blooded agent who would do his job as surely as the man who had spoken to her on the phone. "Don't look at me like that. They would have killed him anyway. It was inevitable. I don't know who they are yet, but I know the type. When it comes to their plots, everyone dies. There is no exchange with men like this. Your friend was dead the moment he took that job, and he was obviously trying to warn you about something. He could have told them where he stashed the package and allowed them to retrieve it and likely kill you as well. He did the right thing by handling the situation the way he did. He kept his bloody mouth shut so you could have a chance. Now get your things so his sacrifice wasn't in vain."

She started to pick up her phone. Maybe she could call them back, offer whoever was on the other end of the line a deal. Maybe she could still save Al. "Simon, you have to let me call back. He's my friend. He was a good friend. He even came out to Venice to meet me once. I can't just let him die."

Simon moved in front of her, his body a wall between her and the phone. "Don't you dare touch it, Chelsea. The mobile and its very-easy-to-track GPS will stay here. You now have four minutes."

Without another thought, she ran to grab her computer. It looked like she wasn't staying in Dallas after all.

Chapter Four

Simon selected a shirt from the dresser and quickly pulled it on, buttoning up with the ease of long practice. He exchanged his pajama bottoms for a pair of slacks and got into his dress shoes. He could put on a suit in less than two minutes. He would have preferred to shave before he headed out, but the fact that whoever was on the other end of that line had known his name meant there was no time for proper grooming. They had to move and fast.

Luckily, he was a man with a plan.

However, the idea of leaving Ian completely in the dark was now discarded. If they knew Simon's name, they certainly knew Ian's. He grabbed his phone and sent a quick text.

Have Chelsea. Trouble on the way. Expect company and watch your back. Will check in later.

He couldn't take the chance that they would go after Charlotte to get to Chelsea. If they knew anything at all about her, they would know she loved her sister above everyone else. He tossed his own phone on the bed. He wouldn't use it again. He had burners in his go bag, but he had something to pick up before they left for a motel and he tried to figure this mess out.

His phone immediately started ringing.

"Are you going to answer that?" Chelsea grabbed her laptop.

She'd managed to put on her shoes. She stopped and stared at him. "How did you have time to put on a suit?"

Because he firmly believed in being dressed for the occasion, and there was almost never an occasion to not wear a suit. He was working after all. He needed to remind himself that this was strictly work. He was nothing more than a curiosity for her.

"I'm a gentleman. I can dress quickly. And I'm certainly not answering that phone." He knew who it was and the minute Ian spoke to him he would take over. Simon wasn't willing to let that happen. He reached into his closet and pulled out his shoulder holster. He slipped it on and quickly checked the clip in his SIG. "Are you ready?"

"Simon, we have to help Al."

She looked so bloody beautiful standing there. Her whole body was soft, entreating him to do her bidding. Her eyes gleamed up at him. He wanted nothing more than to indulge her, but he wasn't naïve. "Your friend is already dead and we will join him if we don't leave now."

Her rich brown hair shook. "He can't be dead. Surely they'll keep him alive for a while."

Simon pulled his jacket on over the shoulder holster. It was perfectly tailored so there was no break in the line. He caught a glance in the mirror. He looked every inch the gentleman, but it was a mirage. Everything about him was a mirage. Chelsea would find that out soon enough. "I assure you he's gone. He either wouldn't tell them where he sent the information and they killed him or he did and they killed him. There is no other option. And either way, they will come here and they will try to take you."

"I turned the locator off on my phone a long time ago, Weston. I'm not a newb."

He wasn't sure what she meant by that but she wasn't thinking straight. "He knows you're with me and he obviously has agents in the area. They're on their way here. It's time to go and you can't take that with you. Pull the hard drive. We need to go."

She shook her head. "It's an SSD. I can't pull the hard drive.

Simon. I would have to take apart the system. I need this computer."

He didn't care that it was a solid-state drive. It wasn't coming with them. "You're not taking it and you know why. I have no doubt you have backups." He grabbed the laptop and tossed it on the bed with the phone.

"I can't access the backups without a damn laptop." She dug her heels in.

He turned and hoisted her up and into his arms. He wasn't going to listen to her complaints a second longer. He couldn't afford to. He had no idea how long it would take the man on the end of that line to send his thugs their way, but he doubted it would be long. The man obviously had operatives in Dallas and they understood Chelsea's circle.

"Put me down!"

Chelsea was spitting bile his way, but he ignored her. She struggled with being out of control, but this was one case where he couldn't give it to her. She didn't understand. Despite her horrible upbringing, she was a little naïve. She'd never really been in the field. Yes, she'd been forced to run, but from what he understood, she'd never had to fight the way she would have to now. She didn't understand how quickly things could go bad. She'd been able to hide behind her screens, but Simon knew the truth. At some point a man or woman's past always caught up with them.

And Chelsea had a hell of a past. It was always just a matter of time before someone came after her.

"I need that computer."

He made it to the door and snagged his keys, though he'd have to dump the car before long, too. Again, it was lucky for her he was a man who planned ahead. He simply needed to pick up a few things and then he'd check them into one of four motels that would likely scare the crap out of her, but they were off the grid and accepted cash. He needed a couple of hours to figure out a plan of action before they made a move.

"I need it."

He stopped because he was an idiot. She sounded scared and tired and she clung to that stupid laptop like a soldier to a gun.

"We have to leave it. I promise I will get Adam working on the case as soon as I can."

"There's too much information on it. Please."

"Chelsea, I can destroy it but I can't allow you to take it."

She would hate it. She would loathe not being in control, but he couldn't give it to her. The look on her face made him feel like he'd been kicked in the gut. It was an actual physical bloody ache to not give her what she wanted. Some Dom he was.

"You're sure?"

"It has to be this way. They're on their way. They'll be here any minute and I can't risk losing you."

She took a long breath and nodded. "You can let me down. I'll do it."

It would be easier if he had both hands, but still, she could be mean. "I swear if you pull anything, I'll haul you to Ian's so fast it will make your head spin."

She smiled as he eased her to the floor. "Like last time?"

It was stupid. He couldn't help but smile back, that first time they met fresh in his mind. "Except I'm ready for your right hook now, love. You won't find me so easy to take out this time."

Her eyes rolled as she straightened her ridiculously large T-shirt. It was at least two sizes too big for her and utterly hid her slender curves. Unlike him, she didn't dress quickly. She held her hand out, silently asking for the SIG. "Yeah, you were so easy, Weston. If I recall you were an unmovable mountain and I was the little gnat trying to get your attention."

She'd had his attention from the moment she'd attacked him. He didn't bother to mention that while her little fists hadn't really hurt, his cock had been aching for hours afterward. He'd turned her in to Ian that day. He didn't intend to make the same mistake again. "I'm trusting you."

She took the gun and flipped the device over so the underside was exposed. She proved she was proficient with firearms, quickly placing two holes in her laptop. "That should take out the chips." She passed the gun back to him, and Simon released a breath he hadn't realized he'd been holding. "I'm ready."

Trust. At least she trusted him this much. He led her to the door, hoping they hadn't wasted too much time.

He worked the alarm, releasing and resetting it so it would be on when they left.

"Stay close to me." He gripped his SIG in his right hand and opened the door, quickly turning right and then left. No one. The hall was perfectly silent, as it should have been at this time of the morning. He waited for a moment, listening for any signs. Nothing at all. He reached his free hand for her. "Come along."

She let him lead her out, waited while he closed and locked the door. "Don't you think they can get in?"

"It buys us a couple of minutes. I have an alarm that the police will respond to. They won't have long to look around." They wouldn't find anything except his sterile condo and her now useless laptop.

And the phones. He started to hurry her toward the lift as he pulled his burner phone and dialed a number he knew by heart.

"Are you calling Ian?" Chelsea asked, but she kept up with him.

"No. Adam."

But it wasn't Adam who answered the phone on the fourth ring.

"This better be really fucking good because I just managed to get to sleep. Whoever the fuck you are, I'm going to find you and tear your balls off and stuff them down your throat and then I'm going to put them on a plane to Europe so they have jet lag."

He didn't have time for Jake's anger issues. The man hadn't been happy with the European assignment. "I've got a situation."

Jake's voice went smooth and professional, any hint of sleep gone. "Do we have incoming?"

It wouldn't be the first time a group had targeted the whole team. They had plans and backup plans, and the first and foremost concern was the team's women and children. "I don't think so. I think they're hunting a very particular game. I have the target and I'll call again when she's secured. I need Adam."

"This is Miles." Adam came over the line as though he'd been sleeping next to Jake, which he'd likely been, their shared wife, Serena, in between them.

"Brick my phone and the target's, too." Adam would render their phones utterly useless and they would be on burners for the time being. The ones they left behind would be good for nothing but bricks, hence the slang.

"The target?"

"You know who she is." Strangely, despite the fact that whoever was looking for her knew her name, he didn't want to say it on a non-secured line. The NSA loved the digital age. They listened in on everything. Beyond whoever was trying to kill Chelsea, he had to worry about the fact that any number of legitimate intelligence agencies might use the situation as a convenient excuse to bring her in.

If they got hold of her, he would never see her again.

"Raging Bitch, then," Adam said.

"I will rip your spine from your body if you call her that again."

"Hey, we're using code names, Limey Bastard."

Whoever let Adam pick codes names needed to die. "Just brick the phones and I'll contact you in the morning."

"Understood. I'll climb the ladder tonight and we'll be waiting for your call." Because neither one of them would sleep now. Simon understood that. They would watch over their wife and son until they got the all clear. Climbing the ladder meant Adam would start a domino of calls to the rest of the team. In minutes, everyone would know something was going on and they would likely be up Simon's ass by morning.

They made it to the lifts and Simon dragged her close after pushing the down button. He didn't want to lose sight of her for a minute.

"Do you need a ride?" Adam asked but Simon could already hear the sound of his fingers pounding on keys. Adam was smart and fast. He would be out in the ether of the web looking for anything about Chelsea. He would have some kind of answers by morning.

"No, I'm calling a cab if I need one. Thanks." He was calling Jesse as soon as he hung up. Now that he thought about it, it would be better to have Jesse with him anyway. They could take Jesse's car and trade it for Simon's extra. Jesse was his partner. While he could call on anyone at McKay-Taggart, he preferred to use Jesse. Jesse was loyal to him. Jesse was his closest friend. Certainly there was the problem of his itchy trigger finger, but Simon wouldn't trust anyone above him.

Simon hung up the phone.

"Where are we going?" Her eyes were up, watching the lights above the lift, her expression tight.

"Someplace safe."

"Do you happen to have a name for this magical safe place?"

Sometimes her humor eluded him. "A motel full of prostitutes and criminals."

"Awesome. I'm really excited about the way the whole day's gone. I should have stayed in Europe."

The door dinged and he prepared to get in. He'd lose the signal in the lift so he'd have to call Jesse when he got to the bottom. He'd have Jesse drive her around town for hours if he needed to, though he should ditch Jesse's Jeep as soon as he could get to his secondary vehicle.

The doors opened and a man was standing there. Tall and lean, there was no question of who he was looking for. Even if there had been, all questions would have been answered as he lifted his gun and fired.

* * * *

Chelsea had only a second to react as the elevator doors opened revealing the next asshole who was trying to kill her. Unfortunately for him, he was also trying to kill Simon. Simon immediately pushed her aside and she hit the wall.

Pure adrenaline pumped through her veins. Her leg gave out and she fell, her ass hitting the floor. Pain flared but she forced herself to her knees. Time was of the essence. She wasn't fast, but she had to be for Simon's sake. He wouldn't do the smart thing. He wouldn't leave her behind and save himself.

The big guy was dressed in head to toe black. He strode out of the elevator, leveling his gun, a Ruger she was pretty sure, right at Simon's head. Terror pulsed through her system. She wouldn't be able to handle watching him die. She couldn't stand the thought of that big, gorgeous man silent and still forever.

Simon was on top of it. Before she could even struggle to her feet, he turned and put a slug in the man's torso. She heard a second shot blare through the hallway. The other man slammed back into the elevator and out of her view. Simon was on top of her. He pressed the SIG into her hands.

"Time to go, love." He hauled her up and into his arms without showing a single sign that her weight bothered him. "I'm afraid this is going to be the quickest of our options. Can you protect my back?"

She was nestled in his arms as he began to jog down the hallway to the stairs. She hated it, but he was right. Even carrying her, he was faster than she was without any impediments at all. Because of her stupid leg she would have to watch both their backs. He carried her high against his chest, allowing her to look over his shoulder.

He opened the door to the stairs and wasn't even showing the strain of carrying both her and his go bag. "There's a service lift at the end of each hall. I'll take us down a few floors and then cut over to them and we'll try to sneak out of the back entrance."

Even though he kept his voice low, it reverberated through the empty stairwell. The lights cast everything in shadows and her heart was still pounding. "I'll feel better when we're in a car."

"Can't take the car now, love. That's why I'm avoiding the parking garage. They very likely identified my vehicle and we know how much these men love a good bomb."

"Shit." She hadn't even thought of that. He was going to lose that gorgeous Audi. "I'm so sorry."

"Don't be. Just reach into my pocket and grab the burner. Call Jesse. When he answers tell him I need a ride to the airport and then hang up. It's code for him to get his arse here and quickly."

They seemed to have codes for everything. She wasn't sure why when they could just as easily say what they wanted, but then she wasn't the cool spy chick. Chelsea did as Simon asked, dialing the number from memory. Charlotte had forced her to memorize the team's numbers in case she found herself in a bind—or with a death squad on her heels. Jesse answered on the second ring and Chelsea gave him Simon's code.

"Understood." The code seemed to mean something to Jesse as he hung up.

"He was a little abrupt. Does that mean he's coming to get us?"

"Yes. He'll drop whatever he was doing and get here as fast as he can. If he was at home that should only be a few moments. He's two blocks down from here." Simon made quick work of the stairs but that was when they heard the door open above them. Simon stopped and flattened against the wall.

"It won't do any good, Weston," a voice from above said. "I'm not alone and while you've got great aim, those bullets you're using won't get through the vests we're wearing. We're far better armed and protected than any army you've come against before."

"Shit," Simon cursed under his breath.

"Fortunately for you, we're also more reasonable than most armies," the should-have-been-dead man said in a flat, Midwestern tone. "All we want is the package Mr. Krum sent to your girl and we'll be more than happy to live and let live. As long as she hasn't opened it, of course. To tell you the truth, we would greatly prefer to employ Miss Dennis than to fight with her."

"You're with The Collective." Simon's arms tightened around her. He had his back out, shielding her from any bullet that might come their way.

She looked up at him. They'd dealt with The Collective a couple of times before. Just a few days ago, she'd been working on an op in Europe involving the shadowy organization made up of some of the world's most powerful companies and wealthiest men. They'd formed a sort of star chamber that oversaw the interests of the companies involved from corporate espionage to murder for hire. They seemed to love recruiting former intelligence agents.

Simon glanced at the door below them and Chelsea followed his line of vision. There were roughly half a dozen steps, but he would have to give up his defensive position to get there. The stairs wound around with a good-sized rectangular space dividing them that would give an assassin a distinct advantage. Simon couldn't see behind him, but she could. Asshole Number One was two flights above them, but he seemed to be standing in the back, unwilling to take the chance that Simon could get a shot off. Chelsea was just waiting for Asshole Number Two, and possibly Three, to show up.

Not that it had mattered. Simon had caught the dude squarely in the chest twice. He should have been dead from the loss of his lungs, but he just kept on talking because The Collective was nothing if not on the cutting edge of technology.

"My team represents a group of businessmen who have a vested interest in the package that was sent to you. It's very important that we have that package returned to us. Miss Dennis, if you'll come with me, we'll allow Weston to live. If not, we'll simply kill him and take you anyway."

Simon's eyes met hers, narrowing, his voice low. "Don't you listen to him."

"Have you thought about what we could do for you?" The man's voice had taken on a soothing quality. "We have medical equipment and therapies that are years away from becoming public. If you worked for us, you would have doctors at your disposal who could not only fix your legs, but make them better than before. And the tech…oh, you have no idea what's coming."

She had no doubt any deal she made with them would be a deal with the devil. "I bet Al didn't know what was coming either."

"That was unfortunate, but I think you'll be smarter than Mr. Krum, won't you? You won't snap at the hand that feeds you. You would be grateful to someone who could fix your legs, wouldn't you?"

The thought of standing tall and straight and pain free whispered through her soul. Wasn't that what she'd always wanted? A way to erase what her father had done to her? A way to be whole again?

"How good are you, love?" Simon whispered the question in

her ear, dragging her out of her very tempting thoughts.

Fuck. There was no doubt about what he was asking. She was an excellent shot. Charlotte had made sure of it. Sometimes the only place Chelsea had gone to outside of her apartment was the gun range. But she'd never had to do it while cuddled up in a man's arms and she'd absolutely never had to do it when she was protecting a man. She simply nodded and prayed she could make the shot when the time came.

Simon's body pressed against hers.

"You're not going to make the same mistakes." Asshole One seemed to really like the sound of his own voice. "Mr. Krum decided he no longer wished to be employed by my boss."

"So you killed him. I think that will get you a severe talking to from the HR department." She kept talking. He had to show his face sometime. He was two flights up. Chelsea gripped the SIG. The safety was already off. She lined up her shot using Simon's broad shoulder to rest her arm.

A chuckle wound its way down the stairwell. "Even your sarcasm would be welcomed, Miss Dennis. We like smart people where I work. So I'm giving you the choice. Come with me or I'll kill your companion and take you anyway."

"They'll kill me no matter what you do," Simon said, his body tensed as though just waiting for that bullet to hit.

Then he would be as dead as Al was and she would feel that ache forever. Life had been so much easier before Charlotte decided to force her into the real world.

"I think I'll take a hard pass on the employment offer." She spoke but she was really thinking about the job ahead of her. He would show himself and Chelsea had to be ready. She had one chance and only one chance because if she missed and he got a shot off, Simon's back was a far bigger target than what she would have to aim at. Simon would go down and Chelsea would be taken in.

Any minute. Any second. Breathe. Focus. Let the world narrow to a tiny pinpoint. That target was all that mattered. It wasn't a human being. It was a target to hit. Chelsea prided herself on always hitting her mark.

"That is unfortunate."

And there he was. She heard him step forward, her entire being focused on one thing and one thing only. There was the light sound of his shoes squeaking across the concrete floor and then his face came into view.

Chelsea pulled the trigger.

Apparently The Collective hadn't prepared the dude for a headshot.

She watched as his gun fell, passing her by on its way to the bottom of the stairwell. The body slumped back, disappearing from view again.

Simon took off running for the door. God. She'd killed a man. She'd done it again. She'd put a bullet in his face and he wouldn't move or walk or talk again. If he'd had a family, he wouldn't see them again. She didn't know anything about him, didn't know if someone would miss him.

She'd only known that it was him or Simon, and there was no choice between them.

"How much time do we have? Is he behind us already?" Simon asked as he raced down the hall.

He hadn't seen what she'd done. He thought she'd just fired and bought them a moment or two. "He's not going to follow us."

Simon turned and Chelsea couldn't help but continue to watch over his shoulder. "Where did you hit him?"

"Headshot. He's gone."

He stopped in front of the elevator doors at the end of a long hallway. He set her down and took the gun back. Pushing the button to call the elevator, he took a long breath and settled his bag over his arm again. It struck her quite forcibly that everything they had in the world was in that bag. She had to hope Simon packed properly.

She hated being out of control. It made her feel small, insignificant—like the child she'd been.

"You had to do it." Simon was staring down at her.

She nodded. It wasn't like it was the first time she'd killed a man. It was just the first time she'd done it with a gun. Her bucket list was getting smaller and smaller.

The bell dinged and the doors opened. Simon was ready this

time. He was prepared to shoot anyone in the elevator.

Blissful silence met them.

"Come on." He hauled her in with him and the doors closed again.

"Do you think he was lying?" Asshole Number One likely hadn't gotten his job because he was such a stand-up guy.

"About there being others?" Simon shook his head, his eyes watching the floors tick away. This elevator was large and industrial, unlike the serene beauty of the ones meant for the residents. The floor beneath her feet was plain metal. "No. I'm certain he wasn't lying about that. The good news is there's no possible way the police aren't coming."

The elevator continued its smooth descent. "Do we want the police involved?"

She had a pretty shady past. Pretty? Try totally awful and dark past. She'd hidden it under various layers of security, but there was always the off chance that someone at DPD would be on top of things and start asking questions she didn't want to answer.

How involved in the Deep Web are you, Ms. Dennis?

Up to my nose, Mr. Cop. I'm so far in that sometimes I can't breathe. Sometimes I'm sure I'll drown in there and no one will know where to look for me. I'll disappear into the code like I never existed at all.

Yep. She didn't want to get hauled to jail. She wasn't completely certain Satan wouldn't leave her there to rot. After some of the things she'd done, she wasn't sure that wasn't where she belonged.

Maybe she should have taken Asshole up on his offer. Maybe she really was one of the bad guys.

The ultimate good guy in her life took her hand again. God, the minute he touched her, she felt warm and stupidly fuzzy. "Stay behind me. I'll pick you up again if we need to."

"I'll try to move as fast as I can." Her weight couldn't be great for his back.

"We're going out the rear entrance. Let me go first and then I'll give you the go-ahead." The doors opened and it was like time slowed down.

Her heart threatened to pound out of her chest. At this time of night no one was in the hallways, but she could hear sirens in the distance.

Simon stepped out, looking one way and then the other before his hand came back, waving her out. She could see the back entrance up ahead. Just another hundred yards or so and they would be out of the building and hopefully Jesse would be waiting for them.

Chelsea stepped out as Simon moved down the hall.

And then she felt something move behind her. Someone had been waiting, hiding. A hard hand clamped onto her throat and an arm snaked around her waist. There was the cold press of metal to her head.

"Don't move a muscle." She could smell cigarette smoke on his breath as he spoke against her ear. "I already called it in. We've got a car on the way so there's no point in trying to get away. Where is Carlson?"

Simon seemed frozen in place. Very slowly he turned, his SIG at his side. "If you're referring to the man who came up to my flat, we lost him in the stairwell."

Chelsea kept her mouth shut. If Simon didn't want him to know she'd killed this Carlson dude, then she wasn't about to tell him. She had to follow his lead. This was his area of expertise but it was hard when all she wanted to do was kick and wail and scream. She hated being held tight, hated the feeling. Her vision started to lose focus and she could smell sweat and the aroma of cigars. Just like that night. He'd wrapped his arms around her and she hadn't been able to breathe.

Not like when Simon held her. She forced herself to fight back. Simon would never smell like days-old T-shirts and the cheap cigars her father's men bought in the bars in Moscow. Simon smelled like sandalwood. Clean. Masculine. Simon needed her to not go all crazy PTSD on him.

Chelsea's brain turned to mush but at least she was still in the here and now. The gun was pointed at her head but the man who held her could easily turn it on Simon and she would be forced to watch him go down.

She'd been selfish. She shouldn't have come here. She

should have gone to the police and taken her damn punishment like a woman. She'd done the crime, but no, she wasn't about to do the time. Not her. She would rather drag the best man she knew into it. It was what she did. She dragged people down. She'd dragged her sister down for years.

"I'll go with you if you leave him alone." The words came out of her mouth in a little sputter.

"You'll go with me, little girl, no matter what I do."

"The police are almost here," Simon pointed out.

She could practically feel the satisfaction oozing from her captor's pores. His hold tightened around her waist. "I think you'll find we have ways to deal with the locals, Mr. Weston. Or should I call you milord? Yes, we know all of you and we have ways to deal with all of you. I would greatly prefer to not piss off the Malones. Malone Oil is affiliated with our organization after all."

"I don't believe you." But Simon had blanched, his face a chalky white.

"Then you're naïve. Why don't we all go back to my hotel and talk this out? I could get your uncle on the line. You'll see for yourself."

"Just let Simon go and I won't give you any trouble."

There was a low chuckle behind her. "I don't think you'll give me trouble. I'll just break your fucking legs again and see that the job is done properly this time. If you give me a moment's trouble, I'll have someone cut them off."

Just the thought made her fight. She struggled in his arms.

There was a loud bang and then the man behind her stiffened and slumped to the ground.

Chelsea shook a little. What the hell had just happened?

Simon stared at the man who had so recently been holding her. He was a heap on the carpet now, his vacant eyes staring up at her. "Sorry. I didn't mean to get you with the spray, but I had to take him out."

"Spray?" Something wet slipped down her cheek.

Simon frowned. "Yes, I was hoping the blood would go another way." He pulled a handkerchief from his slack's pocket and passed it her way.

Who the hell had handkerchiefs these days? Simon really was stuck in another time. She scrubbed at her cheek and sure enough, there was bright blood there. Not once in all her time as a hacker had her computer spat blood her way. It had been so much safer when she was happily behind locked doors.

"Come on. We need to leave." Simon's face had gone completely stony.

"Simon, you can't really think your cousins are involved in this." She'd heard the name Malone Oil come up more than once during missions involving The Collective.

He stared at the man a moment more before straightening his jacket. He strode to the exit and withdrew a card. He slid it through the key reader.

"How do you have a keycard to the service entrance?" She hustled to catch up to him.

"Because I own the building, of course."

Of course. It made perfect sense that he just owned a building in the middle of one of the ritzier parts of the city. Didn't everyone?

Chelsea stopped and stared back. Two down and they would just keep coming. "Simon, maybe you should…"

His hand found hers, pulling her outside and into the gloomy shadows of the trash bins. He tugged her close, dragging her into the dark with him. "Don't finish that sentence unless you want the punishment to start now. If you think for a second I won't discipline you in the backseat of Jesse's vehicle, you're wrong. I will have your pants down and I will tear into your backside if you even contemplate finishing that sentence."

She huddled close, turning her face up to stare at him. "How do you even know what I was going to say?"

"Because I know you. A couple of people are dead and now it's real. You feel guilty and you're going into the martyr phase of your cycle."

She could hear the sirens getting close, very close. Where the hell was Jesse? Knowing him he could have gotten lost. Or found some shiny object and chased after it for a while. "I have a cycle?"

Red and blue lights streamed from the other side of the

building. "Oh, yes, you do, love. It's a never-ending pain in my arse, and the part of the cycle I like the least is the martyrdom followed by the self-pitying cursed one you like to play."

She frowned his way. "Is there anything you do like?"

His lips curled up just the tiniest bit. "Sometimes you forget to hate everything and you flirt a bit. I do like that part." He reached down, brushing his thumb over her cheek. "You missed a spot."

Of dead man's blood. She tried not to think about how utterly pathetic she must look. She was dressed in an XL T-shirt with a snarky saying about T-rexes hating push-ups and a pair of PJ pants covered in puppies. Now she had blood all over her.

And he was heartstoppingly perfect.

She stared up at him and wished just for a moment that she had half of her sister's confidence. Charlotte got all the good genes. She got the beauty and the curves and the…

"Holy shit. I do have a cycle. I think I just hit self-pity."

He frowned even as his head came up and he started to drag her out into the alley. "Yes, I might have mentioned I wasn't fond of that part."

A Jeep turned down the alley, stopping on a dime.

"Our ride's here."

She followed Simon into the night.

Chapter Five

Jesse wasn't alone. Simon opened the door to the back seat upon discovering the front was already occupied by a very wide-eyed Phoebe Graham. She peered at him through the thick glasses she wore.

"Are you all right?" Phoebe asked, her voice tremulous.

She was a little mouse, but one who seemed to have Jesse by the balls. They had started dating only weeks before, but Jesse seemed utterly fascinated by her. She was far too submissive for Simon's tastes, but her very gentle nature obviously called to Jesse.

"We're perfectly fit. I'm rather surprised to see you, Miss Graham." Though he said the words to her, he meant them for Jesse, who should have known there were no civilians allowed during an escape from nefarious forces. "Come along, love."

He would feel better once Chelsea was safely in the car. He ushered her in and then settled himself.

"I didn't have a choice. I was on a date. You couldn't expect me to just leave her. Not when I got that call about the emergency fumigation."

Simon sighed. Emergency fumigation? That was the best he could come up with? Their eyes met in the rearview mirror, and Jesse grimaced.

They had to work on their scenarios.

"I didn't know the bug problem was so big," Phoebe said. "I would have thought a building like this would be very clean. And to think that it could potentially reach all the way to Jesse's place." She shuddered a little. "I don't like bugs."

Luckily Phoebe was a bit naïve. She was the accounting and billing specialist Ian had hired years before. She tended to stay in her office, only talking to Eve and Grace on a regular basis. The men of McKay-Taggart seemed to intimidate her. Until she'd met Jesse and then she'd been so charmingly graceless around him that Simon had to worry about getting a sweet tooth.

"Well, you know what they say about Texas." He fell back on his cousins and the way they liked to talk. "Everything's bigger here. Even the bugs. Scorpions. They sting and hard. We had to kill two of them on our way out of the building, so I think it would be good to put some distance between us and that particular memory."

He heard Jesse curse under his breath as he pulled out of the alley. At least he knew Jesse had gotten the message. Two dead bodies. He would know to avoid those red and blue lights.

He turned left and stopped at the light. Jesse's voice was tight as he tipped his head to the front of the building. "It looks like the situation is well in hand, partner."

Or as he knew Jesse would say if they were alone, holy shit, we were almost fucked. There were two cop cars sitting in the circular drive at the front of the building. There was a uniformed officer standing by his car, his radio in hand. He was shaking his head and obviously calling for backup.

So they'd found the bodies. It was a good thing he'd bricked his phone because otherwise it would be ringing at that very moment. He would be one of the first people they called as the owner of the building. Luckily, he had the building manager's number on file with the security company as his second in command. The poor man would be heartbroken that his lovely building had blood all over it, but he was competent enough.

Chelsea stared out the window, her anxiety a palpable thing. At least she understood what a wretched situation they would be in if they got hauled in by the Dallas police.

The light changed and Jesse very cautiously moved through the intersection. It was one of the reasons he and Jesse got along so well. The younger man almost never panicked. He was cool under pressure, although he had a few triggers that turned him into a beast Simon worried he might have to put down.

"I'm going to drop Phoebe home and then I'll take us to a nice bug-free motel for the night," Jesse said.

"You could stay at my place," Phoebe said quickly and then seemed shocked at her own words. "I mean, only if you want to. I wasn't like saying you had to or anything."

For the first time, Jesse seemed a little flustered. "Uhm, that would be great. I mean I would love to stay at your place, but I can't. I mean…"

Phoebe's eyes widened. "Oh, okay. I understand. I just thought…"

Jesse shook his head. "No. No. I really do want to. I mean, we haven't actually talked about…"

"Yeah. We should talk…"

Simon had no idea how they talked about anything since they couldn't actually finish a sentence in each other's presence. It was irritating. By this point Chelsea would have rolled her gorgeous eyes and told him to make a damn decision. He turned slightly to see a small smile on her face. She shook her head and gave him the universal sign for "they're insane."

They continued to speak in some weird shorthand, or maybe it was just that neither one of them wanted to end the painfully awkward conversation, but Simon had had enough. "Thank you so much for the offer, but I think Chelsea and I would be more comfortable in a hotel. It could take a few days."

"Oh." Phoebe blinked behind her glasses as she turned in her seat. "I suppose I understand. I actually have a really small place so I guess you would be uncomfortable."

"I wouldn't be," Jesse said quickly. "I don't need a lot of space. Trust me. I've been in some of the worst hellholes imaginable."

He'd been in an Iraqi prison, or rather a jihadist one. Jesse Murdoch had been held for a very long time, so long everyone thought he was dead. He'd been forced to watch as one by one, the members of his team were beheaded. He alone had survived, and Simon rather thought that had been a part of his torture, too. Jesse would rather have died than watched his teammates killed. When he'd returned to the States, he'd had to deal with rumors that he'd turned.

Simon knew one thing about the pup. He wouldn't have turned. He would have remained steadfast to his dying breath, but he didn't always think things through. "Jesse, I rather thought you would come with us. We have that case Ian assigned us, you know."

Dumbass. He was getting far too Americanized. He sounded a bit like his teammates now, even in his head.

Jesse nodded. "Oh, right. The case. Yeah, that's why I should go with them. I have work to do."

Phoebe sighed. "Of course. I understand. Maybe some other time. I just thought tonight could be…well, it's all for the best."

"Cockblock," Chelsea coughed under her breath.

Jesse's eyes came up and they narrowed as he stared back at Simon. "It's a really important case."

Yes, he had to hope Jesse believed that or Simon was in for a whole lot of explaining. "Sorry, mate. It is vital."

"Stupid work." Jesse turned toward 75, mumbling under his breath the whole way.

For fifteen minutes they drove in silence until finally Jesse pulled up in front of a nice apartment building in North Dallas.

He hustled Phoebe out of the Jeep and Simon watched as he walked her to the door of her building. Phoebe strode forward, walking better in her heels than she ever had in the office. Curious. She always seemed to stumble along when she was working, but there was something about the way she followed Jesse, something about the easy roll of her hips and how her shoulders had straightened. She looked around and just for a second, Simon saw her eyes narrow as if she was taking in the night around her, evaluating, looking for threats. And then she was right back to smiling. She tripped on the curb, but it seemed an almost practiced thing.

Jesse bought it. He practically leapt in front of her to make sure she didn't fall. She was in his arms and he stared at her for a long moment, no words passing between them.

"Dear god, Jesse's in love." Chelsea snorted a little. "They are going to make the world's least communicative children. If they ever actually sleep together. I heard their first date consisted of watching Harry Potter until Jesse fell asleep."

Jesse shook his head and said something that seemed to make her blush, but he finally got her to the door and kissed her. It was awkward, like all things but killing with Jesse, and yet there was a tenderness Simon couldn't deny.

Jesse was falling for the girl and suddenly Simon wondered about her. It wasn't anything tangible, just a feeling he got from time to time. Sometimes he could tell when someone was lying, and he would have bet in that moment that Phoebe Graham was hiding something.

"Was the first date at his place?"

Chelsea turned to him. "Why, Weston, I would have thought you would be above gossip."

"No one's above gossip." Gossip could tell an agent things that facts would hide. Sometimes gossip had been his best friend.

"Phoebe and I aren't exactly chummy, but Grace said they always stay at Jesse's, though the rumor is they haven't slept together. They've apparently slept in the same place, but not with like sex and stuff. So you really did cockblock the poor guy."

"I'm sure he'll return the favor at the worst possible moment." So she liked to stay at his place. That was interesting, too.

The door opened and Phoebe disappeared inside, taking her secrets with her.

Jesse jogged back to the Jeep and hopped in.

Simon chose to keep his questions to himself for now. Jesse was in deep and he knew well enough that any hint that he had questions about Phoebe would be met with discontent. Evidence was needed and sometimes even that wasn't enough.

"You have the worst timing in the world," Jesse grumbled as he put the Jeep in first and started out of the parking lot.

"It wasn't Simon's fault. I'm the one they're after," Chelsea conceded. "Sorry for interrupting fun time."

"I hadn't even been aware there was going to be fun time."

He cleared his throat. "We decided to take it slow."

Certainly. Simon was entirely sure that had been Jesse's idea. "A very mature decision. You've been dating her for how long?"

"It's only been a few weeks."

"Six," Chelsea piped up. Now that they were away from all the people trying to kill her, she'd perked up considerably.

And good for her since Simon's mood had taken a nosedive. Perhaps he was seeing things that weren't really there. The man from The Collective had inferred his uncle was a part of the organization.

He couldn't believe it. The very thought of David Malone doing anything shady made him sick at his stomach. Ten years before he wouldn't have had a shadow of a doubt, but he'd seen too much.

God, was he actually even entertaining the idea that his uncle was involved? If his uncle was involved, then JT was, too. JT knew Malone Oil like the back of his hand. Simon and Michael had worked rigs during the summers, but they'd always grumbled and complained about it. JT had loved it. Malone Oil was his birthright.

He couldn't be part of The Collective. It had just been a way to get Simon to come with him. That had to be it.

"Hey, you asleep back there?" Jesse's voice broke through his churning brain. "I need to know where to go."

"Head toward Fort Worth. I have a couple of motels in mind. No credit cards. Cash only."

Jesse's eyes widened in the rearview. "Uhm, there aren't a whole lot of those and they tend to charge by the hour, if you know what I mean."

"We're going to one. I have several addresses."

"I don't know what that means," Chelsea said with a shake of her head. "Why would they charge by the hour…oh, seriously? Ewww. Simon, come on. You have to have like a safehouse or something. You own whole buildings. Don't you have just one little tiny house where I won't catch a venereal disease from prostitutes?"

"You're planning on hiring them then? I wouldn't advise it.

If you're looking for a hooker, I can certainly find you a more palatable one than we're likely to come across at a motel. Jesse, do you still have your prostitute's number?"

"Dude," Jesse shot back. "We're not supposed to talk about that around the chicks. And no. I have not been seeing my very nice and well-paid escort for a while. Not since I started dating Phoebe. God, Chelsea. Please don't tell Phoebe. She doesn't need to know."

"But you know I deal in information, Murdoch. I'm going to have to think about it."

He hated it when she joked like that. "You don't deal in information anymore."

"Don't get your panties in a wad, Weston."

He also bloody well hated it when she distanced. When they'd been running, she nestled easily in his arms and clung to him. She'd trusted him with her life and been a damn fine partner, and now she was sitting so close to him but they were a million miles away. "That's ten."

She rolled her eyes. "You can't hold me to that contract."

"Jesse, please turn the car around. We need to go to Ian's place."

"You bastard." Sometimes she pouted like a child.

There were times when he had no idea at all what he saw in her. She was a brat and not always the sexy kind. She was childish and selfish and he should do exactly what he threatened. He should have Jesse turn the bloody car around and wash his hands of her. She was Ian's problem after all. She'd made it perfectly clear that she wanted nothing from him beyond to satisfy her curiosity. He should have taken her up on it and then sent her on her way.

"Just find whatever murder motel is the closest, Jesse," she was saying quietly. "No. We're not bringing Ian into it."

Jesse sighed. "Good because he can yell really loud. Sit back and I'll have us in a rat-infested hellhole in no time at all."

Chelsea sat back. A long moment passed, and Simon decided to give it a night. Just one night and he would absolutely turn her over in the morning. He wouldn't waste another second on a woman who couldn't care about him. He wasn't a masochist.

A warm hand stole over his. "He was lying, Simon. He was trying to throw you off. Malone Oil has been hit more than any other company."

"How do you know that?"

The hand tightened slightly, obviously offering him comfort. "Because when I found out you were involved with them, I checked."

A bitter laugh huffed from his chest. "You wanted to make sure I wasn't a Collective plant?"

Even in the dim light of the car he could see the confusion on her face. "No. I did it because they were involved in the Nelson case and I was curious. But Simon, they were one of Nelson's targets while he was working for The Collective. I think they're clean. If I had to bet on it, I would say that man back there would have loved to have taken both of us in. You would obviously make good collateral against your uncle."

And there it was. A little squeeze of her hand. An encouraging smile on her normally serious face. She gave that smile to so few people. That was why he wouldn't turn her over—because every now and then he saw the woman she could be and he knew he couldn't stop.

She took a deep breath and moved away again, her forehead resting against the side of the Jeep, and they fell into silence.

But just for a moment she'd seen through him and reached out. She'd been the one offering comfort. She'd been the one trying to protect him.

Simon sat back as the miles rolled past and vowed to find a way to reach her.

* * * *

Chelsea looked at the bed that dominated the room. The only bed. Somehow Jesse had managed to find the shitty motel that didn't have two queens. No. It was way worse. It was a single queen and there was no couch. And she was pretty sure the floor was covered in disease. "I think I should sleep somewhere else. We need to find another room."

Blue eyes stared a hole through her. Somehow his eyes managed to be both cold and hot given his mood. The color shifted, lighter, icier when he was angry. As warm as the Caribbean when he was happy.

They often seemed so cold when he looked at her. "You know why we're spending the night here. I explained this to you. This is the only place where I can be sure there are no security cameras and no way for The Collective to trace us. We're staying here."

"I'm sure they have another room, Weston. You don't have to sit up all night." Because there was no way they could share that bed. It was too small. He would take up all the space. He would be on top of her, and they both knew how that had ended the first time.

He locked the door and set down his duffel bag on the table. He eased out of his jacket because the man wore a three-piece suit on the run. She couldn't help but stare at his broad shoulders and the way his vest tapered down to perfectly pressed slacks. He tugged at the silver tie he was wearing, pulling it free and working the buttons at his throat until she could see the start of his truly impressive chest.

God, she hoped she wasn't drooling.

The shoulder holster was the next to go in his inadvertent striptease. "You should get settled in. We have to be up early in the morning. I'll take the side closest to the door."

He couldn't be serious. "Simon, there's not enough room on that bed."

He threw that gorgeous body down, making the springs squeak. "Of course there is, love. You Americans just like to take up an enormous amount of space."

She needed to take charge or she would make a complete fool of herself. Again. "Look, Weston, you turned down my offer."

He turned lazily, one hand coming up to balance his head. He looked like a pinup in a women's magazine—all lean and predatory lines. She could see the write-up in her head. *Simon likes tea, Scotch, and eating subs for breakfast. His turn-offs include everything that comes out of Chelsea Dennis's mouth.*

"Are you talking about your very charming offer to use my body to lose your virginity?"

She hadn't put it like that. "You don't want me. I get it. So let's keep things simple. I hired you. I'm the boss. I'm going to see if I can rent the room next to this one and that can be yours. We have enough cash for three rooms. You and me and Jesse can all have our own."

He didn't move. He didn't have to. She saw the way his eyes narrowed and then his voice came out, low and in that perfect upper-crust British accent that made her nipples hard. Her nipples were really stupid and she wished they didn't like him so damn much. "You're under a grave misapprehension, Chelsea. You are not my boss and you did not hire me. You came to me with a problem and I told you I would solve it. I believe I also mentioned that I was in charge and that was the only way I would do this for you. So you will clean up and take off your clothes and you'll get into this bed and you'll sleep beside me tonight. Jesse doesn't need a room at all. He's watching our backs. I won't make that more difficult for him to do by splitting us up. I'm directing this operation. I explained this to you when you signed the bloody contract. Do I need to explain what the word submissive means?"

Tears pricked her eyes. He was so damn unfair. She had to wonder if she would ever find a man who didn't want to punish her. "You forced me to sign that contract."

Now he moved, rolling to the side of the bed and getting to his feet with pure predatory grace. "I did nothing of the kind."

He seemed very willing to revise history. She wasn't about to let him forget. "If I hadn't signed your contract, you would have let me die."

He sighed, a long-suffering sound. "I certainly would not, and if you think that's true then you don't know me at all. Have we circled back around to the martyr state of your being? Perhaps I should do exactly what I should have done in the first place, what I would have done if you hadn't signed the contract."

That was worse than letting her die. "Please don't call Ian."

His shoulders weren't so straight as he turned and stared at her. "You're reckless, Chelsea. If I give up even a moment's control, I'll lose you, and I can't stand the thought of that. The only way to save you is to be your Master and the only Master you'll accept is not the kind I want to be."

"And what kind do you want to be?"

"Indulgent. Loving. Kind. I want a sub who obeys me in the field because she understands I would never let anyone hurt her. I want the play to just be play. I want a sub who trusts me with her body, who wants me and not just some faceless Dom who'll work her over and then walk away. And I certainly don't want to be a curiosity."

She felt embarrassment flash through her system. If she could take back her earlier idiocy, she would. "I get it. I got it when you turned me down the first time. I can get into bed with you because you won't touch me."

He was suddenly in her space. He'd moved so quickly she wasn't sure how he'd gotten there. One minute there was a bed between them and the next she was backing up until she hit the wall because he was stalking her. She'd gone as far as she could go, but he kept coming. He loomed over her, using every one of his six feet two inches. "I've tried to be polite about this, but you don't want that, do you? You don't want me to be a gentleman about this. You want me to take you because then you'll bloody well get it over with and you can put me in the same box with all the other men who hurt you and used you and cast you aside. I would be just one more villain who did something to you."

She should be shaking. She should be trying to get away. She hated being backed into a corner, but all she could think about was how good he smelled, how nice it had been when he'd let her kiss him and explore his body. "I never said that."

"You don't have to. I understand you, Chelsea. You can't comprehend that, but I do. I understand you like no other man will. So I understand that I have to explain certain things to you." He moved closer until his mouth hovered above hers, his heat sinking into her skin. "I'm going to tell you how this is going to go. We'll get into that bed and I'm going to put my hands on you and I'm going to put my mouth on you. I'm going to taste you. I swear by the time you get out of that bed in the morning, you're going to know what it feels like to come against my tongue. That screaming you heard as we walked in, you're going to make that girl's orgasm sound like the squeaking of a mouse. But the one thing you won't get is my cock. You won't get that because I'm not going to take your virginity because you're curious. I'll take it when you can't think about anything but me. I'll take it when you cry out my name and tell me there's no other man you'll ever love the way you love me. Then and only then will I take what belongs to me. Am I understood?"

She managed to nod.

He took a step back and she immediately missed his heat. His hands went to the buttons on his shirt. "Then take off those bloody clothes and get in bed."

Take off her clothes? Oh, that was what she always tried to avoid so he wouldn't see her scars, so he wouldn't see just how damaged she was. What kind of game was he playing now? First he didn't want her and then he was willing to play with her but not actual sex. She was so confused. Perhaps the best thing to do was a strategic retreat. "I'll be right back."

She fled to the bathroom, flipping the light switch on and then wishing she hadn't. She was fairly certain something had scurried behind the shower curtain. She was going to finally do it. She was going to be patient zero in a North American plague outbreak.

What was she doing? She was picking the rats, or something slightly larger, over the kindest, most gorgeous man she'd ever met? She really was caught in some sort of martyrdom. Poor little Chelsea. She wasn't as smart or as fast as her big sister. Her father had only wanted Charlotte. He'd just taken Chelsea along as a bargaining chip to gain Charlotte's compliance, and when Charlotte fucked up, oh, Chelsea had been the one to suffer.

Chelsea turned on the water to cold and was grateful when it came out clear. She stared at herself for a moment, almost not recognizing the woman she saw in the mirror. She was older, more careworn. She had breasts and hips. Somehow she still saw herself as a child, or at least a teenaged girl who never had to grow up because she'd been brutalized and in exchange, she got to forego responsibility, got to be selfish.

Got to wash blood off her face. Got to run away from

anything that might be good for her. Got to screw up anything that might be good for her sister.

If she stayed here, she would put a wedge between Charlotte and Ian because she'd done such a damn fine job of making Charlotte feel guilty. They were probably fighting over her as she sat here staring.

Charlotte would want to find her as quickly as possible and Ian would be more than happy to leave her in Simon's care. Ian would resent the position Charlotte put him in. He would come to resent the fact that Charlotte tried to put Chelsea first. He wouldn't understand that it was all because Chelsea had taken all the beatings, all the abuse, all the pain. He couldn't understand that one night Charlotte had found her with a dead body pinning her to the bed.

"If you try to get out through the window, I will hunt you down, Chelsea." Simon sounded like he was standing right outside the door.

Chelsea wiped the blood off her face, watched it turn the water pink briefly before disappearing down the drain. It was time to get out of purgatory. Maybe that bomb in a box had been the best thing to happen to her. It let her know it was time to go.

She was going to leave. As soon as she figured out how to get The Collective off her back, she would very quietly do what she should have done in the first place. She would step aside and let Charlotte live her life. She would disappear and then Charlotte and Ian could have little satanic babies and be happy.

Simon could be happy.

But she had a few days before she had to go back into the darkness again. Was she going to be brave or regret every moment she spent not being with him?

The door opened abruptly. Simon stared down at her. "I thought it would be locked."

It had been a good bet. It was certainly the kind of thing she'd done in the past. Now she wondered if she'd been a vicious brat around him because she'd been desperate to get his attention and being mean was the only way she knew how to get it. "I'm not dumb, Weston. I wanted you to be able to get in here as fast as you could in case one of the residents attacked."

He arched a single aristocratic brow. "Residents?"

She shuddered. "I'm pretty sure there's like a possum or something moving over there. Or maybe it's the giant scorpions. I don't actually think we have a ton of those around here."

"Don't joke right now. I want to know what you're going to do. I want to know if you're going to run." He looked so serious she had to sigh.

She'd been lying to herself all along, and having made the decision to leave, she just couldn't do it another second. She wanted to know what it meant to be his, even if it was only for a day or two. "I'm going to obey my Master."

His eyes flared, and she could have sworn his slacks tented in a heartbeat. Maybe she was wrong. Maybe he really did want her. "Chelsea?"

She hoped he still wanted her after he'd seen her scars. She shook her head. "I'm tired of fighting this, but you should know that I'm also scared shitless of the entire sex act."

"We're not having sex."

"So you're taking a Clintonian view of the act?"

It was his turn to sigh. "No cock until you give me what I want."

He was a little arrogant. It was one of the things that kind of got her hot about him. "And what is that?"

"I want you to love me."

"I can't. I don't have that in me." She wanted to. She wanted nothing more than to open herself and love him, but that part of her heart had been burned away. She couldn't love him and even if she was capable, she wouldn't let herself because she was bad for everyone. The best gift she could give him was to leave and let him be free of this weird, painful cycle they were in.

"You have no idea what you could do if you would try." His eyes were intent on hers, staring as though he could impart his will.

The trouble was she wasn't sure she even wanted to try. She'd tried before and it had been a disaster. She'd tried to be good and it never worked out. "I think I know myself better than you think."

"I think you don't know yourself at all, but god, Chelsea,

I'm sick of arguing with you. Kiss me again. I don't get mad at you when you kiss me."

And that was their problem. The only times they weren't arguing or bickering at each other were when they were playing. Kissing Simon had been the most peaceful place she'd ever found. Likely would ever find.

She didn't hesitate. She wanted these moments with him. She went on her toes in that horrific bathroom and forgot about the rodents and the mold and the prostitutes next door and let her lips find his. Warmth immediately flooded her system, and her skin tingled in a way it never had before.

"Why are you afraid?"

She stiffened immediately. She never should have told him.

His hands found her head, softly smoothing her hair back. "Don't. Don't pull away from me. Talk to me. Tell me what the trouble is. We signed a contract and that means your troubles are my troubles. I want to help you, Chelsea."

"When you put it like that it makes me sound like a charity case."

He growled and dragged her against him, letting his hard cock rub against her belly. "Fine. You won't let me be delicate. I want to help me. I want to shove my cock inside you and I can't do that until I figure out why you're so bloody afraid of me and intimacy and being together."

"Can't you let things lie, Simon? I'm tired. I don't want to talk about it. I just want to kiss you for a while and forget about everything else. I promise I'll be good. I won't even try to run away."

"I won't wake up and find you've left in the morning?" He said it like it was a joke, but she noticed the tight set of his jaw. He thought it was a possible outcome.

She had to smile and she let her arms wrap around him. It was so much nicer than pushing him away. Her cheek rested against his chest and she could hear his heartbeat. It was strong and steady, like the man himself. His arms were around her and he surrounded her, cutting off the rest of the world. Why would she run from that? "I told you, I'll honor our contract. I won't run. I'll do what you need me to do until we figure a way out of this mess."

And then she would leave.

His fingers tangled gently in her hair, drawing her face up so her eyes met his. "I will get you out of this. We'll figure out what they want."

She didn't like the thought of that. "And we'll give it to them?"

"No, love. Whatever information you have, we'll make a bomb out of it and shove it right up their arses. We'll laugh when they explode, and they will. I won't allow them to get away with this." Even though his tone was soft, she could hear the will behind his words. He wouldn't stop until he'd done what he said.

She might have to protect her Dom, too. Simon was like a superhero. Strong. Powerful. A little naïve and always preferring to do the noble thing. These men who were after her didn't believe in nobility. She would have to watch his back.

But right now she could watch his front. His gorgeous, sun-kissed front. He'd ditched everything but his shirt and slacks, and his pristine white dress shirt was open and untucked, revealing the most beautiful chest she'd ever seen. She loved the way he looked in his leathers when he walked the floor of Sanctum, but she'd never gotten this close. She'd definitely been a "worship him from afar" girl. Even the one time he'd played with her, she hadn't touched him. She'd done exactly what he accused her of. She'd used him to get rid of her pain and the moment he offered her anything else, she'd called for her sister and pushed him away. She was done pushing him away for now.

"Can I touch you, Sir?"

He shook his head. "Master. I prefer to be called Master. I want to hear it even if it's only for a little while. I'll find a collar for you at some point."

"Simon," she began. She wasn't sure she could handle him collaring her, like she meant something special to him. It would mean so much and it would be a lie because she had to leave when the op was over.

"No arguments," he said, his mouth hovering over hers. "It's in our contract."

He was killing her with that contract. She stared at his lips even as she knew she should be protesting. Such beautiful lips for a man. Plump and sensual and perfect on his face. She managed a token challenge. “You didn’t mention that part.”

Those lips curled ever so slightly in a devilishly sexy grin. “You should have read it before you signed it.”

She’d been impulsive. She always read everything five times and then tried to figure out how the person on the other end of the document was trying to screw her. She was careful but her guard fell asleep around him. Like her walls were tired of holding up and they’d found a safe place to crumble. She hadn’t read the contract, simply signed her name, and if putting a collar around her throat made him feel better, then perhaps she should soften up, too. Just a little. “I don’t like leather.”

“Neither do I. Gold. Your skin looks good in gold. Kiss me, Chelsea.”

She loved the way he said it. It didn’t feel like a demand. Coming from his sensual mouth and in his so-sexy British accent, his words felt more like an entreaty, like a call for something he needed.

No one ever needed her before.

She went on her toes and kissed him again for the second time that night. She let her lips play against his, allowed her tongue to trace the seam of his mouth. His hands moved from her back to her hips, but no further. He seemed determined to play the gentleman. He liked to be in control. He wouldn’t be a Dom if he didn’t, but he held back for her sake.

“Let me see your breasts,” he whispered before dragging his tongue across her bottom lip and making her shiver.

She would have told anyone who asked that kissing wasn’t something she would like to do. It seemed messy. The few times she’d tried it before had been awkward and led nowhere, but kissing Simon was a totally different experience. She’d thought it would be a meshing of lips, but somehow her whole body got involved. Her hands stroked his back. Her chest brushed restlessly against his. Her hips seemed to move to a rhythm of their own.

Her breasts. He wanted to see them. They weren’t too bad. They were small, but perky. He’d seen them before, caught brief glances when she managed to work up the courage to play with him. She could show him her breasts.

Except her hands didn't seem to work.

"Love, this can't work if you won't show me. I can't touch them and lick them and suck on them through your shirt. I can't taste you like this."

That did something for her. Holy smokes. Her pussy seemed to tighten and soften all at the same time. What the hell was that about?

She'd never really felt it before, but it was good. It left her restless, but it was a good restless.

She stepped back because she couldn't do a damn thing with his hands on her. She couldn't even think much less make her hands leave his body.

The minute she stepped away, she remembered where she was—in a rat-infested hotel on the run from people who wanted her dead.

"Don't. We're not here. Not really. We're somewhere beautiful, Chelsea. We're somewhere lovely."

"Where?" Tears clouded her eyes because it had been so long since she'd been somewhere really lovely. She wouldn't have noticed because she never looked around. She kept her head down, watched the sidewalk so she didn't fall. She watched for threats. She never looked at the beauty of a place.

"My home. Norsely. It's beautiful. It's in the country. Everything is green and lush there. My room overlooks the gardens, and during the spring a wind sweeps in and I can smell the roses. It's all in white. White curtains, white linens, white carpet. I open the door to the balcony so the breeze can wash over us. It makes us feel clean and it feels so good on your skin, love. It's cool, but I promise I'll make you warm again."

She closed her eyes and she could see it, feel the breeze on her skin. It made her shiver but he was right. He could make her warm with a single look. Against the white of the room, he stood out. His skin and hair were sun kissed, as though Apollo himself had blessed him.

"You're here with me, Chelsea. Show me how beautiful you are."

She opened her eyes, but all she could see was him. She let go of everything else. She didn't have to be anywhere she didn't want to be. If she wasn't really here, then she didn't have to be afraid. She could be who she wanted to be. She could be brave.

She let her hands drift to the bottom of her T-shirt and she pulled it over her head before she could think about it. She did away with the bra. If she was going to this, she would do it right. "It sounds beautiful. Your home that is."

He'd grown up in a mansion. She'd seen the manor house in pictures because when she was bored she always turned to her favorite subject. Night after endless night she would look for articles about him. When the pain in her leg flared, she looked for pictures of him attending grand balls and graduating from Oxford. She hoped he never found the folders she kept on her servers where she stashed all the information she could find about him and his family. The Westons had been royalty for centuries, coming in and out of favor with various kings and queens but always finding a way to better themselves.

Her father had killed her mother and god only knew how many people. He'd been a criminal and her home had been stolen from someone who owed her father money.

"It is beautiful, but not as beautiful as you."

"Simon…"

He put a finger to her lips. "Hush. I don't want to be forced to punish you. Just agree with me and we'll get along so much better. You're beautiful, Chelsea, and I'll say it until you believe it." His eyes were on her breasts. "Are you really a virgin?"

She nodded. "There weren't many choices growing up and then I was on the run."

She didn't have to tell him anything else. He didn't have to know about that night.

"So no man's ever brushed his fingers over your flesh?" Gently, oh so gently, his fingertips traced a line from her collarbone to her nipples. Like a little butterfly flapping its wings against her skin.

She shook her head. "No."

No one ever touched her the way he did.

With one finger he traced a circle around her areola. She

could feel her nipple tightening, peaking. "No man's ever put his mouth here."

He was going to do it. He was going to kiss her there and she wanted it. Her body felt soft, submissive. Submission had always been just a word for her, something she would say to get what she wanted. She wanted to submit to him, to let him do what he wanted because she had no idea what she could be. That was what he'd said. That she could be more. She wanted more.

"No."

He dropped to his knees in front of her.

"Simon, the floor…" It seemed wrong for him to touch it. He was always so clean.

"The carpet is quite easy on my knees, love. It's chenille. So soft. And you look gorgeous in the afternoon light. The window behind us faces the west. It catches the sunset and it makes your hair come alive. It brings out the red and gold, and sparkles against your naked skin. It makes you look like a goddess."

He leaned his head forward and pressed a chaste kiss against her breast.

Heat flared along her flesh. "Tell me more."

"There's a bed and I'll take you there in a moment." He switched to her other breast, giving it the same tender treatment. "It's quite large."

She couldn't help but smile. "You have a big bed? I would have thought it would be small after your lecture on Americans needing space. You had a brother growing up. Did you share a room with him?"

He chuckled against her skin, running his nose across her as though memorizing her scent. "Don't talk about my brother. He might like to share with his friends, but I prefer to be one on one. And this wasn't my room. This is more like a fantasy I have. A grown-up version. I won't ever live there again. That's my brother's home now."

But he missed it. She could hear it in his voice. "So in your fantasy you have a big bed."

His tongue came out, licking over her and making her squirm. "Yes, we need a big bed for all the things I want to do to you. I don't want it to be staid and plain between us. I want it dirty and rough and sweet and slow and everything that it can be between two people. A Dom needs room to make his sub scream."

She was almost screaming as it was. He licked her other nipple and then took it between his teeth, rolling it gently and then biting down so suddenly she couldn't help but squeal.

"God, I love that sound."

She could feel his whispered words all along her flesh. It made her shiver with desire she hadn't known possible. This man did it for her in every way she'd never imagined. It was like her skin was magnetized and attracted to him and only him.

He sucked her nipple hard, his arms going around her waist and dragging her to him. She let her head fall back. Simon had promised her he wouldn't take her virginity. He claimed he wouldn't penetrate her until she begged for him—until she loved him. She knew only two things in the world. She knew that Charlotte was a devoted sister and that when Simon Weston told her something, he would move heaven and earth to make certain what he said would happen. He wouldn't lie to her. He was the good guy.

She could relax because she wasn't going to give him what he wanted.

She couldn't tell him that she loved him.

God, she wanted to be able to love him. She'd never felt about anyone the way she felt for him but she didn't trust it, didn't believe it could last. She wanted him so badly, but she would have to leave him if only to protect him.

She let her hands find his hair. She had him for the moment and she wanted everything she could have from him. She held him to her breast, reveling in the way he sucked and licked and bit at her. He moved from one nipple to the next and she wondered how it would feel to wear his clamps. He would pick pretty clamps and slip them over her nipples one by one. They would bite into her, a reminder that he was her Master. When he touched her, she would move and whimper and shiver and feel the touch of his clamps.

Maybe she was a little more submissive than she was willing to admit—but only when it came to him.

Simon's hands moved over her back, sliding down to cover her butt. Sweet heat suffused her. Even as he cupped her ass, she wanted more. So much more. She wanted to be exactly in the place he'd described to her. She wanted him to take her to his home and make her his queen, or duchess, or whatever as long as she was his just for a little while.

"Tell me you want me." Simon was staring up at her, his blue eyes hotter than she could ever remember them.

"I want you." It was easy. She could give him that. She wanted him to take her, to be the only man who ever entered her.

Damn it. She didn't mean that. She would move on after him.

And still it was true. "I do want you."

He stood up and hauled her into his arms like she weighed nothing. "Then let's not waste more time."

She agreed. She'd wasted far too much time.

Chapter Six

He was an idiot. What the bloody hell was he doing? He carried her from the disgusting bathroom into the relatively clean by comparison bedroom. He couldn't fuck her here. She deserved more. It was why he'd started talking about his stupid dreams. He'd started having them the night after he'd met her. He was back at Norsely but this time he felt like he belonged. This time he wasn't just the spare. He wasn't always in his brother's shadow, the younger son who screwed up everything. He was a son of Norsely and he belonged.

It didn't matter. He gently placed Chelsea on the bed. He had everything he needed. He had money and a place in the world. He didn't need a stupid manor house. He didn't need his brother to know him.

He did need her.

He was starving for her.

"I'm going to take your pants off now." He was the slightest bit wary. She was twenty-seven. He didn't buy her "I didn't have time to have sex" act. Something had happened. He wasn't a fool. He knew her history. He'd read the file on her and her sister. There had been a reason Ian had put a knife in her uncle's back. And her father… The one good thing Eli Nelson had done on this earth had been to kill the fucker. He'd tortured his daughter. Something had set her off men, and he had to be careful because he didn't want to be just another man who did her wrong.

She was on her back, propped up on her elbows, somber eyes looking down at him. "I don't want you to see me."

Her scars. She was touchy about them. "I've seen you, Chelsea. They didn't bother me before. Do you want to see mine? I've got scars, too. No one gets to my age in this business without a few scars."

She nodded and rolled to her side. She was such a hard case. In order to get her to open even the slightest bit, he damn near had to bleed for her, and yet he shrugged out of his shirt. His chest bore the scars of his youth. She'd likely seen them before, but he hadn't pointed them out, hadn't told her the stories.

He pointed to a long, snake-like scar that ran from his left side collarbone to almost touch his sternum. "Not exactly pretty."

She got to her knees, her eyes widening. God, when she looked at him with that little bit of wonder in her eyes, his cock got rock hard. No woman had ever looked at him the way Chelsea did. She wasn't lusting after his money or the fame that came with being royal. She just wanted what he could give her. "Can I touch it?"

It was going to be a frustrating night. "Yes."

She let her fingertips trace the scar. "Where did you get it?"

"I was fifteen and working for the summer at my uncle's ranch. A calf got stuck in a fence and then I took his place."

"What? What the hell were you doing with a cow?"

It was good to know he could still surprise her. "A calf, love. I wouldn't have been able to get a full-size cow out. Unfortunately, I got stuck and panicked a bit. The barb tore its way across my chest. My uncle's foreman sewed me up. It was also the first time I tried rotgut whiskey. I woke up with a raging hangover, this scar, and my aunt screaming at my uncle."

"Uhm, your uncle is a billionaire. He couldn't take you to the doctor?"

Her hands on his skin felt so fucking good. "Apparently that's not the cowboy way." He couldn't help but grin. "I didn't mind. I just wanted to fit in. I liked riding herd. I understood it. My mother was an equestrian champion in her youth, but I always preferred western tack. Working a horse like that should mean something beyond showing off for a ribbon. There's purpose in riding herd."

So much of his life had been for show, but those summers in Texas held meaning.

"What about this one?" Her fingers moved to a place just above the waist of his slacks. She had to be able to see just how hard his cock was, but she stared at a nasty puncture scar above his hip bone.

"RAF training. I was in a helicopter accident. Luckily I wasn't the one flying." It had been bad. High winds had sent the chopper into a tailspin and they had hit the ground, bouncing several times before stopping. Everyone had survived, but he'd broken his arm in two places, broken two ribs and lost a small portion of his liver. Apparently that grew back. Lucky for him.

"You can fly just about anything, can't you?" She brushed against the scar, staring at it like it was a piece of art she was studying. She seemed to have made a study of him.

"Yes. I flew Tornados mostly." Panavia Tornados, a sleek, styled fighter jet. Sometimes he missed flying. It was something he'd been bloody good at. "But I also can fly choppers and small aircraft. I quite like flying. I've been trying to talk Tag into getting a company jet."

"He's a cheap bastard." She smiled a little. "That's two whole scars, Weston. Not exactly impressive to a girl like me."

"The rest are lower. Do you want to see them?" He took a long, steadying breath.

Chelsea stood. She was obviously awkward without a shirt, and her skin had flushed as though she'd finally remembered where she was. For a second, he was sure he'd lost her and that she'd go back and find her shirt and they would be at another impasse. Then she slowly began pushing the pants off her hips. She shimmied out of the PJ pants and stood in front of him wearing nothing but a pair of panties that a granny likely would throw aside as far too distasteful.

She grimaced a little. "Sorry. I wasn't really thinking I'd be showing off the undies today."

"Chelsea, love, those are about a size too big and the waistband is coming off." It was so unsexy and yet he found it more charming than the woman who had shipped herself to him wearing nothing but a pair of Louboutins and a cream-colored La Perla thong. He wasn't about to have Chelsea escorted out the way he had that one.

She frowned. "I hadn't done laundry. The asshole assassins didn't give a crap that I'd just gotten back from Europe. Though you should know I don't have a lot of pretty things. I don't really need them."

"No, you don't."

She smiled. "Good. I like to be comfortable."

"No, love. Again, you didn't read the contract. No panties at all for you. That should be deeply comfortable and you don't have to worry about laundering them." He loved the fact that she was now standing with him mostly naked and she'd obviously forgotten to be self-conscious. All he had to do was piss her off, and he was very good at doing that.

"You can't take my panties." Her hand went down as though to protect that wretched piece of fabric.

"I can make you give them to me."

She shook her head but there had been no way to miss the way she shuddered. It wasn't in distaste. "I don't think so, Weston."

"Ah, a challenge. I like a challenge." Ever so slowly, so there was no way for her to be startled by the move, he reached out and cupped her breasts again. They were small but beautifully formed, and fit perfectly in his hands. Her nipples peaked again, elongating, and he couldn't help but fall to his knees in front of her. "I'll get them off you. I swear it, and you'll be the one to hand them over to me because you're in control. You know that, right?"

Her voice came out in a breathy puff. "I've heard the whole Dom speech. The sub is always in control. Yeah, sure."

He kissed her nipple. She would look so gorgeous in clamps. He really had to rethink his go bag. It contained burner phones, cash, alternate identification but no nipple clamps, and that seemed like a mistake. Of course he should always have a pair of clamps for her pretty tits. "You're in control, Chelsea. And all you have to say tonight is no. One no and I'll stop and we'll sleep. I won't ever force you to do anything you don't want to do."

"Except not wear proper underwear."

"I want access to my sub's pussy." He could smell her arousal. That sweet, spicy feminine scent hit his nose and it smelled a little like victory.

Her fingers sank into his hair, holding him to her breast, though he had no intention of leaving it. "I thought I wasn't getting any of that."

He circled her nipple with his tongue, palming the other breast. "Any cock? No. Not until I have what I want. I have standards, too, you know."

"Yes, I can plainly see that. It must have been hard to turn down all those women who used to throw themselves at you."

He tipped his face up to look at her. "It wasn't hard, because they didn't really want me. They wanted money or to be in the tabloids or access to my brother. It was easy to turn them away."

Her expression softened and she smoothed back his hair. "I'm sorry. I didn't mean it to sound so…I don't judge. I didn't realize. It sounds like a fabulous life, but if no one really sees you, I guess that would kind of suck."

Ah, the wisdom of Chelsea Dennis. And yet she'd hit the nail on the head. "I need you to see me, Chelsea. I want to see you. We have a lot in common."

She sighed a little. "No, we don't, but I don't really care anymore."

She was wrong, but he didn't want to waste time schooling her. It was past late and they had to move in a few hours. And he really wanted to get those nasty knickers off her.

He tongued her nipples, moving back and forth, giving her stronger suction with each pass. She could handle a good deal of pain, but she'd only ever been worked over in a clinical fashion. The Doms she'd worked with—he wouldn't use the word play—had used floggers to take her to subspace. There was never the promise of anything sexual for Chelsea. She seemed to use

BDSM as an alternative to pain medication when her legs hurt. He wanted to show her it could be so much more. He licked her nipple and then gave her a little bite.

She gasped, but her hands tugged at his hair to draw him in, not pull him off. That was where he wanted her to go.

He continued the nipple play even as he let his hands move lower to cup her ass. That was a gorgeous backside. Full and round, he dreamed of spanking her, of getting her pink and hot and ready to fuck.

He pulled away and was rewarded with a little moan that sounded like disappointment. "Lie down on the bed. I checked it. It seems clean. The sheets smell like fabric softener. On your belly."

Her eyes flared. "What?"

He softened his tone. "I want to touch you. I want to inspect you. Have I done anything that brought you pain?"

She shook her head.

"Then obey me. If you don't like it, you can tell me to stop."

She turned away from him and crawled on top of the bed, giving him a delicious view of her backside.

And her legs.

"God, you've got a beautiful arse."

"I don't know how you can think that word is sexy." At least she was giggling.

He put a hand on her back, loving the silky feel of her skin. "I should be more American? Ass is sexier? I go back and forth. I can use whichever you prefer. I've spent enough time in the States to use the lingo."

It bothered his parents that he sounded so very American much of the time. He was self-aware enough to know he'd likely done it to annoy them. And to feel closer to his cousins.

"It's not about the word. I don't know that a bottom is sexy at all, Simon. I mean, we sit on it. Sure Charlotte always talks about how hot Ian's is, but Ian is a giant walking ass so I guess if she didn't like them she wouldn't have married one."

She had the most sarcastic view of the world. "Do you know what I'll do to your…ass?"

"Spank it?" The question had a little tremble to it.

He let his hand run down to the small of her back. "That and so much more. I'll play with it. I'll rim your little hole with my fingers to make sure you can one day take my cock there."

"We should talk about that," she started.

He gave that glorious piece of flesh he obsessed over a nice hard smack. "I'm not doing it tonight. I am going to do something else." He slid his hand to her thigh. He'd noticed the tightness in her eyes. She could use a session, but again, his go bag was floggerless—another oversight. He had to take care of her in a different manner. He'd studied up on her type of injury. She was a stubborn girl and neglected her body, preferring to use that big brain of hers. She needed a good rubdown, but likely found it far too intimate.

If there was one thing he was going to do, it was give her what she needed.

He slid his hand over her hamstrings, giving her firm pressure as he stroked down her leg.

She squirmed a little. "Hey."

He gave her another smack. "Hush unless you want me to stop."

A groan shuddered through her body as he squeezed her calf. "What are you doing, Weston?"

When she was trying to distance, she always called him Weston. He wanted her purring his Christian name before the night was through. "You're in pain. I'm trying to make sure you can walk in the morning."

"Oh, oh. I shouldn't let you, but do that again."

Yes, that was what he wanted. He wanted her purring. He ran his thumb over a tight muscle, finding the pressure point and pressing down. She groaned again, but after a moment the knot relaxed and he moved on to the next one.

She wasn't leggy like her sister. Charlotte was tall, but Chelsea was more average height. Her legs weren't long, but he liked being bigger than her. He could take her entire calf and engulf it in his two hands. She seemed to relax further every time he did it. Over and over he rubbed, finding the knots and working them out. He slid her socks off and rubbed her feet.

"God, Simon. That feels so good."

"Aftercare. Or in this case simply care. It's what I always wanted to give you." The one time he'd been her chosen Dom, she'd called for her sister after he was done. She hadn't known he'd carefully prepped an aftercare room. He'd borrowed an aromatherapy machine and poured lavender oil in it because it was supposed to be relaxing. He'd made sure the sheets on the massage table had been warmed and he'd stupidly laid out a single, perfect, chosen-by-hand rose. He'd made a complete idiot of himself.

And she'd called for Charlotte.

"Simon, I'm sorry about that day. I was…scared. I don't know. You want more than I can possibly give you." She sighed as he pressed his thumb into the arch of her foot.

He wanted everything from her, but he had to be patient. "We'll take it slow. Are you ready to give me your knickers?"

"No."

He would have to try harder.

"You don't think they're ugly?" Chelsea asked as his hand moved across the longest of her scars.

This was why she'd always held him back. He knew it, but it was ridiculous. There was nothing ugly about her body. She just had a few scars and so did he. "I think you have beautiful legs, Chelsea. There's nothing at all wrong with you."

He straddled her and pushed her hair out of the way so he could get to the nape of her neck. He put his mouth there, nipping and kissing and licking his way down her spine. He loved the way she shivered when he licked the back of her knees. When he'd given her back the full treatment, he flipped her over.

He went straight for her neck, burying his face there while he let his hand find its way down to her pussy. He slid his fingers under the band of her knickers and right across her clitoris.

Chelsea nearly sat straight up.

He eased her back down, his mouth playing at hers. "You like that?"

"Oh my god." She shook slightly and her eyes flared every time he circled her clit.

"Do you know how much better it would feel if it was my mouth sucking at your clit? I want to taste you, Chelsea. I want to shove my tongue up your cunt and suck down all that glorious juice it's making for me. Do you want me to kiss and lick and suck at your pussy?"

"I don't…god, I can't think…that feels so good."

He pulled his hand away. "I told you what I wanted. Are you going to give it to me or should I turn over and go to sleep?"

She closed her eyes and took a deep breath.

Damn it all. He'd overplayed his hand and he couldn't go back now. He should have gotten her hotter, tried harder.

If he went back on his word, he would never be her Dom. He would always be the boy she could do whatever she wanted with and that wasn't what she needed.

"All right then." He rolled off her and got to his feet. "Go to sleep, Chelsea. I'll wake you when it's time to move."

He'd gambled and lost. He turned away and walked back to the small, dilapidated desk. He would sit and watch over her since that seemed to be all she would allow him to do.

It was going to be a long night.

* * * *

When had he become such a drama queen? She'd hesitated for a half a second and he'd gotten up. And she was the martyr? He was turned away from her, his hands on his hips. His head was down and he was breathing heavily.

She had two choices. She could do exactly what he said and turn over and pretend nothing at all had happened and maybe they would be on a better footing in the morning, or she could get him to do that thing he'd said he would do to her girl parts. That thing had felt amazing when he'd done it with his thumb. She couldn't imagine what it would feel like if it was his tongue touching her there.

Of course it could be a truly awful experience. What if she tasted horrible? She'd showered and done all the hygienic things a girl should do. Hell, she'd even shaved, not because she thought some gorgeous British god of a man might want to inspect her lady bits, but because she hated all that hair. At least she was fairly certain she was clean down there, except that she was ridiculously wet, but that kind of seemed to be the point of the exercise.

A weird Venn diagram formed in her head. In the *A* bubble was her pride and in the *B* was her curiosity. She quickly placed peace of mind and safety in *A* and orgasm in *B*. Yep, she was seriously curious about that orgasm. Then there was that place where the bubbles overlapped. Her knickers. She could keep them and her pride or she could give them up and potentially get an orgasm. That was kind of wrong. She would be pretty damn proud if she actually had one, right? It wasn't like this was a game and if she gave in to the Dom she lost. She got a potential orgasm and proof positive that her parts worked like other women's. Circle *B* won.

She sat up. Decision made.

And she was so buying new undies. She bought all her clothes off the Internet and half the time they didn't fit. She needed an upgrade from underwear she could buy in a pack of nine and T-shirts with snarky sayings.

She slipped out of the undies and held them in her hand. She would rather toss them to the side, but he'd been specific. She had to give them to him like a massive granny panty gift. Doms were all about the specifics.

"Simon." She hated standing around naked, but he'd been serious about that, too. And actually it felt kind of nice to not cover up. He hadn't vomited at the sight of her scars. He'd just rubbed her and made her feel really good. And he had some pretty nasty shit on his hot bod. She wanted to kiss and lick his scars, and what the hell was up with that?

"Go to sleep, Chelsea. I'll turn the light off in a moment."

It was time for her to soothe her Dom and give him sweet words and coax him back to bed. "Do you want the underwear or not?"

Yeah, she was probably never going to be that girl.

He turned on her and she was rewarded with the way his baby blues flared. He grabbed the panties out of her hand. "I thought you were done for the night."

She felt herself flush under his stare. "I need time to think every now and then. I just had to make the decision. I decided I want you to lick me because it seems like a good thing to try."

"Not good enough. I told you I'm not a curiosity."

He was a frustration. He was going to make her say it. She needed to be bold and plain. How would Charlotte put it? She wouldn't prevaricate. She would simply use words that would mean something to her man. "Simon, if you don't eat my pussy I'm going to die."

She found herself in his arms again. "That will work, love. I was going to spend the night in throes of frustration if I didn't get my mouth on you."

He lowered his lips and suddenly his tongue was inside, tangling with hers as he backed her to the bed. She loved kissing him. She could lose herself for hours in just playing with his mouth. Now that she was naked, she took inventory of how it felt to be against him. His shirt was off so the hard warmth of his chest met hers, making her nipples peak. Somehow she'd damn near climbed up his body. She wasn't sure how it had happened, but her legs were around his waist and she could feel the material of his slacks against her thighs.

And then she felt the bedspread against her back and his weight on top of her. He was heavy. So heavy. But he was Simon, so she forced herself to take a deep breath and not flip out on the hot guy who was really just trying to give her an orgasm.

"What happened?" Simon's head came up. He looked down at her. "Sorry. I forgot."

He eased his body to the side, sliding over so he could nuzzle her breasts.

How could he have known that being pinned down bugged her? "Forgot what?"

His hand found her now naked girl parts and heat threatened to overwhelm her. "I lost my head a bit. I know it bothers you to have a man's weight on top of you. It's all right. We can do this your way for now."

"How did you know? And I don't think I have a way, Simon." He was confusing her. He knew so much but there was no way he could really know. Charlotte wouldn't have told him. There were no records to find.

He moved down her body again, seemingly unconcerned with her near panic. "You told me you don't like being tied down. My weight on top of you would feel very similar. I've got five and a half stone on you, love. If I'm on top of you, you can't move, can't fight me off. It's all right. And you do have a way. We just have to find it. How do you like this?"

He placed his thumb squarely over her clit, gently pressed down and then rotated it.

Holy mother of… "I like it. You should keep doing that."

She couldn't help it. She pressed her pelvis up, trying to keep that amazing sensation going.

"No." He moved his hand away, proving he was a ratfink bastard torturer Dom. Mean. Mean man. "I think we've adequately found evidence that you like that particular touch. We should move on."

"I hate you." But it was said with a little whine because she kind of wanted to see what else he would do.

He'd moved all the way down her body and off the bed. He was on his knees between her legs. He dragged her further down to the edge of the mattress so her backside was right there. He forced her legs high, spreading her wide.

"Uhm, this feels a little like an exam I try to avoid on a yearly basis." It was awkward. She was fully on display. There was nowhere to hide.

"It's so fucking pretty." His voice had lowered to a sexy growl she'd never once heard from any gynecologist. "It's a lovely pink and coral flower and it's all mine." He leaned over and put his nose right in her pussy and took a deep breath. "God, you smell good. You're going to taste even better."

It was way too intimate. She really should do that "saying no" thing, but her brain just seemed a little fuzzy and able to focus on one thing and only one thing—her pussy and getting him to touch her there again.

"You're so wet, love. Keep your legs spread for me." He let go of her ankles and his fingers were skimming her sensitive flesh.

She planted her heels on the edge of the bed and bit her lip to stop herself from begging him to touch her harder. She wasn't going to do that. Nope. Suggesting that he did anything but what he wanted to do would likely end up with her ass getting all the attention as he smacked it. Smart. She would play it smart because she'd learned that smart girls got all the treats.

Or at least in her fantasy world they did.

"Let's see how you feel about this."

Pure pleasure raced through her veins as he put his mouth right over her pussy and licked along the center. Soft and hot, his tongue covered her. She could feel arousal pulsing through her system.

"You have to talk to me, love. I can't know that you liked that at all if you don't tell me." His fingers parted her labia, his tongue diving deep this time and taking away her will to do anything but remain still for him so he wouldn't stop what he was doing.

How could he expect her to talk? She could barely breathe. "Shouldn't you do that thing where you observe and look for clues? You can't expect me to give you a blow by blow of how this feels."

Something big started to breach her pussy. Her eyes flew open and she looked down. Simon was looking up at her from his place between her legs. He eased one large finger into her channel. "Do you mean that I should apply rational thought and take the fact that your pussy is sopping, soaking wet as evidence that you like having it licked and sucked?"

She nodded, unable to take her eyes off him. His lips—those gorgeous lips—glistened with her arousal. He'd put his mouth on the most intimate part of her. He'd kissed her and lavished affection on her. She would never forget how decadently beautiful this man was.

"Should I take into account that you're soft around my finger and this little jewel is red and wanting and poking desperately out of its hood." He leaned over, and she nearly screamed when he gave her clit another lick.

"You're killing me." She wasn't going to beg. No. She had to keep some pride, right? She had to try to stay her tough-girl self, and her inner tough girl never begged for anything.

He gave her another little baby swipe that brought her right back to the edge. "No. I think I need a verbal clue. You're such a mystery to me that I don't know if I can believe what I'm seeing. I would rather hear it from your lips."

Bastard. Damn it. Her inner tough girl never got any orgasms. Her inner naked submissive girl really wanted one and she didn't give a shit about pride. "Please, Simon. Please. I'm so close. I've never felt this way. I've never…"

He softened. "Oh, love. Not even on your own?"

She shook her head. She could never get out of her own brain long enough to relax, much less come. Her mind was always churning, but he seemed to have the magic touch. He found a way to make her think only of him and what he could do for her.

"Then I better make this good." He winked at her and then she felt that big finger rotate inside her as he lowered his head back down.

She couldn't help it. She screamed out his name as he sucked her clit into his mouth and his finger went to work. He rubbed her again, but this time from the inside. The man had the most magical hands. As his tongue worked her clit, that finger seemed to find some place deep inside her that sent waves of pleasure cascading outward. Her whole body convulsed but in the sweetest way possible. She wasn't in control. He was and he gave her something she'd never known before. Pure and perfect pleasure.

Her whole body relaxed as she came down from the high.

Simon gave her one last kiss and then he was up on his feet, moving her. He settled her under the sheet and tucked her in. He was right. The sheets smelled good and the pillow under her head was a little like heaven. The rest of the place was scary but the bed was clean. She was wiped out. Simon tucked her in and then kissed her forehead.

"Go to sleep."

Her eyes were already closing. She usually fought insomnia for hours, but her muscles felt loose and languid and happy. "What about you?"

He smiled slightly. "Don't worry about me. I'm afraid I'll have to explain an unsightly stain to my cleaner, if you know what I mean."

So he'd come in his perfect suit. Somehow she loved the idea that he'd come while he was touching her.

She watched as he undressed but her eyes closed and she fell into a blissful sleep, thinking about the fact that he wouldn't look so perfect in the morning. He'd have to settle for sweatpants or jeans.

She was pretty sure he would still be gorgeous.

Chapter Seven

Simon finished knotting his tie, frowning at himself in the mirror. It wasn't his best, but it would have to do.

"Where the hell did you find another suit?" Chelsea asked from the bed behind him.

"I had one in my go bag, of course." He might have forgotten to add sex toys to his essentials, but he was never without a proper suit. He turned and caught sight of her in the early morning light. The morning did nothing to aid the décor of the room, but it did wonders for her. She yawned a little, like a sleepy kitten who'd finally been taught to purr.

Even after a thorough hygiene routine, he could still remember the tangy taste of her arousal and how she'd gone wild under his mouth. She'd tried so hard to be ladylike, but in the end she'd screamed out his name just like he'd said she would.

He'd slept beside her briefly. At one point in the night, she'd turned in her sleep and ended up cuddled against his back. Her arm had gone over his waist and she'd hugged him like he was her favorite teddy bear.

And he'd lain there with a hard-on that wouldn't die down. He'd tried a cold shower but now that he was looking at her, he was hard again. Bloody crazy cock of his.

"Jesse's getting us some coffee." She liked hers sweet. He'd made Jesse promise to load up on the sugar.

She was right back to awkward this morning. She held the sheet up almost to her neck. He was going to have to do something about that. "Thanks. Uhm, maybe you could turn around while I get dressed."

He sat down on the edge of the bed. "Now why would I do that?"

She rolled her eyes. Ah, the brat was back. "So I can get dressed."

Poor girl. "You really should have read your contract."

The sheet slipped but only so she could wrap it under her shoulders. Pretty shoulders. He loved the creamy ivory of her skin and the little dusting of freckles across her nose. She wasn't wearing a touch of makeup and it made her younger, so fucking sweet and innocent. Perversely, that made him want to do things to dirty her up.

"What does the contract say?"

He reached out and got a hand on the sheet. "It says that when we're alone, you're naked."

He tugged the sheet and her breasts came into view. He loved the little squeal that came out of her mouth.

"Damn it, Simon. It's cold. You can't expect me to run around naked."

"But you look so good naked."

The prettiest pink flushed over her skin. "You're a weirdo, Weston." But she stopped covering herself and relaxed a bit. "Who the hell has a full suit in his bug-out bag?"

He loved the way she talked and god, he loved teasing her. "First, I would never carry anything called a bug-out bag. You've watched far too many television shows about people preparing for the end of the world."

She grinned, bringing her knees up to her chest and hugging her legs. Her feet were slightly askew and he didn't mention to her that it gave him a lovely view of her pussy. "Hey, I knew crazy-ass preppers before they were cool. And it's a bug-out bag and it contains only the essentials of life, like cash and burners and backup drives. Though that won't really help me since you made me destroy my baby. Oh, and some granola bars and energy drinks. You know, in case I get stuck somewhere. What a real bug-out bag doesn't have is a full suit."

There was nothing he could do about the computer, but he was enjoying the intimacy of sitting with her. "It's the first thing that went into my go bag. We can't let ourselves live like animals, can we?"

"You get a suit and I don't even get undies. How is that fair?"

"I'm not as pretty as you, love."

She huffed a little. "Sure you aren't. The underwear thing, tell me that's just when we're alone. Surely you don't expect me to run around Dallas commando."

That little problem had neatly handled itself. "Unless you have a spare pair in your bag, I'm afraid you'll have to fight the raccoon to get them back. I believe you'll find they're now part of her nest. She'll hiss at you when you walk by to shower, but she doesn't seem to actually bite."

Her eyes had gone as wide as saucers. "A raccoon has my granny panties?"

"I managed to save your T-shirt, but she's also got your socks."

She shivered a little. "I don't like nature. Why does it have to be in our room?" She looked back at the bathroom longingly. "Can we change motels?"

He could do something about that. "Yes, love. We're going to get my spare car and drive a ways out of the city. Perhaps down to Austin. We'll check in somewhere nice with our new identifications and I'll try to get updates from Adam. I promise the next place we stay will be raccoon-free."

"No nature?"

"Absolutely no nature." He should probably try to get her a computer, but he rather liked having her attention on him. The minute he put her in front of a screen, he'd lose her again.

She screamed and jumped on top of him, pointing behind her. "My sock is crawling. It's crawling, Simon!"

He stood up, easily hefting her slight weight. Sure enough, it looked as though her sock was making slow progress across the floor. It was past time to go. Mother Raccoon made an appearance, hissing his way as she dragged the baby under the sock back to the nest. He really should complain to management because thirty dollars a night was far too much to put up with a roommate.

Still, he liked how she clung to him. She wasn't thinking about the fact that she was naked now. He held her tight. "It's gone now. Banished back to the nursery, which also happens to be our loo."

The arms around him tightened, and she buried her face in his neck. "I can't take a shower in there."

"I think you'll survive until I can find us someplace proper." He might not though. His stupid cock was greedy. It was taking all the blood in his body. So hard. Her glorious ass was right there in his hands. Did they really need to leave?

She brought her palms up to cup his cheeks and looked up at him. "No nature."

"None," he promised.

She bit her bottom lip and then did the absolutely unexpected. She leaned forward and brushed her lips against his. "I like kissing you, Weston."

Fuck. She was going to kill him, and he would go out happily if he could just get inside her. "I like being kissed, Chelsea. And my name is Simon. When you're kissing me, I want you to call me Simon."

She kissed him again, a slow play of her lips along his. She'd been awkward the day before, but it looked like his girl was a fast learner. And she was definitely a natural when it came to getting him hot. "All right, Simon. I think if I kiss you for a while, I might not care about where I am."

He knew damn well he wouldn't care. He had a naked Chelsea in his arms. He could be in the middle of Hell and he wouldn't give a damn. He kissed her, not bothering to play it slow this time. She liked kissing. He could work with that. He licked along her bottom lip, loving the way she shivered in his arms. "Is kissing the only thing you like?"

She licked him back, proving she could go with the flow. She took his bottom lip and gave him a little nip that sent a thrill down his spine. "I like it when you kiss me everywhere. I didn't think I would like that, Simon."

He rubbed their noses together, kissing her there, too. There was the sweetest little cluster of freckles on her nose. "Why did you think you wouldn't like it?"

"I thought it would be weird. That's private, you know."

"Not between us it isn't. If you had read your contract," he began.

She groaned. "You're going to throw that back in my face forever. I suppose the contract states that my private parts all belong to you, huh?"

He squeezed her ass. She probably didn't think she would enjoy anal play, either, but he was going to prove her wrong about that, too. "Your private parts are definitely mine. Every one of them. I expressed that in great detail in our contract. Every single pretty bit."

"I'm glad I didn't read it." She frowned suddenly. "What about your parts?"

"Are you asking if my cock belongs to you by right of contract?" He'd been a solicitor after his service was up. It was how he'd gotten recruited into MI6. They'd needed someone to work at a charity they suspected of arms dealing. He knew how to write a contract that would bind them tightly together.

She flushed again, but then her spine straightened. "Yes. My parts apparently belong to you. I want to know what belongs to me."

He lowered her a little so she could feel what belonged to her. He ground himself against her belly. "Yes, love, that's yours. All yours."

It had bloody well been hers since the moment he'd met her. And she could have it when she gave him what he wanted.

"I want to see it, Simon. I want to touch it."

Fuck, he would come in her hand. "All right."

He was just about to put her down when the door opened.

"Hey, nice ass, Dennis. I always knew it would be pretty." Jesse let the door close behind him as Chelsea screamed again.

Simon turned and let her slide to the floor. Cockblocking son of a bitch. "Jesse, could you give us a moment?"

"Yeah, like who just walks in? Dude, what is wrong with

you?" Chelsea used his body as a shield.

Jesse set down the coffee and what looked like donuts. "It's not like I haven't seen most of it before. We go to the same club."

Simon stared his partner down. "We're not at the club now. You can give us some privacy."

Jesse sighed and turned his back. "This is the best I can do, boss. I had to get in here to talk to you. We've got trouble. Have you turned on the TV?"

He reached out and pulled the sheet off the bed, handing it to Chelsea before turning back to Jesse. "No. I'm not even positive that thing works."

The piece of shite telly was mounted to the wall and looked as though it still used tube technology. Jesse proved the thing did work as he switched it on, and Simon was immediately assaulted with the local news that surprisingly enough was all about him.

The bleach blonde news anchor stared into the monitor as she read the latest reports. "The police have issued an all-points bulletin for millionaire real estate investor and security expert Simon Weston after the brutal murders of two local law enforcement professionals at a building he owns late last night. According to police, he's a person of interest in the killings of two off-duty police officers."

"Motherfucker," he breathed. This was serious. The Collective was playing hardball now. He pulled out his burner.

"Ian's having a fucking heart attack. He called me fifteen minutes ago and I swear he made up words about what he's going to do with my innards if I don't give up your location. What does he mean by drawing and quartering me? I didn't think he was very artistic," Jesse said, taking a sip of his coffee.

Jesse hadn't spent much time on the history of torture, obviously, which given his background seemed like an oversight to Simon. So this was how The Collective was going to play? He wasn't without his own connections. He dialed a familiar number and hit speaker. Chelsea deserved to know what was going on.

"Simon, they're looking for me, too." Chelsea had wrapped the sheet around her and she stood beside him, staring up at the screen. Sure enough, her face popped up on the newscast.

His blood practically boiled. The minute her face was known, The Collective might not be the only group after her. "I'm going to handle this."

One ring and then two, and then a masculine voice came over the line. "This is Brighton. You better talk fast because I'm having a shit day and this is my personal line."

"It's Simon and I've got you on speaker, Derek." Derek Brighton was a long-term cop with the Dallas Police Department. He also happened to have been one of Ian's teammates in Afghanistan and was currently a member of Sanctum. He was McKay-Taggart's liaison with the DPD. Simon had to hope he had some answers. "Do you want to explain why you've put an APB on me?"

"Fuck, man." Brighton's voice went low as though he didn't want anyone to hear him. "You need to come in and now. I did not put that call out. I didn't know a damn thing about it until I got in this morning. You want to explain what's happening? I've got two dead cops on my hands and an entire department calling for your rich-boy head. Not to mention the fact that Ian's up my ass. I don't like having that bastard up my ass."

"What you have is two dirty dead cops. They came after me last night in my building and, yes, I put them both down. It was self-defense. Check the security cameras and then get to Chelsea's apartment. Whatever you do, don't start her car. There's a bomb on it. You'll find another in her flat, though she disarmed that one. This is about Chelsea. They're trying to get to her."

"Fuck me hard." His voice got further away. "I'm going to need a bomb unit. Get one together and I'll ride along. I have the address." Derek brought the phone back. "Come in, man. Let me try to work this out for you. I don't even know how the media got hold of this so fast. We have a leak somewhere."

Simon could guess. This was all part of a well-coordinated attack to give him no place to hide Chelsea. They wanted to put as much pressure on him to give her up as possible. "What you have is several members of the force on the payroll of a group known as The Collective. I believe you'll find they also own the bloody media. We've run up against them twice now. Have Ian send you intel on them, but I have to tell you, it isn't much."

Chelsea leaned in. "Simon was protecting me when he killed those douchebag asshats. I'll testify to that. Hell, I killed one of them myself. If you want to arrest him for something, arrest him for stealing my panties and giving them to a raccoon."

"What?" Brighton asked. "Is she there with you? Why did you let her wear panties in the first place?"

He was losing control of the situation fast. "I need to know if you're going to help me, Brighton."

He sighed over the line. "Of course I will. If you killed those men, you had a damn good reason. I know that. I'll help you out of sheer guilt. I've kind of been an asshole to you because I was jealous. I have to make up for it because I found out you weren't sleeping with my girl."

His girl? Was he talking about Karina? He'd never slept with Karina. He turned to explain to Chelsea but she was smiling, seemingly unworried about the possibility of him lying about his sex life.

Chelsea's eyes lit up. "Derek has a girl? Shit. Derek, I told you those Japanese blow-up dolls aren't real girls."

Jesse shook his head. "Didn't you hear? Brighton's finally doing Karina."

That was news to Simon. And not really important at the moment.

"Simon never slept with Karina. She's so not his type," Chelsea huffed. "And good for you, Derek. Oh, Karina would get my panties back. She's a badass. She can take out that raccoon. Derek, I need to hire Karina."

Jesse looked at her like she'd lost her mind. "Dude, the raccoon had babies in your panties. You should hire Karina to buy you new ones."

She pointed a finger Jesse's way. "Good thinking, Murdoch. Tell Karina I wear a six and I like cotton briefs."

"Is she serious?" Derek asked.

Simon took the phone off speaker. "Both of you hush. This is bloody important."

"So are panties," Chelsea huffed and walked to stand by Jesse. She took a Styrofoam cup from him. "Do you have any sugar?"

"I poured half a jar in there for you," Jesse assured her.

At least they had something else to talk about now. He put the phone back to his ear. "How serious is this search of yours?"

"Pretty fucking serious, man. Your face has gone out to every police station in the state. You either need to come in and get this cleared up or get out of town while I try to sort it out. Ian's already hired a lawyer for you. Some new guy from the club. He's all up in everyone's business. He's kind of mean, actually. I think I'll set him on my ex-wife next. You said something about the security feed, but the tapes were blank. The security guard told us it hadn't worked for weeks and you wouldn't fix it."

So his security guard was fired, and depending on Simon's mood at the end of this case, perhaps dead. Luckily his backup plans had backup plans. He was a man who had learned to cover his arse. "I have a feed sent directly to my server." Perhaps the cops would have prevented one thing from happening. The Collective likely hadn't been able to torch everything since the police had been there so quickly. "It's backed up on another server. Adam has the information. He can pull it down for you. Also have him trace Chelsea's phone. We received a call right before we were attacked."

"Thank god, that will help. I'll get on it, but someone has a serious hard-on for you. You need to watch your back."

It appeared they did. "We'll be in the wind in an hour or so. Liaise with Ian."

"Then you'll call him?" Brighton sounded a bit hopeful. "Because he kind of put out an APB on your ass, too."

"I'm going to call him the minute we get somewhere safe. Tell him I'll take care of her and I'll be in contact." He cut off the line. He would have to deal with Ian sooner or later, but he needed to move her and fast.

"Darling, I need you to get dressed. We're leaving in five minutes." He stepped to the door and opened it. The motel was set back from the road. If the motel manager had recognized them, the cops would already be here. Luckily the manager likely didn't want the police involved in anything. He would probably lose the majority of his clientele. Still, Simon kept his head down as they walked into the mid-morning light.

Jesse passed him a cup of coffee. “Drink it. You look like you could use it.”

He needed Scotch, but the caffeine would have to do. “We need to get her out of town.”

“Already working on it. I think we should drive out of the blast zone and then I’ll look into getting us to Mexico or something. Maybe somewhere with a beach. I don’t think Chelsea could handle jungle life.”

No. That much was certain. “We need to ditch your car and get my backup.”

“Already got the keys.” Jesse dangled the keys to the sedan he kept in a garage in Irving, a suburb. He’d taken it out the day he’d come to Dallas, putting the car, which was in another name, and extra equipment in a safe place.

The plate would come up as registered to a John Smith, who had no outstanding warrants and nary a speeding ticket. He would drive exactly two miles under the speed limit and pray they didn’t get pulled over. His plans for Austin were shot. They needed to get out of the state. Once they got out of Texas, he would look into getting a small plane and fly them out.

Jesse was right. They needed to get someplace where The Collective’s wide arms had little reach, and unfortunately, that meant someplace isolated.

They would be on the run and she would be dependent on him. He knew it made him a bastard, but it didn’t sound so bad. He would take care of her, protect her, give her time to really trust him.

He couldn’t think that way. He had to do everything he could to get her life back on track. He had a couple of days to prove to her he was the right man. Of course at this point, all she really knew was that he could give her an orgasm and was a cheap bloody date.

And he had to think about more than just himself. “Are you sure you want to come? We could be gone for a while.”

Jesse suddenly found the cement under his feet fascinating. “I’m not going to leave you hanging. I’m coming with you.”

"What about Phoebe?" He didn't understand the relationship, didn't understand Phoebe at all, but it seemed she was important to Jesse. Jesse struggled to form deep connections, though he obviously needed them badly.

His eyes came up and he shook his head slightly. "She knows I have work to do."

"Does she? Have you told her what you really do?" Despite the fact that she worked for McKay-Taggart, she wouldn't be privy to the more dangerous cases. She was an accountant. She worked payroll and kept the books. She wouldn't have been told that they sometimes worked for the CIA.

"No. She thinks I do bodyguard work. I do sometimes. It wasn't a lie. And Ian won't let me do anything serious." He frowned. "Do you think he's ever going to trust me?"

Well, Simon dragging Jesse into hiding Chelsea wasn't likely to help his case with Ian, but he knew that wasn't the reason Ian was hesitant to really put Jesse in the field. "You know Eve hasn't cleared you."

When Jesse had started with McKay-Taggart he'd been on probation, but that time period had never ended because Eve wasn't happy with Jesse's mental state. He was stubborn, insisting that he was fine, but Eve didn't buy it. Simon didn't either. The reason they'd been partnered in the beginning was so Simon could watch over Jesse. He had triggers and those triggers typically led to him beating the holy hell out of someone. Simon was bigger than Jesse, but when Jesse went to that place in his head, he could take down a bull. Simon had nightmares about having to put Jesse down permanently.

Unfortunately, that was part of their bargain.

Jesse shoved his aviators over his eyes. "Shrinks don't ever like me."

"Eve is quite fond of you."

"I didn't mean it like that. Sorry. As shrinks go, she's a good one. I'm just saying that they don't think I can ever be sane again. I am, you know. I just have good days and bad days, that's all."

His last bad day had put a man in hospital. Lucky for him that man had been trying to kill him at the time. They'd worked a corporate case and when they'd tracked their suspect down, he'd managed to get the jump on them. He'd gotten Jesse in a headlock. Apparently it was something his previous captors had done as well. The suspect had soon found himself with multiple broken bones, including a jaw that would likely never work the same way again. Simon had just barely managed to stop Jesse from beating the man to death.

"I just don't want to come between you and true love." It was definitely time to lighten the mood.

Jesse snorted a little. "I hardly think it's going to be that. A man gets one shot and I had mine. I just really like Phoebe, you know. It's probably for the best that I walk away now before I do any real damage. She couldn't handle my job."

And there was the real possibility that one day he would go ballistic. Jesse was a little like a bomb waiting to go off. When he did, he would likely take out everyone in the vicinity, including the woman he loved. That shite about a man only getting one chance was just Jesse talking out his arse. It was obvious in the way he looked at her that he cared.

"All right then." Maybe getting out of the country would do him some good. "We'll switch vehicles and head for Oklahoma. They won't expect that. I'll hire a plane and perhaps we should head to Europe or the Caribbean. Mexico is the first place they'll look."

Europe perhaps. Greece or Italy. Not England. He wouldn't be going home for a long while. His parents would be horrified, naturally. His brother would just shake his head and tell everyone he'd expected a bad end to come his younger sibling's way.

He hated that he couldn't tell them the truth. Not that his brother would believe him anyway.

Jesse shook his head ruefully as he looked Simon over. "You're going to have to change and lose the accent. I think a Brit in a suit looking for a plane in rural Oklahoma is going to raise some questions."

Simon sighed. Jesse was right. He would have to switch to inferior clothes and try to blend in. But he did an excellent American accent. He'd picked it up during those long holidays spent on the Circle M. "I think I can handle it, son."

Jesse's eyes flared. "Damn, I didn't know you had that in you. I have to take an acting class or something. The only thing I can do is ask where the bathroom is in Farsi. Well, and cuss. I know when someone's calling me a filthy pig in Farsi, too."

Jesse's shoulders tensed, a sure sign he was thinking about his long incarceration and the team he'd lost.

"Let's get Chelsea and head out." Simon stopped, hearing a car pulling into the parking lot. He took a step back, but it was too late. Even before the big black SUV pulled to a stop, the doors were opening and men in dark suits were stepping out, guns pulled.

"Mr. Weston, stand down," a tall man with aviators said, hefting a Ruger Simon's direction. "We've got you surrounded. If you give up the girl, we'll leave you to the cops. If you don't, well, they'll take your corpse, too."

Shit.

The Collective had found them, and they were going to have to fight their way out. Or he could try to play it smarter. They were outnumbered.

He exchanged a look with Jesse. They'd worked together long enough to know each other's tells. Jesse gave him a short nod, letting Simon know he was with him.

Simon held his hands up. "I think we should talk about this. I know where the girl is and I can take you there."

He needed to lead them away from Chelsea. She was a smart girl. She could undoubtedly hear what was going on and there was no way she gave up his game. She would find a place to hide and when they took him away, she could call the rest of the team to pick her up. She would be safe and Simon would just have to stay alive any way he could.

Jesse held his hands up, too. "Uhm, I think I'm in the wrong place at the wrong time, dudes. I was just talking to this guy. I'm going to go and let you all figure this out."

The man who was doing all the talking sighed a little. "I'm not stupid, Mr. Murdoch. However, I am very likely to let you since I don't want to start a war with Ian Taggart. And I think Miss Dennis is here right now. Both of you move away from that door so my men can retrieve her."

"If you think killing me or Jesse is going to start a war with Ian, why do you think he would let you get away with taking his sister-in-law?" He couldn't let them through. They would take her and do god knew what to her. He wouldn't see her again and he couldn't handle the idea of not knowing where she was.

"I suspect that Mr. Taggart wouldn't mind having his wife to himself. We had a plant in MI6 for a while. He told us Taggart didn't get along well with his bride's sister. I would be shocked to find that has changed. Taking care of the brat just might get Taggart off our backs for a while, but everyone knows how he feels about his men. I would rather not kill you, but I will if you don't turn her over."

He was seriously underestimating Ian's care for his family, and that did include his sister-in-law, whether or not they acted like bullying toddlers around each other, but he didn't think the man was going to listen to reason. Maybe he would listen to lies. She had to have heard them. The walls were paper thin. With any luck she'd hidden or had gone out the window in the back, or perhaps trained the raccoon to attack men in black. "I assure you she isn't here. I moved her to a safe location. Do you honestly believe I would bring her here?"

"You better have because you have exactly thirty seconds to produce her or I'll start shooting, and none of us wants that, Weston."

He had to think. He had to figure a way out of this that didn't involve turning her over. He still might have to fight his way out. At least Chelsea would look out for herself. At least she was smart and resourceful and knew when to take off.

The door behind him opened and Chelsea stood in the doorway, dressed in her pajama pants and that T-shirt that did absolutely nothing for her body. She held a hand out as though she could stop a bullet. She wasn't even wearing a pair of shoes.

"Please don't shoot him. I'll come with you," she promised. "But only if you leave them behind."

Simon growled. She'd picked a hell of a time to go into her martyr phase.

Chapter Eight

Chelsea wished she'd been able to find her sneakers. A woman shouldn't have to turn herself over to her probable murderers barefoot. Though it was likely a good thing they would kill her since the parking lot was just as gross as the rest of the place and by walking barefoot, she upped her chance of catching foot syphilis by like a hundred percent.

"What the bloody hell do you think you're doing?" Simon whispered the words her way but she could tell he was yelling at her on the inside. His eyes had gone an icy blue and when he went all icy, she knew she was in trouble.

She was trouble. Trouble for him. Trouble for everyone. She knew what he'd expected her to do. The minute she'd heard the car roll up and the man started talking, she'd looked for an exit. Run. She was supposed to run as far and as fast as her crap legs would take her, but she'd just stood there, listening to the paid asswipe threatening to take out Simon. He only wouldn't because he was afraid of Ian, but everyone knew Ian would be more than happy with him if he got rid of the big guy's problem—her.

Simon wouldn't do it. The big, gorgeous, too-good-for-the-world nutcase would stand in front of that door and let his dead body give her another couple of seconds to escape. He wouldn't do the smart thing and turn her over. And she'd made it so much worse by giving in. He would likely think because they'd shared intimacies, that he had some sort of responsibility toward her. She was sure that there was a "lay down my life for my sub" clause in that contract she should have read.

She didn't particularly want to live in a world that didn't have Simon Weston in it so she'd pulled her big girl panties up—figuratively, of course, god, she wanted some panties; how was she going to explain to her new captors that her previous captor didn't believe in them and could she get some Hanes size sixes?—and opened the door.

But did Simon Weston appreciate her sacrifice? No. The idiot stepped in front of her like he wanted to take a bullet to the chest. She had to hope his suit was also bulletproof.

"When I get you alone, you're getting the spanking of a lifetime," he said under his breath. "Do you understand?"

He sounded really serious. It might be better to go with the murderers. It would definitely be easier on her ass. "You have to let me go with them. We're out numbered."

"They're not taking you," Simon shot back. "Not while I'm alive."

Couldn't he see that was exactly what she was worried about?

Jesse moved to Simon's side. "How do you want to play this, boss? Divide and conquer?"

She had no idea what that meant, but it seemed like a bad idea. "How about give up the girl and live to see another day?"

"Hush. Your input is not required." Simon nodded at Jesse.

That one little nod made her stomach tighten. What were they planning? Why wouldn't they go along with her very reasonable plan of giving up because there was nothing else to do?

"Mr. Weston, I don't want to kill you or your associate, but my partners are not in agreement with me. You took out a couple of our friends last night. I understand that it was self-defense but some of my brethren are a bit more unrealistic. They would love to torture you. And your friend there. We've heard he likes it."

Simon went tense, but Jesse practically froze. "Jesse, you stay calm."

Shit. She'd heard Jesse kind of Hulked out from time to time and smashed shit up, but she'd never seen it. This was what they needed to avoid. "Or we could avoid torture of all kinds and just let me go with the bad guys."

In the end, she kind of was one of them. Despite what he'd said, she didn't have anything in common with Simon. She wasn't heroic. She watched out for herself and her sister, and since her sister didn't need her anymore, it was all for one and one for Chelsea. That was the way it had always been and no amount of hot sex was going to turn her into a mewling love kitten. She was a tough chick, and she knew when the getting had just gotten good.

She was going to die if they shot him.

"She's being reasonable, Weston. Look, there's nowhere for you to run. We've made it so everyone in the country is looking for you. The story is going nationwide as we speak. There won't be anywhere in the States where they don't know your face. That's a pretty bad thing for a spy, isn't it? We might be willing to pull back on that news story and keep it local if this ends here. Otherwise, it might be hard for you to go back to the old career," the tallest asswipe said.

"I'll fix his face for him." The man Chelsea affectionately named Anus Face was staring at Simon, a dark look in his eyes. He seemed to be one of the dickheads who wanted to torture them all. "When I'm done with him, no one will know who he is at all."

"Chelsea, hon," Jesse began. He didn't look back her way, but spoke in an even tone. "I hope you have my back on this one."

He was worried about her loyalty? She was trying to give her damn self up to save him and Simon.

"Yes, you should really have Jesse's back," Simon reiterated.

"I'm going to shoot up someone's front if you don't get out here, bitch," Anus Face said.

"I told you I would cooperate but you have to let them go." She needed to seal this deal or Simon was going to try something stupid. She knew he had a gun on him somewhere. Likely more than one. He could talk about being properly dressed all he liked, but that lovely suit of his also hid a multitude of weapons in a way that Jesse's T-shirt didn't. She could see the holster at the small of Jesse's back and the bulge where the gun was. He was lucky he didn't get called out three times a day for carrying concealed.

His back. Damn it. They wanted her to take Jesse's gun. Divide and conquer. They were going to split up. Jesse would go one way and Simon the other. She looked around the crappy motel parking lot. There was some cover, but they would have to jump to get to it. There was a long box planter that hadn't seen a flower in decades, but it would likely stop a bullet. That was closest to Jesse. Simon's option was a nice brick wall about ten feet to his left.

He would have seconds to make it there before the bullets started. She seriously doubted he was going to just leave her standing there. He wanted her armed. Simon was going to take her with him whether she liked it or not. He was putting her in a box and her two choices were going with his very crazy and likely to get them killed flow or to completely betray him and Jesse and tell the bad guys what they were going to do. She could shout out that Jesse had a gun.

Likely outcome? Jesse shot dead.

She could try to get past them, try to get to the assholes.

Likely outcome? Simon would try to stop her. Bullets would fly. Everyone shot dead.

Damn it. Damn it. Damn it.

"What if I change my mind and I don't want to have anyone's back?" Chelsea asked, tension flooding her. Adrenaline started to pour through her veins, and she longed for her comfy desk chair, her computer, and a cup of ramen noodles. It was pathetic but safe. She never got an adrenaline rush when she was microwaving ramen.

"Then I'll handle things my way, love, and your backside better hope I die," Simon said under his breath. "You have five seconds."

"I'm done playing, Weston." Boss Asswipe took a step forward.

And Chelsea made the only choice she really had. "I'm coming out."

She reached under Jesse's shirt and slid out the SIG he'd placed there. Even as she pulled it free, her thumb found the safety, clicking it off.

"Give me cover," Simon said just as the world seemed to explode around them.

Simon pulled her to the left, taking her with him as he made his way to the wall. Jesse leapt toward the brick planter that ran all the way back to the motel office.

Chelsea immediately started firing. Cover. It didn't matter if she hit anyone. She just needed to make them take cover for the few seconds it would take for Simon to get them to some level of safety. Her feet slapped against the concrete, hitting a rock that seemed to burrow in. Pain flared and her left thigh seized up, but Simon was there, putting his big body in front of hers and twisting around to ensure she found the safety of the wall first.

She heard him hiss as his left arm flew back.

"Oh, god, you're hit." She tried to drag him back, but he stood his ground.

"Watch the left flank. Shoot anyone who comes that way," he commanded as he pulled his own piece and started firing into the parking lot.

Her leg ached and the sound of gunfire filled the air. She glanced over and saw Jesse on his knees, aiming at something she couldn't see.

They were fucked. There was no way the cops didn't show up. The OK Corral seemed to be playing out in the motel parking lot. Surely the police would make an appearance.

Except The Collective seemed to own the police.

Simon's left arm was bleeding, but he didn't seem to notice.

"We've got you surrounded Weston," the boss yelled when the gunfire finally calmed a bit.

"I don't see how. We've taken out half your men," Simon replied calmly.

There was another loud bang and then Jesse's voice rang out. "Three quarters of their men, boss. Wait. Did I do that math right? I suck at math. I'll just kill everyone and call it a day."

"Stay calm, Jesse," Simon said, his voice tight.

Chelsea wasn't sure how they got out of this without killing everyone. The bad guys weren't backing down. She looked to her right, her back to the wall that seemed to be the only thing keeping them alive. She saw a shadow start to slink around the corner.

Chelsea fired and the shadow sank back without a scream. "Simon, I think he's right. I think we're surrounded."

"I have more men on the way," the boss said, his voice perfectly calm. "Lay down your weapons and we still might be able to come to a compromise."

"Please let me go." She was willing to beg him. She was willing to do just about anything to not have to watch him die. Watching him get shot had been bad enough.

"Tag is already on his way," Simon replied. "Jesse will have shot him an emergency signal that Adam can locate us with. He'll be here."

She didn't doubt they had a backup plan just in case they got surrounded by douchebags in a cheeseball motel parking lot, but she did have some questions about how quickly Ian could get here. Despite what his men thought, Ian couldn't fly and he wasn't faster than the speeding bullet that would soon be heading Simon's way.

Jesse was intently keeping his eyes front. He was on one knee, aiming at whoever was in front of him, but he didn't take a shot, which likely meant the other side had found cover, too.

There was another volley of gunfire and it was only chance that had Chelsea turn to see a man creeping up behind Jesse. He stepped out of the dingy hallway and leveled his pistol at Jesse's head.

"Jesse!" Chelsea screamed.

In a single move, Jesse flipped his body back, hitting the man behind him squarely in the midsection. The man hit his ass with a groan as his gun clattered to the concrete, but he was seemingly well trained because he didn't sit back and take stock. He kicked out and caught Jesse in the back, sending him flying forward where he banged against the bricks of the planter. He held on to his gun, but the man behind him wrapped a beefy arm around Jesse's neck and tightened it.

"Shit," Simon cursed. "Chelsea, you have to run if you get the chance. Run and hide and wait for Tag. Do you understand me?"

She nodded because she totally understood the words. The good news was he didn't ask her if she agreed, nor did he ask if she intended to comply. Her answer to both would have been a hearty no.

Jesse was turning a frightening shade of red, but he was fighting. The man who had him in a headlock started to drag him upright. His big chest would be a massive target for the bad guys to play with.

Chelsea tried to line up a shot, but they were tangled together.

Simon took a deep breath and stepped out of his protection.

The world was filled with gunshots again, but Simon was the target now.

* * * *

He was going to leave his hand imprint on that gorgeous ass of hers. No question about it. She would live forever with his mark on her ass.

If he lived, and that was suddenly a big if. He'd already had a bullet burn against his bicep. He could still move the damn thing, but the pain made his eyes almost cross. He was certain it was just a graze, but it hurt. There wasn't time to think about it though. They were pinned down and out of time.

Simon glanced to his right and saw that Jesse was playing dirty and very likely going into a PTSD-crazed state that would cause him no end of trouble. Jesse's eyes had gone wild and a little glassy as he fought his attacker. He'd dropped his SIG as if he didn't even remember he had it anymore. He managed to get his head down far enough that he could sink his teeth into his attackers forearm. There was a loud scream because Jesse wasn't giving the bloke a little nip. Blood immediately began to flow as Jesse settled in like a pit bull who wouldn't give up a nice treat.

Fuck. He had to keep the others off his partner because Jesse couldn't bloody well protect himself when he was in this state. He would think only of killing the people around him because in his rage-addled brain, they all became his former captors. Eve had described it to Simon as Jesse being stuck in a waking nightmare. He really thought he was back in Iraq, fighting desperately for his life, and his senses became overwhelmed with the vision. He wouldn't be able to see straight or think straight until someone knocked him out or managed to talk him down. He was fairly certain there wouldn't be a lot of time to talk him down.

Simon felt a bullet burn past his left shoulder and dropped to one knee, aiming where the bullet had come from. Breathing past the pain, he reacted on pure ingrained instinct. He popped two quick shots and managed to take out his attacker with a direct chest hit.

How many more?

He ran until he was behind the front of Jesse's Jeep. The remaining attackers seemed to be huddled behind their SUV.

How many bodies had he counted? There had been four that came out of the SUV, but they must have come from somewhere else, too, since there had been a fifth man who tried to sneak around to take them out from the side.

The parking lot fell silent, only the sounds of Jesse and his attacker fighting. Simon looked over and Jesse had blood dripping from his mouth, but he managed to get the man off him. It looked like he spat a chunk of arm out. Simon was going to have to talk to him about that. Very unsanitary. Jesse punched out, catching the taller man on the jaw and putting him to the floor.

Simon laid out a line of suppressive fire just as one of the remaining men started to take a shot at Jesse's back.

Return fire hit the Jeep and just inches away from Simon's head. He had to pray they didn't call in reinforcements. He was just about spent. His extra clip was in his go bag. What the hell was he going to do? He prayed Chelsea had run.

And then he saw him. Six foot five, with a square jaw that could have been cut from granite. Ian Taggart was dressed in black sweat pants and a black T-shirt, stalking his prey from behind. Simon couldn't see him clearly, but there was no mistaking that jawline. He was wearing a ball cap that covered the majority of his face as he moved more silently than any big man should. He popped a quick round into the man who had tried to kill Jesse and then faded back behind the opposite wall.

A deep wave of relief sank into Simon's system. The lads were here. If Ian was here then so were Jake and Li and Alex. Adam would be somewhere close, working his mojo to keep the police off them.

There was one last pop and then the lot fell utterly silent except for the sound of Jesse pounding on his victim. Simon took a look around and realized every single human who had tried to take them down was dead on the ground. Tag was going to have his ass, but he was glad for the save.

Now he just had to save Jesse from himself. He got to his feet. He needed to get control of his partner before Tag and the team came out. They were likely doing a sweep to make sure they were completely safe. If he could spare Jesse the rest of the team seeing him like this, he would. He also had no idea what Tag would do if he thought Jesse was threatening the rest of the team. It was up to him to fix this. He'd fucked up and gotten them into this situation in the first place. Jesse should be waking up next to Phoebe and worrying about breakfast, not fighting demons only he could see.

"Hey, partner, it's time to come back to earth. Listen to the sound of my voice." He kept his distance and didn't holster his gun, but he wasn't pointing it either. There had only been the one time he'd been almost certain he would have to put a bullet in Jesse. He never wanted to come that close again. "The rest of the team is here and we're safe. Time isn't on our side. Adam can only keep the police at bay for so long. We need to go."

Jesse straddled the other, his fist moving in a rhythmic fashion, and he was speaking under his breath. The same words over and over again. Farsi. He was saying something in Farsi each time he planted his fist in the man's face.

The dead man's face. There was no way that bloke got off the cement again without the aid of a body bag. Jesse's T-shirt was covered in blood.

"Come on, listen to this accent, brother. You know me, Jesse. It's Simon and it's time for you to stop. He's dead. You did your job. Now come back to reality and we'll collect Chelsea and get out of here."

Jesse's eyes came up as a man in dark pants and a black jacket stepped out from the hallway that led to the office.

"Stand down," the man said. He was built like a brick shithouse and armed to the teeth. Where the hell had Tag gone? "Weston, I don't want to hurt the kid, but I have my orders. I'll put him down if I need to. Get him to back off now."

Jesse got to his feet and turned on the new guy. Something was off. Something wasn't right.

"Jesse? Jesse? Can you come back?" Chelsea stepped out from behind the wall.

"You're supposed to be gone," Simon hissed as the new guy got a good look at Chelsea.

He touched his earpiece and Simon heard him speaking. "Target acquired. Do I have a go?"

This guy was from a different fucking team. This man was military where the others had behaved like hired thugs. Simon looked around and spotted two snipers on the roof. Fucking hell.

A "go" likely meant to put down everyone but his target. Where the hell had Taggart gotten to and why hadn't his team swooped in yet?

Simon held his position, praying no one was coming up on his back. He was fucked and hard if Tag didn't show his bloody face. And he had to deal with the fact that Chelsea was walking toward the crazy killer. She stepped toward Jesse, who had stopped when he heard her voice.

"Chelsea, you can't be close to him when he gets this way. Get behind me now. He will kill you. He'll kill anyone who gets close to him." Pain and nausea threatened to take him out. His arm was killing him, but he kept up a two-fisted hold on the handle. He just wasn't sure who he would have to shoot, the new guy or Jesse.

She just kept walking. "No, he won't. There was a woman with him in that prison. She was the only woman there, and I think he cared about her. He can hear that I'm female. Jesse, it's

Chelsea and you need to help me. I need you. Please, Jesse."

Jesse looked back down at the body next to him and kicked it once and then again. He started speaking in Farsi again.

"He's too far gone, ma'am. Please step back," the new guy said. "I'm required to take you in and get rid of any impediments to doing so. Step back. I don't want you in my line of fire."

"Step back right now, Chelsea." Simon took a step forward and Jesse growled his way.

Chelsea put the gun down and held her hands up. She ignored everyone except Jesse. "Jesse, I'm in danger. Please help me." Her voice was softer than he'd ever heard it before. Was she crying? "Please. I don't want them to kill you. Please, help me."

Jesse stopped and for the first time since the fight had started, his eyes seemed to clear. "Chelsea?"

She sighed and nodded. "Yeah. Hey, I think you should come back here with me and Simon. You have totally killed that dude. He's like dead five times over. Come back here with us because we have bigger problems."

Jesse shook his head. "What the fuck happened?"

"Stand down, soldier." The new guy suddenly had a friend and they both advanced military style, gaining ground while keeping the target in sight. "Drop the weapon, Weston. I don't want to have to explain shooting your ass."

They were surrounded and he had no idea by whom. He dropped the weapon and reached for Chelsea's hand, trying to pull her behind him.

"You guys are pussies. We need to move and now," a voice from behind him said. "You have your orders. Move in."

Chelsea looked over his shoulder. "Holy shit. That is not possible. The universe can't be that mean."

Simon turned, expecting to see something terrible coming his way. The big blond man was a welcome relief. "Tag. Thank god."

Taggart stopped in front of him. He was carrying what looked like a rifle. "How the hell do you know my name?"

Simon felt his eyes widen as he realized his mistake. This was Ian Taggart but at least ten years younger, maybe fifteen.

"What the hell?"

"Doesn't matter. The boss wants the girl and I always follow orders." His face was unlined but grim as he lifted the rifle and fired. Simon heard Chelsea scream and felt the dart decompress, flooding his body with what he hoped was some form of tranquilizer. Otherwise, it was all over.

He fell to his knees, pain flaring. He turned and saw Jesse had taken one to the chest, too.

Chelsea was on her knees, trying to ease him down. "Don't you dare die on me, Weston."

Her face was the last thing Simon saw before the world went black.

Chapter Nine

Chelsea turned and looked at the man Simon had obviously mistaken for Ian. He was practically a dead ringer for her brother-in-law, from his perfectly square jaw to chilly blue eyes, to that deadpan expression that let her know he really couldn't care less that he might have killed a man. "Who the hell are you?"

The big man simply turned, touching a device in his ear. "Target acquired. We have two down. Yeah. Leave 'em or bring 'em in?"

She looked down at Simon even as three other men moved in, securing the perimeter. God, she'd been around military men long enough to know what they were doing. She put a hand on Simon's chest and sighed when she felt it moving up and down. She pulled the dart free and tossed it aside. He needed to wake up and get moving because she needed him. She wasn't about to leave him behind in a dirty motel parking lot to be found by the police and stuffed in a jail cell. The Collective could get to him there.

Or this group. She was so confused. The only thing that mattered was Simon opening his eyes again.

"Come on, big guy." She tugged at the lapels of his ruined jacket. It was dark but she could tell his blood was soaking one side. Tears threatened. He couldn't die. He couldn't. "Wake up. Simon, I need you to wake up. Please. Please."

"Get the luggage, boys. We're moving out." Fake Ian did something very military with his hand, twisting it in one of those gestures only people who served time in some hellhole understood, and the others got a move on.

"Ma'am, I need to take him." A massive hunk of flesh stood over her. Like his brethren, he was all in black, but he'd holstered his weapon.

They thought she was soft, did they? Jesse's gun was close to her knee. She picked it up in a flash. She had no idea where they intended to move his body, and she was the only one standing between Simon and whatever they were going to do to him. She wouldn't let him go without a fight. She pointed that SIG right at his gorgeous face. Did the US military not have unattractive men in it? Couldn't they find a couple of ugly dudes for her to shoot?

"Back off," she commanded. Another one had come in and was hefting Jesse on to his shoulder, fireman style. "And put him down. Wait. Put him in that Jeep. And you, take this one and do the same."

She hoped Jesse's keys were there. She might still be able to make something of this. She might be able to save them.

"Deke, I need you to get a line on the Brit for me," a voice behind her said.

A red dot appeared on Simon's forehead.

Chelsea dropped the SIG. "Don't shoot him."

Fake Ian moved in front of her. "I was trying not to, Miss Dennis, but I will if you don't cooperate. Bear, let's move. We've got incoming. Apparently this one's employer wants to retrieve him, but I think our target is going to be a hell of a lot friendlier if we've got him as a safety measure."

The man carrying Jesse stepped up. "And this one?"

"Boss said to clean up our mess," Fake Ian ordered. "That means leave nothing behind." He touched his ear again. "Boomer, we're ready for the cleaning crew. Make it fast. Our incoming's ETA is about ten minutes out. And make sure you check for security cameras. I know the place is falling down, but that pervert in the office might have eyes in the rooms and I don't want to leave anything behind. Your ass will be mine. Understood?"

Suddenly, the parking lot was filled with men in black moving bodies and cleaning up evidence.

Fake Ian pocketed the SIG she'd dropped as the man he'd called Bear hefted Simon over his massive shoulders like he didn't weigh a thing. "It's time to move, Miss Dennis. This can go one of two ways. You can move your pretty ass or I can move it for you. I will not hesitate to knock you out if you give me a moment's trouble."

"Your way or the highway, huh?" He sounded a whole lot like his doppelganger. "Who do you work for?"

Fake Ian didn't say a thing, merely stared down at her with icy eyes. Now that she was calmer, she could see they weren't identical. This version of Ian was slightly more slender, though there was no lack of muscle on his big frame. He didn't have the same frown lines Ian had, though the way he was frowning, he would get there.

"Stoic type, huh?"

"I'm about to be the shooting type, ma'am. I have extra darts. I would pick you up, but I think you might be a screamer and I really like the quiet type more." He picked up the rifle again.

Damn it. Chelsea got to her feet. "You know how to treat a lady, Tag."

He frowned. "How the hell does everyone know my name? Come on."

She really didn't have much of a choice. She had to go wherever they were taking Simon. She stepped in front of Fake Ian, who also seemed to be named Tag. Which posed another couple of questions.

"Do you know my brother-in-law?"

Weird Clone Tag pointed toward the back entrance of the silent motel. If there was anyone in those rooms, she couldn't tell. "I don't know anyone, ma'am. Left down that hall."

She turned where he told her to, her feet against the cold concrete. "You seem to know me."

"I only know and only care that you're my target. You have information my boss wants, and he's willing to do just about anything to get it."

"So you're what a hired thug looks like." She was really sick of people bullying her. It looked like The Collective had a rival. She wished like hell Al hadn't thought of her when offloading his final confession. Didn't he have other friends he could have gotten into a situation where multiple criminal enterprises wanted to take them down?

The man behind her chuckled. "I like to think I'm prettier than your normal thug. If you want to look at someone ugly, there's my brother right there. Theo, where's the boss?"

Chelsea shook her head as Tag number two stepped out of the shadows.

"He's here." The man named Theo, who fit right into the Ian Taggart look-alike convention, nodded toward the back lot. A limo pulled up on the street. "You know the boss. He's always got to make a damn entrance."

"I'm not getting in that limo." Whoever was in that freaking limo was bad news. She just had to wait a few minutes. They'd said Simon's employer was coming for him. Adam must have gotten that text and the troops were on their way. And then she would have to deal with the nightmare reality that apparently there were three Ians in the world. Four if you counted Sean, who looked an awful lot like the rest of them. But she would take a hundred Ians if they were just the real one because the real one, for all his assholiness, wouldn't let Simon and Jesse get killed, and he wouldn't let her get into that limo.

She looked around and the giant chunk of granite Fake Tag had called Bear was dumping Simon's body in the trunk of an SUV. "No. He comes with me."

She started toward the black vehicle. She would pull him out herself. A meaty arm went around her waist.

Chelsea kicked and thrashed, but it didn't matter. The even faker Tag had her and he wasn't letting her go.

"I'm putting in for combat duty. This one's already shot at me once. Now I think she's trying to deball me."

"She can't take what you don't have, brother. And you're

going to catch hell for not even being able to sneak up on a nerd."

"She's kind of a cute nerd. Hey, if I admit you're hot, will you stop trying to take my head off?"

She brought her elbow back and aimed straight for the asshole's head.

"Chelsea, Chelsea, Chelsea. I thought we were friends." A man stepped out of the limo, his lean body encased in jeans and a white western shirt. His boots hit the concrete and he sighed as he looked her over, shaking that handsome head of his. He was a sun-kissed god of a man, with brown and gold hair and a Southern accent that likely had every woman who heard it melting at his feet.

But he was so not her friend.

She stopped fighting the man who held her and stared at her real enemy. Maybe not an enemy so much as a man who held her life in the palm of his hand and who could rendition her someplace nasty with a single phone call. "Tennessee Smith."

And just like that, her day took a nosedive. It looked like there was a place worse than Hell and it was called the CIA.

* * * *

"You sure you don't want anything?" Ten sat back as he finally gave the driver the go-ahead. It looked like his team of superhot assholes had finished up in record time. "I could have Hutch stop and get you some breakfast. He doesn't mind. I think he's enjoying playing the limo driver. He's more used to driving Humvees, if you know what I mean. He swears he can get this thing through a drive-through line, but I'm not so sure."

The two SUVs the team had been in were already gone, and she wondered how soon she would see Simon again. Maybe never, but it was obvious Ten was going to use him to gain her cooperation.

"I don't want anything from you except explanations." And clothes. She felt ridiculously vulnerable sitting there in a big stretch limo wearing PJs that had definitely seen better days. She didn't even have her bug-out bag. No ID. No weapons. No cash.

Nothing at all. She was completely at the mercy of the Agency, and she was fairly certain they had none.

"I'm sure you do, but I can give you so much more." Ten sat up, and his head turned as a big SUV drove around the corner and motored into the motel parking lot with screeching brakes. There was a shit-eating grin on his face as he settled back against the plush leather seat.

Ian. That was his oversized, environment-killing machine, and he'd probably just moved heaven and earth to find Simon and Jesse, and all he would get for his trouble was an empty motel.

"Can you text him and let him know his people are alive?" She wondered if Charlotte was in that car.

Ten's eyebrow rose. "After I just worked my ass off to cover up any piece of evidence that I was ever there? Not just no, darlin', but hell, no. Besides, I have to admit, I kind of like the idea of the big guy chasing his tail for once. He's done it to me, and I always say turnabout is fair play."

Chelsea was fairly certain Ten never played fair. "Who the hell are those men?"

"They're my men. It's a new project I put together. They're a team I use from time to time when I need to move quickly and cleanly. This is one of our first ops. I think it went well. What do you think, Hutch?"

"I think you owe us all a kegger, boss." Hutch turned the wheel with the cool efficiency of an expert and got them on the freeway. "Though you're going to have some questions. How did that British guy know Tag's name? I heard him and the target there both mention his name. Are we compromised?"

Ten just smiled that laid-back, nothing's-wrong-here-ma'am smile of his. "Nah. It was inevitable. I'd hoped for a little more time, but something came up."

Through the rearview mirror, Chelsea could see the way Hutch's brows rose. "You want to explain, boss?"

"Nope. Get us back to base, Hutch." He pressed a button and the window between the front and the backseat started going up.

Hutch's expression was plain in the rearview mirror and it never changed. He was obviously a man used to getting cut out of the explanations.

Chelsea was not. She was used to knowing everything. "Who are they, Mr. Smith? I think Ian would really like to know that the CIA has a new cloning program and they're using his DNA."

Ten laughed at the idea. "Wouldn't that make the world an easier place? Nah, we could never get that funding through, but I like the way you think, Chelsea. As a matter of fact, I downright admire you. And call me Ten. I really do want to be friends."

"Friends don't knock out other friends and shove them into the trunks of their cars." Somewhere out there, Simon and Jesse were still and unmoving in the fake Taggart's vehicle. She had to hope they were all going to the same place.

Ten shook his head, a sharp movement. "I didn't say I wanted to be friends with Weston, and I wouldn't trust that other nutbag as far as I could throw him. I have to admit, I don't really like the idea of so many valuable assets around a loose cannon like Murdoch. I tried to talk Big Tag out of hiring him, but that man just loves to bring home strays. I'm pretty sure that particular stray is going to bite him in the ass one day. You do realize he killed that man with his bare hands. He also took a nice chunk out of him with his teeth."

She was well aware of Jesse's problems. She was also aware that he wouldn't hurt her. He hadn't been so far gone that she couldn't talk him down. "It was self-defense."

"It's always self-defense in Murdoch's head because he's never really left that prison they had him in, and that makes for a dangerous man."

"What are you going to do with them? And who the hell are those guys who look like Ian?" She was getting really tired of the way he evaded her questions.

"You finally doing Weston?" He gave her a flirty wink that might have set her heart to palpitating, but after being close to Simon, Ten felt like a slick player to Simon's soulful lover.

And Ten was doing it again. He was evading her questions, likely hoping to get her flustered so she would forget everything except what he wanted her to remember. "I can't do Simon when you keep interrupting me, so no. And I'm not forgetting my original question. Who are they, Ten?"

She gave in on the name thing. Maybe he would be friendlier if she gave him a little. One way or another, she knew he was playing some kind of angle. He hadn't picked her up on a lark, and he hadn't done it out of the kindness of his heart.

"I really was hoping to have a little more time with them, you know. I should have known it would all go to hell." He sighed and leaned forward, pressing a button and revealing a nicely stocked bar. "God, I love the rich. Thank the lord for Texas oilmen."

A couple of things fell into place. She couldn't help but remember that Simon's cousins had been arguing about Michael's potential CIA ties and that he'd had friends out on the ranch that week. It looked like he was tied up tight. "You're working with Malone Oil?"

Ten poured a couple of fingers of what looked like Scotch. "They've had a lot of trouble with some of their pipelines overseas. For a while, it looked to be nothing more than the usual mob shit, but I ran across a man in Uzbekistan who claimed that he was working for some corporation. He'd been arrested for trying to blow up some Malone Oil equipment, and he was trying to cut a deal. Funny. That corporation had never heard of him, but two nights later he was found in his very well-guarded cell with three bullets in his torso. I traced those bullets back to a gun purchased by a former MI6 agent. Disavowed, naturally. So I started thinking…"

She rolled her eyes because Ten seemed big on the drama of his job. "It's The Collective. Everyone knows they were behind the problems with Malone Oil in Russia, though one of the douchebags is trying to get Simon to believe his uncle is involved."

"David Malone? Nah. They wish. I think they're going after him hard because they know he would never work with them and he's got serious ties in the government that they haven't been able to break through. How much do you personally know about the group?"

Wouldn't he love to know? She couldn't give up every card in her hand. Not when they were so early in the game and besides, he was distracting her again. It was Ten's best play. Disarm with his good looks. Distract with information that wasn't what she was looking for. "Ian's been tracking them for months and you know it. The assassin was that complete douchebag Baz Champion, who was also working for The Collective, but he's dead now. So cut the bull and tell me who the Ian clones are and why they're working for you."

Ten frowned. "You're really no fun to play with. Fine. I recruit from time to time. I decided a few months back to gather together a special team. I usually use whatever Special Forces team happens to be in the area, but I want something different. I want my team. I want a team that's loyal to me, a team that knows exactly what I want, and I can't get that from players coming off the bench."

"So these men belong to you and not the military?"

"Some of them. Some of them I'm merely in talks with. This was supposed to be a boys' weekend out at the Circle M. We were going to drink some beer, shoot some pool, convince Mike Malone that this is the life for him."

"And you just happened to be in Texas when I was threatened?" She didn't buy that for a second.

"I keep my nose to the ground. I will say that I didn't expect the bomb. Sorry about that. I got my wires crossed. I thought they were recruiting you and I fully intended to not allow that to happen. It looks like they want a little more from you. You want to talk to me about that?"

He was even more maddening than her brother-in-law. At least Ian shot straight. He didn't send a woman down a thousand tunnels to distract her from the one she wanted. "The Viking Twins? Talk or I won't."

Ten sighed as though he hadn't really expected it to work for long. "I look to find really qualified candidates in Special Forces teams. I found Cason and Theo Taggart finishing up BUD/S training. I'm close friends with a couple of the instructors out there and they bring me in from time to time to get my take on their recruits. I was watching the last days of training and then Case walks up and I swear to god, I thought he was Big Tag. I was introduced to him and I immediately started my research.

My buddy who's an instructor there tells me Case has a fraternal twin brother named Theo and the two were flying through training. Said he'd never seen anything like it. Physically, mentally, they're so far above the rest it's ridiculous."

That sounded like Ian, too. "Are they related to Ian somehow?"

Ten's eyes narrowed. "Ian ever tell you about his daddy?"

"We're not exactly close." They mostly just insulted each other and that was kind of crappy. Her sister loved the big guy and Chelsea couldn't be bothered to even try to have a relationship with him. Guilt sat in her gut.

"Well, don't feel bad. He never told me either and we spent some time in foxholes together, if you know what I mean. Big Tag plays things close to the vest. Here's what I found out. Dale Taggart liked to love 'em and leave 'em. He did a lot of playing around. He married Ian's mom and seemed to settle down for a time. He walked out but not before he'd already set up another family in Georgia. He was a salesman and traveled a lot. He'd 'married' Case and Theo's mom during his time with Ian's mom. The old pervert walked away again when Case was sixteen. He died of cancer last year. I'm fairly certain Ian doesn't know about his brothers or he would have ridden in to save them from my tender care."

Ian had brothers. They might only be half brothers, but damn they fit the Taggart bill. Hot as hell and just as sarcastic. "He doesn't know. If he did, he would come after them. Ian believes in two things—the beauty of the power exchange and his family. He takes them both very seriously."

"And I take my country seriously," Ten replied. "I need the best team in place to protect my country. I will do whatever it takes to ensure I get those people. And I take care of them. You should definitely know that."

"How could you not tell him? You're supposed to be his friend."

"I have responsibilities that go far beyond friendship, Chelsea. Ian puts that family of strays of his first. I have to put my country first and that means recruiting and training and yes, if I have to, sacrificing this generation's top talent in an effort to spare all those poor sons of bitches out there from ever having to know what I know."

"And what do you know, Ten?"

"That life is fragile and we're all one step away from getting our asses blown up and the world devolving into utter warfare the likes of which no man in history has seen. Do you know how many ways there are for a terrorist to kill a large group of people? Bombs, well planned attacks, biological weapons, economic warfare. Average Joe sitting in his suburban McMansion and planning his Sunday barbecue has no idea that a couple of keystrokes could bring it all down. I do know. I'm the last line of defense. Big Tag can hold his morality around him like a comfy blanket, but I'm the man who has to ensure this country does not fail. And I will take the best and the brightest and I will train them to fight with me. Old man Taggart might have been a nasty bastard but he had good genes. This country needs Case and Theo like they needed Ian and Sean, and I won't make the same mistakes again. I won't give them up. Those boys are mine and if Tag wants them, well, he's going to have a fight on his hands."

There was zero question in her mind that Tag would have problems with his brothers working for the Agency. Ten would very likely get his fight, but she had other questions. "Why did you save me?"

Ten took a nice drink of that Scotch and seemed comfortable again. "A couple of reasons, darlin'. Like I said, I want the best and the brightest. There's no one in the world quite like you. No one can play the game the way The Broker can. The way I see it, we can help each other."

Like she could help him and he could not put her in a torture chamber. She was pretty sure about that subtext. She fell back on Charlotte's plan. "You know I'm not The Broker. That was Charlotte."

It rankled a bit, not being able to take credit. There was that little piece of her that wanted credit. She was the best. No one could really touch her when she had a keyboard in front of her, but she was also a little bit of an addict and if she let herself, she would become nothing but a hacker, nothing but a fake name on a screen reaching out to other constructs. She would cease to be Chelsea and be something that lived only in the bottomless web.

Ten wagged a finger her way. "Now, now, let's not lie and let's not pretend that I'm dumber than I look. There is no way Charlotte Taggart was The Broker. I know she wants everyone to think she was and on paper, maybe that little story works. But I know her in the real world and she's not capable. The Broker was cold and calculating. The Broker wasn't emotional. She played angles and made money and often didn't care who got hurt. Now that doesn't sound like Charlotte to me. Charlotte is too emotional."

Charlotte was too emotional, too vibrant, too bright to stick to the shadows and do some of the nasty things she'd done. Charlotte didn't even know everything she'd done.

"Don't go looking like that," Ten chided. "You look like I'm insulting you when I'm not. Like I said before. I admire you. I think we've got quite a lot in common, you and me."

Simon had said something to the same effect only hours before and she'd shrugged him off because she knew the truth. There were two worlds out there, Ian's and Ten's. Simon believed in doing good and making things right, and that set him firmly in Ian's world. For all his flaws, Ian tried to do the right things in the right way. He would never sacrifice his men. He would sacrifice himself before he would allow harm to come to his team.

Ten would view himself as the ultimate asset and while he might feel bad, he would do what it took and if that meant sacrificing a pawn, then he would play that game.

Chelsea had played something very similar for years. She'd told herself it was for the good of her and Charlotte, but sometimes she'd done it because it was just fun to watch people jump to her tune. It made her feel powerful, like they could take her legs but she could still beat them. The poor little cripple could make the world go round or she could make it stop on a dime. If she didn't like someone, she could always fuck with his or her life and make it a living hell for months on end. If she decided she needed a little cash, she could take it. No one would notice. A little here. A little there. She'd done good, too. Hadn't she?

Didn't the end justify the means?

It certainly did in Ten's world, but she thought it wouldn't in Simon's. In Simon's world she was just another criminal.

"Why am I here?" She felt heavier than before, weighed down by everything Ten was saying to her. She was closer to Ten than Simon. She belonged in his world, in the dark.

Simon was the sun and she was going to get so burned.

Ten smiled as though he knew he had her. "You're here because I want you, Chelsea. I want to take that big brain of yours and use it to protect this country and our allies. I want to give you the life you've always wanted—to be valued, to be meaningful. I'm your fairy godmother, Chelsea Dennis. You want unlimited resources, I've got 'em. You want free and open access to high-level security. It's yours, Cinderella. I'm inviting you to the biggest ball of them all."

He wanted her to join the Agency, to step into the shadows and never come back out again.

"I'm also here because I have a puzzle and I think you're the one to solve it. I want to know what The Collective is doing and why they want you dead. I'm going to make sure you're alive at the end of this and I'm damn straight going to make sure you're working for me."

Chapter Ten

Simon forced his eyes open, though they seemed so bloody heavy. His whole body seemed weighted down really, and his brain refused to respond to very reasonable requests like *what the hell had happened to him?* And *where was she?*

It was that last question that got him moving. Chelsea. He could remember looking up at her and she'd been crying. Something had happened to make her cry.

Don't you dare die on me, Weston.

The world seemed to rush back in a loud push of sound and light that made his head spin.

Simon sat up and then wished he hadn't.

"Hey, not so fast," a familiar voice whispered. "The sedative can make you a little queasy and I think someone sewed up that gash on your arm so you're probably sore. And keep your voice down. We're not alone."

"Jesse?" He turned and sure enough, his vision faded out a bit and his stomach threatened to roll. His left arm ached, but it wasn't anything he couldn't deal with. It was definitely the way the world spun that threatened to take him out.

Jesse was suddenly there, easing him back down. "Like I said, you'll be nauseous for a while."

At least they hadn't killed Jesse. Quiet. He had to be quiet.

"Where are we? Have you looked for a way out? Where's Chelsea?"

"Slow down, boss." The bed dipped as Jesse sat down beside him. "First off, we seem to be in some kind of dormitory. I kept quiet because I'm fairly certain they're watching us and I didn't want them to know how fast I metabolize that shit. They'll double dose me next time."

"What did they give us? What happened and why can't I remember?"

"Some kind of sedative. Ketamine, I suspect. It's easy to get hold of. It's also got some short-term memory side effects. You might get some flashes, but you won't remember everything."

Simon forced himself to take a deep breath. He looked up at Jesse, who seemed clear and perfectly in control. "How are you so unaffected? I saw them shoot you, too."

"Yeah, well, I've been shot up with about every drug you can imagine. I spent a couple of years in a prison where they liked to see just how much we could take. They liked the whole memory problem thing. I woke up once after they'd dosed me with a dead girl in my room. They swore I killed her and raped her. I still don't know."

The last thing he needed was Jesse's PTSD. "You didn't kill anyone. You wouldn't kill a woman. They lied to torture you."

Jesse turned toward him, uncertainty plain on his face. "How can you be so fucking sure?"

It was coming back to him now. Maybe those affects weren't so bad because he remembered certain things quite vividly. He definitely remembered how terrified he'd been when Chelsea stepped up and talked Jesse down. "I'm sure because you could have killed Chelsea and you didn't."

Jesse touched his chest, indicating his T-shirt. "I've got blood all over me."

He stretched, trying to realign his bloody spine. Whoever had captured him hadn't exactly been gentle. "You don't remember?"

There was a slow shake of Jesse's head. "I go black when I get that way. I was worried it was Chelsea's blood since she wasn't in here with us. I thought maybe I killed her. I saw Ian. I thought Ian was planning on killing me. I was kind of surprised to wake up."

Jesse was not a "glass is half full" sort of bloke. "I don't think that was actually Big Tag. Something's off. As for Chelsea, relax. The blood isn't hers. The last time I saw her she was quite fit. It belongs to the man who attacked you. You took him down quite viciously."

"And then I went after someone else, didn't I?"

Talking was helping to focus him. He tried sitting up again. His eyes were starting to clear. He saw plain oak paneling and a single, small window in front of him. It was covered with an opaque shade, but from the amount of light getting in, he would certainly think they had only been out for an hour or two. The light was strong. Midday or early afternoon almost certainly. He stood up and stretched again, shrugging out of his jacket. "You started to, but Chelsea got in your way."

Jesse was on his feet as well. "Did you stop her?"

"Have you ever tried to stop her? She's quite stubborn." He looked around. The space was small, with only two cots and one door in. He was going to have to take a look out that window to try to figure out where they were. "She had a theory. She thought you would likely attack any man who stepped into your territory, but she was fairly certain you wouldn't hurt her."

Jesse's fists clenched at his sides. "How the hell could she know that? No one should be around me when I'm like that."

This place looked vaguely familiar. Simon glanced around again, his brain finally starting to really function. "She was right. You came down when she talked to you. The minute you realized she was a female, you stood down. You could be high as a kite and you wouldn't hurt a woman, Jesse. They killed that girl and left her for you to find. It was one more way to break you down."

"Sometimes I wished they'd just killed me with the rest of my team," Jesse muttered under his breath.

And there was his survivor guilt. It didn't surprise Simon in the least. Had he gone through what Jesse had, he was certain he would think the same way. In the beginning, he'd thought Ian had paired him with Jesse because they were the two he didn't trust. He'd come to realize the boss had paired him with Jesse because he was the most patient of the team. Li would tell him to shut up and drink it off like a man. Ian would have killed him a long time ago. Alex would talk him to death. Jesse needed to be needed, and Simon understood that.

"Well, I'm glad you didn't. If you weren't here, I'd be stuck with Li and I can't stand that Irish bastard." This place reminded him of somewhere. The wood paneling was reminiscent of the outer buildings at the Circle M.

"You really think I didn't kill that girl?"

He didn't think it. He was sure of it. "You can leave that off your list of sins and help me figure out how we're going to get out of here. We need to figure out where they've taken Chelsea. I take it since we're talking that you've checked the room for bugs."

Jesse stood a bit taller. "No bugs. I checked. I tried to stay pretty still when they dumped us in here, but I've checked the room since then."

"How bloody long was I out?" It unnerved him a bit that Jesse had shaken off the effects so much faster than he had. The floor under his feet was linoleum. A rusty color. Yes, that seemed familiar, too.

"Probably two hours." Jesse moved quietly across the floor. "I woke up in the trunk of an Explorer. The men are military. No doubt in my mind. Special Forces and American. We were on the highway for a long time, and then we turned up a paved road and finally we hit dirt. It was about ten minutes from the paved road out to here. There's one man on the door, and he's supposed to call HQ when we wake up. And there are a lot of cows. When the winds blow the wrong way, it smells terrible. Why would they take us someplace where there are so many cows?"

Simon sighed. Well, there was a reason the place seemed familiar. He was going to kill Michael. Or perhaps relegate him to a long list of people he could no longer trust. Everything fell into place. The linoleum under his feet didn't just remind him of the flooring in the outer buildings. It was the flooring in the outer buildings. His uncle had always been practical when it came to the small buildings the hands could stay in if they had to work overnight. "We're on a ranch. The Circle M to be precise."

"Why would they take us here?"

"Because they're using this ranch as their meet spot. I suspect this entire operation is being billed as a boys' weekend. They likely told my uncle they're out here for some R&R. It's isolated and easy to control the incoming and outgoing flow of information." There would be no handy Wi-Fi signals for Chelsea to piggyback. There was one and he was certain that Ten would control it.

The question was how much had Michael warned his friends about? Simon had spent his holidays on this ranch. There were a total of five small dorms like this across the vast ranch. He and his cousins would migrate around all summer long finding trouble wherever they could. Which one was this?

Ten minutes off the paved road that led to the main house. The shack. That's what they called this place. It was the first of the shelters. It was also the one he'd played in the most as a child. "Are we locked in?"

Jesse nodded. "Oddly enough, I don't think so. There isn't a lock on the door and I didn't hear anything click. I think they're just watching and waiting for us to wake up. There's a guy sitting outside and one other who's checked on him twice already. I heard them talking. They said something about the big house and the boss being there for the time being. Who do you think has us? I didn't think The Collective was this well organized. These are well-trained operatives."

The big house. Yes, he knew that place well, too. Simon hoped like hell that some things never changed. There was a small lockbox under the cot he'd been lying on. Still there. He gently pulled it out. One didn't spend the night on the range without protection. "It's not The Collective. It's the Agency."

The box was slightly rusty, but then David Malone tended to use a thing until it completely wore out. He'd told Simon once that being a chintzy miser was how he managed to stay a billionaire.

With careful hands, he dragged the dials into place. David Malone also never changed his codes. Simon could have easily broken the box, but that would make too much noise and he was a deep believer in finesse over raw power.

"Why does the CIA want us? Shit. You think they're here for me? I'll talk to them. I'll cooperate and get them to let you and Chelsea go. How did you know that was under there?"

Simon rotated the wheels until he'd placed his aunt's birthday. He clicked the button and sure enough, the top came open and he had what he'd wanted all along. A shiny pistol and extra bullets sat in the box. Despite the fact that they were only twenty miles outside of Fort Worth, the Circle M was often plagued with what his uncle called "critters." Unfortunately, he'd lied to Chelsea. There was certainly a lot of nature out here. Luckily, he didn't intend to stay.

"The Agency doesn't want us. They want Chelsea. This is Ten's play to bring her in. He waited until she was vulnerable and now he's going to pounce. I knew this gun was here because I grew up here."

Jesse frowned. "I thought you grew up in England. Is this one of those weird cities that names itself after a country? Like England, Texas? Because that's confusing and you really shouldn't have an accent."

There were days when Li sounded like a better bet, but Jesse was always amusing. "I assure you, I'm as English as they come, but I did spend an enormous amount of time here, which Ten is about to discover."

He made sure the gun was loaded. He wasn't playing around. He was going to get his girl and Ten could fuck himself. He would deal with his cousins later, but this felt like a betrayal of the worst kind. They'd dumped his bloody body in a line shack. Yes, that felt like family to him.

"Someone's coming." Jesse nodded toward the door. Simon couldn't hear anything for a moment but then the sound of thudding boots reached his ears.

"Take the right side," Simon instructed in a near silent voice.

Jesse moved to the right side of the door. He found an umbrella sticking out of a container and gripped it like a baseball bat.

"Don't kill anyone," Simon breathed.

Jesse shrugged as though to say he would try, but he was making no promises.

"Hey, is he awake yet?" a familiar voice asked.

Michael. Perfect.

"Nah, they've got at least another twenty minutes. That was a pretty hefty dose Tag hit him with," another voice said. They were easy to hear. They weren't whispering and standing right next to the door, Simon could make out everything they were saying.

"Yeah, I'm going to take that up with him. He promised me no one would get hurt," Michael complained. "That's my cousin. Do you have any idea what my brother will do to me when he finds out I was involved in shooting our cousin up with horse tranquilizers?"

It was absolutely nothing compared to what he was about to do to Michael. This wasn't a childish prank. Michael had placed his operation in danger. He'd placed Chelsea in danger.

"Your brother seems like a nice guy," the other voice replied. "I think he would understand. This is about national security. Hey, if he needs an explanation, let Ten give it to him. I swear that man likes to hear himself talk. And I never realized how much he looks like that actor dude. Do you think he plays nude bongos, too?"

Michael groaned. "Don't mention that to him. It pisses him off. And we've got to convince Simon to go along with this. Look, I'll take over. When he wakes, I'll talk to him. We grew up together. He'll listen to reason. If I can convince him our intentions were good, I can get him on our side. You go back to the main house. We're supposed to be setting up for a barbecue, remember? If my mom finds out I'm using the ranch as a base of operations, she'll kill me. She only looks sweet. She can make my life hell, Boomer."

There was the sound of masculine laughter. "I love this fucking assignment. It's so much better than Afghanistan. The spy shit is way more fun. I'll save a beer for you, Malone."

Simon held a hand up to let Jesse know to wait. He preferred his odds against Michael alone. After all, he really only needed one hostage.

He heard his cousin take a long breath. "Damn it. Okay. Hey, Si, good to see you. Sorry about my buddies taking you out but your girl is in some trouble and we can help. Yeah, he's going to buy that."

Nope. He wouldn't. He wouldn't buy a word his cousin said and it was deeply interesting to know he still talked to himself. It was something he'd done when they were children, a habit that had always been endearing. But Simon couldn't let that little quirk have an effect on him now. Michael was SEAL trained and Simon was still a little rattled. He was moving more slowly because of the drugs in his system, but luckily he had the element of surprise on his side. And he had Jesse, who was brilliant in a fight if he didn't go crazy.

Simon put his hand on the door. He'd only have a second or two. He took one breath and then two, trying to give the other man time to leave.

Jesse nodded. "He's gone."

Two seconds later, Simon heard an engine and some vehicle drive away. He stared at Jesse, wondering if he wasn't bionic in some fashion. Jesse just smiled. Apparently his good hearing was simply biological. And his ridiculously quick reflexes were likely the same—and Simon was going to use them both to his best advantage.

He held his fingers up, counting down from three to one. When he got to one, he tossed open the door and leveled the pistol straight at his very surprised cousin's head.

"Drop the gun." Michael had a SIG in a shoulder holster.

"Damn it." But he reached out and let the gun drop to the ground. "Happy?"

"Not in the slightest. Don't move an inch."

Michael sighed. "Si, come on. Listen to me."

"That time was done when your friend put a dart in my chest. I want to know what's going on and I want to know now."

Michael's jaw firmed, a sure sign he was getting stubborn. He never liked being put in a corner. "You don't know everything and you're not the only one with a goddamn mission, cos."

"My mission would never have included making you look

like a fool," Simon replied. "Though I suppose it does now."

Where had Jesse gotten to? Jesse wasn't behind Simon and that had rather been the point.

"What are you going to do? Shoot me?"

"If I have to. After all, you shot me."

"That was Tag."

"Yes, I'll be asking about him."

"It's a coincidence," Michael replied. "My Tag's never even heard of your Tag. It's not an uncommon name."

"I seriously doubt that." He might think it was a coincidence, but not if Ten was involved in the game. If Ten was involved then he knew everything. "It doesn't matter. Where is he holding her?"

"This is about the girl, isn't it? Look, man, she's in trouble."

"I believe I know that."

"Serious trouble, Si. People are trying to kill her. I know you have a thing for her. Ten isn't going to hurt her. He wants to help. It's why I was okay being a part of this. We're not trying to hurt her. We're protecting her."

Yes, he was certain Tennessee Smith was doing this out of the kindness of his heart. The bastard would use every trick in the book to recruit her. Ten would play Mephistopheles to her very sweet and hot Faust. Simon wouldn't allow it. She'd signed a bloody contract and he meant to see it through. "Michael, tell me where he's holding her or I'll take your left foot out."

"You wouldn't dare."

Simon aimed and fired at a place about ten centimeters from Michael's boot.

"Fuck!" Michael yelled, but managed to hold his position. "You are a crazy motherfucker."

"I want to know where Chelsea Dennis is."

Michael's eyes hardened. "She's with the boss up at the big house. You going to shoot me now? You better be quick because I'm not alone, little cousin."

"Are you talking about this dude?" Jesse said as he walked around the shack, hauling a large man dressed in black. He'd grabbed his quarry by the back of his shirt and hauled him through the dirt. "I heard him sneaking around the back. He must have been watching the perimeter. It took me a second to get out the window. I was afraid I was going to get stuck for a minute and that would have been embarrassing. Sorry. No idea how I missed him the first time."

Nope. He wouldn't trade Jesse for anyone. "Excellent job. Now leave him and let's go and find my girl and get out of here. I'm afraid I don't feel very welcome anymore. Get the SIG, please."

Jesse picked up the gun Michael had dropped and exchanged it for the one in Simon's hand. He felt better with the familiar weapon. He started moving toward the main house.

He'd read somewhere that no one could really go home again. It just hurt to have that phrase be proven correct.

* * * *

The smell of barbecue made her stomach rumble. Someone really knew how to roast a piece of cattle. And she hadn't had anything to eat all day. "You think I could get a sandwich or is this part of my torture?"

Ten's brow rose up in that sort of sexy way of his. "Now, girl, there's no torture here. Just a really well-smoked brisket that should be served any minute now. Look, there's the waitstaff with appetizers. Like I said, you gotta love a Texas oilman. Tell me something, do you like the clothes? My men aren't particularly good at fashion, but I hear Deke's got five sisters so I gave the job to him. I will say that to my eyes, you're looking mighty fine, Miss Chelsea."

Too bad his eyes weren't Simon's. Still, she couldn't help but admit she felt flattered by his attention. Oh, it was complete bullshit, but he sold it well. Ten had given her the hard sell in the limo and then showed her just what he was offering. Sure, her room here at the Circle M wouldn't be hers, but she got the point. He would lavish her with money and attention and treat her like the cyber queen she was if she would just come and work for him.

She was pretty sure he might even sleep with her. He was just that kind of guy, but she wouldn't be his one and only. She would be strictly business for him, but she was pretty sure he would give it a go if he felt like he could control her that way.

Simon wasn't business. Simon was all about her and she had to really think about what she could offer him. The morning had proven that. Simon was good and she was...difficult to deal with at the very least. If she clung to him like she wanted to, he would get pulled into her shit. He would get mired in it. Dragged down. Just like her sister, and one day in the future he would realize that he needed so much more than what she could offer him.

Would it be different if she took Ten as her part-time, never-wholly-hers lover? Simon would give her everything and in return require her to be his in every way, including changing for him. She would have to shove out of the darkness and into his light.

Ten would be happy to have her in the darkness. He'd made it plain that he would fuck her or let her be. He would find her a lover she liked and then deal with him for her so she could happily do his bidding. Ten would make sure she had anything she wanted.

Except Simon Weston.

He couldn't buy Simon. Ten couldn't turn her into some perfect princess that Simon's family would approve of. Even the Texas branch of his family felt like royalty. She'd been informed that Simon was being held close by and he would wake up and understand that his family was involved and he would want to play things close to the vest. She'd been told that David Malone understood what was going on, but Ava Malone was in the dark and should be kept there for Simon's sake as well as her own. Apparently, they'd kept her away from the news so she didn't know about the warrant. As far as she knew, her son had brought some friends out for the weekend. JT was in the dark as well, though she thought he had his suspicions—especially when it came to her. Michael had talked fast to explain her appearance here at the ranch. He'd told his brother that Simon was on his way.

Was he? She glanced around the yard and wondered if she was doing the right thing. Should she blow this little plan of Ten's all to hell by throwing a fit until they took her to Simon?

Or should she figure out what the hell was going on? That was the question she'd been asking herself from the moment she got in that limo. She'd decided the likelihood of Ten truly hurting Simon was minimal. And she couldn't see Michael Malone allowing his cousin to die. So she'd chosen to play the game even as her heart ached.

She needed to get Ten on her side if Simon was going to be let out of whatever cell they had him in. Once she'd been given her very lovely room in the main house, she'd also been given new clothes. Skinny jeans, a pink tank, and a white *T* that didn't quite meet her waist actually made her look very feminine and curvy. Someone had known her shoe size, but they'd given her a set of medium heels she could barely walk in. They added height, but her leg was already aching. Still she was trying to fit in and that had more to do with the fact that Simon's family was here than trying to look pretty for the men around her. "The clothes are great."

There were a couple of sets hanging in her closet and some bras and—oh thank god—some undies in the dresser of the room she'd been given. They were silky and had matching lingerie that she would never have bought for herself.

God, where was Simon? She couldn't ask because she didn't want Ten to know just how tangled up she was with Simon. He needed to think she was just hanging with him, that he didn't really matter, or Ten would have a massive button to push with her. She'd probably already screwed that up at the motel, but she wasn't going to make it worse.

"They look damn good on you." Ten handed her a glass of champagne. "Here you go, sweetheart."

She took it because she had a part to play. She gave Ten her sweetest smile. "Thank you."

All the while she wanted to punch him in the gut and ask him the question that had been killing her. Where is Simon? Where is Simon? Where the holy living fuck is my Simon?

Nope. She wasn't going to ask. She wasn't going to let him know that she was dying to figure out what had happened to Simon. She was going to flirt and skirt the question.

"So have you thought about my proposal?" Ten waved over

one of the waiters who offered her a ridiculously oversized shrimp.

She took it. "I have but it's a lot to think about. I have to worry about more than just me."

Ten took a sip of his champagne. "Who are you talking about? Charlotte? Because I heard it through the grapevine that she and Ian are thinking about starting a family. You're not living with them. You're not full time at McKay-Taggart. Why is that? You strike me as a girl who likes her work."

She was her work until Simon had come along. Then she'd worried she hadn't been anything at all but the girl who was crazy about him. "Ian and I don't get along."

The smile that crossed Ten's face let her know he was happy with her answer. "Big Tag can be a bit self-righteous. I think you'll find I'm a little more magnanimous. I want you to explore your creative side. There will be no Deep Web restrictions."

Like the rules Ian had given her. He'd told her to stay off the Deep Web for the most part. When he'd needed info, she'd been given the go-ahead because she knew it better than Adam.

Simon had protested.

Again, what kind of future could they really have? He wanted her to love him, to be the kind of girl she just wasn't. She wanted to sleep with him, to know what it felt like to be with him but to keep some very needed distance.

Ten got in her space, his big body brushing against hers as a twangy country waltz started playing. "You want to dance, pretty girl?"

Yes. So badly. Just not with him. It was so frustrating. Ten was offering her everything she wanted. Free access to all the information she could handle and a team at her back, him in her bed when she wanted him and no need to say I love you.

She took a sip of champagne. Ten was the whole package, so why was she hesitating? "I would love to dance. I just can't."

His face split in a gorgeous smile. "Of course you can. Just follow my lead. That's actually really good advice for life, Chelsea. Follow my lead and I'll make sure you get everything you want."

What she wanted was to see Simon. She just wanted to see

Simon, but she had to be patient. The last thing she wanted was to get them moved to a more secure location. Simon knew this ranch. Ten might not understand it, but Simon had the upper hand here and she wasn't going to lose it for him. Patience. He would want her to be patient.

He took the champagne glass from her and threaded his hand through hers, leading her to the patio which served as the dance floor. Ava Malone and her husband, David, were already out there along with Theo Taggart and a pretty blonde woman who had been introduced as Beth and who couldn't seem to take her eyes off JT.

Ava was a lovely woman with auburn hair who appeared to be in her late forties, though Chelsea was pretty sure she'd read the woman was sixty. Her husband was a burly man whose hair was graying but his body still bore the muscular fitness of a man who worked for a living.

Ten started out slow, which was good because she really was terrible at dancing.

"Hello, dear," Ava said as they met on the floor. "Are you having a good time?"

She still had a British accent. She was Simon's aunt, his father's youngest sister.

"Yes, everything is lovely," Chelsea replied, trying to concentrate on the steps. Why did everything have to be so hard? The other women on the floor made it look effortless, but she had to think about every step.

"I can't wait to see Simon." Ava moved with grace. And she had that smile on her face that told Chelsea her husband had done a brilliant job of keeping her away from the news. She had to wonder what would happen when Ava eventually discovered the truth. "It's been a while."

David frowned as he twirled his wife around in time to the music. "Too long. That boy's avoiding us, I tell you."

Ava shook her head. "He certainly is not. He's been busy with his new job. That's all. You know how single-minded that boy can be. Chelsea, dear, how did you say you were connected with my nephew?"

The last thing she wanted to do was lie to Simon's relatives.

But how exactly did she say "we're locked in a power struggle because I want to jump his hot bod and he won't take my virginity until I tell him I love him. Which I don't. Because I can't." Yeah. That probably wouldn't go over too well. "We just work together."

"At that security firm? David, why don't you move our security to them now that Simon is working there. I really prefer to keep it in the family."

"I've got in-house security, baby. And then there's Michael's firm, of course." He gave Ten a pointed look.

Yeah, David Malone should probably leave the spy stuff to his son.

"Michael hasn't exactly signed on as of yet," Ten said with a sure smile. "I'm looking to seal that deal this weekend. He seems to get along really well with the rest of the team. I think he would fit in perfectly, and with all his experience as a SEAL, he would move right to the top."

"Well, I for one will be happy to see him leave the military," Ava said with a sigh. "It's bad enough to have JT constantly on oil rigs in the middle of warzones, but Michael actively seeks battle."

"He's served his country." David frowned at his wife. This was obviously an argument they'd had more than once.

Ava soothed her hands over her husband's chest. "And I'm proud, but I'm also very happy that he's settling down. The corporate security world isn't the same."

Chelsea exchanged a look with Ten. He winked her way as if he enjoyed pulling a fast one on Simon's aunt. What she didn't know was the corporate world was one long war after another.

"What do you say we go somewhere and talk for a while." Ten pulled her close and whispered into her ear. "You know I can give you more than Big Tag can. And Simon is a Boy Scout. He's never going to understand you the way I can. Let's go somewhere and talk."

And he would attempt to seduce her. He was attractive and smart. She could handle him because he wouldn't push her the way Simon was. It made sense to go somewhere quiet and see if Ten could move her.

She just wasn't going to do it. She might end up taking Ten up on his offer of employment, but she suddenly knew without a shadow of a doubt that she wouldn't go to bed with him. Not ever.

Damn it. She was going to die a virgin because she didn't want anyone but a British do-gooder Boy Scout who always acted like a gentleman.

"Sorry to interrupt this little party, Aunt Ava," a familiar voice said.

Simon stepped up and he wasn't alone. He was making a human shield out of his cousin as he stepped onto the patio. He had a SIG shoved under Michael Malone's ribs.

Every man in the room stood up and suddenly Simon had five guns pointed his way.

"Give me Chelsea Dennis and I won't gut my own cousin. Do you understand me, Ten? Get your bloody hands off her this very second or I swear I won't give a damn who I kill as long I get to you," Simon said.

Gentleman? He didn't look like a gentleman now. Well, he kind of did because he was still in his dress shirt, slacks, and vest, though there was blood on the shirt. It didn't matter. Without the jacket, he was predatory and lean and so gorgeous it kind of hurt to look at him. But it was the gleam in his eyes that really got her. He was dangerous. He was on the edge and it was all about her. He wasn't a gentleman. He was her Dom and she was in serious trouble.

Jesse winked her way as he obviously lined up a shot in Ten's direction.

Ava had gone a pasty white but she kept her stiff upper lip as she turned to Chelsea. "Just work partners, then?"

Yes, that cover seemed to have been blown all to hell.

Chapter Eleven

Simon didn't feel even vaguely civilized as he watched Chelsea step back from Tennessee Smith. He felt like shooting the bastard. His hands had been all over her. There had been no mistaking how the agent's big palms had been inching their way down to her ass. And she'd been smiling at him. Dancing. She'd been bloody dancing with the bastard. She never danced and she never wore heels but she did both for Ten.

"Hey, cos, could you maybe let up on the gun a little. I think you're going to crack a rib," Michael managed to say.

"I think he should drop the damn gun all together or I might have to ruin this little party by splattering his brains all over this lady's nice garden," the man who had to be Ian's brother said.

His aunt stepped up. She walked right up to the man who had at least a foot on her and seven stone of muscle and pointed a well-manicured finger his way. "If you lay a finger on my nephew I swear I will make your life a living hell. How dare you threaten him in his own home?"

The big guy had the grace to flush but he didn't drop his weapon. "Mrs. Malone, he has your son in a hostage hold. He's the one who's threatening your blood, ma'am."

His aunt's eyes narrowed as she placed herself between Simon and the big blond man. "If Simon is using Michael as leverage then I say Michael has been doing something he oughtn't."

A low laugh came from Simon's left. Sure enough, JT stood watching with an amused look on his face and a beer in his hand. "I think you were right, brother. Simon can look after himself. Momma, did you just figure out Mikey's using this weekend getaway to recruit for the CIA?"

Ava's jaw dropped open.

Michael managed to put a hand up. "Momma, just listen to me…"

"Hey, let's all calm down." Ten stepped up. Of all his men, he was the only one who wasn't pointing a gun, which was sad because Simon wanted so very much to kill him. "Case, boys, let's drop the weapons. Simon, as you can see I wasn't hurting your lady love there." He frowned back Chelsea's way. "You were lying about sleeping with him. I'm surprised."

Chelsea stood still, her eyes moving around as though looking for an exit. She was about to find there wasn't one. Not from him. "I didn't lie. Not exactly."

Ten's men holstered their weapons and the testosterone in the yard seemed to go down significantly. He wasn't really going to kill his cousin. He eased up and let Michael go. "She signed a contract with me. She's mine and she's going to stay mine."

Ten snorted a little. "Oh, you're toeing Ian's line then. I always said that man should have been born about three hundred years ago."

"Does he know he has two brothers?" It was the only explanation. The two men in front of him had to be related.

"I might have failed to mention that fact to him," Ten confirmed. "It wasn't something he needed to know."

"What are you talking about, boss?" the taller of the two asked. He had roughly an inch and a half on his brother.

Ten held up a hand. "That's a discussion for closed quarters. Stand down, Case."

Case stood down, but there was no way to miss the look in his eyes. He didn't like standing down. He would prefer to fight it out.

His cousin turned and proved he preferred to fight as well.

Simon took a hard punch to his face that almost had him seeing stars. Bastard wanted to play? He might not be at his finest, but he was righteously angry and ready to take it out on anyone. He would have preferred Ten, but he would take a stand-in at this point. Simon reared back and got Michael with a quick uppercut to his chin that sent his cousin flying back.

Michael hit the ground but was on his feet in seconds, wiping blood from his cut lip. "You want to play, Si? You think I wanted it to turn out this way? All you had to do was listen to me for ten minutes. You owed me that."

"Simon, you need backup?" Jesse asked, his expression as bland as if he were watching two friends playing tennis.

Something nasty had taken root in his gut. "I can handle the little SEAL on my own, brother."

Michael's eyes widened. "Oh, you think you can? You think you can take me on? I let you get the drop on me, pretty boy. I know you like to play at being tough, but we all know you won't get that damn suit of yours dirty in order to play with the big boys."

"Mike, shut that shit down. He's family. Can we sit down and talk about this?" JT suddenly seemed to be the voice of reason.

"Simon," Chelsea walked across the patio wearing a pair of fuck-me heels. She'd put them on so she could dance with Ten. "Come on. This isn't you."

No. Being the tough guy wasn't him. He certainly couldn't handle an American operative because he was just a dandy in all their eyes. Everything he'd done, none of it mattered. He utterly ignored Chelsea. She'd obviously made her bloody choice. "I don't get my suit dirty because I don't have to to take you down, Michael."

He feigned moving to the left. Michael was bigger than he was, but he was also less agile. When Michael came after him, it was easy to sucker punch him right in the gut, momentarily taking away his ability to breathe. From there, he used his elbow to break his cousin's nose and when Michael went down to his knees, he kicked him in the groin for good measure.

"Shit," JT breathed. "I don't think he likes being called a

pretty boy, Mike."

Michael managed to hold up his middle finger.

Simon straightened his tie and turned to his aunt. "Hello, Aunt Ava. Sorry for showing up unannounced."

She held her cheek up for his kiss. "Don't worry, love. I'm thrilled. I'll set up a bedroom for you unless you're really leaving us so quickly. Michael, do go and get cleaned up. You know I detest blood at my parties. As for the rest of you, you're all on probation, including you, my husband."

Uncle David was giving Michael a hand up. "Damn it. I told you she would find out."

Ava shot his uncle her sternest look. "I always find out." She turned to Ten. "Mr. Smith, if that is your real name…"

Ten stepped up, right beside Chelsea. "It is, ma'am. I'm sorry to have to fudge the truth a bit, but my mission is to help your husband with some of his problems overseas. While we were here, we found out about Miss Dennis's issue, and that really is a matter of national security. We drugged your nephew because I needed to speak with Chelsea privately and he wasn't about to let me do that."

"I bloody well wasn't," Simon said under his breath.

"His associate is also on several watchlists," Ten said, staring at Jesse.

"Watchlists?" Chelsea asked, but Simon noticed she didn't move away from Ten. "Why would anyone be watching Jesse?"

"Because Mr. Murdoch is dangerous and your friend there refuses to see it. The United States government would still like to know how he managed to survive when the rest of the team didn't," Ten said.

Simon was just about to start another fight when his aunt jumped in. She walked right up to Jesse and looked him in the eyes.

"Well, he looks perfectly fine to me," his aunt said and she held her arm out, fully expecting that Jesse would understand she was giving him the honor of escorting her. Ava Weston Malone might live on a ranch in Texas now, but his aunt had never forgotten that she was the daughter of royalty. "Shall we? I find the barbecue tiring. I believe I would like more civilized refreshments, Mr. Murdoch. I think I shall ring for tea."

"Okay." Jesse frowned a little, but offered his arm. Simon nodded approvingly. He'd been attempting to civilize the younger man. "But I've never really liked tea."

"Oh, heavens, it's not really tea, young man. I'm going to call for the good vodka. My husband has driven me to drink. But calling it tea sounds so much more civilized, don't you agree? Simon, dear, you should join us when the spy shenanigans are through. I'll have new clothes brought up to you. Despite what Michael said, you do seem to have gotten your clothes a bit dirty. It doesn't suit you."

Jesse walked into the house with his aunt, leaving him alone. Only his aunt would call what had just happened spy shenanigans.

Chelsea started to take a step forward. She wobbled a bit on those heels she'd worn for another man. "Simon…"

"Don't. I completely understand." She'd made her choice, but he still owed his boss and that meant he couldn't turn her over to Tennessee Smith. "Get your things together. It's time I took you to Ian."

Ten's eyes narrowed, and Simon got the feeling that the guns were going to make another appearance now that his aunt was gone. "That's not going to happen. We're going to keep Ian out of this."

"Says you and what army?" Simon asked.

"The one I brought with me," Ten replied. "You make no mistake, Weston. I will not allow you or Chelsea to leave this ranch until I've had my say, and even then I might take her into custody."

"Because you want to fuck with Ian?"

"Because she is a valuable asset and I won't allow anyone to blow her up. Not while I'm breathing. I waited until you were awake because I was going to give you the courtesy of a debrief. I have valuable information on who's trying to kill Chelsea Dennis."

"And you couldn't have mentioned this before?"

"Before or after you were getting your ass kicked in a motel she had no business being in. I won't leave her with you because you have no idea how to take care of her. You'll dump her someplace where any idiot could get to her."

Guilt churned in his gut. He'd done the best that he could in the time he'd had, but she'd still been placed in harm's way. It was only luck that Ten's men had shown up or they might have been taken out. "What kind of intel do you have?"

Ten sighed and his shoulders finally relaxed. "Now, that is something that can only be discussed after I get some of that very delicious barbecue. The good thing about being out in the open is we can talk in the open. Let's sit down and have a beer and figure out just how fucked we all are."

Chelsea turned her face up to him, obviously looking for guidance.

He walked past her. He was certain Ten could help her find her way.

* * * *

He was freezing her out and she wasn't even sure why. Chelsea stared across the table as Simon tipped back a beer. She'd never seen him drink beer, but he'd taken the bottle when JT had offered it to him and gone back to looking broody and gorgeous and being noncommunicative when it came to her.

"You want some more brisket?" Ten asked, pulling the chair beside her back and sitting down.

She shook her head. "When are you going to debrief us?"

Ten sat back, his lean body relaxed. "Malone offered us use of his office after lunch. A couple of my boys are checking it out right now. We'll sit down and I'll put my cards on the table and you can put your cards on the table and we'll see how our hands play out."

Simon's eyes found hers. It was a little like getting hit with an arctic blast. He was brutally angry with her and she couldn't figure out why. Could he really be so angry about getting knocked out that he blamed her, too? Was he pissed that she'd gotten to stay conscious?

She didn't understand men. When she'd looked like crap he'd been all over her. The whole time she'd been changing and trying to look halfway decent, all she'd been able to think about was him and where he was and how he was doing and yes, she'd wondered if he would like the way her butt looked in the jeans and if he thought the heels were pretty enough for her to deal with the discomfort.

He didn't like any of it.

Chelsea stood, her decision made. Until someone was willing to give her some answers, she didn't need to sit here and watch Simon not looking at her. "I'm going to join Mrs. Malone and Jesse."

Ten frowned. "I don't think that's a good idea."

She frowned right back. "I don't care. Do you know what else I'm going to do? I'm going to find a computer and I'm going to send a message to my sister. I'm going to let her know I'm okay and that she should stop worrying about me."

"Absolutely not," Ten replied, setting down his fork. "I told you, we're silent when it comes to Ian."

"Do you think I can't reroute a call? I can send that call through so many places Ian could never figure out where it's coming from. I'm not stupid, Ten."

"Neither is Adam," Ten replied. "And I assure you Adam is waiting for that call. He's been waiting for it since the moment you went missing."

"I'm better than Adam. I've already proved that. I had him jumping through hoop after hoop back in St. Augustine. I can do it again." She was tired and scared and she wanted to talk to her sister.

"Have you thought about the fact that Ian could act out?" Simon asked, his voice lazy as though he couldn't really care less about the outcome of this silly little argument.

"What are you talking about?" Ten leaned forward.

"I'm talking about the fact that Ian is smart. He'll put together the facts and come to the conclusion that The Collective has his sister-in-law and two of his men. I firmly suspect that's exactly what you want him to believe."

Ten shook his head. "No. I want him to stay out of my business."

Simon huffed, a surprisingly elegant sound. "Then you're

going about it the wrong way. All you've done so far is poke the beast. He won't stop, and he has no idea what faction or company of The Collective is involved, so he'll roll the dice. He'll go after the most likely and he'll start a war. If I know Ian, he'll go straight to the CEO of whatever company he thinks has the most influence and torture the poor bloke until he gives in. And he'll do it again and again and again until he finds what he needs, which is you. What do you think Ian's going to do to you when he realizes all it would have taken to avoid that bloodshed was a phone call? You think you're playing a game and you're winning. Perhaps you think at the end of this he'll buy you a beer and agree you're the shit, as you Americans like to say. He won't because he isn't playing a game. He's fighting for his family and he won't ever forgive you. And I assure you, Ian Taggart will never forget. If you want any hope of a working relationship with the man after this is over, allow her to call and explain the situation. Better yet, you call him yourself and then let her talk to her sister, which is all she really wants in the first place."

Ten's jaw went tight and then he stood up. "Fuck. Boomer, is your head clear enough to go and find me a laptop?" He frowned Simon's way. "Jesse's lucky he didn't kill my man."

Simon's lips curved up slightly. "Boomer's lucky, you mean. He was armed to the teeth after all, and Jesse just had an old umbrella. Not even a fair fight."

"Come to the office in five. You'll get your call." Ten stalked off.

And she was left with Simon. "Thanks."

"I was only being honest with him. Perhaps I should have kept my mouth shut and allowed Ian to take care of the problem."

Meaning let Ian kill Ten. "I think it's better this way."

"You would, wouldn't you?" Simon stood up, leaving the majority of his food untouched. "I believe I'll go clean up before our debrief. JT, could you show Miss Dennis to your father's office? She has a call to make."

He nodded her way and then walked off, one of Ten's men following him at a distance.

JT shook his head as he finished off his beer. "Dayum, that

man is pissed off. I've never seen him so mad." He chuckled a little. "Of course, I've also never seen anyone take my brother down. That was fun. It makes up for the total clusterfuck of a party."

"I'm sure he'll apologize," Chelsea murmured as she stepped out of the stupid shoes. There was zero reason to wear the things if Simon wasn't around.

"Nah. Mike was asking for it. He should have sat Simon down and told him what was going on."

"Why didn't he?"

"Because despite what he said back in Dallas, he still views Simon as a kid, too. Mike likes to play the badass, and I'll admit that he's good at it. He was the one who beat the shit out of anyone who bugged our cousin. Si was a scrawny thing when he first showed up here. Scrawny and shy. He was different, and different isn't always celebrated in a small town."

She could imagine that this place had seemed like an alien world. Like Russia had been for her. She'd been young and she'd lost her mother, and she hadn't even known the language. Charlotte had been the one to stand up for her. "So he still thinks Simon's soft. I can assure you he's not. He's done some truly heroic things in the short time I've known him."

JT started walking toward the main house, opening the door and letting her through. "I can imagine, but it's hard for us because we still see the kid we need to protect. I assure you it wasn't Mike's choice to knock him out, but Mike apparently has orders to follow."

And it was easy to see JT didn't approve. "You don't want your brother in the military."

He laughed but it was a rueful sound. He walked toward a grand set of stairs. They might call this place a ranch, but the main house was a mansion. "I don't understand a bit of it. All the lies, the subterfuge. I don't get it. It's the one thing I don't like about running my business and it's the very thing Mike runs to and wraps his legs around."

She wondered if Charlotte thought the same thing of her. Charlotte hated the information brokering and Chelsea loved it. They started up the stairs, Chelsea moving slowly because her leg was aching. She was fairly certain she wouldn't get a rubdown tonight. She was on her own, but then she'd known that would happen. "Why did Simon spend so much time out here?"

"You gotta understand a little about our childhood. My aunt and uncle are good people, but Simon's brother was sick for a long time as a kid. He doesn't like to talk about it, but Clive had cancer when he was a kid and Simon pretty much got shipped off to boarding schools and then to us for long periods of time. He was five the first time they sent him to school, and I would be shocked if he spent more than a handful of days a year at home until he was a teenager."

And yet he dreamed about it. When he talked about the place, he made it seem magical. How lonely had it been for him? A little boy with no real home. A boy who had been shoved to the side. "He would come here when he wasn't in school?"

"My momma insisted on it. The only real fights she's had with her brother have been over Simon. It got really scary with Clive for a couple of years. I think my uncle thought he was sparing Simon from seeing what his brother was going through. I don't know. Maybe I would do the same thing. I've never almost lost a child, but I do know Simon probably felt left out. I know he and his brother don't get along to this day. I also know that he damn near killed Michael and it was over you, so we're about to have a little talk."

He stopped at the top of the stairs and his demeanor turned on a dime. All she'd seen of him up until this point had been the flirty cowboy and a man who was worried about his family. The air around her nearly froze with the intensity of his stare and she remembered that JT Malone had been groomed to run a multibillion-dollar company. He understood the art of war, and the man definitely had intimidation down.

"You don't want me anywhere near your cousin." It was a good bet. The Malones were the kind of family that married British royalty and likely wouldn't want their blood lines cheapened by a criminal with no family ties beyond a Russian mobster.

"I think Simon needs a woman who knows what the hell she wants and that obviously isn't you," JT replied. "Or maybe you do know what you want and you think you can have your cake and eat it, too."

She'd never really understood the point of that saying. "Why bother to have cake if you can't eat it?"

"You need to choose and you need to do it fast. If you're going to choose Simon, then stop flaunting your relationship with that fucking CIA agent. I won't let you play my cousin for a fool. He's in deep with you, and I won't let you screw your lover under my roof while you're keeping my cousin on a string."

Chelsea couldn't help it. It was so deeply unfair as to be ridiculous, and she had to laugh. "You think I'm sleeping with Ten, but I'm keeping Simon around if I need a little extra on the side. Is that it?"

His eyes narrowed to hard emerald's that let her know he didn't appreciate her laughter. "If you want to call it that, I won't argue. I won't let you use him and I sure as hell won't let you play him in my house. You want to sleep with that douchebag CIA asshole, go ahead. Hell, I saw how Mike's friends looked at you. Sleep with them, too. Leave my cousin out of it."

"God, I love being called a whore."

"I didn't say that. I don't care what you do or how casual your relationships are. Hell, I would be a hypocrite if I did, I just know that Simon can't handle them. He needs stability."

Tears pricked her eyes, and she kind of hated JT in that moment. "I'm not sleeping with Ten, and you can breathe a sigh of relief because I'm not sleeping with Simon either. I don't sleep with anyone. You get that? Anyone. Not in my whole pathetic life, so you can go to hell. If those men are looking at me, it's with pity. Do you get it? Just stay out my way and I'll stay out of yours."

She turned to walk down the hall. She could find Ten on her own. Naturally, her very graceful retreat was completely fucked up when her leg gave way, and she started to head to the floor. Humiliation swept over her when JT caught her and lifted her up, setting her on her feet.

"I am so sorry, Chelsea." He kept his hands on her as though he was afraid to let go. "Are you serious? Are you really not playing him?"

"I have never played a man in my life, Malone." She was suddenly ridiculously weary. "And it really doesn't matter because he won't talk to me now."

"Because he's jealous as hell."

"What are you talking about?"

JT gave her a brilliant smile. "You really don't know? How the hell are you so naïve? A woman like you should have been manipulating men for the last twenty years."

"I would have been seven."

"Yeah, that's what I'm saying. Trust me, Southern girls are taught two things from birth: how to tease their hair properly and how to get what they want out of a man. You have no idea what was going on out there, do you?"

"I didn't have some debutante childhood. I was too busy trying to survive my mobster father, and then I was on the run for years. I didn't have a lot of time to take Flirting 101."

"I'm going to have to have that story sometime, but for now, you have to fix him."

"How? I know Simon is mad at me. I guess he's mad because I put us in this position. I was supposed to hide and run when I could, but I couldn't leave him behind."

For every bit of intimidation he'd used on her before, he was grinning at her brightly now. "He's not mad at you. He's a little boy who got his favorite toy taken away."

She didn't understand a word he was saying.

Ten stepped out of a room down the hall. "Dennis, you got your call."

"I have to go. I don't think you have anything to worry about, JT. Nothing's going to happen."

JT grinned. "I don't have anything to worry about. Now I can just sit back and watch the show."

He was weird. So was Simon. She rushed down the hall as fast as her bum leg would take her because at least she could talk to Charlotte.

Ten ran a hand through his hair in a way that let her know his call with Ian hadn't gone great. He gestured her inside David Malone's big office. "All you need to do to connect the call is press send. The call will terminate in two minutes."

She sighed. Amateurs. "Really? If you let me set it up, we could talk all day and they wouldn't be able to trace us. Did Ian not agree to let you handle things?"

"The bastard promised he'd find you and take my balls off when he did. I tried to explain the whole national security issue, but he believes only in the United States of Ian. Chelsea, this is important. If you tell your sister where you are and Ian fucks everything up, I could lose control and you won't like who takes over after me."

That she believed. Besides, she didn't particularly want to involve her sister. She didn't even understand what was happening yet and why Ten thought it involved the whole nation. "I won't tell her."

"Two minutes and don't think no one's listening."

She really didn't care. She was so damn confused about everything that she really didn't give a flying crap if Boomer or Hutch or any other silly-named soldier heard her crying to her sister. She was already tearing up as she sat down at Malone's oversized desk and hit the button that connected the call. "Charlotte?"

"Chelsea?" Charlotte sounded a little panicked. "Chelsea, are you all right?"

Ten was standing in the doorway. "Tell her you're fine. Calm her down."

Yeah, that wasn't happening. "I'm not okay because you always said Simon liked me and then I thought you were right and you were wrong, Charlotte. He hates me, and I don't even know why."

"Jesus," Ten said under his breath.

She ignored him.

"Hey, honey, what's happening?" Charlotte was using that patient voice she always used when Chelsea got upset. "Ian's flipping out."

"I'm fine physically. I really am. Tell him we're all fine and Ten is making sure we stay that way, but I need you to tell me how to deal with a man who's mad at me. Normally I would just get on the Internet and do something horrible to him, but I just want to make him like me again."

"Is she talking about Simon?" a feminine voice asked. Serena.

"Chelsea, everyone's here. We're all worried about you, and Ian wants me to force you to give us verbal cues about where you are, but now I am so much more interested in this. Are you sleeping with Simon?"

"I told you," another voice said. Grace. The gang was all there.

"He's being weird about it. He won't sleep with me until I buy him flowers or something but then Ten shot him with a tranquilizer dart and he took me to a party and I knew Simon would show up so I got pretty and wore heels and everything and Simon's mad at me."

"Ten took you to a party?" Charlotte asked. "If Ten was with you then he probably got twelve kinds of handsy. Did Simon see?"

"I did not," Ten said under his breath.

"When Simon showed up, dragging a hostage by the way, I was dancing." She was starting to see where this was going. Was JT right? Could he seriously be jealous? "With Ten."

She heard Serena and Grace start to talk in the background about spankings.

"They're right," her sister said, and Chelsea could practically see the grin on her face. "You're getting spanked. But first, you have to soothe the beast. I know this goes against your nature, but you need to be so submissive around him. He won't expect it, and it's going to throw him for a loop."

"Give him wide eyes and then let them slide away like he's too much too look at," Grace said. "It'll make him feel like he's in charge."

"She does that to me all the time," Sean said in the background. "Brat."

"He's jealous and men hate feeling that way, especially Doms. You have to soothe him, Chels. Is he being good to you?" Charlotte asked, her voice serious again.

He was better than anyone except her sister. "Yeah."

"But he won't sleep with you. You have to fix that."

She couldn't help but smile a little and she wished the whole damn world wasn't listening to her conversation, but given her prior profession, it was probably karma. "He kissed me and I liked it. I loved it."

"He kissed you? Where?"

"Charlie! Give me that phone." Satan was in the house.

She could hear Charlotte moving, likely running from her husband. "Tell him to kiss you everywhere and I love you. My time is running out and he is not getting my last few minutes. You stay with Simon and Jesse. You trust them. No one else. And know we're coming to get you."

"You tell Taggart that if he impedes me in any way, I can shove him in a cell somewhere," Ten swore.

"Tell Ten to screw himself," Charlotte yelled back. "Love you."

"I love you," she managed to say before the connection was cut.

Ten was rolling his eyes her way. "I did not need to hear half that conversation."

She missed her sister. She missed the girls. She almost never actively took part in their conversations because they talked about their husbands and their kids and weird things like which wine paired with fish at a dinner party. All she knew how to do was microwave Hot Pockets, but she liked to listen to them. She liked to listen to Avery and Serena and Grace and Eve and Charlotte. Now that she had something to say to them, she might not get to see them again.

"Hey, I'm sorry, Chelsea." Ten stepped back in the room. "Damn it. I know you won't believe this, but I don't like to make women cry."

"I don't cry." She never used to. She even missed Satan.

"I kind of thought you didn't myself." Ten took a knee in front of her. "You might take me up on my offer but you're not going to take me up on my more personal offer, are you?"

"No. I'm not going to sleep with you."

"Because you're in love with him."

She shook her head. "I can't be in love with him. We don't fit, but I want to spend time with him. I know I'm wrong for him, but I want a night, a day, a week. Whatever time I have."

"You belong working for me. You know that, right?"

She belonged in the shadows, doing bad things for the right reasons. She nodded.

"He won't understand you." Ten seemed grave, maybe a little sad. "I know you want it to work, but unless you can change, I don't see how. You're brilliant, Chelsea. You've got one of the top minds of your generation. It's being wasted by Ian. Come with me and I swear, I'll make sure you have everything you need. And if you want to spend time with Weston before we head back to DC, then I'll help you do that, too. Your sister was right. You have to calm him down. You have to show him he's in charge and you're okay with that."

She shouldn't have anything else to do with him. It was obvious to her that she should take the job with Ten. This probably wasn't the last time her past would come back to haunt her, and she had to think about those women she loved to listen to. She had to think about their kids and who was going to get caught in her line of fire.

"You can't prosecute Ian for anything. No matter what he does. No cells."

A single brow arched over Ten's eyes. "Are we negotiating?"

She nodded again, unable to speak for a moment. This should have been her dream job. If he'd offered it to her six months before, she would have jumped on it and gone happily into whatever bat cave he wanted to put her in, but Simon had ruined it and now all she wanted was him and she couldn't have him for all the reasons she couldn't stay.

"All right then. Let's talk and then we'll bring Weston in. He can have you until this is over, but then we're leaving and he can't know where you are. I'm not saying you won't see him again. Nothing so dramatic, but you won't be in touch with him on a regular basis."

She sat back in her chair, feeling a little older than before. "You have to get Jesse off the watchlists."

He frowned. "That will be hard."

"So will leaving my family."

"Done."

"You have to fix things for Simon. The police are looking for him. His reputation could be hurt. He could be in serious legal trouble."

"Done." He looked up at her. "Chelsea, whatever you can think up, I can make happen. You know you can watch over all of them from this seat I'm putting you in. Despite what Tag might tell you, I believe in family, too. Now let's talk about how you're going to get Weston into bed since it looks like I'm playing your fairy godmother for the night."

Ten got to his feet and started to talk. Chelsea listened because if there was one thing she wanted more than anything, it was one more night with Simon Weston.

Chapter Twelve

Simon walked down the hall, trying not to look at Tennessee Smith so he wouldn't feel the desperate need to punch his nose through the back of his face. He could do it. All it took was the right amount of pressure in the right place and suddenly his face wouldn't be so movie-star pretty anymore.

He had to get hold of his violent tendencies. He'd already assaulted his cousin, though at least JT was still talking to him. And his aunt had given him a perfectly pressed three-piece Hugo Boss with Louis Vuitton loafers that made him feel vaguely human again.

"We'll get started in five," Ten called down the hall. "Did you tell Jesse or is he still taking tea with the ladies?"

Simon didn't bother to turn around. "He'll be here."

He'd already spoken with Jesse, and they had a plan to leave as soon as possible, which looked to be some time in the night. He would drag Chelsea kicking and screaming.

God, he hoped he didn't have to drag her out of Ten's bed.

It made him physically ill. The thought of her in Ten's arms made him see red, and he had to check himself.

He entered his uncle's office. It hadn't changed much. It seemed to have gotten updated paint and carpet, but the giant longhorn head was still over the mantle. Lou, his cousin's had named it. He'd heard his uncle tell more than one VP that they would take Lou's place if they didn't get their jobs done.

He hadn't gotten his job done, and now he had more problems than he liked to think about. He was wanted by the bloody police. His uncle was already working on getting the charges dropped, but he had to be quiet about it. His aunt had been kept away from the tellies and apparently his parents hadn't heard the news yet.

They would be thrilled.

Chelsea walked in. She'd gotten rid of the shoes, but she'd changed to a ridiculously low-cut blouse, and she seemed to be wearing a bra that made her tits round and glorious.

She walked in, her left leg obviously stiff. She needed to be off it, to have it rubbed and stretched. Ten wouldn't do that for her. She would find that out. Ten wouldn't take care of her.

"Hey." She stood back as though hesitant to approach.

"Are you feeling all right?" He could do the small-talk thing.

"I guess."

So no small-talk then. He turned and looked out of the windows, hoping the meeting would start so he could get this over with. He would retreat for the evening and make plans and then when he kidnapped her at three or four in the morning, he could gag her and they wouldn't need to talk.

"Are you all right?" She stepped up next to him. "Master?"

He turned, his every instinct on high alert. "I'm perfectly fit."

She turned her face up and then her eyes slid away from him. "I don't know why you're so mad at me, Master. I know I was supposed to run, but I couldn't leave you out there and I think I was more afraid of the raccoon than I was of the guys with the guns."

What was she playing at? "You disobeyed a direct order."

She nodded. And then she was suddenly in his arms, her body crashing against his chest. He stood there for a moment, his brain still seeing red, but his cock was already in charge because his arms went around her body, holding her tight to him. "I was really scared, Simon."

"Perhaps you were at the motel, but you got over it quickly.

You seemed perfectly happy when I found you in the courtyard." His actions didn't match his words because his fingers were moving to tangle in her hair, dragging her head back so he could look into her eyes.

She stared right at him. "Was I supposed to rage at him? Should I have kicked and fought? Simon, I can't do that. I'm not strong. The only thing I could do was to play his game until I got you back. I'm sorry. I wasn't trying to get close to him. Please, you have to know that."

"You were dancing with him."

"No one ever asked me to dance before. I wasn't sure what to do. I was really bad at it, and the whole time I kept thinking about you on the boat and all those women."

He shook his head. "On the Royale?" His cover on their last op had been as a dancing instructor on a cruise ship. One of the benefits of his upbringing had been learning to dance. Mostly ballroom. He could waltz, foxtrot, and tango. He picked up rhythms easily and since he'd been living in Texas, he'd learned the Latin dances. Dancing, he'd learned, was a damn fine way to get a woman in bed, and that was precisely why he objected to her dancing with Ten. "Why would you think about that?"

He'd relaxed his hold and she sighed and let her head rest against his chest. "Why do you think? I was in the security room when I was working my shifts. There were hundreds of cameras on that boat, but I just watched you most of the time. I definitely watched you dance. You were so graceful. You looked beautiful dancing with those women. You were in a tuxedo and they were in those designer gowns, and I knew I would never be the woman you danced with. I would always just be the girl who watched you like a weirdo stalker."

She was manipulating him. He was suddenly certain her talk with Charlotte hadn't just been about whether she was healthy. She was being honest with him, open and vulnerable, and it didn't mean a damn thing that he knew she was doing it on purpose.

"I could teach you." Right. It felt right to have her in his arms. He'd been jealous. Couldn't she be jealous, too? What real reason could she have for disarming him? He couldn't provide anything for her that Ten couldn't. Ten was in the position of power, so if she was coming to him, she had to be doing it for a different reason.

She moved up on her toes, bringing their faces closer. "Just kiss me, Master. I was so scared they killed you. Please don't be mad at me for the rest of the night. And don't make me sleep in a different room. I want to be with you. For however long we're thrown together, I want to be with you."

She was tearing down his every defense. Damn it. He should be harder. He should be able to walk away, but his mouth just kept getting closer to hers. "You know what I want from you."

"You want me to love you. I don't think that's a good idea. Please can't we negotiate, Master?"

His dick really wanted to negotiate. His cock wanted to give every concession to her if she would just let him inside. He'd yanked his own cock in the shower while thinking about her. He could barely breathe. He wanted her that badly. How could he really show her what they could be if he didn't take her all the way?

"Do you two need a room?" Ten's flat voice broke the moment.

When Simon looked over, Ten was standing just inside the doorway as his men walked in the room. There were eight of them including Michael, who looked like he'd gone a few rounds with a heavyweight. Simon couldn't help the little satisfaction that ran through him. His cousin thought he was a lightweight? Now he knew.

He turned but wouldn't let Chelsea go. His arm slipped around her waist, binding her to him. "I suspect we can hold off for a while if you're ready to give me some explanations."

Ten nodded, but his expression was dark. He didn't look like a man who was okay with getting cut out. He would be even less happy when Simon took her away from here. "I will as soon as your partner gets his ass up here."

As the rest of the group settled in, Michael stepped up.

So he was going to get the speech, the one where he was no longer welcome around here because he was far too much trouble. Well, it wasn't entirely unexpected.

"You're a bastard, Si," Michael said.

Simon made sure his expression never changed, but he could feel Chelsea tense beside him. "My parents were married when I was conceived."

"You're the asshole," Chelsea began.

He had to shut that down quickly. "Chelsea, be quiet. You disobeyed me earlier and there will be punishment for that. Don't add to it by placing yourself between me and my cousin now."

She frowned. "But yelling at people is all I really do well." An evil little smile lit her face.

Oh, he definitely had to shut her down. "And you're not allowed to cyber bomb the man."

Michael's eyes went as wide as all the swelling would allow. "Cyber bomb?"

"He means I could make your life hell with a few happy keystrokes, buddy." Chelsea was suddenly standing taller.

Simon sighed. "She's not going to ruin your identity or set you up on one of those fetish dating sites."

"Oh, that would be so much fun. Navy SEAL seeks Master to dominate him. No calls necessary. If you're man enough, show up at 101…"

Michael pointed a finger her way. "You are not doing that. And I wasn't coming over here to fight. I was coming over to apologize. I never meant to hurt you, man. I was following orders and sometimes that has to come first. You remember."

Yes, it was precisely why he'd gotten out of the military and then MI6. He'd never liked following orders. It was his cousin's whole life. It was perfectly possible that Michael had believed him to be in real trouble and Tennessee Smith had convinced Michael this was the way to get him out of it. At the end of the day, everything was Ten's fault. "It's all right, Michael. And I offer my apologies for breaking your nose."

Michael shook his head. "Hey, it gave me the chance to punch JT so we stay identical. He was pissed. And I'm now a little scared of your lady there. JT really likes her, by the way."

Everyone liked his sub it seemed. His aunt had asked a million questions, none of which he'd answered because he'd been in a terrible mood. He was still in one. He was surrounded by people he didn't trust, and he was going to have to take sides against Michael and his Malone relatives again. His gut was twisted by the thought of having to deal with the charges against him. He was in serious trouble.

And none of it mattered because she was curling against his body as though she wanted to sink into him.

He had another bloody hard-on. What the hell was he going to do? He'd promised he wouldn't fuck her until he was sure of her, but she was the most elusive thing he'd ever met. If he didn't have her soon, he might never.

But he was going to get his discipline in first. Oh, he wasn't going to let this evening pass without some serious punishment. He would have her screaming for him by the time he was done.

Her deflowering wasn't going to be sweet, but he intended to make sure she remembered it for the rest of her life.

"Take a seat, gentlemen. I need to explain how I found out about the plot to bring Chelsea Dennis in." Ten sat at the head of the table, his men around him.

Simon gestured to the only two seats left just as Jesse walked in the door. He'd cleaned up, and it looked like his aunt had worked her magic. Jesse was looking rather civilized in a pair of slacks and a light dress shirt. He'd forgone the tie, but likely lost the battle over the dress shoes. His normal boots were gone and in their place was an elegant set of loafers.

"I'll stand," Jesse said, moving to Simon's back.

"No. It's okay. You can take the chair." Chelsea put both hands on the table in front of her and started to lower herself down.

Startled, Simon caught her before she could hit the floor.

She looked up, a soft smile on her face. "Thanks. I don't do that very well. I guess I should practice more. And do a whole lot of yoga."

He had to stop because she was so beautiful and felt so damn right in his arms. "What are you doing, Chelsea?"

She bit that bottom lip, and he couldn't help but wonder what her mouth would look like wrapped around his cock. "I didn't read our contract, but I do know that most Doms like their subs to sit at their feet for long talks. Was that in our contract?"

What kind of game was she playing now?

"Dennis, could you do the submissive crap quickly?" Ten asked, his expression deeply irritated. "I have a meeting to run here."

Her eyes widened and her skin went the prettiest shade of pink.

"Get the chair." He wasn't about to have her sitting at his feet during a meeting. They weren't in a club and this wasn't a McKay-Taggart meeting where no one would question or look down on a woman sitting at his feet. There was nothing he wanted more but this wasn't the place. "Sit down. He needs to start the meeting."

She flushed again, red this time as embarrassment flooded her system. She pulled away and straightened up, all her easy sensuality fleeing in a second. "Oh, uhm. Yeah. Sorry." She moved to get the chair, and he realized this was her concession.

He had two choices and he wouldn't get a second chance. She'd tried and she wasn't the kind of girl who would try again. She would go back into her shell.

She'd flirted with Ten. He should let her sit in her chair and not give a goddamn that she was hurt. It didn't matter. She'd made her choice.

Or had she? She was naïve enough about men and sex that she could think she could handle Ten. She could think she was doing good for their little team.

No one ever asked me to dance before.

He was an idiot. He reached out and grabbed her hand and pulled her to him. "You sit in my lap. That's what's in our contract. Jesse, take the chair."

He tugged on her hand until she moved, falling on his lap. It was an easy thing to maneuver her where he wanted. Her arms went around his neck and her head fell against his shoulder.

And he felt that odd peace that came to him when she wasn't railing or yelling or pushing him away. When they finally connected, he felt something deep inside fall into place. This sense of contentment was why he kept trying, why he would likely always keep trying. He smoothed back her hair and let her settle down as Jesse sank into the chair beside them.

"Really? You're going to play it that way?" Ten asked.

He didn't give a damn what Ten thought. "You can conduct your meeting or I'll take my submissive back to our room. She's tired and has had a long day."

"What's a submissive?" The slightly smaller of the new Tags leaned over toward Michael. "Is that what the Brits call a submersible? Because we don't really have anywhere to put that out here."

Jesse leaned over, his voice low. "It's good to not be the dumbest person in the room for once."

Ten's brows raised, but he ignored Jesse. "You boys haven't kept up with your erotic romance reading, have you? One of the things you should know about the McKay-Taggart team is every man among them is into BDSM and they tend to call their women subs. That's short for submissives. They want their women to submit in the bedroom, but don't take that term too seriously. Those women will cut a man who isn't their Dom down to size."

"Sometimes we cut our Doms down to size, too," Chelsea said with a smile.

"So this dude who supposedly is my brother and who might show up here at some point in time to get his ass kicked is also a complete pervert," Case Taggart said with a nice long roll of his eyes. It was obvious Ten had filled him in, but he still wasn't impressed with his new family.

Chelsea sat up. "Hey…"

And he gently brought her back down. He didn't need anyone to defend him against perfectly reasonable accusations. He was a pervert. He enjoyed it immensely. It was so much more fun than being vanilla. "Darling, relax. If all Ten brought us here for is to call me names, this is going to be a short meeting. And I, for one, will pay to watch that little boy over there get schooled by his brother."

"He is not my brother," Case said, his ice blue eyes narrowing. "He's just some dude who happens to share my DNA. He can bite me for all I care."

Oh, Ian wouldn't just bite him. He would have the poor boy for lunch, and likely sooner than he thought. "Could we move on?"

He wanted to get her alone. He needed to figure out how to handle her. Hell, he needed to figure out how to handle the whole situation. His intentions were pure. He wanted to get her away from Ten and protect her so Ian had time to figure out exactly what was going on, but how was he going to do that when his face was all over the evening news?

It was something to think about, but more than that he had to ensure her loyalty to him and not to Ten. When the whole thing went to hell—and he was certain it would—he needed to make sure it was him Chelsea looked to to save her pretty ass. There was one way he knew of to gain a woman's loyalty and that was treating her right in the bedroom. Chelsea was addicted to the pleasure he could give her. What if he showed her even more?

Or perhaps he was just trying to come up with any excuse to get inside her. He no longer cared.

"I started receiving some intelligence that certain factions within the group we call The Collective were looking up information on the shadowy figure known as The Broker. For those of you who haven't read my memos—yes, Boomer, I write those for a reason and not for you to doodle on—the woman currently purring like a kitten in Weston's lap is The Broker."

Chelsea sat back up. "I'm not purring."

Simon eased her back. She certainly had been. "My client refuses to confirm the identity of the person known only as The Broker. On advice of counsel, of course."

"You aren't licensed to practice in the States, Weston," Ten shot back.

"I believe you'll find I am." Or he would be after Chelsea hacked the bar's website and made him a member. "I'm Oxford trained. Certain companies find my experience in European law very useful."

"Malone Oil included," Michael added. Or rather lied. He'd never worked a day for his uncle in a legal fashion. "But my cousin's resume isn't on trial here. Now I did read the memos, unlike Boomer, who doesn't read anything that doesn't involve sports scores."

Boomer frowned. "I got ADD."

Michael moved on. "So let's just say that somehow this group, for whatever reason, decided that Chelsea here is The Broker. Why were they looking for her, and what does any of this have to do with the death of a federal judge?"

Now Simon was the one sitting up a bit straighter. "Federal judge?"

Ten held a hand up. "I didn't send you the memo. All right, here's how this went down. I've got an operative of my own in place at a corporation I know is in The Collective."

"Then why the hell don't we shut the corporation down?" Jesse asked.

Simon could answer that one. "We very likely don't have enough proof and besides, I would bet anything that key politicians in several governments hold stock in the corporations."

"I've already proven that." Chelsea sat up but kept an arm around Simon's neck for balance. "After that douchebag Baz died, I got into his laptop and found some information on a couple of the companies. They have a firm grip on a bunch of American, British, and EU politicians, not to mention ties to several criminal organizations."

"And those are just two of the smaller companies," Ten continued. "There's no telling just how deeply entrenched The Collective is within our government, although it seems to me they haven't managed to make great headway with the judicial branch if they're doing what I suspect they're doing."

"You think they're assassinating judges who might find against them?" It wouldn't be unheard of. Trials cost time and money, and a class action could cost a company everything. Even a large corporation would likely prefer to settle lawsuits rather than waste resources. "Why not settle?"

"Because this was a case of patent infringement and there's a couple billion on the line." Ten's fingers drummed against the desk. "This particular case involves crystal technology."

Chelsea squirmed a little, making his dick jump. "Seriously? Holy crap. I need to read that. I heard there was a breakthrough."

Theo leaned in. "What are you talking about? I get the feeling it's not new-age crystals."

She was squirming again. He'd noticed when she got excited it was hard for her to stay still. Unfortunately, her excitement was doing amazing things for his cock. He had to hold it together so he didn't end up making another mess of his trousers. "Quantum computers are the way of the future, but we don't have the means to power them yet."

"Quantum computers are the ones that would use qubits versus bits, correct?" Case Taggart proved he didn't have the same problems as Boomer.

Chelsea nodded. "Yes. The computers we use today run on bits. 1s and 0s. So they operate in one of…you know what this is actually very mathematically interesting. Can I get a white board?"

He had to reign her in or they would all get a lecture on quantum supposition. "Darling, let's skip the mathematics and just say that any number of corporations would love to get their hands on the next evolution in computer technology. The crystal would replace the storage systems we use now. Quantum computers are so fast they tend to overheat and burn out very quickly, hence the ones in development now are kept in sub-zero temperatures."

Chelsea turned slightly to look at him. "You know about quantum computers?"

He let his hand slip to her hip. Her face was the nicest shade of pink. "Of course. I try to keep up. Later, if you like, we can debate whether or not quantum computers disprove the Church-Turing thesis."

The sexiest little huff came out of her mouth. "Not in their current iteration but surely later they will. I can't believe you know what that is."

He'd kept that in his back pocket. At first he'd simply wanted to understand her world, and now he realized he could get her hot just by proving he had a brain in his head. "I look forward to the debate."

"I think they're having math sex," Jesse whispered to Theo.

Ten huffed. "Yeah, well, they need to have it on their own time. And it's more than corporations that want that technology. The NSA is very intrigued and honestly they don't care who comes up with the tech as long as they get their hands on it first."

"You believe the NSA is involved?" Simon asked. He didn't want to have to deal with both the CIA and the National Security Agency. Their turf wars could get a man killed. Or a woman.

"The NSA is always involved," Ten replied. "And that's what makes this a delicate operation. The judge in this case was a deep believer in intellectual property rights. He tended to side with whoever could prove they knew the property inside and out. It was a fairly good bet that in the case of Coleman vs. the Nieland Corporation, the little guy was probably going to win. Even if he hadn't, the judge had put an injunction on any further development or use of the tech until the trial was over."

Simon could see the outcome of that particular order. "And Nieland's stock took a hit."

"It plummeted. They lost roughly half a billion in a week."

That was enough to kill for. "How did the judge die?"

Ten's eyes tightened. "That's my problem. The man had a heart attack."

"There are several poisons that could mimic or cause a heart attack."

"No. The toxicology reports are all clean."

"If The Collective can kill a judge, they can surely buy off a coroner and some lab techs," Chelsea said. "I could try to find some connections if you would let me have a laptop."

"I bet you would find connections to all kinds of things." Ten shook his head. "No. You can answer some questions for me though. My corporate mole ran across your name and a Dallas address in the same file as some notes on the court case. I can't find the connection, but I'm thinking you might. That wasn't the first time they came after you. Weston wouldn't have you in that sleazy motel if he'd had another option. Tell me something, why didn't you call in Big Tag?"

"Chelsea didn't want to involve her sister," Simon explained. It wasn't the entire truth, but Ten didn't need to know everything. "How did you find us?"

"The minute I connected Chelsea's name to the case, I had someone watching her."

The man they'd code named Ace held up his hand. He was a

tad bit older than the rest, with a little gray at his temples, but he had a lean body corded with muscle. "That would be me. I got to follow you all over Dallas. You couldn't have stopped somewhere for a sandwich or something? I got a little loopy from hunger. Next time think about your potential stalker and take a break."

He could buy that Chelsea wouldn't notice a tail. She'd always relied on Charlotte for that and she'd had a rough morning that day. But she hadn't been alone that night. "And you're trying to tell me you tailed us to the motel?"

Jesse leaned forward. "I can bust a tail. We didn't have one that night. I would have known."

"Would you?" Ten asked. "I assure you, you had a tail and you should be damn glad you did or those boys would have mowed you down the next day."

Simon held his tongue but it didn't completely make sense. If Ten had known where they were why would he wait to take them? Had he been watching them the whole time? Jesse would have felt it. Jesse always knew. He had a sixth sense about it. If Jesse said no one had been following them, then no one had physically been following them.

Someone had been smart. Someone tagged Jesse's car.

And there was only one person who could have done that. Bloody hell. He would have to use that little piece of information for later. The last thing he wanted to do was tip off Ten that he was on to him.

"What else do you have?" Simon asked. "This can't be an isolated incident."

"I don't think it is. I have four deaths I think might be linked. A US attorney, a whistle blower and two judges. Mostly cardiac incidents. One had a bad reaction to medication. Now all of these people were in their late forties through early sixties."

"That makes sense because they were at the top of their game and to get to that level in the federal court system, they're going to be mature," Ace said. "This could all be coincidental."

"Could be," Ten allowed. "I don't think so. They'd all been involved in cases that directly affected large corporations. I haven't been able to link them to The Collective definitively, but the ties are there. I just have to find them."

"What does your guy on the inside say?" Jesse asked.

"Who said it was a man?" Ten got a shit-eating grin on his face. "You a sexist, Murdoch? It doesn't matter. My insider is working on it, but for now we need to figure out why they want Chelsea."

Chelsea sat back, curling her legs up and letting her face rest against his shoulder.

It was a signal. She was letting him take control. He could tell Ten however much or little he wanted. She was ceding control.

In this particular case, sharing information could only help him. Any information the CIA and Ten could gather would aid them in figuring out where this package of Albert Krum's was. "Is the flow of information going to go both ways?"

Ten tapped the folder in front of him. "I didn't give you this information for my health. Yes. I'm offering to show my hand. You show me yours."

"Chelsea is acquaintances with a man named Albert Krum." He knew the language to use in case Ten was taping this conversation. He wasn't about to call Chelsea The Broker or place her in the crosshairs. "I believe she met him while she was living in Europe."

"I came across him on a dating site," Chelsea said.

Cheeky girl. He stroked her hair as he spoke, deeply enjoying having her close. He didn't give a damn what the rest of the men thought. It seemed to be calming her down and it was definitely making him feel better. "Krum was a hacker, a very good one."

"Was?" Case asked.

Chelsea's arm tightened slightly around his neck, the only sign that the conversation was bothering her. This was what she was so good at. Anyone watching her would think she was barely listening. She looked bored, but Simon knew the truth. She felt everything deeply, but she'd learned to never show it. He had to make her understand that it was safe to share those fears and feelings with him. He let his hand slide along her spine, firm pressure because she reacted so well to it. She relaxed against him.

"It's our belief that Mr. Krum was killed by The Collective. The night she was sent the bomb, they called her."

Theo held a hand up. "I've been monitoring Dallas Police bandwidths and that bomb was a dud. It was meant to scare the holy hell out of her, but it wouldn't have gone off. The one on her car actually had a message on it. Some sort of code."

Chelsea was up on her feet. "Can I see it?"

Ten nodded.

Theo passed her a piece of paper.

"While she's looking at that report, you can tell me what happened with Krum," Ten said.

"They called and put Mr. Krum on the line. He claims to have sent Chelsea a package, though she didn't receive anything." He watched her as her eyes ate up that report. Ian was wrong. She needed to work and she needed to be important. He understood why he'd placed her on the sidelines, only using her when Adam was out of pocket, but Chelsea needed more.

"She'd been in Europe," Ten mused. "Have we checked her apartment complex? Did they receive her mail?"

"Al didn't have that address," Chelsea stated. "And this isn't a code. This is another address. A Deep Web addy. I need a computer and I need Internet." She frowned Ten's way. "Come on. No one is going to do this better than me. You can stand over me and watch me, but let me put my hands on this sucker."

Simon leaned forward. "This is about her. She should have some say in what goes on."

"Hutch, give her yours and watch her. I don't want to tip anyone off as to where we are." Ten nodded the big guy's way. "Hutch is our communications specialist."

Hutch stood up, gripping his backpack and zipping it open to slide out a sleek-looking laptop. He was no more than twenty-five and had the kind of rugged good looks that screamed all-American. He grinned as he flipped open the top and powered it up. "Hutch is damn glad to get to see a master at work. The others might not know who you are but I do. Well, I know who some people think you are—allegedly, counselor. You want me to ping this signal around for you?"

Chelsea's eyes lit up the minute that computer was in front of her. She was an addict, but it didn't have to be a bad thing. She would always need the power she felt when she was hacking, but he could turn her just the right way so she was doing it for good instead of just doing it. She simply needed a firm and loving hand. And he needed one, too. He'd just started to recognize it. He needed her to give him a reason to get up in the morning, to color his bland world.

"I can handle it, Hutch," Chelsea said, her hands already flying across the keys.

Boomer held up a hand like he was still in grade school. "Uhm, I'm going to get called a dummy for asking this, I'm sure, but what's a Deep Web?"

Chelsea never looked up even as she answered the question. "Think of the Internet as being a massive piece of property and the web addresses are real estate they sell. The www is a part of town that's easy to get to, safe for the most part until you add in a couple of words like anal hotties or free movies. Then it gets a little skeevy and someone's coming out of it with a virus."

"Don't all sites have a www?" Theo asked. He sat next to his brother, and Simon had to stare from time to time. They weren't exactly twins to Ian and Sean, but it was easy to mistake them on a casual glance.

"Nope. Not at all," Hutch replied. "The Deep Web is off the beaten path, so to speak. These are sites that can't be indexed by normal search engines. You can't type in a name for these sites and find them. You have to know the very specific address. It's kind of like a speakeasy. You better know the code word to get in or you're on your own."

"Like Silk Road?" Case asked.

Chelsea's brows rose and he loved how cute she was when she was serious. "Yes, like Silk Road. Which despite reports, I had nothing to do with. Nothing. Mostly."

"How about my client declines to answer on the grounds that every little sound she makes tends to incriminate her," Simon offered, giving her a warning glare. Ten didn't need ammunition.

"Fine." Chelsea went back to concentrating on the screen in

front of her.

Ten stood and walked around the table so he had a view of what Chelsea was doing. “So Krum found something that incriminated The Collective and he mailed it to her? Are we sure we’re talking about snail mail here? Why wouldn’t he just send it to her digitally? I thought all the hackers avoided the post office.”

Simon was fairly certain. “He said he sent her a hard copy.”

Chelsea sighed a little. “I just don’t know where he would have sent it to. He knew how often Charlotte and I moved and we haven’t talked much since Satan took over my life.” Her eyes strayed to Case. “That’s my name for your big brother, and he could so kick your ass. Hey, does the smaller one cook?”

Theo stared at her, obviously offended. “I’m not exactly small. I’m six foot three for god sakes. He’s only got an inch or two on me. And for your information, I’m pretty good. I’m not chef quality or anything, but I had to learn because our mom worked so much and Case there can burn an egg just by thinking about it.”

“Yep, Little Tag Two,” she said under her breath as she went back to work. “I got it. I’m going in. There’s no way anyone can trace this signal. I’ll get in, download whatever it is they want us to see, and get back out before they even know it.”

“How did they find us the first time?” Simon wondered.

Hutch had an answer for that. “Traffic cameras. You didn’t switch cars after the initial pickup. It would have been hard because not every intersection has a camera, but we know they’ve got some people on DPD, so they could track you and figure out where you stopped.”

“It’s probably how Adam did it,” Chelsea explained. Her face went white. “Oh god.”

Ten frowned. “Hutch, take over. Simon, she doesn’t need to see this.”

But he did. He nodded at Jesse, who had Chelsea pulled back as fast as he could get her up and out of her seat. She was shaking, but Simon had to see for himself.

It was a video playing on a loop. There was a woman kneeling in what looked like a hospital room. White and sterile,

Simon could almost smell the bleach. But the man who entered the picture wasn't a doctor. He was dressed in a suit with a mask covering his face. He stepped up to the camera.

"Mr. Krum, you missed your deadline. I believe we promised you a penalty." He stepped back from the camera and it was all over in an instant. The man placed his pistol at the woman's temple and pulled the trigger. Her body slumped over and the floor wasn't white or sterile anymore.

"We want the files you stole and we want them now. You have four hours. We have your sister, too. She has four hours to live."

The video went blank and then the man was on again. This time he was alone and someone had cleaned up that room.

"Miss Dennis, I'm sorry for the shock. I'm sending you this video so you understand the history of our interactions up to this point. Unfortunately, that woman's four hours were up a long time ago. So were her mother's when our very reasonable request went unmet. Apparently our employee, Albert Krum, has mistakenly sent you a package that belongs to us. The bombs you discovered are meant merely to show you that we do mean business. We know where you live, where you work, where you play. We know who you care about. We don't want for those packages to be sent to your sister or perhaps to Mr. Weston. You look him up far too often on the Internet, dear. You're getting a bit sloppy in your retirement. We'll call you this evening. Find the package or Albert will be joining his mother and sister and then we'll be forced to start looking at your family. Until then."

Simon looked over and Chelsea had her stoic face on, but she was pale, far too still.

Ten took a long breath as he stared at the screen. "Hutch, I'm going to need another secure line. No matter how the man feels about me right now, there's no way I'm not warning Tag. Chelsea, where would he send the package?"

"I don't know. It wasn't like I got a lot of packages while I was moving around the world trying to keep one step ahead of my father's men. It was a bad bet to leave a forwarding address," Chelsea said.

Simon moved toward her, but when he put his hand close to

hers, she moved away slightly.

She was shutting down again and at the worst possible moment.

Ten flipped the laptop closed. "Let's clear out and I'll make my call. I want every man looking into this Krum guy. Connect him to a corporation and that corporation to a lawsuit. I need straight lines to and from, people. And figure out where he would have sent this mysterious package of his. Weston, make sure your people get some sleep. We're moving in the morning. Don't ask me where. It's better you don't know."

The room emptied as Ten and his men went to find another, more private location. It wasn't lost on Simon that Boomer and Deke stayed behind. Their guard. It was good to know there were only two of them.

He could handle two of them, but not until later. Now it was time to truly bind her to him because he was going to make his move and he needed to make sure that when he did, she was by his side.

Chapter Thirteen

She wasn't going to cry. She'd done enough of that. It was time to face the facts. She'd gotten them in this mess and working with Ten was the only way to get them out of it. She stared out of her balcony at the massive moon overhead. It didn't look so big when she was in the city, or maybe she just never looked up long enough to really see it.

Three hours had gone by and she still couldn't get the sight of that poor woman kneeling on the floor out of her head. Jesse had pulled her away before the shot that ended the woman's life, but she could imagine it. She could certainly imagine feeling utterly helpless and alone in the world. It made her sick. Al's whole family was dead. Al, with his shy smile and big eyes hidden behind thick glasses. He'd been a little chunky and the dude could have dressed better, but the time they'd actually met he'd been funny and sweet. He'd run all over Venice with her. It had been weird because she hadn't pictured him that way, but he'd been one of the first real friends she'd made during those years on the run.

The sound of boots moving across the patio below brought her out of her reverie. Case Taggart had taken Boomer's place manning the outer perimeter. She was sure if she opened her bedroom door that Theo would be pacing the halls.

Where was Simon? Was he still sitting downstairs talking to his aunt? Ava had finally caught a little of the evening news, and the very elegant lady had proven she knew a whole bunch of curse words.

Tag the Third looked up and nodded before continuing his sweep.

So much trouble over one little package, but then that might be the story of her life.

A restlessness took over and she couldn't stay cooped up a second more. She needed to see Simon. She needed to come clean with him and get him the hell out of this op. The Collective would use him against her and she couldn't allow that to happen. She would just walk right up to him and tell him what she was going to do. She was never going to be his girlfriend or sub or whatever he wanted to call it. She was going to be Ten's broker.

She crossed over to the door after pulling a robe over the gown Ava Malone had dropped off at her room. Deke had forgotten about PJs and apparently Simon's aunt was a deep believer in wearing elegant things to bed. It was a far more feminine nightgown than she would ever wear, but it was all she had at this point. White and silky, it covered everything. It also had a plunging neckline and a thigh-high slit, but luckily it came with a long-sleeved robe that when knotted properly formed a sort of elegant silk muumuu. At least that's what she told herself.

She opened the door, perfectly ready to walk out and face down Simon. Theo was standing right there, his hand up as though ready to knock. He looked so much like Satan and Sean it was a shock to see him there. "Hey."

He nodded. "Hey. Uhm, the British guy asked me to bring you to him. He's in a room at the end of the hall. I don't know why he couldn't get you himself, but I had nothing better to do so I said yes."

Good. At least she wouldn't have to look for him. "All right."

Theo held a hand out, gesturing toward his left. "His room is in the east wing. God, that's weird. The rich are different. I grew up in a double wide. No wings there."

She started walking beside him. He slowed to match her

pace. "I've lived just about everywhere and it's all the same. It's the people in the house that make it livable. Not the house itself."

Sometimes when she slept she dreamed about the little house they had on the Carolina coast. She could smell the Atlantic and hear the waves. Endless waves like possibilities.

You're like those waves, baby girl. You can go anywhere, be anything.

Her mother hadn't been great with metaphors and then she hadn't been anything at all.

She'd been a wonderful mother. She'd surrounded her daughters with love. She just hadn't been able to protect them when the monster came back for her.

"What's he like?" Theo asked, his voice low.

"Ian?"

"Yeah. I'm just curious. I didn't tell Case this, but I knew Dad had another family. I found pictures in the closet once. They were way in the back with some of Dad's old things. When I took them to my mom and asked about it, she didn't know. They fought that night. Worst fight ever and I never asked again because I didn't want to see that look on her face."

"Well, you would know if you'd gone into the Army instead of the Navy. Big Tag is a legend. He and Sean were both Green Berets. Ian got recruited into the Agency but then he met my sister and she died, and he was framed and he said fuck it, because he says that a lot, and quit and opened McKay-Taggart in Dallas. His hobbies are cussing, shooting people who annoy him, oddly enough gossiping, and he's got this weird affinity for Guns N' Roses." Every time that one song came on, Ian and Charlotte would mysteriously disappear. "I think he's got a man crush on Axl Rose."

Theo shook his head. "He killed your sister?"

Oh, that was a long story. "Nah. She faked her own death so we could get away from our Russian mob father, but it cost Ian his career and he was pissed when she came back. She showed him her boobs and it was okay."

Maybe it wasn't such a long story. If she showed Simon her boobs again, would he forgive her?

"I'm confused. I don't know if I want to meet him or not.

Case says no."

"Oh, then you should totally be like your doppelganger and say yes."

The sweetest smile curled Theo's lips up. He was quite stunning when he wanted to be. "His name is Sean? What's he like?"

It was nice to know one of them was curious. "I like Sean. He kind of lives to poke his brother, but they're really close. He got out of the business for the most part, though he helps out from time to time. He opened a restaurant."

When he really smiled, he could light up a room. "Wow. That's kind of cool. I guess when I think of Taggarts I think of military men. It's nice to know we're expanding."

"You should meet them."

His glow dimmed, and he shook his head. "Nah. That's not a good idea. Case wants to do this thing with Ten. We have to keep real low profiles."

They had to stay in the dark. Their only real friends would be in the program. Anyone they met in the outside world would be given a happy little lie. She was likely going to be spending a lot of time around Theo and Case and they would forever be reminders of the life she almost had.

They came to the end of the hall, and she could hear music playing through the closed double doors. She stopped and stared for a minute.

"You okay? If you don't want to see him, you don't have to, but I kind of thought you had a thing going," Theo said.

"What gave me away? Was it sitting on his lap during a business meeting or him nearly killing his cousin?"

"It was the way you looked at him. You looked at him like he was the only man on earth. No one ever looked at me like that. I got kind of jealous and I don't even know you. Did I get it wrong? Are you scared of him?"

She was scared of so many things, but not him. Never him. Not in any physical way. "I love him and I shouldn't. I can't because I'll get him killed in the end."

"A woman looks at me like that and maybe that's worth dying over," Theo said. He took a step back and a rueful grin crossed his face. "If you need anything, I'll be out here."

Ah, the night watch. "I bet you will. I promise not to bust out."

He gave her a little salute. "See that you don't."

She turned back to those doors and forced herself to walk through them. He was probably ready to talk strategy or to go over her memory again in hopes of figuring out where the package might be. She would just walk in and treat him like a coworker. That would be for the best. Talk about the case and then tell him what she'd decided.

She opened the doors and her jaw dropped.

His room was a suite and he'd moved the furniture all to the side so there was a large space in the middle. The room was lit with what looked like a hundred candles. There couldn't be that many, but they sparkled like diamonds illuminating the night.

He stood in the middle of the room. He'd left off his jacket, but he looked utterly masculine and immaculate in his dress shirt, vest, and tie. His slacks were perfectly pressed, and she had to sigh over just how hot he was. The Taggarts of the world might be rugged, but she would take Simon any day of the week. He was perfectly polished and smart and she'd seen him in a fight. For her, he was the perfect man.

How the hell could she give him up?

All the reasons flooded back, but they didn't matter because she had one more night with him. "Hey. I was coming down to see you. What's going on?"

His eyes heated as he looked her over from head to toe. "I was going to call Jesse in for a late-night supper. I thought he would appreciate the romantic gesture."

"Come on, Weston. Let me off the hook. What's going on here?" She kind of couldn't breathe he looked so good. "Aren't we supposed to be working?"

He stepped toward her. "I'll leave that up to Ten. I wanted to find a way to apologize."

"For what?"

"For being angry with you when I shouldn't have been." There was a single strand of golden hair that fell across his forehead, the imperfection making him look younger, happier than she was used to seeing him. "I was wrong about you and Ten. I'm sorry. My only excuse is that I was horribly jealous."

He held out his hand, offering to bring her into his circle, the one filled with candlelight and soft music. She hesitated. "Why me?"

"What?"

"I don't understand this." She didn't trust it for a second. "Why me? I'm not beautiful. I've got a bad attitude. I push people away. So I have to ask—why me? Is this some sort of game to you?"

His hand came down and he stepped toward her, his face going dark as he left the light. "I don't play games like this. I knew I wanted you the minute I met you. Perhaps it makes me a masochist, but I wanted you the second you planted that little fist in my face. I wanted you because it would be a challenge and I've had so few of those."

A lie. Now that she knew about his childhood, she could partially see that the elegant clothes and sophisticated veneer were there to protect him. "I don't know that I like being pursued because I'm a challenge."

He laughed a little. "It's been a while, love. I think I would have given up by now if there was nothing else in it for me. We're a lot alike, you and I. If you would just see past the outer parts of me, if you would really see me…"

She would see the lonely boy inside the man. Like she was still a girl who had her life ripped out from under her. One day she'd been playing in the shoals, up to her ankles in sand and sea. She'd been beloved, and the next she'd been taken around the world to a place where she was used as nothing more than a way to force her older, more beautiful sister to do their father's bidding.

They had more in common than she liked to admit.

"I don't know that I can be the woman you need me to be." That was the real reason she'd stayed away from him. She was afraid he would need her to change and that she wouldn't be able to.

His hand found hers. "As my cousins would say, bullshit. I don't believe that for a second. You went into the information brokering business because you needed to be powerful. You were on the run and you had to find a way to protect yourself and your sister. And then you liked being powerful for a change."

"Yes. Yes, I did." And that would be all she would have when she worked for Ten, but at least she would feel useful.

"I can give that to you in a way that doesn't hurt anyone. Chelsea, you're bloody brilliant. You can find anything. What if you decided to find people? People who get lost? My cousins and I grew up with a girl named Dana."

"The redhead in the pictures with JT and Michael?" She'd seen a couple of pictures hanging on the walls. She'd caught JT staring at one of them.

"She was a family friend, and at one point we all thought she would marry JT. She went missing a while back. It's a long story, but I believe she's on the run and she was pregnant when she left."

"With JT's baby?"

"No. She married someone else and it got her into a spot of trouble. I've looked for her and I can't find a trace. I'm going to ask you to take over the case. Find her for us. Chelsea, find her and then we find another case and you spend your life reuniting families or hunting down people who need to be found. There's power in that. Can you see it? You could be a force for good in the world, and that isn't something to be taken lightly or thrown away on a whim. You were given a gift, and it is not yours to waste. You can be so much more."

She was good at finding people. They always left a trail behind. Even when they left the grid, almost no one could stay off it forever. She could find loved ones, hunt down criminals.

Find secrets and play in the cesspool. That's what she'd do because she'd made her bed long ago and now she had to lie alone in it.

"I'll find her." She would use every tool in the Agency's pocket to find JT's lost girl. It was one thing she could give to Simon. "I promise."

His smile was brighter than all the candles. He moved into her space and his hands found her face, tilting it up so she was staring into those warm blue eyes of his. "I knew you would say yes. Now say yes to me again."

She wanted to spend her life saying yes to him, but she would take one more night. Looking up at him, she realized she needed this. Wasn't tomorrow soon enough to face reality? Shouldn't she get one beautiful memory of him? "Yes."

"You don't even know the question."

She sighed and moved closer to him, feeling a little drugged by his nearness, the romantic candle light, the soft music. "We both know I'll sign anything you put in front of me, so why not just say yes to all your questions?"

"Dance with me."

She took a step back. It had been one thing to sway slightly to country western music with Ten. That had been more about Ten using the moment to talk to her than it had been about dancing. Simon could really dance. Like a professional. Like the guys on TV. She could barely walk. "Simon, I don't think that's a good idea."

He reached down and gripped her hand, bringing her back to him. "I think it's a brilliant idea. I think you'll love dancing. Come on, love. Do you know what it was like having to take bloody ballroom dance classes at the age of eight? Embarrassing. Humiliating. Foolish. You can make it all worthwhile. All that torment could finally be made into something good because I'll get to be Chelsea Dennis's first dance. I'm ignoring that shite with Ten. He can't dance to save his life. He was just trying to get his hands on your bum."

Heat flashed through her system. "He was not."

Simon loomed over her, and his hands were suddenly on her waist, sliding over her hips until they found the cheeks of her ass. She had to remember to breathe. "Oh, yes he was. He was trying to cup this luscious flesh and drag you close so you would know exactly what he could offer you."

She could feel Simon's offering against her belly. His cock was long and thick and she really wanted to see him naked, to touch him and taste him the way he'd tasted her. But she didn't want to fall all over him and make an idiot of herself. "Why don't you kiss me, Simon?"

He lowered his head, his lips hovering against hers. She

could feel his heat right there and she shivered, waiting for the sensation of his mouth brushing hers. He stopped just short. "After you dance with me."

He stepped back, bringing his body upright to his full height. His shoulders squared and he held out a single hand. It was an aristocratic gesture, his demeanor reminding her that he was a nobleman. "This is a waltz. Let me show you."

"Simon, I'm not even wearing shoes. And this robe is just a little too long."

"Then take it off. Drop the robe and we'll pretend you're in an elegant evening gown. You won't need shoes because I promise, your feet aren't going to touch the floor. I told you I want you to experience the feeling of dancing. I can teach you later, but for tonight, I'll dance for both of us."

She had no idea what he meant, but it was obvious he was going to have his way and she had to admit she was curious. He was hard to turn down when he stood there like a decadent dream. She unbelted the robe. It wasn't like he hadn't seen everything and the white gown did make her skin look sort of pretty.

"Oh, remind me to thank my aunt." He was staring at her breasts.

"I don't think your aunt meant anything by it." But she kind of wanted to thank her, too. Up until now, he'd only seen her in snarky T-shirts. At least he knew she could look like a lady when someone gave her the proper clothes.

"My aunt can be a tricky one, and she tends to know what she's doing. Come on." He held his hand out again and this time she took it. "Stand on my feet."

She looked up at him, but he had his Dom face on. She nodded and stepped onto his loafers. Her feet fit almost entirely on the bridge of his.

"All right, put your left hand on my shoulder," he instructed as he took her right hand in his and held it out to the side in a formal dance position. She'd seen people dance on TV, but she'd never once thought to do it herself. She was too awkward, too closed off. "Look into my eyes. The glorious thing about the waltz is we never break contact. I hold you tight the whole time.

Trust me, love."

He moved his foot slowly, as though getting used to her weight. He stepped out with his right foot and followed with his left, turning slightly. Awkward at first, he never stopped looking at her, never gave her a moment to look at anything but him.

After a moment, he seemed to get comfortable and that innate grace that was such a part of him took over. He moved across their little dance floor in sweeping motions. Chelsea held on for dear life at first, but after he really picked up the rhythm, she relaxed in his arms. He wouldn't let her fall. He wouldn't misstep and send them to the floor. He would carry her when she couldn't carry herself.

"Let go," he whispered to her. "Let yourself just feel for once. Let me give this to you."

She looked into his eyes and let her inhibitions go. She gave over to him, finally really understanding that submission didn't have to mean that she was weak. It didn't have to be a means to an end. It could be a gift—from sub to Dom and from Dom back to sub. The music flowed through her and for the first time in her life she felt like she was floating. Maybe not the first as she flashed back to a time when her mother twirled her around and around until they were both laughing and fell to the sand together. Freedom. She hadn't felt so free since she was a child.

A wild joy took up in her heart and seemed to flow through her veins as Simon whirled her around. His hands tightened as he picked up the pace with the next song. She was floating, flying and it was all because of him.

"Please make love to me." The words came out naturally, without her even thinking about them.

Simon stopped, his eyes finding hers. "That is going to have to do."

Chapter Fourteen

He'd promised to make her scream his name and beg him, but getting a sweet and polite request from Chelsea Dennis was almost a miracle. She'd said it and his cock had practically jumped around in his trousers. He hadn't actually planned on keeping her to his ridiculous vow of that first night, but hearing those words from her mouth were sweet indeed.

Without another thought, he leaned over and hooked his arm under her knees, lifting her against his chest. The bed wasn't far away and he wasn't going to waste another bloody second. Months and months had gone by as his dick languished, waiting for her to catch up. He couldn't see a point in spending another second not buried deep inside her.

Except for the fact that she'd never had a man buried inside her before. He was the first and meant to be the last, and that meant not mucking it up like an untried schoolboy. He stopped, taking a deep breath.

"Simon?" Chelsea was looking up at him. He'd expected a bit of fear, but she was frowning his way. Her narrowed eyes gave him the clear impression that he'd already made a mistake.

"I'm going too fast."

"You are going way, way too slow. Don't you have something you want to say to me? Something beyond 'that will have to do'? That's horrible. I expected better from you."

He couldn't help the grin that crossed his face. Most women would already be all over him, demanding their pleasure, but not his Chelsea. "Don't I get credit for all the candles and the dancing?"

She softened a bit. "Yes, but something more along the lines of 'you look pretty let's go to bed' could go with it."

All of that brash wit of hers fled and she was a bit timid again, as though he wouldn't think she was pretty. "You're gorgeous and I want to make love to you. I made that plain from the beginning. I want to take you in every way a man can have a woman, but we're going to go slow and easy."

"I don't want to go slow and easy. Simon, I think about you all the time. I think about the gentleman you are, but when I close my eyes and see you and my whole body clenches in anticipation, it's not the gentleman I see. It's the Dom. I want my Dom."

"Don't tempt me." He was barely leashed as it was. He wanted her so badly and he didn't want to make sweet love to her. He wanted to fuck. He wanted to take her hard but only after he'd mastered her body. When she'd taken his discipline for her disobedience and she looked up at him with wide pleading eyes because she couldn't stand another moment without his dick inside her, that was when he would take her.

But he didn't want to hurt her. He didn't want to frighten her.

"Please, Simon. I don't want you to treat me like I'm made of glass. I feel that way far too often. I want to know what it means to be your sub. Even if it's only for a night. Please. I want to be yours, really yours."

He entered the bedroom and set her on her feet. This guest room used to be Dana's. It was feminine, but not frilly. The cream colors complemented the gown Chelsea was wearing that he really was going to thank his aunt for. He'd seen her in the baggy shite she used to conceal her beauty and versions of fet wear, but this Chelsea was soft and sweet, with beautifully feminine curves that made his mouth water. Her breasts were round and upright in the bodice and he could see a hint of the legs she always tried to hide. If she wanted her Dom, she was going to find out there was absolutely nothing she hid from him.

"Present yourself to me."

Her eyes flared for a second and then her jaw went firm, stubborn as she started to lower herself. He caught her because she really hadn't read that bloody contract. He had to work on her lamentable lack of attention to any details that had nothing to do with computer code. "Most submissives greet their Doms on their knees, but I don't want that from you."

"Because you think I can't do it?" There was that stubborn little girl who so often came out any time she was challenged.

"Because I think it would be uncomfortable for you, love. The presentation is merely a formal act of submission meant to let both parties know it's time to play. Many times it's a gift to the Dom because the sub wouldn't get on his or her knees for anyone else. You have other acts you can give me, acts that prove you belong to me and me alone. When the other subs get to their knees, you'll walk up to me, invade my space, and wrap yourself around me. You'll say the following words. 'I offer myself to you, Master.'"

She frowned. "I think I would rather get to my knees."

Because she would see that as less intimate. Well, she said she wanted her Dom. She was about to get him. Hardening his voice, he pointed to the bed. "Put your hands on the mattress, palms flat, and get your backside in the air. Now. It's a count of twenty but I will add ten for every moment you hesitate."

"I didn't know."

"You didn't know you were supposed to obey your Dom? I'll have to take that up with Ian since he assures me you were properly instructed in how to behave around a Dominant partner." He gave her a stern glare. Did she think he was a pussy Dom who would sit back and hope she obeyed him? "That's another ten. We're up to thirty, love. Do you want to make it forty?"

She turned and walked to the bed, her head held high. She placed her palms on the cover and leaned over.

Not nearly good enough. He had chosen their protocol in deference to her legs, but there was nothing at all wrong with her ass. "Higher. You'll get that luscious ass higher for me."

There was no way he missed the hitch in her breath as she resettled herself, her legs spreading slightly, her back flattening out.

"Would you like to explain to me why you can't obey?" He actually liked this part. It was all play and he would stop the minute she protested, but he rather enjoyed being the big bad Dom.

"I was just asking a question."

He smacked her cheek through the gown. "What do you call me?"

"Master. I was just asking a question, Master."

How quickly she forgot. Another smack. "It wasn't a question. You stated that you would prefer to greet me in another fashion than the one we agreed upon. Don't you dare say you didn't know. It was laid out for you. Now, tell me why you won't greet me the way I wish to be greeted."

"I'm sorry," she breathed. "I don't know why. It really wasn't a hard thing to do. I'm just not used to being intimate and when I thought about doing that in front of everyone, it made me nervous."

Finally, a bit of honesty. "Because you don't want anyone to know you belong to me?"

Her head shook. "Because I always worry that if people know I'm soft, they'll know how to hurt me and I'm sick of being hurt."

More sweet honesty. It made him even more hopeful than her agreeing to go to bed with him. Chelsea hid everything. She hid behind her smart mouth and her computer. She hid behind her sister. He didn't want her to hide anything from him. He wanted to lay her open so she would know she could trust him. "I can't promise that no one will hurt you again. I can promise I'll protect you from anyone who tries."

"Why did you hit your cousin?"

"Because he tried to keep me from you." He let his hand run along her cheeks, feeling her through the silk of her gown. That would have to go, but he wanted to enjoy her on every level. "I won't let anyone do that. As long as you accept me as your

Master, I won't let you do it either. I'll be honest and open with you and I expect the same. I won't close myself off."

"You never told me about your brother."

His cousins had been busy. He hadn't really intended to talk about his family because they weren't a part of his life in the States. But she was quite smart. She knew exactly when to play her cards. "Fine. I'll talk while you take your punishment. And you should be deeply glad that I've decided to forgive you for disobeying my very direct order concerning running." She hadn't done it for selfish reasons. She'd tried to save him. He found he just couldn't punish her for being loving. Maybe he was the pussy Dom. "But if you disobey next time, I swear you won't sit for a week."

"I'll do it next time, Simon. I can't run when you're in danger. I can't. And you should understand how different that is for me. I spent my life running. There are two people I can't leave behind. You and my sister." Her head drooped. "Maybe more. I've gone fucking soft. I don't think I could have even left Jesse behind."

Because she was starting to feel for her family. This was what he'd been working toward. He'd been working toward making her a part of the team because the team was a family—the one he'd been looking for all his life. He might complain about Ian from time to time, but he was a good brother. He'd found a whole brotherhood, and he wanted Chelsea to love them, too. "Because you're brave, love. I can't fault you for being brave."

He could adore her for it though. He'd lied. He'd been intrigued that first day when she'd given him her best uppercut. He'd thought about her, but he hadn't fallen until later. A few days later, he'd found her crying in the office. He'd asked her what was wrong and she'd stood up, thrown her shoulders back and sniffled. She'd told him that she was scared because her sister was going to leave her. But she'd shut her mouth and gotten on the plane that took them to India and she'd supported Charlotte ever since. She might call Ian Satan, but she'd allowed her sister to find love when she hadn't had to. Charlotte would have given in, but Chelsea backed off. She still called for

Charlotte from time to time, but it was only because she didn't have her own lover, her own man. It would be different from this night on.

Chelsea would reach for him. She would be his—to protect and care for. To provide her with affection and everything she needed.

"God, Simon. It doesn't feel like punishment. It feels so good." Her ass wiggled a bit. She enjoyed a bite of pain. Her needs dovetailed neatly with his own. "How do you make that feel good?"

She was harder core than many subs he knew. She truly liked the pain. He smacked her a little harder, watching the way she shivered. "I know what you need." Two more. He kept count in his head. Later, he would hear her count it out for him, but apparently they were having a therapy session. "What do you want to know about my brother?"

"Is he okay?" Her breath hitched as he drew the gown up, but she managed to not protest.

Smart girl. He pushed the gown up over her cheeks until he could see the perfection of her backside. Pretty skin, beautifully round and made to hold on to while he fucked inside her. And she wanted to talk about Clive. "He's perfectly fit. I take it my cousins told you about his childhood illness."

He discovered he liked the leisurely nature of this particular session. So many times a spanking was rote and something to get over quickly, but he could take his time with Chelsea. He'd delivered discipline in sessions created to give the sub what she requested. He'd been a rent-a-Dom. He'd worked Karina over many times and never once had he stopped and sighed over how lovely she was and talked about himself in the midst of slapping her ass.

"JT said he had cancer." A whimper came out of her mouth, finding a straight line to his cock. He loved her little sounds.

And damn but he loved the scent of her arousal. He could smell her. She was getting ripe and ready. Three quick smacks had her shaking, but she held her position. Yes, this way he could keep her on edge, never knowing exactly what he was going to do next. He let his fingers skim her flesh as he spoke.

"They found it when he was seven and I was four."

"And they sent you away?"

"Not at first. I was too young. I had nannies. A couple were good. A couple were bad. For the next ten years, our lives revolved around my brother's blood counts and his chemo. I'll be honest, I was grateful at times to go to school or to come here because even when I was home, it wasn't mine. Not really."

He never talked about this, but somehow it was easier this way. They were alone and he could touch her, feel her soft skin. He was further from those years in this place. He peppered her cheeks with quick, sharp slaps.

She shuddered. "You're killing me, Master." She took a long breath. "Were you lonely?"

He chuckled a bit. "Yes, darling. I was a lonely child. I didn't just miss my parents. I missed him. He was a good brother and then he was gone. They didn't want me around him much because his immune system was so damaged. They spent a year in Zurich at a treatment facility. I saw my mother once that year. She came for family day, but all she talked about was how well Clive was doing and how we could all be together again soon. He took a turn for the worse a month later."

"So you didn't get to go home. Don't forget my thighs. Please, Master."

He didn't have his kit or he would get his flogger out. Though this was a ranch and he knew where the crops were kept. He might have to make a stop at the barn later. For now he gave in because she'd said that one little word. He laid stinging slaps to the backs of her thighs, satisfied when she groaned. "No, I didn't go home. I was told by everyone that I should stay out of the way and pray for my brother and simply be satisfied that I had my health. I lived to come here, you know. I counted the days. The first time I came here I was seven and my aunt insisted. She came over to England and flew back with me. She escorted me to and from all those years. She insisted she liked the time alone with me. I liked the time alone with her, too."

He had no idea what he would have done without Ava Malone. She'd opened her home and her family and would have been perfectly pleased to have kept him full time, but his parents insisted that he was likely the future duke and had to be schooled properly. He'd rebelled by trying to sound as American as he could around his parents. They'd shuddered when he'd first used the word "y'all." It was still there in his speech. He wasn't quite British and not fully American.

He moved to her other side, sad that her punishment was almost over. He counted out the last ten in his head and then sighed. "You did beautifully, love."

"It's over?" She sounded disappointed. "But I didn't find out the end of the story."

The end of the story was an easy one to tell. He let his palm find her cheeks, loving the heat there. Even in the soft light he could see the pink sheen to them. "My parents found a new therapy and Clive made a full recovery. He was sixteen. I was thirteen. He was a complete stranger to me. My parents returned home and I was expected to pretend nothing had happened. I threw the biggest fit when they wanted me to go with the family for holiday. My mother finally decided I wasn't worth arguing with and I came here and they went to Spain. And that was how we spent the rest of my youth. I was the odd child they didn't understand. I heard my father once say how grateful he was Clive had survived because I wasn't a worthy successor."

"Simon," she started.

"I'd gone a bit wild by then," he admitted. "I was almost always in trouble for something during my adolescent years. My brother no longer wastes his time on me. You smell so fucking good."

His fingers came up against the sweet softness of her pussy. Wet. She was so wet. She'd liked her spanking. "Tell me something. Do you get this wet every time you have a session?"

She gasped as he found her clit and let his thumb ease over it, pressing lightly. "No. God, no. I don't. Unless it's you."

That's what he wanted to hear. He let a single finger split her labia, working its way inside. She was going to be so bloody tight. Her pussy was clenching around just his finger. What would she do when it was his cock working its way inside?

"Do I have to stay still? Because I don't want to."

But he was having so much fun torturing her. "You're not to

move until I give you leave."

"Damn it."

He hadn't told her not to curse so he let it pass. He pulled his fingers out and brought them to his mouth, licking the taste of her off them. So sweet and perfect. She was like the sweetest treat to him.

"I don't like your brother." He could hear a little pout in her voice. "Though I will confess, I also don't like you very much right now."

He could handle that, but he had to admit some things to her. "He went through a lot, Chelsea. He's just a man. Through all of his treatments, he managed to maintain perfect scores on all his tests. He would study and work even when the chemo made him deathly ill. Or so my parents tell me. I admired him, but he was a stranger to me after all those years. I can see now he tried to be a good influence, but I had my brothers."

"JT and Michael."

"Yes. And Clive isn't all bad. It turns out he's actually quite the pervert. Imagine my surprise when he showed up one night at The Garden with his two best friends and shared girlfriend. That was a bit awkward." He touched her ass again, loving the way he'd marked her. It would be gone by morning, but he would enjoy it tonight.

He wanted to forget about his brother, who he hadn't talked to in months. His brother and their very uptight parents thought he'd made a horrible mistake when he'd used his law degree to join a charitable organization instead of making money. His trust fund wouldn't last long, they'd said since he seemed to spend money on women and luxuries. They had no idea he'd already been recruited into MI6 and given quite a budget to keep up appearances.

Then he'd left United One Fund and MI6 to come to America and that had caused the biggest lecture of his life. He was a lost soul according to his father—unable to follow through on anything, and Simon couldn't tell him the truth about the part he'd played.

And now they would likely get the news at some point that he was wanted for murder. Excellent.

"Can I move, Master?"

He sighed, wishing JT had kept his big mouth shut. "Of course."

He reached out to help her balance. She turned and immediately hugged him, wrapping her arms around him and holding him close. Her head found his chest and she plastered herself against him, leaving no space at all between them. "I offer myself to you, Master."

He let his arms wrap around her, let her fill his senses. She so rarely showed softness and this was all for him. It felt like the gift it was. He let his hands find her hair. So often she put it up, but for him she let it flow down her back. "I accept you, love. You understand what I mean when I say that? I mean I accept everything about you."

She shook her head slightly. "I don't deserve that, Simon. I don't. Some of the things I've done…"

"You did because you were trying to survive. Darling, you didn't have an aunt who came and brought you home twice a year. You were alone with a monster."

Her head tilted up. "I killed a man, Simon. I was fifteen."

He'd known there was something. It didn't surprise him that it was this. The tells were all there. She was nervous around men. She'd made it to twenty-seven without trying sex. His heart ached for her, but he kept his expression soft. "He tried to rape you?"

Her eyes filled with tears and she nodded. "He was drunk and he told me my father wouldn't let anyone near Charlotte but I was fair game because he didn't give a shit about me. He snuck into my room when Charlotte was gone. She'd left me with a knife and I used it."

Because she'd been brave. Even as a child. "I promise you if he wasn't dead, I would kill him for you."

"And I would kick your brother in his non-cancerous balls for you."

Like he'd said, they were quite the pair. "I want to take you, Chelsea. I want you to accept me into your body and let us be lovers. Can you do that?"

"Yes. I want you. It was a long time ago. I still see it

sometimes, but I want to leave it behind me. I want to be with you."

He had plans to be with her forever, but he would take tonight to start with. "I'll handle this however you want. I'll be as gentle as you need me to be."

"I don't want you gentle. I want you. And I want to serve my Master before he serves me." She bit her bottom lip and her hands went to the straps of her gown. She let the straps drop and the gown pooled around her feet leaving her body on display.

"God, you're beautiful." He knew what that had cost her. She struggled to see herself as a physical being, but he was going to make her believe she was the most gorgeous thing on the planet if it was the last thing he did. He reached out and cupped a breast. Soft and perfect in his hand. The nipple peaked immediately. "And you should be very glad you were obedient. I'm sure whoever bought you day clothes included knickers."

She sighed as she curved her body to his touch. Such a sensual little cat. "I wanted to, but I thought you would be opposed to them."

He didn't particularly like the idea of her wearing clothes that one of Ten's men had purchased for her. As soon as they escaped, he would buy her a new wardrobe. "Definitely opposed to them. You really look best when you're just like this."

She shook her head. "I have no idea how you get me to do things I never dreamed of. Like I never thought I would beg a man to let me kiss him."

"You don't have to beg." He leaned over.

She put a hand between them. "I wasn't talking about your lips, Simon. I want to know how you taste, too. I want to know what it feels like to lick you and suck you. Is that good dirty talk?"

He had trouble answering since all his available blood had just rushed to his cock. "Yes, I think that will do." She knew how to push all his buttons. Nothing got him into pure Dom mode like a sub on her knees taking his cock between her lips. It had always flipped his switch and the idea of Chelsea being the woman to do it nearly made him come then and there. But he had to take care of her. "Get on the bed. You'll be more comfortable there."

Her lips turned down in a little pout. "You don't want me to?"

He tangled one hand in her hair and pinched her nipple with the other. Hard. "Obey me. Now. Or we'll start this all over again. Don't think for a second I won't torture you all night until I get what I want."

It was gratifying to see her turn and hurry toward the bed.

He made quick work of his vest and shirt. If he could dress quickly, he was a sprinter when it came to getting a suit off. He set them aside and toed out of his loafers. He glanced her way and she was sitting on the bed, her eyes wide as she watched him.

He undid his belt and went for the zipper on his slacks, more slowly since his cock was already fighting to be free. He eased the waistband over his hips and let them drop. He stood in front of her, not giving a damn if his slacks got wrinkled. He was focused on her. And she was focused on that part of him that was aching and needy.

"You couldn't be built on small lines, could you?"

"We'll fit perfectly. I promise." He strode to the bed, unwilling to wait a second longer. If she did that thing where she took her time and memorized him, he might explode. "Touch me. Stroke me. Use a firm grip and make me feel it."

She reached out and suddenly he couldn't breathe. He was surrounded by her heat, and she seemed determined to obey his instructions. She took him firmly in hand and stroked him, her eyes watching his cock as it started to weep with pre-come.

"Yes, being close to you gets me hard and having your hands on me makes me want to come. Don't ever doubt for a moment that I want you."

She stroked him, pumping him with her small hand. "I don't understand it, Simon, but I'll be honest. I don't care tonight. Tonight I just want to be with you. Tomorrow I'll deal with all the questions."

He would make sure she didn't have any questions. After tonight she would understand that they belonged together, that she didn't have to worry about being alone because she would be with him.

"Am I doing it right? I want to be good at it."

He was going to come in her hand if she didn't stop. He pulled away because he wasn't ready for that yet. "You're bloody perfect, but you better understand that you only practice on me. That's a hard limit. You're mine."

The sweetest smile lit her face. "I'll have to let all my other suitors down."

"Well, you'll certainly have to tell Tennessee Smith to keep his bloody hands off you." The next time Ten tried it, Simon would take his hands off. Permanently.

Her smile faded. "I'm not going to sleep with Ten. I only want you, Simon. I've only ever wanted you."

He climbed on the bed, lying back and spreading his legs wide so she was in between them. His cock jutted up, almost reaching his navel. "Prove it. Lick me."

She couldn't seem to meet his eyes. She was back to staring at his dick. "I've never done this before."

Yes, he'd gotten that when she'd told him she was a virgin. He hadn't imagined she'd been giving men hummers in lieu of sex. "I'll teach you how to suck my cock, Chelsea. Lean over and lick it."

She obeyed, moving to a position that had her on her hands and knees, but with the mattress beneath them, he was fairly certain she was comfortable. Tentatively, she brought her head down and her tongue came out, caressing him and making his eyes roll into the back of his head.

"Just a little play, love. I won't last long and I really want to get inside you. I don't think I can go another night without sinking into you. Lick the head. Taste me."

She gave his cockhead a long lick, drawing that drop of pre-come into her mouth. Pure pleasure threatened to curl his toes. "You like this."

"Yes. I like it a lot." It was taking everything he had to not take her hair in his hands and force her mouth down. "I'll play sweet tonight. Later, I'll very likely fuck your throat and it won't be sweet or pretty. I'll force you to take my cock deep and I'll come straight down your throat. I'll be rough. It's going to be hard for me not to, but I'll try."

She didn't move from her spot, simply continued to use her tongue on him. "I want you rough. I want you every way I can have you. I want to eat you up."

He watched as she opened her mouth and proceeded to prove she was serious. His cockhead disappeared into her mouth, pure heat nearly burning him up. He couldn't help it. His hands moved to her hair. Soft silky stuff. He let his fingers dive in and tangle up. "You're going to do what I tell you, love. While we're in bed, I'm in charge. I won't hurt you, but I will have you. Can you trust me?"

She kind of mumbled around his cock. He let up. He was already being rough with her and he just wanted more. Her head came up and that killer smile was back in play. "Yes, Master. I can trust you. And you taste good. I could suck your cock forever, Simon."

Fuck. He'd always known she would be a fierce lover if she let herself go. This was what he wanted. He didn't want some mouse of a woman to submit to him—someone who would submit to any dominant male. He wanted to earn the submission of a strong woman. One who would only submit to him and no one else. "I'll take you up on that."

He drew her head back down, bringing her lips back to his cockhead and pressing inside. So hot. So sweet. So damn good.

Over and over she drew on him, sucking hard once she found a rhythm. She might not have sucked a cock before but she was doing it perfectly. Her tongue ran all over his flesh, making him pulse and writhe. He fisted her hair, needing more.

"Take all of me." He wasn't going to be satisfied until he found that soft place at the back of her throat.

Inch by inch, she worked her way down, taking more and more of his cock. She was methodical, even as he was being driven slowly out of his mind with lust. Every lick and swipe of her tongue brought him closer and closer to the edge.

More. He needed more and she was going to give it to him. He pulled gently, forcing her on his dick, taking more territory, getting closer to what he really wanted.

She hummed, the sound spreading across his flesh like a

song in his soul. This was what he'd wanted with her. He'd felt this connection the moment he'd seen her, and this was the inevitable conclusion of that fateful day. Connection. Completion. He would have it finally when he took her.

He felt it—the soft back of her throat, but if he let her go further, he would come and he wasn't doing that tonight until he was buried inside her cunt.

"Stop." He tugged gently on her hair. Later, he would allow her to suck him dry, but not this first time.

She was still sucking, still working him over and he tugged harder. Finally she came free. "But I want to finish."

"And I want to finish and I can't do that until you take me inside." The time was right. It was time to make her his, time to complete this insane journey they'd been on so they could finally start their lives together.

* * * *

Chelsea forced herself to breathe as she watched Simon reach for a condom. It was surreal. He was going to do it. He was rolling that condom over his big cock so he could fuck her. She would know what it meant to be Simon Weston's lover.

Even if it was only for a night.

She shoved aside her guilt. It wouldn't work in the long run, but she could give him everything she had tonight. She could close her eyes and hold on and maybe it would be enough to dream about for the rest of her life. When she was all alone in some DC hidey-hole, she would close her eyes and think about the one night where she felt loved.

Sucking Simon's cock had been a revelation. She'd been utterly sure she would hate it. It would be something she simply got through so she could get to the good stuff. She'd loved it. She'd loved how her scalp lit up when he tugged her this way or that, pulling her down so she was forced to take more of that magnificent dick inside. He'd tasted good. Clean and salty. She licked her lips just thinking about how it felt to lick the slit of his cock and know it was all for her.

"You're going to make me come just looking at me like that,

love."

And she loved listening to him talk. His voice had gone deep and dark, commanding. "Theo says I look at you like you're the only man on earth."

He shook his head as he finished rolling the condom on. He was on his back, his body laid out like a feast for her senses. Every muscular line was tense and ready. He stroked himself as he looked at her with hot blue eyes. "I am the only man on earth for you, and let's not talk about Theo or any bloody Taggart. Come here, Chelsea. I want you to control the penetration."

He readjusted, moving his body so his back was against the headboard and he was sitting, waiting for her.

So awkward and yet her body pulsed at the thought. He was waiting for her to climb on top. He was offering her control. With shaking hands, she moved between his legs and as gracefully as she could she straddled him. She wasn't thinking about how she looked or moved for once. Her body suddenly wasn't a betrayal. It was an instrument of pleasure, a way to show this man how much she cared about him, how much she loved him. She might never say the words to him, but she could give him this.

His cock was suddenly pressed against her pussy and it was so big.

"Kiss me." His hands were on her torso, smoothing and easing over her skin. "Just kiss me for a minute."

She lowered her lips to his and there were those hands again, pulling her close, holding her tight. Any fear that crept along her brain was firmly shoved aside. This was Simon. He'd been protecting her since the day they had met. She'd never believed in some mystical one person who could make her complete, but Simon had proven her wrong. She felt more like herself when she was close to him. It had scared her at first because it seemed like the real Chelsea felt things more deeply than the woman she'd forced herself to become. She'd dulled her own senses so nothing could hurt her again, but she'd also given up on love and excitement and joy. They were roaring through her now as her breasts cuddled to his chest, her legs against his, and she could feel that masculine part of him twitching to be inside her. His tongue delved deep and there was no more awkwardness. All she could think about was being one with him.

She let her hands find his hair as their tongues tangled together. Soft and silky smooth. His hair flowed to smooth skin covering hard muscle. She could spend hours just touching him. Her nipples were hard and rasping against the faintest hint of his chest hair. Her backside was still aching from his discipline, but it was a good ache. She would feel it all day tomorrow. She thought about all the little bratty things she could do so he would spank her again.

BDSM had been a form of therapy for her, but now she could see why her sister liked to play. It was all a private game, an intimacy between lovers so they didn't have to draw a line at the bedroom. They could take their sensuality into the world and never have to close it off. Simon would be able to look at her, raise that one aristocratic brow, and remind her of just how good it felt to be naked and submitting to him. He would look at her across the boardroom table and with nothing but a gesture of his hand let her know what he would do to her later so the anticipation could build until she was bursting with it. She could spend her days being intimate with him without ever taking off her clothes.

But she wouldn't because they only had a day or two.

She forced that thought out of her head. She wasn't going to taint this time with him by thinking of the future. She let her tongue run across his bottom lip, nipping him lightly.

"Don't tempt me, love. I'm going to go easy on you this time, but after you're used to a good long fuck, I'll do you hard. I'll get you on your hands and knees and slap your arse while I fuck inside you. I'll get those tits in clamps and make you ride me so I can watch them bounce." He reached out and gave her nipple a hard twist.

She felt that like her breasts were a direct line to her pussy. She was so wet, but he liked that. She couldn't help herself. She rubbed against his cock.

"Oh, fuck that feels good." His hands tightened. "Stop playing with me. Take me."

His hips thrust up, sending his cock to run over her clit.

Sparks seemed to light along her skin as she lifted up and could feel his cockhead against her pussy. She looked up and Simon was looking down, his eyes watching the place where she was about to take him inside. She couldn't see it, but he was intent, all of his focus centered on the core of her being.

She eased down, taking him in inch by inch, letting him fill her up. Tight. She felt so tight, like her skin was too small for her body, but she wasn't about to stop now. She needed to know where this sensation would lead her.

"You feel so good." He gripped her hips, helping her to balance.

He felt perfect. So big there was a streak of pain, but she kind of liked that, too. The discomfort sizzled along her skin, warring with the pleasure and forming a new kind of sensation that threatened to overload her system.

She worked her way down, taking her time because she wanted to remember every second. She memorized the way he looked, decadent like a king allowing his mistress to please him. She memorized how hot he felt against her skin and the way she could feel his heartbeat thundering in his chest. She memorized how her body seemed to tune to his, as though in that one moment she wasn't a separate entity anymore. She was one with him.

Discomfort flared as she took another hot inch, but it was just one more sensation to be had now. Their pelvises finally met and he was deep inside. No distance between them. No space.

His eyes came up and he held himself hard against her body. "Are you okay?"

Even when all his primitive instincts should be taking over, he stopped to make sure she was fine because that was the heart of who he was. She loved him so much. She just wished she could be worthy of him. She leaned over, not giving up an inch of his cock, and kissed him. "I'm perfect."

His lips curved against hers. "You certainly bloody feel that way."

She rotated her hips and pleasure flared. "Oh, my god."

He thrust up. "No. You say my name when I'm fucking you, love." He did it again, moving her with the strength of his hips alone. "Say it. Say 'fuck me hard, Simon.'"

He really liked to hear her get dirty it seemed. That was easy though since she thought dirty thoughts about him all the time, much less when he was actually rubbing her from the inside out. "Fuck me hard, Simon. I want it, Master. I want your cock."

Something seemed to break and he wasn't lying back anymore. He moved, his hips rolling hard against her as his dick shot up. He bounced her, making her breasts jiggle, but she couldn't think about anything but the way his length was moving. Up and around and out again only to forage back in hard. Even from beneath her, he dominated. There was no question of who was in control. He was. Simon moved her up and down on his cock. Each roll of his hips brought her closer and closer to the edge. She caught the rhythm and found a way to move with him. When she leaned forward slightly, his pelvis rubbed against her clit and she couldn't hold on a second more. She wanted him deeper, harder, faster. She held on to his shoulders and fought him, pushing down on his upswing so she took every single inch of his cock as deep as she could.

"That's right, love. Ride me." His hand disappeared between them and she felt the pad of his thumb find her clitoris. He rubbed hard and it was over.

She cried out as she came. He'd been right. She couldn't think of anyone but him. She simply called his name again and again.

Before she could come down, he flipped her over. She found herself on her back, looking up into the most beautiful eyes she'd ever seen.

He hesitated, his dick still huge inside her.

He was scared, she realized. Scared that she wouldn't like this position. He didn't have to be. She liked everything with him. She let her hands find that rock hard backside of his and gave him a squeeze. "I'm fine, Master. I'm good. Better than good. Please fuck me some more. I want to fly again."

He stared down at her, his face so serious, but his hips moved, dragging his dick in and out. "I like this, love. You should know I like penetration and I like to make it last. I'll wake you up every morning with my cock in your cunt and I won't stop until you've screamed out my name at least three times. I promise you, I won't let you start the day without it. Now that I've had you, I'll be on you all the time. You won't be able to get me off you now."

He fucked her hard, making her feel every inch as he slammed into her again and again. Pleasure built as he managed to hit some magic spot inside her body, and she came again, this time even stronger than before.

Simon's big body stiffened as he dove deep, grinding into her, pouring out his come. He thrust once and then again and then he relaxed, rolling to her side.

Peace enveloped her like a blanket. It seemed to start at her toes, where their feet met, and it rolled all the way up her body. Simon's arm tucked around her waist as he pulled her close. Her back was warmed by his chest as blood pumped through her veins. She was so aware of her body in that moment. Aware of how her heart was beating. Aware of how her skin felt like it glowed and how her breath seemed to move in time to his.

His hand slid over her breast, cupping her and drawing her back against him. "Are you all right?"

She couldn't find the energy to do anything but nod.

His breath was hot against her ear. "I'm glad. You won't regret being with me, Chelsea. You'll see. I'm going to take care of you. We fit. I hope you can see that now."

She loved how sweet he was. He wasn't a man who held back his feelings. He offered them to her. She couldn't turn him down. There would be time enough for that later. "I know we do. I never fit with anyone the way I do with you, Simon."

He chuckled, the sound caressing her skin as he eased back. "I'm going to clean up and when I get back, we might just start all over again." He kissed her cheek. "Don't go anywhere."

As if she would leave him if she didn't have to.

She sat up and watched as he walked away, his magnificent ass in view.

She was in love with Simon and she would never fall in love again. He was the be-all, end-all of men, and she had to let him go to save him. Ten had been plain. He would clear Simon's name if she worked for him. If she didn't, it could take years to undo what The Collective had done. Simon was in America on a visa. He would be deported and he wouldn't be able to work security. He loved his job. It was all he had. She couldn't be the reason he lost it.

And she was certain this wouldn't be the last time someone came after her. If she was working for Ten, he could protect her and no one could use her love or her family against her. She would utterly break ties and let everyone know she couldn't care less. It was the only way to protect them.

She bit back the now hated tears. She used to only cry during scenes, but the Chelsea Simon brought out was a weepy girl.

One night. Maybe a week. Ten would let her keep Simon as long as the op was going. When they found the package, she would have to give him up.

Stolen time. That's when all her happiness occurred. Pockets of time she carved out of all the bad shit. Like the days when she and Charlotte would decide they couldn't take another moment being cooped up and they would risk being seen in public. They'd gone to a beach in Thailand and soaked up some sun with the tourists. They'd walked around Munich and visited the church where legend had it the devil had left a single hoofprint in the entryway. And Venice. They'd met Al. Al, who was gone now.

Hey, you remember the fun we had in Europe? When we spent that weekend there? That was a good time.

He'd mentioned it in the middle of their conversation before he died. Had he been hoping that reminding her of the good time they had would sway her to save him? She would have saved him if she could. How could he be gone? He was right. It had been beautiful. But they hadn't been all over Europe. They'd only seen each other in Venice. Why had he said Europe?

I'm so sorry, Chelsea. I wish I'd kissed you that day. Sometimes I still feel the wind in my hair and the sun on my face. I really do. That was a beautiful day.

Code. Al believed in code. Al believed that there was power in words and their meanings, and just because a word had a definition didn't mean it couldn't bring up other connotations.

Sometimes words were keys meant to unlock memories that would lead to the truth.

Al was gay. He would never have kissed her, but that day had been meaningful.

And the place. Because she'd loved Venice, and as she did back in those days, she'd opened an account at one of the local banks. She'd needed an address so she'd bought a small apartment. It had seemed smart to keep a network up. She and Charlotte had kept several of their former hideaways. They had a small bungalow in Bali, a postage stamp of an apartment in Tokyo, a brownstone in Manhattan, and a third floor walk-up in Venice so they would always have somewhere to run. It was in another name, but Al knew about it.

And now she knew where the package was.

He'd sent it to her Venice address. If he'd been a normal person, she'd wonder how he'd gotten it since the property was in another name. Al was smart and knew her fairly well. It would have taken him the work of a few hours to find her Italian residence.

He'd sent the information to Venice.

"Love, do you want a shower? You can join me. I'll clean you up and then get you filthy all over again."

"Oh, please don't. I really can't live through that again," a deeply sarcastic voice said from the outer rooms.

Chelsea sat up, her whole body tense. She thought she would have more time. She thought she'd have at least a whole night with him. But that wasn't to be.

Ian was here and her time was up.

Chapter Fifteen

Simon slipped into his loafers, his whole body still humming. Now he had a double dose of adrenaline. Between the thrill of finally getting Chelsea under him and then knowing he was going to get away, he was kind of hard again. Kind of? Damn. He needed to get the randy fellow to give him a moment's breath. He had to find a way through it since there was no way he was getting at Chelsea again until they got through the next few hours.

He had no idea how Tag had slipped past Ten, but he was certain that he'd taken care of the situation. If Ian was here, Ten was taken care of for the moment, but that moment wouldn't last forever. Unless Ian had killed the bastard, the Agency would be hot on their trail again in the near future.

He stepped out of the bedroom, once again properly dressed and ready for whatever was going to come their way.

"It's romantic." Charlotte blew out the final candle before glaring at her husband.

Ian shook his head. "It's not happening. It's dangerous. Look, he was trying to burn the place down. I think that was Simon's version of escaping. The British have funny ways, baby."

He couldn't help but chuckle. God, they were going to be

interesting in-laws. "Charlotte is right. It was romantic. We're smarter than you yanks. Brits can even be romantic on the run. Are you ready?"

He glanced at Chelsea, who seemed utterly horrified that her sister and brother-in-law had caught them in bed together. Well, she'd been caught in bed and he'd been caught with his willy hanging out. Standing at attention actually. Charlotte had given him a thumbs-up. Ian had made a vomiting sound and told him to lock up his junk.

"You know they're joking with us, love. Ian and Charlotte aren't exactly prudes. I think they're probably more relieved than anything," Simon said with a chuckle. "Most of the team thought this was inevitable."

"I need to talk to you." Chelsea was back in her robe and gown. As clothes to run in went, they were definitely prettier than her PJ bottoms and dirty T-shirt, though he suspected they were less practical. He was sure she would disagree, but it would have to do.

Still, shouldn't he take a few seconds to explain to Ian about the baby Tags running around the ranch? He walked up to Chelsea, wishing they'd had more time to spend alone. He'd intended to cuddle her, to make her genuinely comfortable being intimate with him, but that would have to wait. They had to escape first. As much as he loved his cousins, he wasn't going to trust Chelsea's safety to the Agency. "Of course. When we're at the safe house we can talk as much as you like. I think Ian won't object to my staying with you now that he's seen I can turn pyromaniac to please you."

He kissed her forehead.

She pulled away. "Simon, this is serious."

He should have expected that she would struggle. He didn't have time to deal with her lamentable habit of taking two steps back for every forward movement. Besides, he knew how to handle her now. He would simply get her back into bed and fuck her until she agreed with him. He led her to the door to the living area. "Yes, getting away from here is serious. I have no idea what Ian's plan is. For that matter, I have no idea how he found us."

He walked through the French doors and realized Ian and Charlotte weren't alone. Adam and Jake stood in the room with them, both armed to the teeth.

Adam gave him a grin. "We're here because it turns out I'm way smarter than The Broker there. Hah, girl. Did you really think I couldn't trace that call? Amateur."

Chelsea frowned. For just a second she was her arrogant hacker self again. "Uhm, back up, buddy. You didn't beat me. Did you really think Ten would allow me to ping that call around the world? No. You beat some twenty-two-year-old nicknamed Hutch. Or maybe that's his real name. Maybe his mom watched too much TV in the 70s."

"Damn it." Adam sighed in disappointment. "I thought it was you."

Jake chuckled. "He's been high-fiving people on the street."

Ian shook his head. "Yeah, well, he's also lying because all he could do was trace the call to a satellite. We're here because apparently no one messes with Momma Malone. Let's move. The van is waiting."

"What do you mean?" Simon asked as he took Chelsea's hand and followed Ian and Charlotte out into the hallway. "And we have to get Jesse."

"I sent Jesse out to the van," Jake said as he and Adam took their six.

Ian started down the main stairwell. Something serious had to have happened for Ian to boldly walk into the living room.

Chelsea gasped and stopped, turning her head. "Is that Theo? Oh, god, is he dead?"

Simon turned and sure enough, Theo Taggart was laid out on the floor, his weapon at his side as though he'd been trying to get to it even as he'd fallen. Simon noticed what Chelsea hadn't. There was a nice-sized dart sticking out of Theo's bum. Oh, he really hoped his cousin didn't get renditioned somewhere nasty. This particular plan had JT written all over it.

"He's sleeping," Ian said. "And I would like to point out that I did nothing but come here to collect my property. Property that Ten stole, so when he wakes up all pissy, I hope someone points that out to him."

Simon was sure that if Ian had taken Theo out himself, he would likely have questions. He hustled Chelsea down the stairs. She seemed reluctant to leave Theo behind. When they reached the bottom of the stairs, he saw JT and his aunt were in the spacious entryway.

JT winked. "I'll be sure to take the credit. They always underestimate me because I'm the pretty one. I slipped a little Mickey into their beers. The ones who weren't drinking, Momma took out with the tranqs they used on Simon and Jesse. Seriously, you should have seen the look on that Ten fellow's face when he realized a five foot nothing woman had taken him down. You have about twenty minutes before they wake up."

His aunt walked up to him. She was a good foot shorter, but she was still the ultimate figure of loving authority in his life. She smoothed down his tie. "Simon, do you want to stay with these Agency people or do you prefer to go with the very familiar-looking Mr. Taggart over there?" She sent Ian a frown. "You stay back until he makes his decision. I can take you out too, young man."

Had he felt bad about coming home? "I think I'll go with my team, Aunt Ava. And thank you for allowing me to make the decision. If we'd stayed with the Agency, I'm not sure what they would do with Chelsea. But we really do need to get out of here. Ten will probably wake up in a bad mood. JT, you know Michael's not going to be happy with you. Neither is your father. He's obviously trying to get the Agency to help with Malone Oil's overseas problems."

JT shook his head. "Don't you worry about that. It's been a while since Mike and I beat the shit out of each other. It'll be like old times. As for the other, well, I think Malone Oil has been fine on our own for a long time. It's time my father and my brother remember that family comes first."

It did. Sometimes a man's family went past blood. He turned to Ian. "I'm sorry. I thought I was doing what was best for her and for the team. I should have sat down and talked this out with you."

"Damn straight, brother. But I really do understand." Ian put an arm around Charlotte. "The Dennis women can drive a man crazy. Let's get out of here. Alex is waiting in the driveway with the van. We're getting out of Dodge for a while, if you know what I mean. We're dropping Adam and Jake off and then we're heading for a safe house. We'll figure out what the hell's going on before we surface again."

Chelsea tugged on his hand. "Simon, I just need a minute."

"All right." She was likely still worried about dragging her sister in, but she had to see that Charlotte wouldn't be anywhere else.

Just as he was turning to her, Jesse crashed into the room and he wasn't alone. A very angry Case Taggart was holding him by the back of the neck, leveling a SIG at his head.

Ian rolled those blue eyes of his. "I thought I told you to go to the van."

A grimace crossed Jesse's face. "Yeah, I got waylaid, boss. Sorry."

Case stopped, not letting up on his grip. "I don't think you're going anywhere. Not a damn one of you."

His cousin hadn't been very thorough. "I thought you took them all out."

"I was sure I hit him. He went down." JT shook his head.

"I found Ten and knew something was up," Case shot back. "You hit my wallet, asshole, but I played along. And you owe me thirty bucks because it was a good wallet that now has a hole in it. Look here, I don't give a shit what kind of family problems Mike has. Obviously he's got issues he needs to deal with, but I will defend my team and my mission. I'll shoot every single one of you fuckers and I'll start with this one."

"Holy shit," Charlotte said, her eyes widening. Her mouth dropped open. Yes, she'd obviously gotten a good look at Case.

"Jesse, you stay calm." The last thing he needed was a Jesse meltdown. It looked like the Taggart family reunion was going to happen here and now.

"I'm cool," he said, his hands up. "It's hard to be afraid of him. I really just can't stop thinking of how much he looks like Ian. I keep expecting him to smack me upside the head and tell me I'm an idiot."

"I'm going to blow your head away, asshole. I want to know

what you shot my brother full of." Case's question was directed at JT, who was now standing directly in front of his mother.

"Nothing but what you used on my cousin. He'll wake up," JT said, his voice steady. Simon had to give it to him. He was cool under pressure.

"He doesn't look like me," Ian was saying. He turned his head a bit as though considering the problem from all angles.

"Are you kidding me?" Charlotte pointed Case's way.

Ah, so they were going to go the chaos route. It was a good play, especially since Simon sincerely doubted Case wanted this to end in multiple dead bodies. So Ian and Charlotte would argue and distract Case while someone else used the cover to deal with the younger man. Simon watched as Jake and Adam exchanged a glance.

"He looks nothing like me, Charlie." Ian crossed his arms over his massive chest as if to say clearly *I'm not a threat. Look, I can't even reach for a gun.*

"He's like your twin," Charlotte argued back, looking every inch the impatient wife.

Jake nodded slightly and moved slowly back.

Adam stepped up, covering his partner's move. "I think Big Tag's right. That dude is way more attractive and younger. He doesn't have all of Tag's frown lines. Dude, smile every once and a while."

"Shut up all of you," Case said. "I don't care who you are. You're all going to stand down. I want the redhead to come over here and take the zip ties out of my pocket. She's going to tie up the big guy first and the rest of the men, including that traitor over there."

JT simply shook his head. "This ain't going down the way you want it to, man."

Ian was suddenly deeply serious. "My wife isn't doing anything, and you might not care about who I am but I damn straight want to know who the hell you are. I take it my bastard father wasn't happy simply walking out on me and my brother. The fucker couldn't get a vasectomy, could he? Tell me you're some sort of distant cousin and that the Taggart genes just run true."

"He's your brother, Ian," Simon said quietly.

"I am not his brother." Case's voice cracked just the slightest, the only way Simon could tell he was at all emotional. "My brother is laid out in that hallway with a dart sticking out of his thigh."

Ian shook his head. "There's another one of him? Older or younger?"

"Younger, but only by a couple of minutes. They're fraternal twins, but it's easy to see who's the leader. His brother's name is Theo and if I had to guess, I would bet Case has spent his life looking out for him. Much like you and Sean." Ian had to understand that Case would be serious about his brother.

Ian held up his hands and took a step up. All the while, Jake had been moving, clinging to the wall like a ghost. "I understand what it means to be left behind and to have to grow up really damn fast because someone is depending on you. Tell me he stayed with you. Tell me he got a second chance and turned out to be a good father."

"He left when I was sixteen. Not that he was much of a dad before that. Stand down, asshole." Case's eyes moved right to Jake. "Move back with the group or I take out someone's kneecap."

Jake stopped, holding up his hands as though he'd only been taking a leisurely stroll. He rejoined Adam.

Ian nodded. "I think I know this story well. Dad takes off for parts unknown leaving you and baby brother. You had to watch out for him because your mother had to work."

A hard huff came out of Case's throat. "My mother became an alcoholic who could barely get out of bed to buy another bottle of vodka. I kept everything together. I did that."

"If I had known about you…" Ian started.

"You never even looked for the old man or you would have found us," Case began. He stopped and shook his head. "It doesn't matter. Like I said, you're no brother of mine."

"Oh, but that's where you're wrong," Ian replied. "Blood means something to me. Brotherhood means something to me and that's exactly why Ten recruited you. That son of a bitch."

Jake slipped closer. Case's whole focus was on Ian. "He

recruited us because we're the best."

"Oh, brother, you're not even close yet. And you tell Ten that I'll have a talk with him soon and he won't like what I have to say."

"You forget that I have the upper hand," Case replied, sounding just as arrogant as Big Tag ever had.

"And you forget that I always have backup. Alex, take him easy," Tag said.

Simon saw what he hadn't before. Alex McKay had come in from the side door, very likely shadowing Case from the moment he took Jesse.

He put his SIG to the back of Case's neck. "Ease down slowly. I don't want to kill a Taggart, but I will if I have to."

Case cursed and Simon let out a sigh of relief when he finally lowered his weapon and let it drop to the floor.

Jesse moved out of the way, striding to Simon's side.

Case stared at Ian. "We'll be coming after you and I swear I'll be the one to take you down." His eyes strayed Simon's way. "We don't leave team members behind either. You should be ready for that."

It was Simon's turn to stare because he didn't think that had been directed at him. He looked down at Chelsea, who'd gone a pale white. Was she terrified that Ten would keep coming after her? He'd failed her once by letting Ten get the jump on him. Was she afraid he would prove incompetent again? She had to know he would lay down his life to keep her safe.

Ian stepped up and stood in front of his brother. Now that they were so close, Simon could see the differences. Case was definitely younger than Ian, his hair threaded through with bronze where Ian's was pure Nordic blond. Case was just the tiniest bit shorter than his brother, but his shoulders were just as broad and his nose had been broken at some point giving what likely would have been a perfect male-model face some real masculinity.

"And you should know that this is far from over, brother," Ian said before nodding to Alex.

"You're not…" Case's defiant words were cut short by Alex bringing the butt of his SIG down on Case's head. The younger

Taggart dropped to a heap on the floor.

Ian stared, all joking gone from his expression. "How did I not know this? What the hell am I going to tell Sean?"

Charlotte was there with him, her arms going around his waist. "The truth. Ian, this isn't your fault. You couldn't have known about this."

"But Ten did." Ian's lips curled up in a nasty snarl. "Ten fucking knew."

"Yes and I'm sure he also knew that if you had any conception you had a couple of brothers out there, you would go after them. Ten's got a job to do, too. You know he's had a hole in his operation since you left. Don't start a war with him until you talk to him." Charlotte seemed determined to be the voice of reason.

Alex shook his head as he looked down at the currently defunct Case. "That is so weird. And he's got a Southern accent. Even weirder. Did I hear him say there's another one? Should I bundle them up for transport?"

Ian shook his head. "No. We'll deal with them later. We have to get Simon and Chelsea out of here and now. Adam?"

Adam didn't need more than that to know what Ian was asking. "I'm on it. I'll get everything about them to you in twenty-four hours. I'll find out what they eat for breakfast and how often they crap, Tag."

The slightest smile tugged at Ian's lips. "I think I can live without the last part, but thank you, Adam." He turned back to JT. "Mr. Malone, I owe you a favor. I expect you to collect one day."

JT nodded. "I suspect a favor from you is worth something, Mr. Taggart."

Chelsea pulled her hand out of his. "Simon, I'm not leaving this house."

He turned and sighed. She could be difficult at times. "I promise I'll get you clothes once we're out of here. I suspect Charlotte might have already handled that problem."

He grabbed her hand again and started toward the driveway.

Charlotte jogged up beside them. "I did indeed. I have a bag packed for little sister." She lowered her voice. "We're driving to

Florida. We're going to hide out in the condo. It's under a fake name that no one will tie to us. You'll see. A little beach time and we'll figure this whole mess out."

Chelsea dragged her heels. "No. I'm not going. Simon, I want to talk to you, but we're out of time. I can't go with you."

He stopped as they made it outside. The night was warm and quiet except for the sounds of crickets chirping. It was peaceful, but frustration built inside him. Why did she have to make everything so difficult? "You can and you will. Charlotte wants to be here. I was wrong to not involve her. I was wrong to take you away. We're a team and we stand by each other."

She shook her head. "No. We're not a team. Simon, I never meant to leave with you."

The rest of the team was moving. Alex sighed as he jogged by and opened the driver's side door. Jesse patted him on his back. Even Jake and Adam sent him sympathetic glances. Because they all knew he was in over his head with her.

It was time he took charge. He was sick of his brothers looking at him like he was a pathetic chump who couldn't handle his submissive. "Get into the van right now. I understand you're afraid and we'll talk about it later, but right now you will get into the van and keep quiet. You will obey me or I swear you won't be able to sit our entire ride to the condo."

Charlotte winced, but Ian was right behind her. "Not a word, baby. This is Simon's gig."

At least Ian was willing to back him.

Chelsea was so fragile looking in the moonlight, but she shook it off and he watched as she pulled that armor around herself again. Gone was the vulnerability, like it had never existed in the first place.

"No. I'm not going to obey you, Simon. Or you, Ian. I'm staying here because I work for Ten now. I chose this and there's nothing you can do about it so get out of here and don't worry about me anymore."

It took a few seconds for the words to really penetrate. She'd done what? "He blackmailed you."

She shook her head. "No. He didn't blackmail me. He offered me power and money and that's what I want, Simon. I'm sick of all of this. I want what I had. I want to be The Broker again. I'm sorry. I should have told you, but I also wanted to sleep with you."

He was trying to let her words sink in. "And you knew I wouldn't if I thought you weren't serious."

She shrugged as though it wasn't a big deal. "I told you I was curious."

He felt like she'd kicked him in the gut. He'd been nothing but a curiosity for her? He'd invested in her, sacrificed for her and she'd lied so she could sleep with him and satisfy her bloody curiosity?

"Chelsea, you don't mean any of this," Charlotte said slowly. "What's going on? What did Ten do? And Ian, I take back everything I said. Go to war. Kill that fucker."

Chelsea turned on her sister. "Don't you dare. I won't have you ruining this for me. You have your comfy little life. I want mine now. I don't want to be Simon's sweet little sub, popping out his kids and making sure his suits are pressed. I'm smarter than that. I deserve better. I deserve the life Ten is offering me and I won't let any of you hold me back. Do you know how pathetic I've been? Pretending to be Adam's little assistant or some shit. I'm smarter than all of you combined, so I'm leaving and I'm not looking back."

Charlotte's eyes had narrowed. "You better rethink this whole thing because this is not going to go well for you. I'm going to give you some sisterly advice. I don't know why you're doing this, but you're going to lose this battle and you're going to have to grovel. Apologize to him right now and maybe, just maybe he'll calm down in a few months and you'll have a shot with him again. You are throwing away something special and you might not get another shot at it. He's been patient and kind, and for some reason I'm pretty sure he loves you and you're about to kill that emotion. It's not something you want to be responsible for. So throw yourself at his mercy and tell him everything right now."

It might work. If she was hiding something, if Ten had convinced her there was a greater purpose in working for him, perhaps he could consider it. He actually felt a little hollow. He didn't want to consider it. Suddenly, he rather wanted to be done with all of it. Months and months he'd spent pursuing her and it was all for nothing. Worse than nothing, actually. She'd actively lied. She'd known how he felt and used it against him.

He straightened his shoulders. He was once again the object of everyone's pity. Just a left behind boy.

Maybe Chelsea could finally teach him what nothing in his life had.

"Simon, I'm sorry." Her lip trembled, but perhaps that was an affectation, too. She'd gotten good at manipulating him. "I didn't mean to hurt you, but I want to stay with Ten."

It was time to let her go. Once and forever. He took a deep breath and gave her his most serene smile, the one he'd perfected over years and years of telling everyone he was all right. "I understand. Come here. Give me a hug and we'll be done."

"Simon," Ian began.

She practically ran into his arms. "I'm so sorry."

In one swift move, he turned her and got his arm around her neck. She couldn't be left behind, but he didn't trust her to come quietly. She would put everyone at risk including herself and that couldn't happen. "I'm sorry, too, love. This is probably going to be quite painful."

He pressed on her carotid artery, depriving her brain of blood. It was a move he'd practiced hundreds of times and had perfected. In the hands of an amateur, it would be dangerous, but he knew exactly what he was doing. She slumped over, completely unconscious.

Charlotte was crying as he lifted her up. "You're a good man, Simon. She didn't mean any of that. I know her. When she's backed into a corner, she spits bile but it doesn't mean she doesn't care for you. I've watched her since she's met you. She's crazy about you. She's hiding something. You'll see. I'll go make a place for her."

Charlotte was an optimist of the highest order. He'd required one thing from Chelsea. Some modicum of trust and the tiniest bit of honesty. He was willing to look past every other problem, but she didn't really want him. Not for any length of time. She'd wanted someone to fuck her and he'd been enthusiastic. She would likely just move on to Ten now that she knew she enjoyed sex.

Ian stayed behind, his expression grave as he looked Simon's way. "Are you sure you want to come with us? I can handle it from here if you want. I can drop off you and Jesse and you can head back to the office with the rest of them."

He said nothing, simply held her knowing this would be one of the last times. The last time. Funny, he should have known the only way she would be sweet and docile in his arms was when she was unconscious.

Ian put a hand on his shoulder. "Man, I know where you are. Charlotte's high if she thinks everything's going to magically be all right. You need a little time. If you need to take a step back, I'll understand."

Dump her on Ian. He could dump her here and now and go back to his regularly scheduled life. He likely wouldn't even have to see her again.

Or he could use her the way she'd used him. He hadn't even fucked her arse yet. He hadn't done half the things he wanted to. He could prove to her that he was the boss and she meant nothing to him.

Idiot. He was a bloody idiot because he was making excuses. Even as she ripped his heart out, he was trying to find a way to stay close to her.

"I'll finish the op." Simon hauled her to his chest. She weighed next to nothing. Despite the fact that she'd just betrayed him, he couldn't leave her alone. He couldn't turn her over to Ian and just hope that she was all right. He shouldn't care and eventually, he wouldn't, but he couldn't just walk away yet.

He would do his job. His job was all he had left.

He carried her to the van and settled her in then got into the back. He got in beside her, but kept his eyes front. She would be out for a while and then he would have to deal with her bile. For all the false sweetness and affection she'd given him, she would likely equal it with her nastiness.

Alex took off, leaving the ranch in the dust. His real home. Despite the fact that his aunt had helped him, he had to wonder if he'd be welcome again. His uncle was indulgent with her, but he had a breaking point and Simon was a little afraid that JT might have found it. It seemed all he'd managed to do was cause a massive rift in his family.

All of them it seemed. Ian was sitting next to Jesse in the very back and he turned to him. "What the fuck did you think you were doing? I understand what Simon was doing. He was following his dick. Your dick isn't involved so you should have had a brain in your head. Who do you owe your fucking loyalty to? You should have called me the minute you realized Simon was running. My goddamn number should have been the only thing on your brain and yet you just did whatever the hell Simon told you to. Who are you loyal to? Decide right fucking now. Are you loyal to him or me?"

Shit. He'd done this to Jesse, too. "It's not his fault."

"Shut up, Simon. This is between me and him. I want to know and you better think about it. Who is your first loyalty to?"

Jesse's face went blank. He stared straight ahead. Ian was treating him like he was a new recruit straight off a damn bus and meeting his drill sergeant for the first time. "It's to Simon. My first loyalty is to Simon Weston. He's my best friend."

Charlotte winked at Simon.

And Ian put a hand on the back of Jesse's head. "That's right, Murdoch. That's your fucking partner and you take care of him. If he wants to do stupid shit, you go with him and make sure he doesn't die. We have partners on this team and we back them. I've got Alex. Jake, the poor asshole, got stuck with Adam."

Adam sat in the front seat next to Alex. He lifted his hand, sending Ian his middle finger. "Fuck you, Tag."

Ian ignored him. "And Li has that bottle of beer he never seems to finish. Or maybe he just starts 'em faster than my eye can track. You did good, Murdoch. I might be pissed as shit, but he's your partner and you take care of him." Ian sat back and Simon took a deep breath. "I found a lot of blood at that motel. You do that?"

Jesse nodded. "I lost it."

"And we'll deal with that, too. I promise, man." He reached out and smacked Jesse upside the head. "But what the fuck were you thinking letting that dumbass mini-me get the jump on you?"

And Big Tag was off. He was yelling about anything and anyone who came into his bloody head. Charlotte gave Simon a smile. She was on the other side of Chelsea's unconscious body.

"He's been worried. You have to let him yell for a while. In the meantime, I'm supposed to make a list of all the places we lived so we can try to figure out where this package thing went. It's a long damn list," Charlotte admitted.

But he could narrow it. "You kept up addresses everywhere?"

She shook her head. "No. Just a couple of places. Our favorite places."

But Al had only talked about one place. Damn it. He'd been off his game. He'd been thinking so much about Chelsea that he hadn't really thought about the problem at hand. Why the hell had Al spent so much time reminding her about Europe if he wasn't trying to warn her? And there was really only one place in Europe to go. He thought back to that night. Al had mentioned Europe, but Chelsea had told him that Al Krum had met her in Venice.

Al Krum had been rather brave. He'd lost his family and his life and he'd still attempted to give Chelsea a chance at getting out of this alive.

"We need to get to Venice."

And then he could finish this thing forever.

"You want to explain?" Ian asked.

He turned so he was staring out into the night. He'd never really belonged here. It was a temporary home at best, like all places in his life.

"Certainly, but Adam should find us a plane because we need to get to Italy." He began his explanation, vowing silently to finish the job so he could finally let her go.

Chapter Sixteen

Chelsea came awake slowly, the world foggy and vague. Sound. She could hear something that sounded like thunder. No. Not thunder. Engines. She knew that sound.

Chelsea forced herself to sit up. Damn it. What the hell had happened and why was she so lethargic? Her body felt heavy, her eyelids barely able to open. For the first moment her vision was dimmed, but slowly the world started to come into focus. Yes, she had to focus.

Take stock. Figure out where you are.

She was in a chair, a seat belt around her middle. To her right was a small window.

Chelsea groaned. Damn her sister. She was on a plane. How the hell had they gotten her on a plane?

"Morning, sunshine," Charlotte chirped from the seat beside her. "Aren't you super happy to be awake? Rise and shine. We're somewhere over New England. That makes me think of crab cakes. Damn, I'm hungry."

"How long was I out?" She was suddenly aware of an aching pit in her stomach. Simon. The last thing she remembered was Simon's face. He'd gone a careful blank, but not before she'd seen his hurt. It had been right there in his eyes. They'd widened and he'd looked down at her like she'd stabbed him in the heart and he was trying to find a way to make sense of it. And then the emotion had blinked from existence because he wouldn't share with her anymore.

She'd killed it. She found it threatening and scary. Simon's love had been something she didn't understand so she'd done what she did with all things she didn't understand; she'd gotten rid of it.

Oh, god, what had she done?

Charlotte looked down at her watch. "A couple of hours."

"What?" Simon had done something to her. God, Simon had opened his arms and she'd walked into them, and if she needed any explanation of how thoroughly she'd killed any love he'd had for her it was there in the fact that he'd done that to her. Simon, who was always so careful with her, who rubbed her legs when they ached and placed his body in front of hers so he took whatever came her way, had pressed on her carotid until her brain no longer had the blood flow to properly function. It was a martial arts move and dangerous as hell. She could have died and apparently that had been fine with him.

And what had she expected? She'd basically told the man she'd used him for sex and that he wasn't good for anything else.

Misery swamped her, a familiar friend. She understood misery in a way she just didn't comprehend happiness. Happiness was climbing to the top of the building and feeling like the king of the world before the inevitable multistory fall broke her again.

Focus. She had to focus if she was going to deal with the situation. "I should have been out thirty minutes tops. Less really."

"Oh, I dosed you with sedatives for transport. We had to do a little creative manipulation of the system. So we drove to Dallas and got on a Malone private jet and took it to Houston, where we then logged a flight plan for that plane to Phuket. Derek and Karina met us there. They're flying as you and Simon and they're so grateful for the honeymoon. It might involve a little gunplay, but apparently Karina hasn't killed anyone in a while and it's made her cranky. Meanwhile, we're taking this Malone jet to Canada."

"You drugged me like I'm a rabid fucking dog you needed to keep calm?"

Charlotte sighed and smiled. "Yes. Excellent analogy. I'm so glad you understand. We changed planes and used aliases. New ones. Adam can work fast when he has to. It's just the five of us now. You and me and Simon and Ian and Jesse. Ian tried to tell Jesse he would handle it, but he took that whole partner speech seriously."

Partner speech? She had to shake her head to try to clear it. She wasn't sure what Charlotte was talking about, but one thing penetrated her brain. Simon was still here? It didn't matter. It would be better if he'd left. She would have one less person to deal with. Her sister could be obnoxious. "Why? Why the hell did you do this?" She tried to stretch, but her leg was aching terribly. "I told you what I wanted. I'll just walk away when we land. This was all for nothing. I'll call Ten and he'll come and get me."

Charlotte picked up her glass from the table in front of her and turned her chair. They weren't flying commercial. It looked like an executive jet. Was Simon in the cockpit?

Cock. She would never see his cock again. She was going to miss his cock forever.

"Ten is spitting mad." Charlotte leaned over like they were gossiping about boyfriends or something. "He called Ian and left the nastiest voice mail. Something about murdering him but only after he's played with his innards. He actually used the word innards. That boy's country comes out when he's mad. So, tell me how it was with Simon. Was he as good as he looks? Don't tell Ian, but the whole suit thing kind of does it for me. He wasn't a gentleman in bed, was he? He was all nasty, right?"

He'd been perfect. He'd given her everything he had and she would dream about him for the rest of her life. "It's none of your business. When do we land?"

"Not for a while. We have to change planes again. We're going to bed down in Toronto for a bit. We're doing the equivalent of making sure we don't have a tail so we won't be where we need to be until sometime the day after tomorrow. Which gives us time to talk because that's so not fair. I totally told you all about Ian."

"I didn't want to hear it." Her sister was big with the over share. "I still don't. I'm glad you're happy with Ian and all, but I don't want to be here. Are you really going to keep me against my will?"

She could still salvage this. If she got back to Ten, or even just got to talk to him so he knew she hadn't run willingly, he would probably keep up his end of the bargain. Probably.

She had to make sure Simon was safe. He couldn't spend the rest of his life on the run because she'd gotten him into a bad situation. Or worse, he wouldn't run. He would turn himself in and face murder charges and The Collective probably had really good lawyers. He would get sent to prison and likely murdered himself. She couldn't be the reason that happened.

Charlotte's eyes narrowed. "You don't know what you want."

Frustration welled. "I do. I just don't want the same thing you want so you think I'm wrong."

"I know you're wrong."

She sighed, so tired. "I don't care. Unless you're going to continue to drug me, I'll find a way to leave. You can't keep me here."

The glass knocked against the tray table, and Charlotte's hands made fists in her lap. "I'm so sick of this. Do you understand what a fucking brat you are?"

She understood that quite well. "Yep. Which begs the question of why you won't let me go."

"Because I love you. Because you're my sister, but I'll be honest, I'm getting really sick of how weak you are."

Weak? A surge of red-hot anger flowed through her. "You think I'm weak? I'm the one who had to take all the beatings, all the pain, so the beautiful Charlotte Denisovitch could stay daddy's little princess."

"Yeah, such a princess. He loved me so much, Chels. He wanted me to become his assassin because he thought having a pretty teenage girl killing his enemies was amusing. Yes, I was so happy to be his favorite. I did it. I killed people for him to save you. I did things you can't imagine for you, and you're the little shit who wasn't grateful for any of it."

Charlotte wanted to do this now? Oh, she could do it. This was a long time coming. "I lost my fucking legs for you. I ache every single day because I was the whipping girl."

"No. You lost them because you're too weak to fix them." Charlotte's pretty face was red with anger. "Yes, something horrible happened, but you're the one who refused to recover."

"I was a girl. What did you expect from me? I managed to walk again." Battered, that was how she felt. Charlotte's anger was beating against her like a damn hurricane.

"But you wouldn't do the work it took to be really strong."

How little she remembered. "You're so good at rewriting history. Do you honestly believe he would have taken me to a therapist?"

Charlotte leaned forward. "I would have. I would have risked everything to make sure you got what you needed. I would have done whatever it took, but you retreated. You were too scared. And after I did what I had to do to take that monster out, you still wouldn't do anything about it."

"We were on the run. What did you want me to do?" They often hadn't known where they would be in the next hour, much less had a life that allowed for scheduled appointments.

"I wanted you to fight for yourself."

The accusation cut deep. "I've fought for myself my whole damn life."

"No, you've accepted what you were given. You've waited for the universe to crap all over you because you got dealt a shitty hand. You've let him win. He wasn't the only thing in your life, but you let him win."

She had to shake her head as the unfairness of Charlotte's words hit home. "How can you say that?"

A little of Charlotte's anger seemed to flee as she sighed and continued on. "Because I've watched you. You would rather just sit in that fucking chair and have a half-life because you're so damn scared. You think being The Broker made you powerful? It was like playing a video game for you. Those people weren't real. Those hacker friends of yours would have sold you out in a heartbeat."

"Al didn't." At least she'd had one person to depend on.

"Fine, great. You had one friend and you mostly ignored him until you needed something from him."

The words pierced her. Like a video game? Had she really been that person? She'd shuffled the players around, sending real information or false leads depending on who had pissed her off that day. Sure the people she'd dealt with had been the bad people of the world, but their actions had affected the innocent and she'd been the shadow behind it all.

She'd started because they'd needed information to be safe, to hide from the syndicate. She'd continued because they'd needed money, but even after they had plenty, she'd reveled in it. She'd gotten addicted to being the all-powerful Oz of the Internet.

But when she drew back the curtain, there was only a broken little girl who'd never cared enough to put herself back together.

Had she let one person, one monster ruin her life even from the grave? Had she become nothing but a shadow?

You could be so much more. Simon's words whispered through her brain.

Could she?

"Why did he hate me?"

Charlotte stopped, her mouth dropping open. "Are you talking about our father?"

Chelsea nodded. It still hurt. He'd been a terrible human being and she could remember his face as he'd beaten her. Hatred. Pure hate. In his own perverse way, he'd loved Charlotte, but there had been nothing but hate for Chelsea.

Tears dripped from Charlotte's eyes.

"You have to tell her now." Ian stood up. He'd been sitting behind them and Chelsea hadn't noticed. Great. Satan had witnessed her humiliation. He likely thought she was weak, too. "If you don't, I will."

Tell her? "What?"

Charlotte's face was pale as she turned back to Chelsea. "He wasn't your father, sweetie. Adam caught it. He was making sure all records of the two of us were erased."

What was she talking about? "I did that."

"Not the new ones. You had blood tests on your last checkup."

The one Charlotte had dragged her to. The doctor had tried to set up PT on her legs, had advised her yoga classes would help her mobility, had said any number of helpful things that Chelsea ignored because she knew the truth. They wouldn't get better. "Yes, I remember."

"Adam has a file on all of us. Including everything he could find out about our parents. I have Dad's blood type. You don't. You don't have Mom's either." Charlotte sat back. "I found out a couple of months ago."

Her father wasn't her father? "Why didn't you tell me?"

"Because I took it a step further. I think I found your dad. Mom had a professor teaching her Russian. He was at a university in Moscow. He was killed the day Mom left. I think he was trying to meet her. I think they were trying to run together. She got out. He didn't."

Her father wasn't her father. Her father had been some no-name teacher who'd been dumb enough to fall for a mobster's wife. Her father had been the dumbass who thought he could run with her.

Her father might have loved her.

Ian held a file in his hand. "This is what we've dug up on him. He did have your blood type. Vladimir Denisovitch hated you because you were a symbol of your mother's betrayal. At some point, he put it all together and when he found her again, he took it out on you."

She took the file and opened it. There was a picture of a smiling young man. He was accepting a small medal. She could still read Russian with ease. Pavel Yokin was accepting first prize in a poetry writing contest for students. Then another about his first book being published. He'd been a gentle man, a man of letters. He'd written poetry. She could read it. She could learn about him.

"And you've kept this from me?" She looked up to see Charlotte crying.

"I was afraid."

"Afraid?"

"Chelsea, my father killed yours."

"Vladimir killed lots of people."

Charlotte reached out, but then pulled back as though she knew Chelsea wouldn't want to be touched. "Do you remember the day he came back for us? He tried to leave you. I didn't understand. I didn't even realize he'd killed Mom. I just knew I was being separated from you. I begged him. He would have walked away from you then and there. You would have been scared, but someone would have taken you in, someone who wouldn't have brutalized you. This is my fault."

She could have been spared. She would have mourned her mother and sister, but she likely would have found a decent life.

A life without Charlotte.

She'd spent so much time dreaming of some other existence. Now that she knew that life could have been hers, she knew bitterness should have been welling up inside her. She should have been left behind and given a chance.

To grow up without Charlotte? To send her into the hell without anyone to hold on to?

She turned away and looked out at the night. It was dark, but the clouds turned everything to silver.

You could be so much more.

What would she give to spare herself pain? Would she send Charlotte off on her own? Would she give up her sister?

Would she give up those moments with Simon for a life free of pain?

God, she was an idiot. No one got a life free of pain. No one. She'd been dealt a shitty hand and decided to not even bother to play the game. She'd hidden and let herself be made small by a man who wasn't worth anything. She'd decided to merely accept survival.

You could be so much more.

If she changed. If she accepted that the past wasn't something that defined her. If she decided who she wanted to be. The man who she'd called father had told her she was weak and useless and she'd believed him.

She glanced back down and there was a list of her true father's books. The first caught her eye. *Dare to Dream.*

She'd stopped dreaming a long time ago because it seemed naïve. But she'd just realized something. Naïve people were strong. Naïve people changed the world because they actively believed they could. There was strength in that. Power in that. Her mother had fought. Her father had died. Both had been brave. Her sister hadn't given up. Not once. Not ever.

Why were they less meaningful than Vladimir Denisovitch?

She'd chosen this.

And she could choose again.

She stood up because there was one thing she could give her sister here and now. She could give her some freaking peace.

"Chelsea?" Charlotte asked as she moved past her toward her big brother-in-law who she'd fought with from the moment they'd met.

Ian. Big dumbass who acted like he couldn't care less and did everything he could for the people around him. Even the ones he didn't like. She'd thought she and Ian were alike. Both cynical and sarcastic, but Ian had a heart and she'd tried to kill hers long before.

"Thank you."

Ian's eyes narrowed. "Why?"

"For being good to my sister and to me. Thank you, Ian." She walked right up and put her arms around him.

"What the hell do I do, Charlie?" Ian asked, his arms at his side.

"You hug her back, asshole. She used your name and everything. You hug her. Now."

Very slowly his arms came up and enveloped her in what had to be the most awkward hug of her life. "Okay, but if she kills me it's your fault."

Chelsea felt Charlotte move in behind her. "She's not going to kill you. She's forgiving me."

Well, at least her sister knew her, but she was wrong about one thing. "There's nothing to forgive on your side, Charlotte. I'm just trying to make it up to you."

"Couldn't you bake cookies or something?" Ian asked.

"No." She was horrible at baking. And cooking. And most everything at this point, but it was time for her to try. And it was past time for her to admit some things to her sister. "I did blame you, Charlotte, and that wasn't fair. Forgive me."

She felt Charlotte rest her head on her shoulder. "Always. Forgive me for being selfish and taking you with me."

She'd just been a girl. She couldn't have known. Chelsea had been a girl, too, and maybe it was time for both of them to forgive the children they'd been. "I wouldn't change it. Do you understand what I'm saying? I've spent a lifetime wondering about what I would be if only a few things had been different, but I know something now. I wouldn't. I would leave it all the same with one exception. Me. I would change me."

She could still change her. She could be more. So much more.

"I love you," Charlotte said.

"I love you, too."

"I'm still being hugged and I didn't do anything wrong," Ian complained.

Her brother-in-law was always going to be an asshole. And she wouldn't change that either. She broke away, letting him off the hook.

She turned and looked up at her sister. "I don't know what to do about Simon. I love him, but I have to leave him. I have to leave all of you. I made a deal with Ten. He's going to make sure Simon doesn't face any charges."

Ian snorted. "I already did that. Ten? Like I need fucking Ten to fix that problem. The new guy was on it. Mitchell Bradford. Nastiest lawyer in Texas. He's been trying to get into Sanctum. I've turned the fucker down three times because I don't need his money, but I do like having him in my back pocket. Life is about timing. It wasn't time for him to play at Sanctum until I needed a massive favor from him. Now we're all happy, including Simon in there who everyone including the DA now agrees was merely defending himself. I might have had to work a little dark magic on that one. Don't tell Derek."

Charlotte's eyes got round. "Shit. Tell me you didn't."

"Mitch worked a deal, but she was the holdout. It's not forever. It's one year and I can't kick her out." Ian shuddered a little. "Maybe Derek won't notice his ex-wife is suddenly in the dungeon."

"Not a chance," Charlotte said. "But we do what we have to. So see, Simon is fine. You don't need Ten."

It had all been for nothing. Absolutely nothing. Simon hadn't needed her to protect him. He hadn't needed her at all.

"Chelsea, are you all right?" Charlotte asked.

She shook her head. "I took the job with Ten to save Simon. I did it all for him, and there's no way he'll believe me."

"He will if you keep telling him. You just can't give up."

She had to completely change her thinking. Could she even get out of her promises to Ten? Should she? None of it mattered if she couldn't get Simon to believe her.

Ian sent his wife a grimace. "You're about to plot. I can't listen to this. It's against the guy code. I'm going to join Simon."

"We have to go to Venice," she said quickly. They did have a job to do after all. She needed to get out from under The Collective's threat no matter what happened between her and Simon.

"Well, of course you knew. You simply didn't bother to tell me. We already figured that out." Simon stood in the doorway to the cockpit, his eyes as cold as ice. He shook his head dismissively and turned his attention to Ian. "We touch down in Toronto in an hour. We'll rest and refuel there. Adam says all the records will be changed by the time we take off again. If Derek and Karina don't fool them, then records will show five people matching our description disembarked in Toronto and this Malone Oil jet suddenly belongs to a Canadian game show host. Apparently he's a friend of Adam's. Where does Adam come up with this shite?"

Ian moved toward Simon, slapping him on the shoulder. "He's got a damn creative mind, my friend. Let's talk. Jesse, move your ass. It's your turn to watch the chicks. Watch out. Apparently now they spontaneously hug you."

Simon disappeared again and Jesse sidled through the slim door, allowing Ian to take his place.

"Hey, don't try to escape, Chels. I'm kind of sleepy so I'm going to take a nap if it's all right with you. Let me know if you need a hug or something. Apparently you do that now." Jesse sank into Ian's old seat.

Charlotte took her hand. "It's going to be all right. If there's one thing I know about, it's how to get a man to forgive you for a massive mistake. You just have to follow a very simple plan."

"I don't think it's going to be that easy." He'd looked through her like she wasn't there.

"Are you willing to try?"

Chelsea took a deep breath. She'd given up trying long ago, and it had been a mistake. "Yes."

She leaned forward and did what she should have done months before. She listened to her sister.

* * * *

Simon looked out over the Atlantic. Nothing but water as far as the eye could see. London was somewhere north in the distance, but he wouldn't be going home anytime soon. He would want to avoid the inevitable lecture from his family. Despite the fact that Ian had gotten him out from under the cloud surrounding the deaths in his building, his parents would likely have heard of it. Just because he wasn't guilty didn't mean he would escape their judgment.

They'd spent the night before on the plane. It had been comfortable enough, but he'd dreamed that Chelsea had escaped, running back to Texas and Ten. He'd been surprised to wake and see her curled up with a blanket next to her sister.

They hadn't said more than two or three words to each other.

"You know she thought she was saving you," Ian murmured from his seat next to Simon. He was leaning back, his body relaxed, his eyes covered in a pair of mirrored aviators.

Perhaps his parents' wasn't the only judgment he couldn't escape.

"I don't care." It was ridiculous. She'd truly believed Ten could manage things Ian and Derek couldn't? Ten had very little pull in the States. Now if they were in a foreign country, Ten would be their guy. If Simon didn't throttle the fucker the next time he laid eyes on him.

"Good." Ian crossed his arms over his chest and yawned a little. "Just wanted to be able to say I did my part, man."

"Consider it done." The last thing he wanted to do was a postmortem on his non-relationship with Ian's sister-in-law.

Another moment passed in blissful silence.

"Ten's a good recruiter, you know," Ian said. "For all I'm unhappy with the fucker at the moment, I have to say, I'd probably do the same thing in his shoes. Hell, I got recruited by Ten. Yeah, he knows exactly what to say."

Ian rarely talked about his days with the Agency. "What did he use on you?"

Simon had always known he would join the RAF at some point. Every Weston did. And he'd been so desperate to be seen as a Weston, though he wasn't sure why. By that time his relationship with his parents was distant. Pleasant enough, but he could always feel his father's disappointment in him. Yet, he'd chosen a profession where he couldn't tell his father what he did.

Chelsea wasn't the only one who was damaged.

"He played on my god complex," Ian replied. "I'm not sure if you know this about me, but I sometimes have issues with needing to be in control."

It took everything he had not to roll his eyes. "Yes, I'd heard that about you."

A little smirk curled Ian's lips up. "I get better as the years go by. But back then I definitely had some issues with being out of control. I thought the Army would help. Drill sergeants in the Army break a man down. I mean a good DS will use every form of mental conditioning you can think of to break you to the US Army's will."

"Yes, we have something similar." Just because they had different accents didn't make the British military any more civilized. It was the job of every military in the world to break down and rebuild its soldiers, to break their old loyalties and forge new ones.

"And the whole time I was getting my face shoved in the dirt, all I could think about was rising through the ranks so no one could pull that shit on me again. I kept a list of everyone who fucked with me." He chuckled a little. "When they eased up a couple of weeks into Basic, everyone else would beam with pride when the DSs would praise them, but I knew it was one more way to control me. They couldn't work me with praise or pain. Only Ten ever figured me out."

Because Ten was smarter, sneakier than the rest. He would have to be to do his job. He would have to be good at reading people, at knowing how to get them to do his bidding. "He played on your protective instincts?"

"In a way. He bought me a beer after my unit had worked with him on an op. He was smart enough not to flatter me. He just sat there and told me stories about some of the work he'd done and how good it felt to be free of the constraints of command. He talked about the men who make sure this country is free no matter what they have to do. They made the calls in the field."

Yes, he could see how that would appeal to Ian. He would be doing good, but on his own terms.

Ian sat up and stared out over the ocean. "When he talked about his work, man, I knew what I wanted to do. It was more than just making the calls in the field. It was about the responsibility. I would be responsible for the safety of my country, actively out there making sure the people I gave a shit about were safe. That was all a man like me could ever want, right? I was naïve. I bought into it. Don't get me wrong. Ten is necessary. I was naïve to think that was all I would ever want. I was stupid to think that I could watch over them and be uninvolved, but at the time it sounded so good. I could tell myself I loved them but I didn't have to have all those messy emotions and shit. It actually still sounds kind of good."

He had to stop Ian now. He wasn't going to sit here while Ian tried to paint him into a corner. "If you're trying to make some sort of comparison between yourself and me, you're completely wrong. I've spent my entire bloody life trying to make ties, doing anything I could to make the people around me accept me. I was one of those idiots who wanted the respect of my superiors. Desperately so. I just kept fucking it up. So don't compare us, Tag."

"I wasn't comparing you to me. You're probably one of the

smartest men I've ever met, Simon. I knew it even during the UOF op. Why do you think I scooped you up? And don't think I didn't fight for you. I sat down with Damon after you resigned. I talked him into accepting your resignation when he didn't want to. His intention was to tell you you weren't allowed to resign and put you back in the field."

Simon shook his head, trying to digest that piece of information. He'd resigned his position with MI6 over a mistake he'd made. He'd allowed himself to be led into false information and tried to use it to break Ian's team. He'd been on the wrong side of that fight. "Why the hell would you do that?"

"Because I wanted you working for me. Because I do the same thing Ten does. I recruit the best men for the job, and I want them to be loyal to each other and to me above all else. I've handpicked every single one of you. Even Jesse. If I can get Jesse's fucking head on straight again, he'll be an amazing asset. Every one of us has fucked up in the past and we all deserved a second or third or fourth chance to be everything we can possibly be. The Army did teach me that. I'm just a better me out here in the world, and I'm definitely better as a man than an operative." He stood up and stretched as much as the cockpit would allow. "And I wasn't comparing you to me. I'm far more like Chelsea. Chelsea is the one who thinks she has nothing to offer anyone past her work. She's the one who could be easily manipulated by a devil's bargain offering her a way to protect the ones she loved. For all her big brain, she reacts to things without thinking. If it involves an emotion, she goes on instinct and her instincts are shitty."

"I don't want to talk about this." He was through. Perhaps one day he could forgive her, but she had zero interest in changing. She would never trust him, and he couldn't live waiting for the next time she "protected" him.

"Good. Talking is stupid. We'll drink when you're not in charge of flying a tin can through the air. That's what men do. I always knew you would fit in here, Weston." He sat back down and propped his feet up. "Besides, I bet Chelsea will be happy working for Ten in the end. I just get nervous with all Charlie's talk about babies. That woman is after my sperm. I tried to tell her that any child of ours would likely come out of the womb guns a blazing. There won't be a brain in that boy's head. I guess I was kind of hoping he would have a smart cousin to balance him out."

Sneaky bastard. "Just because you're going to allow your sperm to be stolen doesn't mean I'm offering up mine."

But he'd thought about it. He'd thought about having children with her. They'd be smart. So smart. They'd have a ton of family around them, including their brutally obnoxious and stubborn uncle.

Who'd fought for him. He'd always thought Ian felt a bit sorry for him. In truth, he'd never really understood why Ian had made the offer. He'd leapt at it though. It had been a lifeline. He couldn't go back to legal work. Not after he'd had a taste of undercover work. It was in his blood. He'd been convinced he wasn't good for anything else, couldn't want anything else.

Could Chelsea really have thought she was helping him? It didn't matter in the end. He couldn't trust her. She couldn't change. She'd proven it. Either she'd told him the truth and she really wanted to work for Ten and leave him behind or she'd lied to him. He could stand for neither scenario.

She'd known where the package was and withheld it from him. Likely, she'd intended to go to Italy with her new boss.

"By the way," Ian began, "that was one hell of a choke-out. I've wanted to do that to her since I met her."

He needed to get away for a moment. He stood up. "Can you handle the autopilot while I get a cup of tea?"

He needed far more than caffeine, but he wouldn't get that until they touched down.

"I might not like being in a small metal can over a sea of sharks, but I can handle the autopilot. Actually, I've always wanted to land one of these suckers. Maybe…"

"Not as long as I'm breathing, boss." He turned and walked out of the cockpit. The kitchen was toward the back. He had to step through the cabin. He had to admit that his uncle knew how to travel. An executive jet with twelve comfortable seats. He'd been surrounded by wealth all his life, but the Malone fortune far eclipsed the Weston's. It hadn't always been that way.

Jesse was snoozing in his seat. Charlotte was curled up reading and Chelsea was staring out the window. She'd changed into a breezy skirt and a top that showed off her breasts.

Now that he couldn't touch her again she decided to dress to show off. Well, naturally. Their relationship never had good timing. He walked past her without another glance. She wouldn't matter after a while. She would be like all the rest of them, in his past. He would move on and…what?

Get married? Perhaps but he worried he wouldn't feel for another woman the way he did Chelsea. Keep working? Certainly, but wouldn't he wonder where she was and what she was doing?

He moved into the small kitchen area and looked through the cabinets to find the tea bags. They were woefully inadequate, but would have to do until he could hit the ground and find the nearest bar.

He needed to get her out of his head. Time. Space. That was the only thing that would do it. Eventually she would be a distant memory, something he only thought about from time to time.

"Simon?"

His cock wasn't going to forget her at all if she kept showing up. "I'm just getting a cup of tea. I'll be out of your way in a moment."

"I wanted to talk to you."

He turned to her. He could make this quick. "Did you or did you not mean what you said at the ranch?"

She never apologized, simply blazed her way through even when she was wrong.

"No. Not a word of it. I'm so sorry I hurt you but I thought it was for the best because you were going to be brought up on charges for killing those men."

She was playing him again. She had to be. "It doesn't matter. I really don't care."

"If I believed that I would want to die." Her eyes didn't quite find his. "I would like to know what my requirements are, Master."

His cock jumped in his pants but his stomach took a deep dive. "Our contract doesn't matter anymore."

Her eyes finally came up, a hint of a challenge in those dark orbs. "Doesn't it? I didn't negate it."

She was not going to do this to him. "You did when you told me you were leaving."

"Did I? I would like to see it. I think I need to read that clause."

Fuck all. He hadn't written it so he had an out because he hadn't dreamed he would need one. He'd given her a very specific out, but he was in for the duration of their time together. "Chelsea, you can't expect that there is a contract after what you did."

"I just said some words. I didn't use my safe word. I didn't say we were done. I would like to see the terms of my contract so I can know what my rights and responsibilities are. If you don't have a hard copy, I can read it on Charlotte's phone. Don't tell me you didn't write it on your laptop because I know you did and you saved it. You have backups. Just give me the server name and I'll get it myself."

She was right, of course. He had saved it. He was a creature of routine and he'd hit *save*, so it was on his backup. He'd modified one he'd written for the subs at Sanctum. One of the first things Ian had asked him to do was rewrite the contracts. He'd written them for The Garden so he knew what he was doing. He'd fucked up because he'd known what he was doing and then he'd written the contract to suit his stupid romantic sensibilities. He'd been an idiot. He contemplated lying to her. Telling her anything that would get her off his back.

Or he could be honest and fuck the shit out of her. His cock was in firm control now. He could stay within the confines on their contract and spend the next week or so fucking her over and over again until he screwed her out of his system.

"I don't like the look on your face, Simon. Please don't lie to me." She stood there, her eyes softer than he could remember.

But he could be cold. She'd made him that way. "I wasn't thinking about lying to you. I was thinking about using the contract to fuck you until I don't care about you anymore."

She sighed, a relieved smile coming over her face. "Oh, that's good."

Had she listened to him? "I said I want to fuck you until I don't want you anymore."

"I won't ever stop wanting you." She turned her face up to his. "I'll take what you give me, Simon. A day. A week. A lifetime. Eternity. I'll take it all because I love you and I won't stop trying. I screwed up. I should have talked to you and I know that now. I shouldn't have made a unilateral decision. I'm so sorry. Please forgive me."

Chelsea Denisovitch was asking for forgiveness? "Are you asking as Chelsea or the bloody Broker?"

"Both because they're both me. I did terrible things as The Broker. I did some good things, too. But I want to be Chelsea now. I really want to be Chelsea Weston, but I know I screwed that up."

What the hell game was she playing now? It was messing up his head. "You're going to work for Ten."

"I might have to, but I'm going to negotiate new terms. Even if you won't forgive me, I'm going to stay in Dallas. I'm going to have a relationship with my sister and whatever little demons come out of her union with Ian. I was scared that I would hurt her. Hurt you. But she says I would hurt her more by walking away. What do you say? I didn't think I deserved you. Should I walk away? Or stay and fight? I can't pretend we don't know each other. I can't just be polite, not when we're working together. I want the terms of our contract. I insist on them."

She insisted? Oh, he could comply. He let his hand find the back of her neck, drifting up and into the soft nest of her hair. He tangled his fist there. "You want me as your Dom? Our contract was written for the duration of this operation. I don't have a way out. I locked myself in. You can merely say you're done and everything ends. Do you know what I'll do to you?"

Her face fell a little, but she didn't back down. "Probably something a little nasty. Are you going hardcore?"

"You have no idea. Continue down this path and you'll have my cock up your ass before you know it." He wanted it. Blow jobs might be his trigger, but he never felt more alpha than when he was fucking a sub's tiny asshole. And Chelsea was the ultimate sub, the one who wouldn't submit. If he could get inside her, could make her bend to his will—what a fucking high.

A high? He was fooling himself. It was trust and love and submission rolled in one gorgeous ball and he wanted it more than he wanted to live another moment. He wanted to fuck into that tiny hole and know she was submitting to him. He'd been her first and damn but he wanted to be her last.

"Show me your tits."

Her eyes wrinkled, her face turning down.

"You want to be my sub? You obey me. Show me your tits."

She took a halting breath as though fortifying herself, and for a moment he thought she would walk away. And then her hand moved to the bottom of her blouse and she pulled it up and off her torso. She wasn't wearing a bra. Her breasts were right there on full display. Pink and brown nipples. Small but full.

The bloody tea could wait.

Chapter Seventeen

Chelsea's whole body woke up, every cell seeming to sing with anticipation as Simon's hand came out and covered her breast. She loved his hands. They were big and strong and callused in a way she wouldn't have thought a royal's could be, but then Simon was an enigma. He was a code she couldn't crack and all the more attractive for his mystery. She could really spend a lifetime trying to figure the man out.

God, she hoped she got to.

"Drop the skirt and pray you aren't wearing knickers, love." He pulled his hand back and leaned against the counter, his eyes on her. Cold. The blue was like steel now and she needed to see she could melt it just a little.

Patience. Charlotte had counseled patience. She'd put her Dom in a bad situation and now the lion had a thorn in his paw and it wouldn't be easy to take it out. She had to be steadfast.

Patience had never been her strong suit, but she had to change if she wanted any chance at all with him.

The good news was her sister gave great advice. When she'd asked Charlotte for some undies, her sister had shook her head and told her to get used to going commando. Chelsea hooked her thumbs under the waistband of her skirt and pushed it off her hips. When had it gotten easy to be naked in front of him? He'd given her so much, but this ease with her own body was the greatest gift of all. She'd always hated the way she looked, but how could she not be at peace when he looked at her that way?

Would he still look at her the same way? It suddenly occurred to her that he really could have some revenge here and now. He could turn cold and mean. He could tell her she wasn't pretty enough for him and send her away. If he stared through her and ridiculed her, would she be able to handle it? She might deserve it, but she wasn't sure she could take it coming from him.

"Fuck, you're gorgeous."

Never from him. Even when he was angry with her, he wouldn't hurt her. He might be a mystery to her, but she'd figured out the depths of his kindness. "I love you."

He shook his head. "I don't want to hear it. I might be willing to play with you for the duration of our contract, but I won't hear those words and don't expect them from me."

"Just because you won't hear them doesn't mean they aren't true, Master." She had to give him everything until he finally realized she wasn't going anywhere. She'd hit him where he was most vulnerable. She'd told him she was abandoning him.

His jaw tightened. "Turn around. Palms flat on the wall. This isn't the same as before. This isn't some love affair. This is a D/s relationship and nothing more. There's punishment and pleasure, but that's all. You will serve me. I'll keep you safe. At any time, you can end it."

"I'm not going to end it. I don't want it to end."

"Chelsea, I don't know what's made you change your mind, but it's not going to work. It's best we let it go now."

"I have until the end of the op."

"Then turn around and accept my discipline."

She turned because he likely needed this. She could handle just about anything as long as he didn't send her away.

Fire licked her as Simon's hand came down on her ass, peppering her with slaps. He didn't count, simply spanked her like he was never going to stop. The pain flared and heightened her senses, making her skin come alive.

"What is my first rule?" He slapped at the fleshiest part of her ass. She felt that smack all along her spine. There was no doubt. Her Dom was pissed.

But he was still here. He was still hers and she had a chance. "To obey you in the field."

Another walloping smack nearly jarred her teeth loose. "And did you disobey?"

"Yes, Master. I did." She wasn't going to argue with him that she'd done it with the purest of intentions. He'd let her off the hook when she'd placed herself in danger the first time. He wasn't going to do it now, and she had to show him that she could bend. "I'm so sorry. Please let me make it up to you."

Charlotte would be proud. She'd told her to memorize those words because she would likely be using them so very often.

"Do you think sweet words are going to save you?" Another nasty smack.

Her eyes were watering, but she felt the clench of arousal deep in her body. She would take him here and now knowing fully well that her sister would probably hear her. It didn't matter. All that mattered was being near him, proving to him that she'd made a terrible mistake and they belonged with each other. He'd been right. They did have so much in common, so many things to bind them together. She had to hold on to those things.

"I don't need to be saved from you."

She could hear him breathing. He wasn't nearly as unaffected as he would like her to believe. "You might not think that five minutes from now. Stay where you are. Don't you move."

He was leaving her here? Standing naked in the kitchenette? She kept her mouth closed because her ass was already aching. He would come back. Surely. At some point. He wouldn't land the plane with her standing here naked. That would be dangerous and he was a good pilot. Of course, there were still hours and hours until they touched down in Venice. He could torture her for a decent amount of time.

"Uhm, hey, I was just grabbing a drink." Jesse's lips quirked up as he crossed to the small fridge. "Pissed off the Brit, huh?"

Yep. This was torture. She was naked and couldn't move or she risked pissing off her Dom even further. Just the day before, she likely would have screamed and jumped for the bathroom, but she'd finally figured it out. She had a choice. She could run for that door or she could accept that Simon needed this and take a deep breath and stop being a scared child. She was naked, but there wasn't a person on the plane who would be shocked to find her naked and waiting on her boyfriend to come back to torture her a little more. Hell, Ian would probably cheer. She knew her sister would. Jesse, for all his weird post-traumatic stress problems, had never been anything but kind to her. What was she so afraid of?

"Yes. You could say that. He's mad at me for disobeying him. I don't think he likes my new job."

Jesse leaned against the wall, seemingly at ease with the whole naked female thing. "Well, he usually just yells at me."

Chelsea frowned. "You like killed a dude with your bare teeth. I was just exploring other job options."

Shit. She needed a filter.

Jesse just grinned. "I was smart enough to not sign a contract that said I get my ass whipped." His light dimmed a little. "But I'm sorry I scared you."

"You didn't scare me. Not at all. It was gross though, and I think you might need a tetanus shot, but that guy was an asshole. He would have killed you. It's okay."

"So we're cool?"

"We're cool, Murdoch. You're a good guy. I'm happy to be your friend, and I know if someone else tries to kidnap me, you'll take care of it in the messiest way possible."

His hand came up in a mock salute. "Will do. And might I say your ass looks mighty fine even when it's red. I think he left a handprint."

"You've said enough, Jesse," a cold British voice said. "Take your drink and leave."

Jesse gave her another wink. "Will do, boss. I'll let Charlotte know the kitchen is closed."

"You do that," Simon said.

Jesse walked away and she turned her head, trying to see what Simon was doing. He was carrying a leather bag. Shit. He'd gotten his kit out. Damn it. She was in trouble.

"I thought you didn't have your kit."

"Ian was kind enough to bring it with him when he realized we would be leaving Dallas for a time. Charlotte brought some of your things and Ian brought my kit." He set the leather bag on the counter. "You didn't move."

"You left very specific instructions."

"Tell me you wouldn't have hidden a week ago."

She was fairly certain that he would know if she lied about this. "I thought about it even today."

"What changed?"

How should she explain this to him? "You think I'm pretty. You think there's nothing wrong with me."

"I've always thought that."

"Yeah, well from today forward, I choose to believe you." That was what had changed.

His voice went low, the words coming out in the sexiest of rumbles. "They all know you're back here. They all know I'm going to do something nasty to you."

"Yes." And that didn't horrify her the way it would have before. Maybe it was time for more truth. "Charlotte was the one who found me after Victor tried to rape me, so I think it's only fair she knows I'm getting something good for a change."

He paused, and for a moment all she heard was the whine of engines. "That's not fair."

She had zero intentions of playing fair. This was the most important game of her life, and she intended to win. "I was just explaining my thinking, Master. Is there really a handprint on my bottom?"

She felt him touch her, his fingers grazing the skin he'd punished and making her shiver. "I was hard on you, but you should expect that from now on, and no, there's no print. There's only a lovely shade of pink that will likely be gone in an hour or so. Jesse was teasing you. Do you really consider him a friend?"

"Yes. He's my friend." She might have just realized it, but it was true. The only reason she hadn't gotten close to anyone had been her own standoffishness. When she looked at the situation through new eyes, she could see everyone had tried. Adam constantly tried to battle her for hacking dominance—like that would happen—but it was his way of reaching out. Eve had asked her to lunch a few times. Chelsea thought it was so she could psychoanalyze the new girl, but what if it had been about friendship?

"Flatten out your back and don't move."

What was he doing? "Simon?"

A hard smack to her ass. "Don't question me. You have a safe word. You can use it. Until then, flatten your back."

She did as he asked. Yoga lessons were definitely in her future. So was a whole lot of rehab. If he didn't take her back, he would have to watch her change because she wasn't going to slink away and hide. She was done with that. He'd brought her into the light, and she wouldn't go back to the shadows.

"This is going to be cold. Don't move or I spank you again and we'll start over."

Her brain nearly short fused as she realized what he was doing. Warm hands parted the cheeks of her ass and then she felt something cool and slippery. "Holy shit. Are you plugging me?"

"Yes and if you move again, I'll grab the ginger lube. I really wanted to. I want to punish you, but this isn't about punishment. This is about preparation. It's a small plug. You'll wear it for a few hours and I'll move you up to a bigger one until you can take me." The evil bastard was already pressing against her asshole though he wasn't using a plug yet. His fingers were massaging in the lubricant. He worked in slow circles, opening her up bit by bit.

Pressure built, but she didn't complain. Simon wouldn't hurt her. Anything he'd done to her before had brought only pleasure. And she had to admit that she wanted him to take her in every way possible. She wanted to submit to him because she could, because he was worthy. Now that she thought about it, he'd submitted to her for months. He'd been patient and kind, allowing himself to be teased and taunted and frustrated by her. Most men would have given up, but not her Simon.

She groaned as he gained ground, his finger just sinking into her asshole before coming back out again. He rimmed her, sinking in a little and then massaging her before pulling back out and starting the process again.

It was hard to stay still, but somewhere along the way she found an odd strength to it. She was doing what made him happy. It was only okay because he'd earned it and wouldn't abuse it. She wouldn't ever be able to do it all the time. She had to be an equal partner in life, but this was something different. This was something just for them. There was a deep intimacy in knowing she would only ever do this for him. If he left, she might be able to take another lover some day in the distant future, but she would never ever take another Dom.

"Relax for me." His voice had deepened, and she wished she could see him. She loved watching his eyes heat up and those sensual lips of his curling in desire.

She took a deep breath and let her body relax. She wanted this. She needed this, needed to be open to him.

She felt it all along her spine as he pressed the tip of the plug to her and pushed it inside. Electricity seemed to spark up her backbone and the pressure flared as he dragged the plug back out and then slowly pushed it back in again.

"You like this. You should see what I see. You should see how pretty this is. It's going to be so much better when it's my cock your little hole is trying to strangle." He placed his hand on the small of her back as he fucked the plug in and out. In and out.

He was going to drive her insane.

Just when she was about to beg him for more, he pressed the plug deep and it stayed there. He sighed and stepped away. She heard water running in the sink.

"Wear it until I tell you it's time for it to come out. If you lose the plug, there will be punishment and I'll apply the ginger lube. It burns, but it will serve as a reminder to not lose your Dom's plug. You can get dressed again."

It took a moment for the words to sink in. He was leaving her like this. The bastard. The fucking bastard. He'd gotten her all hot and bothered and now he was going to punish her by walking away and withholding affection.

She managed to stand, though her legs were a bit stiff. She breathed through it and got ready to tell Simon where he could shove his fucking plug. And then she watched him. His movements were stiff, lacking his normal grace. He was turned away from her as he washed his hands and cleaned down the countertop, but his back was stiff. He was hurting too.

For months and months she'd let him get close only to push him away again and again. Didn't she owe him that patience she'd promised her sister? It was time to act. She'd spent her entire life reacting. She never thought, simply got mad or hurt, never considering the other person's feelings. A child. She'd been a child, but if she wanted him, she had to become something more.

"Can I make you some tea, Master?" A simple gesture and yet he was always the one to ask if he could bring her coffee or a snack when they were in a meeting. Never once had she returned his kindness.

He stopped and turned slowly, as though he was afraid of what he might find. "What did you say?"

She stood in front of him, naked and vulnerable and calmer than she could have imagined. He wasn't calm. Underneath his placid demeanor he was a storm of emotions, and she'd put him there. She'd brought back all his old fears and only she could make them go away again. He needed her. "I asked if I could make you some tea."

He stared at her a moment before asking a question of his own. "Why?"

"Because I think you would like it," she returned evenly. He was obviously going to be stubborn, but she had to get through it.

"I told you to get dressed." He was staring at her breasts and there was no way to miss the erection he was sporting.

Now was the time for honesty. "I'm terrified of bending over, Master. I think I'll try to find a robe or something. I really should have thought about tossing my clothes on the floor."

He was suddenly in her space, backing her to the wall and pressing his body to hers. "Why are you doing this?"

He was close again. She'd worried she would never feel this close to him. "I love you, Simon. I want to be good for you. I want to make you tea when you're tired and I really want to keep this plug in so you don't get mad at me."

His hands tangled in her hair, tugging her head back so she was forced to look up at him. He stared straight at her, his mouth faintly cruel. "It won't work. I'm done, Chelsea. I won't trust you again."

His mouth hovered over hers. It didn't feel like he was done with her. His words were meaningless against the slow grind of his cock against her belly. "I'll earn it this time. I didn't earn it the first time. It was a gift and I didn't understand what I was missing. I know you're mad and you have every right to be, but I love you."

"You chose Ten."

"I thought I was saving you, but maybe it was the easy choice to make, too. I won't say that's not possible. I've spent a lifetime trying to hide. I'm done. I found the one thing worth fighting for."

He chuckled but there was little amusement in the sound. "Are you trying to say that's me?"

More honesty. "No. It's me. You made me realize that I matter, that I have something to give you and it's not mine to throw away. I love you. That love is yours. It's not mine. It's simply the truth. I love Simon Weston and I'm going to do everything I can to make him love me back."

"It won't work, but I'll take the sex." He turned her around. "Hands on the wall."

She wanted to kiss him, wanted the intimacy of being face to face with him, but a beast was raging in her Dom and he needed the distance. He needed to tell himself this was merely sex, but she knew the truth. He couldn't stay away, wouldn't be able to if she really opened herself. Her own fears had been his ally, but the war had turned.

She heard the drag of his zipper, the tearing of the condom, but the time between those sounds and the feel of his cock pressed against her pussy was lightning fast, as though he couldn't stand another moment.

He'd been so gentle with her before and now he was rough, the other side of the man. He gripped her hips and shoved his cock inside in one hard thrust.

So full. Oh, between the plug in her ass and the massive cock invading her pussy, she could barely get a breath.

He fucked her hard, never relenting a second. The minute he

fucked inside, he dragged himself right back out. All the while she felt the pressure of the plug and the way his dick jostled it, bringing to life nerves she hadn't known she had. She pressed back, not wanting to lose the feeling.

"That's right. Fight me for it," Simon groaned as he slammed inside again. "You don't get an orgasm without earning it."

She pushed back, catching his rhythm. Heat flushed through her system. She could feel him pounding into her and she pounded right back, giving as good as she got. "More. God, Simon, I need more."

"I knew it would fucking be like this." He brought her up on her toes with his next thrust. "You're so fucking tight. I can't last, but don't think I won't be back. For as long as this op lasts, you're mine to fuck and discipline and I'll take you three or four damn times a day."

His hand moved from her hip to find her core, his thumb pressing on her clit.

The orgasm flashed like fire through her body. She couldn't contain her gasp or the little scream that came after. She yelled out his name, and in that moment she didn't care who heard her. He was all that mattered, and maybe that was the way it should have been from the moment she knew she cared for him. She'd placed everyone else first.

As he stiffened behind her and thrust in one last time, she vowed to put his needs first, before her own because that was what people in love did.

He slid out of her and stepped back, and she heard him toss the condom in the trash and zip up. "Get dressed."

He was cold again, but she saw through him. Or maybe she was naïve, but she preferred to be naïve when it came to him. She stepped up to him and put her arms around him. He stood still in her embrace and after a moment, she backed away. He wasn't ready yet.

He bent over and picked up her clothes. "There's a shower in back if you want to clean up."

"Thank you." She took the bundle he offered her. It was going to suck to get into those clothes and not lose the freaking plug. "Can I make you some tea?"

He stopped and turned again as though remembering why he'd come back in the first place. For a second she was sure he would tell her no and walk away. "Thank you. I like…"

"One sugar, no milk." She'd watched him enough to know his habits.

"Yes." He started out and then turned back. She was in his arms again, enveloped by him.

He kissed her on the top of her forehead. "This doesn't mean anything. It's just after care."

Oh, but it felt like love. "Yes, Master."

He straightened up, fixing his tie. When had she started finding suits so sexy? "Don't lose the plug."

He turned and left and Chelsea happily made tea. Naked. It gave her deep pleasure when Ian walked in, made a vomiting sound and ran away.

Her day was looking up.

Chapter Eighteen

Simon paid for the private boat with a credit card Adam had approved and turned back toward the dock. The office he stood in was slightly gloomy and he could smell the sea, but the light outside was brilliant even this late in the afternoon. He had to breathe a sigh of relief. Their passports had worked perfectly and he had yet to detect anything out of the ordinary, but he was nervous. He glanced outside, the reason for his nerves currently looking at the Adriatic.

Chelsea stood with Charlotte on the dock outside Marco Polo airport waiting on the private boat that would take them to Venice. In the past, she always looked a little lost when standing in a crowd. Her eyes would be on the ground, but this time, her face was turned up to the sun and it lit her a little like a halo.

What the hell game was she playing at? She wanted to fix his tea and play house with him?

Wasn't that exactly what he'd wanted from her the whole time? Not exactly the fixing his tea part, though it had felt nice and rather domestic to have her bring it to him. It was all about her bending the slightest bit. Didn't he want to show her that they could work? When he'd taken her on board the plane, she'd been everything he'd hoped she would be. Fierce. Giving. Loving.

Why couldn't he believe it?

"Could you ease up on the nudity thing when it comes to my sister-in-law? I nearly hurled."

Ah, the dulcet tones of Ian Taggart. Luckily he had an answer for his boss. "No."

"Seriously, all I get is a no?"

"Yes. My sub. My rules. You can stay out of it." No matter what happened, Ian wasn't going to be in control of his relationship. He was certain Ian thought he was the head of the family, but Simon wasn't so sure he was family yet. Possibly never. He would always be waiting for her to walk away and it wasn't as if she'd said she'd stay with him. She'd simply told him she loved him. He knew better than anyone those three words didn't mean a person would stay with him.

"So you two are all right? You're going to keep her so she doesn't show back up at my place again?"

He was so bloody nosy, and Simon wasn't convinced that this was all about keeping her out of Ian's hair. "We have a contract in place and she insists that I honor it. That contract is over the moment we solve this case and she's safe. After that, I assume she'll be wherever Ten places her." And that would be classified. He might see her again, but it would be sporadic and never for long. She would be far too valuable for Ten to let her keep her own place. She would likely live in Agency approved quarters. "What has Adam learned about Chelsea's flat?"

Ian stared at him for a moment, but then sighed. "I should have known you would be the tough one. British reserve and all. All right. He's popped into the CCTV around the area. Cannaregio. One of the quieter, more residential areas of Venice. It seems like Charlotte bought the flat in full and set up a routine maintenance plan. Apparently this was what they did those years they were running. A cleaning woman comes every two weeks and dusts and wipes down counters. She keeps things in ready in case one of the owners returns. She has a key and so does the super for the building."

They began to walk out as the line moved. Simon could smell the ocean. From this vantage they couldn't see the city, only the waters of the Adriatic that would take them to the lagoon. "Would they leave any packages in the flat?"

"No idea," Ian replied. "I don't know if she would have to sign for it. They have all kinds of taxes on products coming into Europe. It's possible it's still at the post office because there wasn't anyone home to sign. The Italian postal service is fucked up, man. Do you know the one place you can't buy a stamp in Italy? Yeah, the freaking post office. Great food, weird services."

Americans always thought their ways were the best. Though he'd seen Italian post offices, so he didn't disagree. "We can't just walk in."

Ian pulled his ball cap down as they walked into the sunlight. "No. I looked through some of the surveillance footage Adam tagged. I don't like it."

He should have done that himself, but he'd been busy flying the plane. "Anything suspicious?"

"A little glint of light that goes off from the same angle every fifteen minutes or so."

Hell. "So they have someone watching. How do they know? The property isn't in her name."

"Her friend could have told them. I think that's likely. Or they found the address on his computer. I don't care how much he resisted. Everyone breaks in the end," Ian said.

It was frustrating to not know. "Then why are they parked outside her flat? Why haven't they just taken the bloody evidence?"

"I have a theory but you're not going to like it."

He knew what Ian was going to say. "They want Chelsea as much as they want that package."

Sometimes it was hard to be in love with one of the world's greatest criminal masterminds. He stopped. He had to stop thinking that way. He hadn't really been in love with her. He'd been fascinated by her because he had a soft spot for hard cases. Anywhere he went, he was always drawn to a challenge. He needed to be necessary and that was the bane of his existence because she certainly didn't need him. She was strong and once she decided to, she would be so strong she might never need anyone again. She would disappear into the work Ten gave her and cease to need affection at all. She would become the robot she'd always bloody wanted to be. No one would stop her.

So why had she stood there naked and vulnerable and offered him tea. Stupid tea. Why had it tasted better because she'd made it? Why had it made him feel good?

He pushed it all aside as he considered the problem. "We have to get her out of this. The Collective is known for giving up arms to save the body. If we can figure out what company is involved and expose them, it's likely The Collective will leave her alone. They won't need her anymore if they think we're satisfied with taking down the single entity."

Ian nodded as they approached the women. "I think we have to go for the throat, but only of the company involved. We've seen that they don't have a problem cutting their agents loose when they fuck up. We have to hope it's the same here. Simon, you know I want to take them down."

"We can't. Not now. They'll use her as a pawn." And he couldn't allow that to happen. No matter how much he wanted to crush the whole organization, he had to protect her first. "I know she's your sister-in-law. We'll play this your way."

"So I'm taking over the op?" Ian's voice got tight.

Simon turned. This was his out. He would give it over to Ian. He could still help, but he wouldn't run the thing. He wouldn't be in charge of her. Oh, bugger all. "No. It's mine and you know it."

Ian slapped him on the shoulder and smiled. "That's because your dick is in charge and your dick is stupid. It's so fucking good to know. You're always so stoic and intellectual and shit. It's good to know deep down your dick is as stupid as the rest of ours. Hey, Jesse. We're following Simon's cock so we're all going to die."

Sometimes he hated Ian.

Jesse simply gave him a grin. "Hey, he's my partner. I gotta follow him even when his dick is a little crazy. Although, I will say, it might not be as crazy as I thought. Chelsea looks good."

He was going to kill the little shit. "Say one more word and I swear you'll swim to the hotel." Jesse closed his mouth, but his eyes were lit with glee. It was good. So often he was dark and there was a sadness in his eyes, but something seemed to have changed, as though Ian telling Jesse he was Simon's partner had given him something real. Jesse was his partner and there really was no reason for jealousy. "She did look lovely though."

Jesse just nodded.

Ian held his stomach. "Sanctum is never going to be the same. I gotta deal with seeing my sister-in-law running around with her boobs hanging out." Ian sobered and looked at Simon. "She looks happy, Si. I've never seen her look happy. She's been through a lot. Sometimes a woman goes through what Chelsea goes through and the damage is permanent. And sometimes, she just needs the right man to show her it isn't all bad. I think the damaged ones become the best lovers. At least I hope they do."

He truly identified with Chelsea. He saw himself in her.

Charlotte and Ian had worked out. Why the hell couldn't they?

"Chelsea," he called for her.

She looked up, her eyes eager as they found his.

When he motioned for her to join him, she practically ran his way. She smiled up at him as she nestled close. It was unselfconscious, that movement of hers. She simply took her place at his side and her arm wound around his waist as though it belonged there.

And his arm wrapped around her shoulder. "Stay close to me."

"Yes, Simon."

If only she would always say yes to him.

* * * *

Chelsea loved Venice. She'd loved the city the moment she'd seen it and back in those days, she hadn't really looked up from her computer long enough to see much. But something about Venice called to her. She stood up on the boat that was driving them toward the lagoon. One minute all she could see was the Adriatic, and then a left turn and Venice rose like a jewel from the ocean. It made her breath catch, but no more than the man who stood beside her.

Simon's hand was on her waist as they watched the city

come closer and closer. "You don't leave my side unless you're with Jesse or Ian. Am I understood?"

Something about the dark, possessive way he commanded her sent a shiver down her spine. He didn't want to lose her. He was serious about not losing her and she couldn't believe it was all about the mission. "I understand. And you stay safe. I don't want you going off alone."

He turned his face down slightly, and she thought for a moment he would argue with her. He sighed and then went back to staring at the city. "All right."

She tamped down her irritation. They were going into the world's most romantic city and she got a feeling he would fight her every inch of the way. She looked to her left and Charlotte and Ian were standing together. Ian was behind her, his body protectively curled around hers as the wind whipped through her hair. He put his chin on her shoulder and Chelsea could tell he was whispering in her sister's ear. Charlotte's smile curved her lips up. He was likely saying something naughty.

Husband and wife. Despite the fact that they were a D/s couple, they were always a husband and a wife first, with all the rights and responsibilities inherent with being in love.

All of her rights were in some contract she hadn't read.

Simon moved in closer as he spoke. "When we get to the hotel, I expect you to settle in. I've been informed that the place has Internet. You can use the laptop Adam sent for you and start trying to put the pieces together. We need real information we can use, not just Ten's rumors and innuendo."

She turned her face to his. "I already know what company we're looking at. I'm sure of it. Only one had pending court cases with all the victims. I put it together after I brought you the tea. Malone Oil pays for some serious satellite Internet."

"Well, of course, you did." He sighed a little, and she could tell something she'd done had disappointed him. "Tell me."

She hesitated. Normally she would bluster her way through, but Charlotte had done a number on her. She'd given her a hard lecture on being honest and vulnerable with the people she loved. Simon was the chief person she loved, so she couldn't give him an arrogant grin and tell him how smart she was no matter how much she wanted to. "Why are you mad at me? Did I do something wrong? I had the laptop. I thought you would be happy I figured it out."

His face was a stony mask. "I'm sure Ten will be. Do you need to call him?"

Jealous. He was jealous. "No. Simon, I don't have a thing for Ten. He just offered me a way to help you. I took the job because he said he would get you off the murder rap."

"I certainly didn't ask you to save me. I could have gotten out of it myself. Has it occurred to you that I have a degree in law?"

He was splitting hairs, and she couldn't win if she played that way. She needed to make him really understand. "What do I mean to you, Simon? If you don't need me to care for you, then what am I to you? Because I honestly didn't think about anything but saving you from the cops. I saw that news spot on TV and I knew I had to make things right."

He stopped, looking the slightest bit startled. "I didn't need your help. I could have handled it myself."

Honesty was kind of awesome. Honesty had that gorgeous Brit on the ropes. "I didn't think. I saw the person I loved might get hurt and I did whatever I could. We didn't have time to talk about it. So I need to ask you again, what am I worth to you? Did you just want sex? Don't I get to stand up for you? Protect you when I can?" It was time for a gamble, but it was a meaningful one to her. "If you just want me in bed, you should tell me now."

She couldn't be meaningless. It was why she really thought she should work out terms with Ten. Ian didn't need her. He had Adam. She could do good work for Ten. She just couldn't be in his cave. She had to be with Simon.

His jaw locked and she worried he was about to turn away. He might join Jesse, who was watching the boat captain's every move, ready to shoot the dude at the first sign he wasn't on the up and up. Finally he reached for her hand and tugged her close. He put her in front of him as they made the turn into the grand lagoon. He covered her back with his body, his arms coming around to surround her. "You're an unconscionable brat and don't think anything of this. Our cover is as vacationing lovers.

We have to stay close. Now, tell me what you know."

So he wasn't ready to answer her questions but he wasn't willing to turn her away either. She would take his affection. She sighed and let her head roll back to rest on his chest as the boat cut through the lagoon. Around them, gondolas made their way through the water, the familiar red and white shirted gondoliers using poles as they sang in deep baritones.

She was here with him. Here in Venice. She would take this lovely time with him and then she would watch over him even if he didn't want her anymore.

Her love…it was meaningful. It had value. It was a gift and a gift didn't have strings. A gift didn't require anything. She loved him and it had made her a better human being.

A deep warmth suffused her. "I love you."

He stiffened behind her, but he didn't move away. If anything, his mouth got closer to her ear. She was sure he would say he was trying to make her hear him better. All she felt was his heat. "Just tell me."

"Nieland Affiliates. They're a parent corporation. A major conglomerate. Three of their subsidiaries have ties to potential multimillion-dollar cases that were either being tried by or in the courtrooms of the victims Ten identified. It's the only company that has ties to every victim. All but one of the cases—the one dealing with the patent—have either been dismissed or given a ton of time for both sides to deal with the loss."

Many times, the longer a trial went, the less chance the defense had. Oftentimes witnesses died or complainants got sick of waiting and accepted a pennies on the dollar deal.

"We need whatever's in the files Al sent you to prove it," Simon murmured. His cheek was against hers and the world got quieter as the motors on the boat slowed and they entered the canals.

He leaned into her, his body curling around hers as though he'd detected a threat. As they moved from the grand lagoon into the smaller canals, the buildings around them towered over, each a testament to Venice's long history. The boat slowed and the city seemed to quiet, the sun blocked by the houses that surrounded them.

Something about the whole thing worried her. "Why would they need Al?"

Al was a hacker, not a doctor. He wouldn't know about poisons. He certainly wouldn't administer them. He rarely left his place. She simply couldn't see him assassinating anyone.

"Perhaps they wanted him to change the medical records." Simon's voice went low in deference to the change in noise levels.

She lowered hers, too. "Anyone with half-assed skills could do that. Al wouldn't have taken that job. He liked a challenge."

She thought back to the things he'd said to her. He'd said something about not understanding what he was doing. He'd hacked a password but that didn't necessarily mean he knew where it had led to.

He would have seen it as a challenge, one he likely got paid well for.

How would a hacker kill someone?

"Oh, shit. Did they have pacemakers?" Now that she thought about it, it made sense. "I bet they either had pacemakers or someone changed their medical records so they got something that would kill them. Like a prescription. I think I read in one of the files Ten had that the DA who died had a prescription for high blood pressure. It would be fairly simple to get into a pharmacy's system and change the records—especially if someone working for The Collective changed the drugs to something lethal. There are a lot of pills that look alike. Then they could change the toxicology records, but again, that's fairly easy. But hacking the code to a pacemaker, now that would be a challenge."

Charlotte moved closer, Ian following behind as the boat turned again. Chelsea could see the brilliant white arches of bridges ahead of her.

The Rio de Palazzo. She recognized the gorgeous white bridge spanning the river ahead of her. The Bridge of Sighs.

The boat slowed further in deference to the gondolas all around them.

"Didn't this come up years ago?" Charlotte asked.

Years before, when Dick Cheney was the vice president,

he'd had his pacemaker taken utterly offline out of fear it would be hacked. The Secret Service would protect vulnerable politicians, but no one would likely think about lesser civil servants. "Yes, and it was proven that it is possible to hack into a system and send a deadly charge through a device, though until now I haven't heard of anyone actually doing it."

"What would he have sent you to prove it?" Ian asked.

Chelsea stared at the bridge. The late afternoon sunlight was shining on it, making the elaborate arch look pearly and perfect. Her head should be on the case, but all she could think about was the legend about the Bridge of Sighs. "He could have printed out a record of his work. He was damn good at his job. He could have sent it to himself and printed it out. Apparently they checked his work and found out about it."

The boat floated toward the bridge where it was legend that if lovers kissed under the bridge at sunset in a gondola, they would be together forever.

She seriously doubted she would get Simon in a gondola any time soon. She would be lucky if he flew back to the States with her after it was over.

Ian glanced around. "We'll be at the hotel soon. I'll check out Chelsea's place and talk to the housekeeper. You two keep your heads down and stay in the room. I don't want Chelsea out on the streets until she has to be."

Chelsea frowned. She didn't want to be left out. If Simon had his way, he would likely leave her with Jesse as a bodyguard. Not that she didn't like Jesse, but she wanted the time with Simon.

"Hush," Simon said in her ear as the shadow of the bridge began to cross. "Obey him. We'll keep our heads down and get through this. Turn around."

The sunlight disappeared and the world seemed to narrow down to just him as he leaned over and thrust his hands in her hair. His mouth covered hers in a hungry kiss, forcing her lips open as his tongue surged in. Just like that she didn't care about anything but the feel of his body against hers. If he'd stripped her naked, she wouldn't have cared. When he kissed her like that, she was his.

And then the sunlight hit her face again and he broke off the kiss.

He glanced back at the bridge.

He knew. He knew the damn legend. Maybe they weren't on a gondola, but he'd kissed her and she definitely sighed.

His face went blank again and he turned her back around. "It's our cover."

"Of course," she replied, happy he couldn't see her smile.

Chapter Nineteen

Simon looked out over the small canal outside their hotel. It was quiet outside of the well-traveled portions of the city. Not that he'd seen them. Forty-eight hours in and all he'd seen was the outside of Chelsea's flat.

And Chelsea. He'd seen plenty of her. It had taken everything he had to send her to bed without him the night before, and he was coming up on the time when he would have to do it again.

Could he do it again? Could he lie on the bloody couch with his cock pulsing against his belly while she was asleep in the next room? Could he take another night of knowing she was soft and warm and he was a fool?

He stared out and wondered what he was waiting for. Was he really not going to take what she was offering? He kept telling himself it proved he was in charge and that he could take her or leave her. It was his choice. He wanted her to know that he was the Dom and she was the sub and she should stay in her place.

The problem was he was rather miserable.

The real reason he hadn't let himself sleep with her the night before was he didn't trust himself not to get on his knees and beg her to stay with him. God, he was a fool.

He could hear her talking in the bedroom. Charlotte was

with her. She'd barely left her sister's side except to sleep. He'd walked them down the narrow streets to a quiet restaurant where they had dinner while Jesse prowled around the outside and Ian finished his investigation.

Simon knew he should have been the one to question the housekeeper, but he couldn't leave Chelsea. He couldn't trust her to anyone because the instant he closed his eyes at night, she disappeared. She would be smiling up at him, her face more open than ever before, and he would reach for her and she would disintegrate in front of him, that damn smile on her face like it didn't matter she was leaving him.

He ran a frustrated hand through his hair. He needed this whole thing to be done. He needed to move on. Sometimes it was better to simply pull the bloody bandage off and get it over with. Let the misery start now so he could get used to it.

"And you're all right with everything?" Charlotte was asking.

"What do you mean 'everything'?" Chelsea sounded curious.

"You know, everything about sex." Charlotte was speaking cautiously, as though she didn't want to scare Chelsea off.

He was relegated to eavesdropping. It was pathetic. And yet, he couldn't quite move away until he'd heard her reply.

"Well, I'm pretty pissed I didn't get any last night."

He had to smile a bit. She had been upset. She'd walked out wearing nothing at all, her body a beacon in the night, and he'd been the bloody bastard who sent her away.

Why had he kissed her under the bridge? Because he'd wanted to. Because he'd wanted for a minute to believe that some stupid mystical power could grant him a wish—that they would work.

Charlotte snorted. "I'm talking about how scared you've always been because of what happened."

"I was at first, but he's Simon. I can't be scared of Simon," came the sure reply.

Because he wasn't worth being scared of. He wasn't as masculine as the rest. He was far too concerned with the cut of his suit to be taken seriously. It was the story of his life. He was tired of it. He certainly didn't want it from her.

There was a little knock on the door before he heard it opening and Ian walked through. He was dressed in black, a cap on his head. He looked like a burglar, which was fitting since he'd likely broken into the flat.

"Did you find anything?" Simon stepped away from the door as Jesse joined Ian.

Jesse seemed to be the only one having a good time. He'd stopped at every gelato stand in the city. He took a bite of his current obsession before he talked. "I got to beat the shit out of a guy."

Ian nodded. "And he didn't even flip out. That's why he got gelato. I'm trying this whole new 'positive reinforcement' training with the puppy. So far it's working. And don't freak out. We needed a distraction so we found a pickpocket, flashed some cash, and drew his ass where we needed him. It worked beautifully. I'm pretty sure they didn't see me slip inside. They were too busy watching the fight."

"What did you find out?" His impatience was getting to be a problem.

"The housekeeper said she left the notice of the package delivery on the bar in the kitchen." Ian pulled out a little slip of paper. "Which is exactly where it was. I should have bought her a gelato, too."

It didn't make sense. "Why would Krum send her a package that had to be signed for? He knew she wasn't in Venice."

"He couldn't be sure," Chelsea said from the bedroom door.

Charlotte joined her husband, taking her place at his side. "You look hot when you're committing criminal acts."

He grinned at her. "I try to keep my boyish physique for you, baby. Simon, there are a million reasons he could have done it. He didn't want it to fall into anyone else's hands. When I think about it, it's a pretty decent plan. Chelsea's the only one who can get it. She has to show ID and the post office is fairly safe."

No. He could see where Ian was going with this and it wasn't happening. "I'm not sending her to get that package."

Chelsea's chin came up. "Simon, it's the post office. It's out in the open. I'll be fine."

He had other plans because he didn't like any of this. "We'll call in another female operative. Get Damon on the phone. Surely he knows someone. We'll fake her identification and send her in. Damon can have someone here in a few hours."

London wasn't as far away as Dallas. It was a good plan.

"I can pick up the package," she said stubbornly. "I can do it in the morning and we don't have to fake anything. I still have that ID."

"Simon, we'll all be there, but we also need to get this done. We need to settle this op and get back home," Ian explained.

"I'm not on your timetable," Simon shot back. "This is my operation and we'll do it my way. She stays out of it. As a matter of fact, why don't we send both women home? Ian, you can escort them. Jesse and I will handle everything from here."

That got the Dennis women yelling. They both turned on him, and Ian's hand shot out as he took a step back like the bloody coward he was.

"You are not sending me home, Simon Weston," Charlotte was saying as she wagged a perfectly manicured finger his way. "She's my sister and that takes precedence since you're not willing to marry her. Hell, put a collar around her neck and then maybe, maybe I'll concede, but this whole 'it's my op' business isn't going to fly."

Chelsea had an argument of her own. "You can't send me away. I'm not useless, Simon." Her face had gone red. "Can't you see this is why I have to work for Ten? At least he'll let me do something. I can't live this way. I can't be meaningless."

Why did she willfully misunderstand everything he said? "I'm not trying to make you meaningless. I'm bloody well trying to keep you alive."

Even Jesse had stepped away from the fray. So much for having his back.

"What does being alive mean if you don't trust me?" Chelsea threw his way.

"How can you expect her to live like that? And you can't expect me to walk away and leave her. She's my sister. You screw with her, you get me, so whatever kind of fight we're going into, you better understand that I'll be right there," Charlotte explained.

"No, you won't." Ian's voice had gone dark, without a hint of his normal sarcasm.

She turned on her husband. "Yes, I will. She's my family."

Ian's eyes were cold as he looked at his wife. "She's not the only part of your family that you're putting in harm's way. I allowed you to come with me, but the minute I feel you're in danger, I will carry you out of this country kicking and screaming. You're the one who wanted this. You're the one who pushed for this. You got it, Charlie, and now you have to deal with it. That baby in your belly is my son, and I can assure you I will keep him and you safe. You wanted to see what kind of father I would be? This is it. If I tell you to get on a fucking plane, you will get on that damn plane or the next nine months of your life are going to be very boring."

Chelsea's mouth dropped open. "Charlotte?"

Damn it. "Ian, how could you bring her along?"

Ian turned that nasty frown his way. "Because she's my wife and I didn't fall in love with her because she was some docile little woman. She needs to be here. She needs to be with her sister and Chelsea needs to deal with this. She needs to know she's important in and out of bed. That's why I'm here. That's why Charlotte is going to play it safe, but she's going to back up her sister because that's what family does."

Did she really think he didn't want her for anything but sex? She'd spent years in her sister's shadow being used by their father as nothing but a way to control Charlotte. She'd probably felt so small. He knew how that felt—to be insignificant, tiny, meaningless. She'd found a way to make herself meaningful, though she'd become a criminal to do it. How hard had it been for her to go from being truly powerful to where she was now? This was where Ten had hit her.

Or was he being too cynical? Yes, she missed the power she'd had, but all she'd asked to do was to help him with the mission. Which really was all about her.

And she'd said she took the job with Ten in a naïve attempt to save him. Chelsea wasn't naïve. She was hard to her core and she'd gotten soft for him. If he pushed her away, would she retreat?

"Charlotte, are you really?" Chelsea asked, looking at her sister.

"I think so because I really, really want that gelato." She eyed Jesse.

"I am on it," Jesse said with a salute. "Strawberry? Chocolate? I think they had tiramisu."

"Yes," Charlotte replied.

"All right then, I'll get some kind of holder. Boss, I think those two need some time alone. I'll bring the vat of gelato to your room," Jesse said, opening the door and holding it there.

That was his partner, backing him up and right into a corner. He wasn't ready for this. Not even close. He wasn't ready to make a decision about her yet.

Charlotte gave her sister a hug. "We'll talk later, but I'm not going anywhere without you."

Chelsea took a step back. "You have to. You have to think about the baby and Ian. They have to be your priority now. You did a good job with me. I promise you I'll prove it, but I have to take care of me now. No matter what happens, I love you and I won't let you down."

Charlotte turned his way. "Simon…"

"And you're done." Ian gripped his wife's hand. "Their fight, Charlie. We have enough of our own, and it seems like baby sister can stand up for herself. Simon, call me later and let me know if I'm going home. I'll have Damon ready to take my place. I meant it. This is your op, but you should think about what I said."

And Chelsea was his problem. His. Maybe Chelsea was just fucking his.

The door closed behind them.

"I can't believe she's pregnant."

"I can. Those two have zero discretion and they really should learn to lock doors. I can't count the times I've walked in on them." Now that he was alone with her, he wasn't sure what to do. "Perhaps you should get ready for bed."

She shook her head. "Not until we talk this out."

"There's nothing to talk about. I'll think on it tonight and give you my decision in the morning."

Tears suddenly glistened in her eyes. "Please don't do this to me. I know I deserve it, but I'm asking you not to. I'm begging, Simon. I can take it from anyone else. Not from you."

"I'm not doing anything but my job, Chelsea. I'm not doing this to hurt you." He was doing it to protect himself. He'd been stupid to try. He had no idea why he had to fall for the hard cases. He would find someone sweet and simple and build a life. He turned away and walked back to the window, needing a moment away from everything.

"He barely talked to me except to tell me I was ugly and fat," she began in a halting voice.

"Chelsea, you don't have to do this." He didn't need to hear it. It was one thing to read it in the files and hear Ian relate it. It was entirely another to hear it from her trembling voice.

"It's funny because I went from my mom, who always told me I was smart and pretty and that I could do anything, to a man who spit on me more than once. At least I understand it now. He hated my real dad. At first he let me stay with Charlotte, but then she refused to do something he wanted and I got sent to the servant's quarters. I actually liked it down there. The housekeeper would sneak me desserts and she was kind to me. The problem was the doors didn't lock down there."

He turned, ready to tell her to stop, but she wasn't looking at him. She'd sat on the couch, her body curling up as though to protect herself. As though she needed to protect herself from her own words, the past rushing in. He stopped. She never spoke of these times in anything but a sarcastic voice or to put a wall between her and the rest of the world. Now she was simply telling him, sharing the pain with him. Like lovers should.

"How old were you, love?" He didn't even try to stop the endearment. She was his love. It might never work, but she was his love and always would be.

"I was fifteen at the time. I'd already had my legs broken by then, but I could walk. One night one of Vladimir's men decided that if the boss cared so little about me, he could likely get away with raping me. I still remember waking up to the smell of cigars and then all that weight pressing me down. I couldn't breathe. It was dark so I couldn't see. When I tried to scream, he put a hand over my mouth and then I really couldn't breathe."

"Come here." He sat down on the sofa, unable to stay away from her a second more. "Sit in my lap."

She scrambled to get to him, her very gracelessness utterly endearing. He used to have to trap her into affection and now she ran to him. She settled herself on his lap and her head found the crook of his shoulder. "I killed him, Simon."

A fierce relief went through him. "I'm glad."

It saved him the trouble. If she hadn't, he would be hunting a Russian mobster.

She sat up, wiping away her tears. "You don't understand. I really killed him. I had a knife under my pillow and I…there was so much blood."

He eased her back down. "You did what you had to. It's nothing to be ashamed of. I would have done the same thing. It was brave, love."

She'd been so young, in a foreign country with no one but her sister and a powerless housekeeper to protect her.

"Charlotte helped me bury the body. Neither of us wanted to know what Vlad the horrible would do to me if he found out I killed one of his men. I wanted to die. I remember sitting there and thinking that I should just get it over with. I didn't, of course, because I couldn't leave Charlotte. Why didn't you?"

So she finally understood. Chelsea was often so wrapped up in her own trouble, she didn't think about others'. Another way she was changing. She finally understood that they had both been deeply marginalized during childhood. "I don't know. I guess I always had hope. I hoped that once Clive was well, they would see me again. At the darkest times, I thought if Clive died, then they would finally need me. Not the best of me to think that way, but true. I wouldn't have wanted it, but it went through my head. Besides, I was always waiting for Aunt Ava to come. I had those summers."

"And I had years of my mother's love. I've started to wonder why I let the bad stuff wipe out all her love. I listened to him. I don't eat a lot because I'm worried I'm everything he said

I was. I deny myself because I listened to him. Why is it so much easier to hear the bad stuff?"

He needed to inundate her with the "good stuff" as she put it. "You're beautiful. I think you're gorgeous."

"I have no idea why, but I'll take it."

"Why do you want to work for Ten?" He needed to know so he could let her go if he had to. He needed to know this was what she wanted, needed.

Her face turned up. "I didn't at first. I really did take the job to protect you. But I've thought about it. There's no place for me at McKay-Taggart. You don't need another Adam."

"I told you what I thought you should do."

She nodded. "And I'll do some of that, too, but I'm addicted to the adrenaline of hacking. I know you wish I wasn't but this is who I am. I'm willing to do it for good reasons, but I need to do it. I need to look at this massive, twisty turny maze and know that I'm the only one who can get through it. I need to know that I can make a difference."

She was really going to leave him just as she became everything he thought she could be. Giving. Kind. Loving.

She'd made her choice and it wasn't him.

He let his hands drop. "All right then. Go and get some sleep. You're going to pick up that package in the morning."

It might be the only thing he could really offer her. One last mission before she started a new life.

She didn't move, simply looked at him with wide eyes. "Simon, please don't push me away."

She wanted a few more nights? Part of him thrilled at the idea. Maybe just one more night since they would likely get the package in the morning and then be on their way back to Dallas. One more night with her. One night to memorize her so he could remember every inch of her body later when he was all alone. One more night to imprint her on his brain.

And yet it was somewhat cruel of her. She wanted more from him. She couldn't realize how much she would take.

"Take off your clothes." Who would watch over her when she was far from him? Who would push her to take care of herself? To be better? To find her place in a world that seemed to have none for her?

He was going to be all over Tennessee Smith. He might not be able to have contact with her, but he would let Ten know that if she was ever hurt, ever neglected, he would answer to Simon Weston.

She stood up, the sweetest smile on her face, and pulled her T-shirt over her head. No more silly sayings on her shirts. Charlotte had packed them for her and she was dressed for maximum impact to her man's senses. She wore jeans that hugged her every curve and a V-neck that showed off her breasts.

If she'd remained his, he had a plan to fill out those curves. It was as he'd always expected. She stayed thin for reasons that didn't make sense. He would have fed her chocolate and wine and rich foods until those curves filled out and she couldn't help but look healthy and happy and full.

He watched as she undid her bra and her breasts bounced free. Lovely. He would love them small or round and full because they were hers. He'd found that his physical type changed when his heart was involved. She was lovely because her soul called to his. If she stayed the way she was, he would love her as long as she was happy. It was happiness that made her glow, and he hoped she found it in her new life.

He couldn't make her stay. He accepted that one truth of life as she pushed her jeans off her hips and proved that Charlotte knew about the no knickers policy. He had to set her free so she could fly.

"Present yourself to me." He'd chosen that stupid protocol as much for himself as for her. He needed her affection more than he needed to be in control. She sighed and found her way into his arms, winding her limbs around him.

"Hello, Master." She cuddled her head on his chest.

Perhaps he wasn't as masculine as the others. He really did need this. He needed the love and affection from his chosen submissive more than he needed anything else. He needed the right to adore and protect her. The rest of the contract was fluff. He wanted the right to love her and have it returned to him.

In the end, what he truly wanted was a marriage, but he

wouldn't get that.

"I want to push your boundaries tonight, Chelsea." He had one more night with her. He would take it. "Can you trust me?"

"I trust you like I've never trusted anyone but my sister, Simon. You're my family, too."

But not her husband. She would likely look back on her life and see him as a bridge. He'd shown her she could love and she would do so again. She would find the man she couldn't let go of.

And he would stand in the shadows to make sure if that man ever fucked her over that he paid. He would be her guardian angel from afar.

"Then get on the bed."

She gave him a wink and then walked to the bedroom, her left leg limping slightly. He would have to take care of that.

While she was walking to the bedroom portion of the suite, he walked to the closet and grabbed his kit, his dick starting to throb. There was no question that part of his anatomy was thrilled with the situation. His bloody cock was ready to play. It didn't seem to understand that it was the last time it would for a long time.

He was going to take her ass. He was going to take that last piece of her virginity because it was bloody well his and he'd earned it. When she went to her perfect man, she would have to remember him.

He grabbed the kit and stalked to the bathroom, cleaning the never before used plug. He'd bought it for her. He'd also bought the rope he brought along for her and the crop and vampire glove. She liked sensation play. Oh, she would tell whatever Dom she found that she merely wanted a flogging or a spanking, but he'd pushed her further and found how beautifully she responded to having her senses engaged.

He carried the kit and plug with him into the bedroom and found her waiting for him.

She'd opened the window, letting the moonlight in. It caressed her skin, making it beam like a pearl in the night. Her nipples had already tightened into little pink nubbins. "It's so much bigger here. The moon, I mean. You're always big, my love."

He hoped Ten had a teeny tiny cock. "I want to tie you up."

Her breath caught, but she nodded. "All right. I can handle it. You can get me out fast if I can't, right?"

He had a knife in his kit for just such an occasion. "Of course. Let me tie you to the bed."

She took a deep breath and then laid back, her arms spreading out like an angel spreading her wings. She gripped either side of the headboard. "Yes, Master."

He'd thought she was beautiful before, but her unselfconscious sexuality called to him. The sight of her spread out and waiting for his pleasure burned into his brain.

He gripped the soft jute rope in anticipation. She would be helpless, trusting and needy. He could do anything he liked to her once she was tied up, and he intended to bring her pleasure like nothing she'd ever felt before.

"Up a bit more." He helped her move a bit and slid a pillow behind her upper back to raise her up. He wanted her to be able to see what he was doing to her.

His hand slid up her arm until he found her wrist and he made his first knot. He took his time, allowing the rope to slide along her skin like a lover lavishing affection. One knot and then two, never so tight she couldn't move a bit but enough to keep her there.

"Are you afraid?" If she was, he would forego this bit of heaven.

She shook her head. "I love you. I'm not afraid of you."

Because he was safe. He realized that now. He was a safe way for her to find the real world again, but she would move on after him. His safety couldn't bind her to him. It could only set her free for the real love that he was sure she would find.

He moved to her wrist, letting the rope lick along her flesh before he knotted the rope, holding her surely. It was the only way he could bind her, hold her tight. It wasn't forever, but he would have a night of pure bliss.

He stood up, fully dressed to her naked. He rather liked that. She was naked, open and waiting for him. So beautiful in her wantonness.

He stood back and watched her for a moment. "Do you have any idea all the things I want to do to you?"

Her voice went low and there was no way to mistake the way her nipples tightened further. "Everything, I hope."

"You have no idea." He wanted to fucking brand her. He wanted his name tattooed on her flesh so every other man who happened to see her beauty would know it belonged to him.

He wanted to have her in every way it was possible for a man to have a woman. He wanted her on her knees with his cock shoving its way to the back of her throat. He wanted to know she walked around with his come in her belly. He wanted her tied up and down and begging him for release.

He would settle for a little torture.

He grabbed his deerskin flogger. The falls were super soft. It was a good place to start.

With a practiced hand, he struck her breasts in a rotating motion, the falls hitting her softly. He found a rhythm that had her eyes closing and her body relaxing. Something about the thuds seemed to get to her. She subbed out quickly, her body relaxing and her brain seeming to go somewhere else.

He couldn't have that. He wanted her here with him. He would let her find her subspace, but not so quickly.

He reached out and gave her right nipple a hard twist.

Her eyes came open and her mouth formed the sweetest *O*. Yes, his cock would fit quite nicely there. "You want me to count?"

"No." This wasn't punishment. This was pleasure, and he wanted her with him. "I want you to look at me. I want your eyes on me. And keep your legs spread wide. I want to watch your pussy get hot and wet."

She nodded. "It's pretty much already there. Always is with you. I didn't know what that meant until I started playing with you."

He brought his wrist back, flicking it neatly before bringing it down on her thighs. It occurred to him that she seemed very open to answering questions this evening. It might be his last chance to ask. "Why? Why me?"

She gasped as he continued, but kept her eyes steady on him.

"You're my type. I didn't know I had a type until I met you. Now I know what I need. I need a Brit who's half aristocrat and half cowboy. I need a man who carries a full three-piece suit in his bug-out bag. I need a man who craves afternoon tea and thinks any Scotch under fifteen years is a travesty."

She made him sound like a snob. He kept up the slow and rhythmic flogging. "So you want someone civilized."

Again, it made sense. He was utterly unlike Denisovitch's thugs. She would turn to him because he was so different.

Her eyes narrowed. "You're not civilized, Simon. Never think I don't see through your gorgeous trappings. Do you think I don't know what you're capable of? Do you think I didn't watch you that day in Goa?"

He stopped. She'd been with him and Ian and Sean in India when they'd finally taken down Eli Nelson. Simon had been assigned to watch from the cliff tops as Sean, Ian, and Charlotte met with a prince on a boat in the middle of the Arabian Sea. Chelsea was supposed to have been safe in their beach bungalow. She shouldn't have seen the insane chance he took when he realized Ian was in trouble.

"You were watching?"

Her lips curled up. "Yes, I was. I saw you cliff dive and swim what had to be at least a half a mile. I had binoculars. I watched you sneak on that boat. Tell me something. Did you bother to take off your tie, Simon?"

He hadn't. He'd ditched his jacket, but kept the vest and tie. "No."

She sighed, her eyes soft. "I think about that a lot. Especially at night. I think about it and imagine that you're coming for me. I imagine that I'm on that boat and you can't wait another minute to fuck me so you jump off that cliff and you swim for me and you're hot and hard when you find me."

He was fucking hot now. Every word from her mouth went straight to his dick. "I would. I would jump off a bloody cliff if it meant getting inside you. Do you want more?"

"Fuck, yeah, I want more. I want everything you can give me. I've spent the majority of my life with my sexual experience being summed by my almost rape. I'm leaving it behind. I want it to be all about you. All about my love, my Dom. Give me everything. I promise I won't be scared."

"Because I'm not like the men you knew." He was as far from the man who'd tried to hurt her as possible.

She growled a little his way. "Because I love you. Because you can be dangerous, but not to me. Because every cell in my body lights up when I think about you. I love you like I didn't know I could love anything in my life."

He would take it.

He pulled the vampire glove on his hand. It was a black glove covered in soft faux fur that covered prickly metal tacks. Soft and smooth and then a bit of bite, it was just what he needed to make her squirm and to give her what she wanted.

"Are you ready, love? Because I think it's time to get serious."

It was time to live in the now, because the now was all he had left.

Chapter Twenty

Chelsea shivered as he ran the soft part of the glove over her breasts before he flattened his palm and she felt the hard edge of the tacks.

A low moan came from the back of her throat as it scratched over her flesh, sending crazy sensations along her skin.

It was nothing compared to what he was doing to her soul. He was here with her. She'd told him her darkest secret and he'd just held her and told her he was proud.

She relaxed. Not even the bonds bothered her since he'd been the one to tie them. She trusted him. Simon Weston knew how to care for a woman, and she was so happy to be the woman he gave a damn about.

Her toes curled as he got back to the flogger. The sound nearly made her brain turn off in the most pleasant way. She loved the sound of the thud and the massage it gave her skin.

He brought her right back to reality by running that damn vampire glove over her breasts. She couldn't help the gasp that came from her throat as he flattened out and the sting hit her.

"I love how pink your pretty skin gets," he said.

She looked down and sure enough, there were thin pink lines where the glove left its mark. Four little scratch marks that proved he'd been here with her. They would be gone before morning, but she kind of wished they wouldn't leave. She liked having his mark on her. She suddenly kind of understood why people liked tattoos. She wanted a little "I love my Brit" on her ass. "I think I need a little more, Master."

His gorgeous blue eyes narrowed. "You think you're in control?"

Her damn womb spasmed at the sound of his deep, dark voice. Yes, she'd brought out the Dom in him. "No, Master. No. Please. Please, don't flog my pussy. Please don't run that horrible glove over my tender flesh."

He chuckled. "I won't throw you in the briar patch, either, love."

He brought the flogger down gently on her pussy.

It didn't hurt, just a nice thud that got her to shivering as he moved to her legs. He pounded at the large muscles of her thighs, massaging them with the deerskin falls of the flogger. She loved to watch him work but so often she was holding on to a St. Andrew's Cross or lying on a spanking bench on her belly so she couldn't see him. The position he'd chosen wasn't normal, but she loved looking at him while he worked her over. There was an intensity in his eyes and his body moved like it did when he was dancing. He couldn't help it. He'd been born with a natural grace that was infused in everything he did.

His wrist flicked and another delicious thud echoed through the room before he ran the vampire glove over her leg.

She couldn't help her moan as he started just left of her pussy and worked his way all the way to her toes. She yelped a bit as he playfully ran the exposed tacks over the tender bottom of her feet.

"Little brat thinks she'll always get what she wants, does she?" Simon asked, his voice a wicked growl.

All she really wanted was him, so yes, she thought she would get what she wanted. If the crazy erection he was sporting was any evidence at all, it wouldn't be too long. Still, she knew the game he wanted to play. She bit her bottom lip and gave him her widest-eyed stare. "No, Master. I just want to please you."

He grabbed the pillow her head wasn't resting on. He tossed aside the vampire glove. "Hold your hips up."

Now her eyes were wide because she wasn't sure what he was doing. She did it anyway. If he wanted a little creative torture, she would go with it. She planted her feet on the mattress and forced her hips up. Her leg seized, but Simon was right there.

He shoved the pillow under her ass and then helped her down, his big hands easing the tension from her leg. "I swear I'll have you in a yoga class if it's the last thing I do."

She sighed because it always felt so good when his hands were on her, strong fingers stroking all the pain away. She would pretty much do anything he wanted. He couldn't know how crazy that was. "Yes. Just name the time and place and I'll do it."

A frown passed over his face, but he seemed to shut it down. He got to her feet and placed one in between his hands. Warmth encased her. "Do you know what I want from you tonight?"

"Pillow sex?" It finally hit her why he'd done it. "My ass. You want my ass."

He brought her foot to his lips and kissed the arch. "Yes. I'm going to take you there and I'm going to make you like it. But not until you're begging me for it."

"You like to make me beg," she groused. "How about I just beg for it now?"

He lightly bit her foot, making her jump. "Brat. I'm in charge. This happens when I want it and how I want it, and don't you dare forget it."

He dropped her foot and stood up, his hands going to the knot of his tie. She watched him as he undid the tie and then unbuttoned his vest and dress shirt. Inch after inch of gorgeous skin was uncovered. She watched as sculpted muscles moved, divesting himself of the clothes he damn straight wasn't going to need.

He settled the shirt, tie, and vest on the dresser and then turned to his kit.

"Shouldn't I be on my belly?" She kind of thought hands and knees were required to make this work.

"Questioning me again? For your information, I have you right where I want you and your commentary outside of screaming in pleasure and calling out my name is not required.

Spread your legs."

She swallowed as she noticed the plug in his hand. It was big. Really big. How the hell was that going to fit? But then it was probably a smidge smaller than Simon. She took a deep breath and spread her legs wide, keeping her feet flat on the mattress. It put her on full display. There was no question of where Simon's eyes went. He stared at her for a moment, that massive plug in his hand. He stared at her pussy.

"It's lovely. Do you know how pretty you are, love?"

It was hard to feel self-conscious when he was whispering reverentially about how gorgeous her girl parts were. "No, babe. I haven't taken a mirror down there lately."

His eyes lit up. "Oh, I can change that."

He grabbed his kit and came back with it, setting it on the floor by the bed. He settled a towel next to her and placed the plug and what looked to be regular old, wouldn't-have-her-anus-screaming lube on top of it. She breathed a sigh of relief. And then she grimaced because the bastard apparently carried around a damn mirror.

"I want you to look at yourself."

"Come on, Simon."

He reached up and tweaked a nipple, sending a nice bite of pain flaring through her system. "Who's in charge?"

He was and he seemed damn intent on reminding her. "You are, Master."

He brought the mirror between her legs. "Then look. I want you to watch."

The mirror had a flap that came out and allowed it to sit on the bed between her legs. Sure enough, she could see the folds of her pussy and beyond. Because the pillow gave her height, she could see the little pucker of her asshole. Between the pillow behind her back and the one under her butt, she could see the whole show.

Simon lay beside her, his hand on her belly. "Isn't it pretty? Do you want me to tell you all the things I love about it? I can show you now. Look at how this pretty pussy flowers open for me."

His hand slid down and she had to catch her breath as his

fingers slid through her labia. She could see how his fingers moved over her delicate flesh. It was another type of dance, and naturally Simon knew all the moves. Pearly fluid pulsed from her core, coating his fingers and making it easy for him to slip against her flesh.

He dipped a finger in. Just one. So much less than she needed. She was aching and empty without his cock. "I love your cunt." He rotated that single finger deep inside her. "Do you know what it feels like when this cunt locks down around my cock?"

The temperature in the room seemed to rise with every nasty, hot word that came from his mouth.

She shook her head.

"It's as close to heaven as I've ever gotten." His hand moved again, that finger fucking deep and then drawing back out. "Look at all that cream."

Her arousal coated his finger. "You do this to me. I never did this before."

"You didn't know how hot you could get. Now you do." He pulled out and brought his finger to his mouth, sucking the juice off it before leaning down. "Taste yourself."

He brought his lips to hers, and she could taste the lingering arousal. Tangy, just the slightest hint of something sweet. His tongue swept over her lips and met hers. Their tongues played for a sweet moment and then she gasped when she felt his fingers on her clit.

"Oh, Simon." She tried to hold herself still, but it was hard.

Simon's head turned down, his eyes on the mirror. "Yes, I love this little jewel, too. Look at it. It's all ruby red and ripe for the plucking. Look at how it swells for me."

Her clitoris was on display, poking out of its hood and begging for the attention of his thumb, his teeth, his tongue. It didn't matter. She just wanted him to touch her, but he kept skirting around the nubbin. Pure torture. He was trying to make her crazy.

"Please, Simon."

His thumb did a long slow circle around her clit. Pressure was building inside. She couldn't help but squirm. "Please what, love?"

"Please touch me."

With a naughty grin, he very gently touched the tip of his finger to her swollen clit. Barely any pressure. If she hadn't been watching in the mirror, she wouldn't have known he'd done it at all. "There."

Bastard. "Harder, please. Please, Master. I need more."

"Then ask for what you really want, brat."

He never gave her an inch. "I want you to touch my clit and make me come. Please, Simon. I can't breathe."

"Tell me this is the prettiest pussy you've ever seen." He pulled apart the petals of her sex, showing her in the mirror everything she had to offer him. "Tell me you understand how beautiful it is."

"It is the only pussy I've ever seen quite like this so yes, it's very pretty and I think it's beautiful because you love it. Anything you love has to be beautiful, Simon."

"I'll take that. Now watch what happens when I play with that clit." His thumb found her clitoris again, but this time he was serious. He pressed two fingers into her pussy, fucking in and out while his thumb pressed hard on her clit.

The orgasm flashed through her like lightning striking metal. It started in her core, but sizzled along her every nerve ending. She kept her eyes open, watching even as she cried out. She watched as his fingers came out saturated with her juice, her arousal and orgasm making every inch of her flesh look dewy with cream.

"See, beautiful." He licked her off his fingers again, and she let her head drop back.

She wasn't sure how beautiful she really was, but he made her feel that way. As the languor from the orgasm spread through her, she had only one thought.

She would do anything to stay with him. To never leave him.

* * * *

Simon glanced at the clock. It was hours and hours before

dawn, but time seemed to be moving at the speed of light. This was possibly his last night with her. He wanted to make it count.

He licked the last of her orgasm off his fingertips. He loved the way she tasted. Feminine and delicate, with a hint of sweetness and a whole lot of spice. Perfection. He could eat her pussy for hours and still not be full, but that wasn't his goal tonight.

He wanted that sweet little hole.

He glanced down her body and looked at her through the mirror. She'd been an obedient girl, keeping her legs spread wide so he could see. Her pussy was beautifully swollen, a testament to how hard she'd come. Her labia was engorged and a lovely combination of peach and ruby red, but her arsehole was still tight and puckered and pink.

Lonely. It was lonely. Her pussy had all the treats. He'd been terribly neglectful. It was past time to make up for his horrible favoritism.

He let his fingers get saturated in all that sweet arousal again before letting them make their way toward that little puckered hole.

The minute he touched her, her head came back up. He was happy she seemed to not mind the restraints because they held her tight for him.

"Look in the mirror and tell me what you see," he commanded.

"Your finger is on my asshole."

He rimmed the tiny hole, thinking about just how tight she would be on his cock. She was going to strangle his dick. He would have to fight for every inch. "What does it feel like?"

He pressed against her, but not into her. He let his finger run the circle.

She shivered. "Pressure, but not pain."

"That's what I want." He let his pinky finger slide right over her entrance and pressed gently. Chelsea's sweet hole clenched, trying to keep him out. "Don't think you can win this war, love. I'll get in there. I'll claim that territory. It's going to be mine."

"It would be so much easier if you let me turn over." She panted a bit as he pressed further.

Easier, but not so much fun. “I want to look into your eyes when I take you. I want to know I’m not hurting you. I want to see them widen when my cock surges inside.”

She clenched again, this time around his finger. “What if I don’t like it?”

“Then I’ll stop.” But she would. She’d responded beautifully to everything he’d given her. He pressed in again, loving the way she began to flower open for him. He watched carefully, examining the way the little hole blossomed.

He caught her eyes. She was watching in the mirror, her skin flushed a pretty pink and her nipples standing at attention. She liked to watch, the dirty girl. That was just the way he wanted her. There should be no barriers, no room for silly embarrassment between them. They should be able to explore their sexuality in whatever form it took. That was true intimacy—no walls between them.

No job that would take her away from him. She could tell him she loved him, but the distance would do its work. He wasn’t a fool.

“Don’t move, love. I need to clean up.” He rolled off the bed, striding to the bathroom.

He washed his hands and then looked at the man in the mirror. He’d forced Chelsea to stare at herself in the mirror, but he barely recognized the man he saw. He was used to seeing a cultured man with a civilized mask. The man who looked back at him was primal, barely leashed. He couldn’t wear that damn mask around her, couldn’t hide who he was.

He wore that bloody mask too often. He’d worn it since the moment he realized it only mattered what people saw.

Chelsea was the first woman to see past his outer trappings. She’d seen the violent predator underneath his placid façade and she wasn’t scared. No, she wanted him.

He shoved his slacks off, freeing his cock. He didn’t need clothes around her. He’d keep them both naked for as long as he could, fucking her over and over again as though he could imprint himself on her.

He stalked back into the bedroom and there she was, laid out for him, every inch of her on glorious display. She was tied down for his fucking pleasure and he meant to take it.

But he was a kind Master. He had plans for her. He wasn't going to just leave her little pussy alone. No. He had plans to fill her up.

"God, you're beautiful." Her lips curved up. "I can call you that, right? Or should I say handsome?"

"You can call me anything you like, love, as long as you let me shove my cock up your pretty backside." His cock strained, standing up and pulsing, but Simon was determined to do this the right way and that meant torturing his sub for a while.

He picked up the plug and lubed it thoroughly before placing it against her hole. It was bigger than the one she'd worn on the plane, but she'd handled it so beautifully he wasn't worried. She could take him. She would open for him and take him deep inside.

He rimmed her with the plug and though she clenched at first, she took a long breath and relaxed. The plug slid in easily. He fucked her with it for a moment, watching the plug sink into her body and then pulling it almost all the way back out.

He looked up and she was staring down at him, her arms still tied to the bed. She clenched around the ropes, her hands making fists.

"Tell me how it feels," he said.

"Like you're inside me. I want more. I want to feel you and not that plug."

He had something else he wanted her to feel. He picked up the vibe he'd bought in the hopes one day he'd be able to use it for just this purpose. It was a little U-shaped device that started humming the minute he pressed the button. One side was meant to sit on her clit and the other to slide up inside her body and stimulate her G-spot. She didn't need lube for the vibe. Her pussy was soaking wet. He slipped the humming vibe in her cunt and then settled the outer piece over her clit.

"Simon!" She nearly shouted his name. "Oh, my god."

Her body was vibrating, her hands so tight around the rope.

"Don't lose my plug or I'll take the vibe out and we'll start again with a nice long spanking." He prayed she took it seriously. He didn't want to start over. He was minutes from being where he wanted to be.

"I won't. Oh, oh." Her body shook as she came again. "It feels so good."

He bet it did. He was stimulating every nerve she had in her pelvis. He wanted her relaxed and ready for him. He wanted to make her crave his cock in her every hole, to miss it when they were apart. He climbed on the bed, straddling her torso. "Suck me."

Her head came up and her tongue licked along his cock. She showed no signs that his weight bothered her. Her eyes were on his cock as she sucked the head, running her little tongue over the weeping slit of his dick.

She hummed along his skin, licking and sucking as her eyes rolled back and her body clenched again.

Yes, he could feel her orgasm through the moans and groans that vibrated against his skin.

Her tongue whirled around his cock as she sucked him hard, her eyes steady on his. She was open and vulnerable. He'd never dreamed she would let him in with such sweet invitation. He let his head fall back and gave over to the sensation of her mouth sucking him down. Servicing him. He would be her slave in their daily life, working to make sure she had everything she could want, but here, oh, here, he was the Master and she the sweetest sub imaginable.

She sucked him deep. He opened his eyes and watched as those lips of hers moved across his dick.

He wasn't going to last long if he let her go much further. "Stop, love."

She gave him one last drag and then a shaky smile. "Simon, the vibe is killing me. I don't know how much more I can take. Oh, my god."

Sweet torture. "Let me give you something to take your mind off endless orgasms."

He leaned over and worked on the tie that bound her right hand.

"I'm okay. I don't need to be set free," she said, her arm dropping.

He freed her second arm. "It's for me. I want you to touch

me."

He needed more than just her tied up. He needed her hands on him, stroking his skin, reminding him she wanted him, too. He wanted her arms around him when he took her. If he had forever, he'd tie her up and down and any way that would bring them both pleasure, but he likely only had tonight and he wanted to be surrounded by her. The memory of her clinging to him would be something he held on to.

He moved off the bed, grabbing the lube and slicking up his cock before removing the mirror and taking its place between her legs.

He was shocked at how his hands were shaking. Never had he wanted anything as badly as he wanted her.

She looked up at him, a quizzical expression on her face that rapidly softened, and then she was reaching for him. "I want you, Simon. Oh, wow, that still feels amazing. Simon, I want you. Please come inside me. I want you to be my first in every way. I love you."

Her first. He wanted to be her last. He leaned over and kissed her, his lips brushing hers in an oddly sweet kiss before he got to his knees and gently eased the plug out. He watched as she tried to clench down, unconsciously trying to keep the plug inside.

He had something else to give her. He pressed his dick to the little rosette of her arse. It was still slightly open from the plug and he took advantage, pushing in until his cockhead was inside.

So hot. His heart rate tripled and the pleasure nearly sent his eyes rolling in the back of his head.

Chelsea reached for him. "Damn it, you just have to be bigger than the plug."

He couldn't help but chuckle. She did this to him. Only Chelsea Dennis, of all the women he'd ever met, could take him out of himself with just a few words. "It's going to get better, love. I promise. So much fucking better."

He pressed in, feeling the drag of that damn vibe on his dick. God, no wonder she'd come twice since he'd put the damn thing in her. It tightened her up, but worse, he could feel the vibrations all along his cock.

"You like that." Chelsea was grinning up at him. Yes, this was why he'd chosen this position. He wanted to look at her, be joined with her in more than just the physical.

"I love it." *I love you.* He wouldn't give her that because she was leaving, but it didn't make it any less true. He pressed forward, gaining ground. Her asshole clenched around him, the feeling making his heart pound.

He thrust in and pulled out, trying to give her time to get used to his size, but she moved her pelvis. He slid in, almost to his balls. So tight. So perfect.

"It's killing me," Chelsea breathed. Her hands were on his waist, nails starting to dig in.

"Just wait." He pressed in ruthlessly. They hadn't gotten to the really good part yet. He wanted to watch her when he showed her exactly how good it could be. Every inch he gained seemed to go straight to his balls, tightening them up and readying them to go off. To give her his come. It was only right because it was hers. It fucking belonged to her.

He settled in, his balls finally caressing the globes of her backside. He couldn't go any further. She'd taken every inch of him. He held himself there for one moment, enjoying the feel of being as deep as he could go. He reached out and touched her breasts, tweaking her nipples so she gasped and squirmed on his dick.

"Hold still," he commanded. He needed a minute, too. She was too tight and the feel of the vibe threatened to unman him, but he was determined that she would come again. He wanted to feel her come, watch her.

"It's too much." Her jaw tightened.

"Give me a second." He started to pull out, slowly so she would have the chance to feel it.

Her eyes widened, rounding out, and her mouth opened. "What is that?"

"That's why you let me do this to you, love. That's what this is supposed to do." He went slowly until he was almost out and then slammed back in. He found his rhythm, one sure to make her crazy. He thrust in and dragged out and then pounded in again, making sure to grind against that vibe on her clit.

She spread her legs as far as she could, shoving her pelvis up and fighting to keep him inside.

He let go. He wouldn't last long, but he could feel her getting ready to go off again. Her whole body convulsed around his and he couldn't hold out a moment longer. His balls tightened and he dove in one last time. Her arsehole closed on his cock and he shot off in seemingly endless streams of come. Pure pleasure jetted through him, and he was more connected to her in that moment than he'd ever been to another human being in his life.

He slipped out of her body and let himself go limp. Every ounce of energy had been drained and a sweet pulse was pounding through his system. His head found her breast and he let himself lie there.

And then remembered how being caged bothered her. He started to push himself off, but her arms came around him, holding him tight.

"Don't go. I like it. I like being close to you," she whispered as her arms wound around his body.

Don't go. He wouldn't ever go, but he didn't have the choice. He sighed and let himself relax. "I'm not done with you."

She chuckled a bit. "I wouldn't dream that you were, Master."

He wouldn't be done until the second she walked out, and even then he feared he would never stop loving her.

Chapter Twenty-One

Chelsea wished Simon would look at her. Since they'd sat down for breakfast, he'd completely ignored her. He was busy staring at a paper she wasn't entirely sure he could read. Did he speak Italian? Or was he just avoiding her?

"Could I have the butter?" Surely he would have to look up to pass her the butter.

Nope. He was far more graceful than that. His eyes never left the paper in front of him as he passed her the small dish. "There you go."

She took it and set it down because she'd lost her damn appetite. He was utterly maddening. He'd made love to her the night before over and over again like he couldn't breathe if he wasn't on top of her. He'd taken her pussy and her mouth and god, he'd taken her ass. She'd never felt closer to another human being than she'd been to Simon in that moment. She couldn't have imagined how amazing that had felt.

Though she was a little sore this morning and the man who'd made her that way had gotten up and been all dressed and perfectly pressed and right back to his British reserve. Her passionate lover had been replaced with a man who seemingly had no interest in her at all.

Maybe honesty would shake him up. "Could you pass me a

bag of frozen peas?"

His eyes finally met hers. "What? What on earth do you want with frozen peas at this time of the morning?"

Apparently the Brits weren't big on anal sex aftercare. "My anus is swollen because someone shoved an extra-large rod up my butt."

His lips started to curl and then a calculating look came over his face. "You're sore. You should stay here today. I'll get you an ice pack. If you're sore, you can't run the way you should."

She couldn't help the growl that came out of her throat. "I can't run the way I should period. The state of my backside is meaningless. We're not putting the op off. I was just trying to get you to talk to me about last night."

And he was right back on the paper. He flipped it over. "What about last night? It's inevitable you're going to be a bit sore your first time. I'm sorry about that."

He was so frustrating. "I'm not sorry. I get the sore part. You're a big guy. That's not what I'm really talking about. I'm trying in my not so subtle way to have a relationship talk. I want to know if last night was real." She had no other way to ask except the obvious. She didn't want to, but she was supposed to be working on honesty. "Do you love me, Simon? I told you I love you."

She'd gotten utter silence back from him. His body had made promises though. His body had worshipped hers. That had to mean something.

"You say you love me, but you're still going to work for Ten." He took a sip of his coffee. Apparently tea was for afternoons. His brows had climbed in a way that made the question really more of an accusation.

"I told you why I want to do that. I don't have a place here. Ian doesn't need me." She had to find a way to make him understand.

He sighed as though dismissing the entire conversation. "You'll do what you need to do. I'll do what I need to do."

"What does that mean?" She really wanted to halt the conversation all together. It would be so much easier to retreat, to act like the night before had meant nothing to her. She could pull her armor around her and go right back into her safe little shell, but she was so sick of that shell. It was lonely in there and being a coward proved she hadn't changed. "Simon, I really don't understand what's going on. Could you please tell me? I'm not asking to be a bitch. I'm asking because I'm really confused. You said you wanted me."

"I did. I do. We're quite compatible in bed."

She let a moment go by, waiting for him to say something more. He sipped his coffee and ate his toast.

She needed to know once and for all. "What happens when I get this package and we neutralize the threat?"

"You go your way and I'll go mine." He sat back and sighed a little as though the whole conversation was really boring him. "Our contract is over the minute the op ends."

She nodded and stood. It was time to walk away. He'd wanted her and he'd had her, and apparently that was enough for him. She would go and get cleaned up and dressed and she wouldn't sleep with him again. It hurt too much when she loved him and apparently he didn't even like her anymore. She'd done her best and it hadn't been good enough. All that was between them now was that stupid contract.

She stopped at the doorway, the words coming out of her mouth before she could think to call them back. "What did I do wrong?"

"Excuse me?"

In for a penny… "I'd like to know what I did wrong. I'm not good with relationships so I don't really get why you don't like me anymore. Could you just tell me what all this was about? I promise I won't yell or throw a fit no matter what you say. I just…I would rather know."

His jaw tightened. "You didn't do anything wrong."

"Why did you pursue me if you didn't really want me then? If I didn't do something wrong. Was it a game for you?"

"I don't play bloody games and I don't like the one you're playing right now. What else do you want from me, Chelsea? I've given you everything. I've allowed myself to look like a fool over you."

"So you are mad at me?" She felt like she had whiplash and

she felt like she was twelve again and trying to figure out why a man who should love her suddenly didn't.

Let it go. Let that go and see Simon for who he is. Nothing in your life is going to work if you can't let go of what that monster did to you. He wins every time you push someone away.

"I'm mad at myself, Chelsea." He stood up and started to pace, his body long and elegant in his suit. "I should have known better. I should have understood that it couldn't work. I'm not going to fight you. You've made it plain what you want."

"So you're mad I want to work for Ten. Why? Did you think I would be happy staying at home all the time?"

"I gave you a perfectly good alternative. You could become a missing persons expert."

"And I'll look into it, but Simon, you don't get to choose my career." Had he thought once he got her in bed that she would be so enthralled with him she would give herself up? "You really did just see it as a challenge, didn't you? You wanted to see if you could change me. If you could make me into something I'm not."

"That's not true," he shot back.

"From where I'm sitting it is. Here's the funny thing. You really did change me. You really did show me I could be something more. I wish you could have loved me. I really do because I love you, Simon. I realized something last night. I've spent most of my life wanting to go back and make all the bad stuff go away, but I would have been different. If I hadn't gone through that pain, I would have had a different life, one that didn't lead Charlotte to Ian, one that wouldn't have led me to you. So I think I'll take the pain because I wouldn't change a minute of it. Not even this one. I really do love you."

His face went a vibrant red and his hands were suddenly fists clutched at his sides. "Prove it. Bloody well choose me. Stay with me. You say you love me, but you're walking out…"

There was a knock at the door and Simon turned. She watched as he seemed to shake off the volcanic rage that had threatened to explode. He was always in control. Oh, she'd seen his dark side, but never this rage, this passion that had almost consumed him.

Walking out? What was that supposed to mean?

The door opened and Ian walked in, his face flushed. He moved with none of his natural grace. "I'm taking Charlotte to the hospital."

She completely forgot about their fight, her heart suddenly in her throat. "What? Why? Where is she?"

"I've called in and they're waiting for us. She's with Jesse waiting for the water taxi. She's spotting. Heavily," Ian explained.

Oh, god, she couldn't lose the baby. "I should go with her."

Ian shook his head. "Please, let me take care of her."

Because if she was there, Charlotte might turn to her sister when she should look to her husband. Chelsea nodded, tears in her eyes. This was yet another thing she had to let go of. She had to honor her sister's husband. "Of course. Please let me know if she's okay. We'll get the package so as soon as she's ready, we can go home."

Simon shook his head. "We can't. We're down a man. We're not doing this today."

"It's your op," Ian said, his face pale. "You have to do what you have to do, but I need Charlotte well. I'm worried the stress of having Chelsea targeted is getting to her. I'm sorry, man."

Simon held out a hand. "There's no need. Call us if you need anything. We'll come down with you."

Ian's head shook. "No. Just keep her safe here."

What he didn't say, Chelsea surmised, was that he didn't want to make a vulnerable Charlotte a target because she was too close to Chelsea. Ian turned and walked out, and Chelsea couldn't stand the slump to his shoulders that told her he wasn't sure tragedy hadn't already happened. For all he'd said he wasn't sure he wanted kids, Chelsea knew he would ache forever if Charlotte lost this baby.

Whatever was going on between her and Simon had to be put aside. "I'm going to get that package."

Simon stared at the door Ian had just left through. "I can stop you. I can keep you here."

"Don't. I owe her. She's my sister and she's in trouble because of me." She had to make him understand. "We can do this. You and me and Jesse. All we have to do is walk into the post office and pick up a package. It will be fine."

"We wait."

"And if Charlotte loses the baby? Or if they save the baby? We just expect her to wait here until you're sure no one can touch us? I get that somehow I've disappointed you. I didn't turn into the person you wanted me to be, but this is who I am, Simon. This is who you made me. I can't run anymore. You took that away from me. I have to stand and fight for the people I love. I already let my friend down. I can't let her down, too. Yes, you can stop me, but you'll take something precious away from me."

She'd just found her courage, her willingness to sacrifice. She couldn't be put in a cage again, slotted into a little box where she was meaningless.

Simon stood there for a moment and when he turned around, he was calm and placid again. "All right then. Get cleaned up. Dress in nondescript clothing. Nothing that would bring attention to yourself. Hat and sunglasses. We'll walk about for a bit to make sure no one is following us before we go to the post office. We'll leave when Jesse gets back."

She turned away, knowing she'd won the battle, but terribly afraid that she'd just lost the war.

* * * *

Simon felt the sun on his skin and wished they were exactly what their cover was—two tourists on vacation, taking in the sites of Venice. Two lovers on holiday.

Not two agents who could barely speak to each other about to embark on something dangerous.

Her hand was in his, but she wasn't clutching it the way she had before. Since that moment she'd learned her sister was in trouble, she'd been all business. Once he'd told her the op was a go, she'd pulled away from him.

What game was she playing? And why did he find himself hoping he could get her to stop playing it?

"Piazza San Marco," she said with the slightest hint of a

grin. "Where the only thing that outnumbers the tourists are the pigeons."

St. Mark's Basilica was to his left, the grand church rising up from the piazza. There was already a long line waiting for tours. Straight ahead was the lagoon, the emerald waters just beyond the two massive granite columns that held symbols of the two patron saints of Venice, St. Theodore and St. Mark. He could see the gentle sway of gondolas in the lagoon.

And lots of pigeons to his right.

One landed right on his bloody shoulder. He shuddered and nearly jumped a foot to get the blighter off him.

"You're afraid of birds," Chelsea said, a light coming over her face for the first time. "Oh, my god, the great secret agent is scared of a little bird."

He wasn't afraid exactly. He simply hated them because they were winged rats with dead black eyes. And that had been an awfully big bird. "I don't like anything that can land on me."

"You were a pilot. Shouldn't birds be like your brothers or something." She seemed deeply amused as he jerkily sidestepped another bloody pigeon. It was one thing he definitely preferred about the States. Birds in Europe were so much more entitled. Birds in Texas ended up on his plate.

"My brother doesn't carry a million different bacteria in his beak." Clive merely carried judgment and intolerance in his system. Simon was used to both.

She smiled at him, the same open smile he'd started to crave. "I so wish I had a video camera. I would watch that again and again."

"We should keep moving," he said, beginning to walk. There was a set of shops ahead that seemed relatively pigeon free. He touched his earpiece. It was flesh colored. When they'd switched to this piece of technology, he'd allowed his hair to grow out the slightest bit, covering the receiver in his ear. This particular earpiece however only went to one other person. "How are we doing?"

Jesse was set at the post office. He'd followed them briefly and then wound back around to make sure there was no one waiting for them. "I'm in place, partner. I've got eyes on the site and I haven't seen anything that looks like a tail."

It was precisely why Ian had broken in the night before. They wanted to keep the watchers watching the wrong place. Adam had put out false information that Chelsea would be in Italy in two days.

By then, hopefully, they would be gone.

Jesse continued. "And according to the big guy, Charlotte is resting comfortably for now. They should have some test results shortly."

"Excellent. We'll pick up our package and then prepare to leave." He didn't even want to examine the bloody thing until they were in the air. He would, but the instinct was strong to grab it and run and not look back. He was being far too cautious. He knew it. This was why he shouldn't have kept control. He was too close to the mission, but he couldn't leave it in another's hands, either.

He was stuck. Like he was stuck with Chelsea.

"The place looks crazy crowded though. The post office that is. They've got people in a line outside just to get a number to get in," Jesse explained.

He didn't want her out in the open. "We'll grab an espresso and give it fifteen minutes. Call back then."

He let the line go dead.

"What's wrong?" Chelsea asked as he led her to the line of shops on the edge of the piazza. He could smell the rich espresso and cappuccinos the cafés were pouring.

"There's an issue at the post office." He should have thought about that, should have planned to be there at the least busy time.

"Ah, it's packed. Yeah, they can get that way. There's usually only two people working and one of them is always on break, and let me tell, you don't complain or they kick your ass out and you have to go to the back of the line. The joys of government jobs in Italy. Do you know how hard it is to get fired here? Impossible. So they treat it like their own little kingdom. After the first time I got kicked out, Charlotte wouldn't let me go back. Naturally they all loved Charlotte." She sighed. "Any news from the hospital?"

"She's doing fine. They're running tests and they'll know

something very soon." If there was one thing he could believe about her, it was that she adored her sister.

What had it taken for her to let Ian go without her? A few months back, she wouldn't have. She would have been right in that taxi with them, causing trouble and forcing herself into their marriage.

What had changed? Had it really been him?

"That's good. I hope." She stopped when he did, walking from the sunlit square into the dark café.

"Do you want anything?" It was as good a way as any to pass the time and likely cheaper than taking her to the Louis Vuitton store he saw up ahead. Though he would really like nothing more than indulging her, he doubted she would take him up on it. After all, he'd been a right bastard to her.

She gave the barista a tentative smile. *"Un espresso, por favore."*

"Due," he said, holding up two fingers, though he knew how to count in Italian. Just not much more. He could speak French, but most Italians hated the French as much as they did the English. He wouldn't even go into how they felt about Americans.

She nodded and turned to begin her process.

"I'm sorry about this morning." He didn't really have any right to treat her like that. He'd been angry, hurt, and he'd taken it out on her.

"Me, too. I wish I understood."

He sighed. He couldn't comprehend how she was confused. "I don't think a long distance relationship is going to work. Ten isn't exactly going to allow you the freedom to date who you like."

"What are you talking about?"

Maybe it was easier to have this conversation in public where he wouldn't give in to his need to shout. "You'll be wherever Ten says you'll be and I'll be where Tag needs me. How did you see this working, love? You tell me you love me and then you turn around and make it impossible for us to be together."

"Simon, I work from a computer. I can be wherever there's

Internet."

She was being naïve. "He won't allow it."

"He will if he wants me. Now that I know he doesn't have you to hang over my head, there's really not a lot he can do. I guess he could arrest me."

He felt his fists clench, the very thought causing his blood pressure to rise. "I'll kill him. Don't think I can't do it."

Those lips curled up again. "I know you can, babe. I'm not stupid. I know there will be times when you're somewhere in Europe and I'm stuck in the States, but that's kind of the way two income households operate and I need to work."

"I don't want you to work for Ten."

Her shoulders squared as though ready for a fight. "I don't think it has anything to do with distance. You don't trust me."

He rarely really trusted anyone at all. "I certainly don't trust Tennessee Smith."

She put her hand on his arm. "I don't want Ten."

"You say that now."

She sighed, obviously frustrated. "All right. I won't take the job with Ten. Are you going to get a say in any job I do take? Can I only take the ones you approve of? How long will it be before this comes between us again? I'm willing to change to be with you. You were right. We're very much alike and you have issues, too. Are you willing to deal with them to be with me?"

He thought about Ian. It must have gone against every instinct in his body to allow Charlotte to come to Italy, but he'd done it because she needed to be here. Even though it might have cost him, Simon rather thought Ian would make the same choice again because that was who Charlotte was.

Chelsea was becoming something new, a better person, but she would always chafe at restrictions that didn't make sense to her.

Would she ever understand that he needed her close to him to feel safe? Was it fair to her? Was he really expecting her to live in his back pocket? Or should he examine himself and realize that he wanted her at home waiting for him, dependent on him. And that wasn't her. This was a woman who not only ran when she needed to, she'd built the only business she could. Did he really want to make her dependent? He hadn't fallen in love with her because she was docile. Was he trying to make her into something she wasn't because he couldn't trust her as she was?

He needed to let her go.

Or could he just love her and hope for the best. Wasn't that the essence of faith? The universe wasn't going to open up and promise him that everything would work out, that he would have what he wanted.

All he could do was love her and hope that she loved him enough to not leave.

Was that what a marriage was for? Two people who loved each other enough to stick it out. It might not work, but he couldn't know if he didn't try.

He had three choices. He could let her go. He could push her. She'd never had a lover. It would buy him a lot of tolerance. He could bend her to his will, but there would likely be a cost.

Or he could take that mighty leap and just maybe get everything he hoped for.

"Simon?" Chelsea tugged on his jacket. "Simon, I can't believe what I'm seeing."

He brought his head up and there was a man in a black hoodie, despite the heat of the day. He strode across the square toward the little café.

A bright smile crossed Chelsea's face. "Al!"

"Chelsea, no." He reached out for her, but she was moving too quickly and she obviously hadn't figured out what he had.

"Mr. Weston," a low voice said from behind. "You should probably let her go. Don't worry. We'll take you with us when we go."

He felt something hard press into his spine. Gun.

He had to hope that Chelsea would forgive him when he killed her friend because there was only one reason Albert Krum was alive and walking toward her.

Al was The Collective.

Chapter Twenty-Two

Chelsea couldn't believe what she was seeing, but she kept her voice down. It was like a ghost had appeared in the middle of the city. "Al? Is that you?"

He grinned her way. "Yes. God, Chelsea, it's good to see you, baby."

She had zero idea why he'd called her baby, but maybe his near-death experience had made him more affectionate. A huge weight lifted from her shoulders. She hadn't gotten him killed. "I thought you were dead."

He hugged her, pulling her into his arms and squeezing tight. "Definitely not dead. I need your help though."

Nothing added up. She'd been so sure they would kill him. Simon had been sure. "How did you get away?"

"I'm really smart."

A cold chill went through her. That wasn't an answer and now she was actually thinking. She'd just reacted when she'd seen him, her relief a palpable thing. But now she had to think. He really should be dead. There had been zero reason for The Collective to keep him alive after they'd realized she wasn't going to be allowed to turn herself in.

She pulled back, but he kept his hands on her elbows, holding her fast. He was stronger than she remembered. Or stronger than he'd wanted her to believe? He was dressed differently than he had before. When they'd met, he'd worn baggy clothes. He'd either lost weight or he'd been hiding his true form. Either way, it was time to retreat. "I should get back to my partner."

His hands tightened and there was a cruel twist to his lips. "Your partner or your lover?"

Shit and double shit. Simon was going to kill her. She brought her eyes up, really looking at him. They'd been friends through e-mail and the Internet. They'd only met once and yet she'd run to him. She hadn't thought about anything except the fact that she hadn't gotten him killed. She was an idiot. "You didn't get away, did you?"

He started to turn her around, his hand firmly on her arm. He was far more muscular than she'd assumed. She was forced to move with him, and her heart started to pound. Simon was standing at the bar of the café, but he wasn't alone. There were two men right behind him, very likely with guns pressed to his back. One was tall and muscular and seemed to be talking to him. The other stood back, his face a grim mask.

Slowly Simon stood up, his eyes finding hers. Arctic blue. Yes, she was definitely in trouble.

"I didn't have to get away from my own men. I did have to find a way to get you away from your new friends, and that proved far harder than I could have imagined." He dragged her into the café. "Don't scream, baby, or I'll have Gio or Bill put a bullet in your boyfriend's back. I'll be honest, I never thought you were the pretty-boy type. I kind of got the idea that you were afraid of men. It was why I decided to play gay when we met. I realized you would be more comfortable with me if you thought I wasn't after your body."

"Why are you doing this? Let Simon go. He has nothing to do with this." Chelsea wasn't even sure what "this" was, but she couldn't stand the thought of him getting caught up in the trouble she didn't even know she had. Her mind was still trying to wrap itself around the problem. She tried not to look at Simon, but her eyes kept finding him, assuring her that he was still alive.

"You brought him into this when you ran to him. I had to do

a nice little scramble. I thought I would be the one you called for help. Why do you think I sent those fake bombs? You were supposed to call me and I would have been the white knight. The first bomb was meant to send you straight into my arms. I put the Deep Web addy on the second one to throw the police off, but it came in handy. I was going to use the whole 'Al in danger' thing in case you called the police, but I didn't think you would. Now, I'm glad I had it as a backup. I don't like having to scramble." He nodded to his thugs. "I think we can take this party home, boys. Maria, thank you." He gave the barista an arrogant smile. "You've gotta love mob-run establishments. I've had fourteen places on the lookout for you and pretty boy here since the minute I found out you were in Venice. It was clever to sneak in on a private plane, but it's so easy to bribe officials here and you stand out. You can't quite fake walking properly."

"They were looking for a girl with a limp." He was right. There was very little she could do since she'd refused therapy up to this point.

He smiled oddly her way. "Hey, don't think it bothers me. I kind of like the idea of the cripple queen taking out her enemies from the shadows. I always adored your backstory. It's why I decided to befriend you. You amuse me. I'm quite obsessed at this point."

A few things were falling into place. "There was never a package."

"Of course there was. It just wasn't what you suspected. After I realized you weren't doing what I expected you to do, I had to figure out a new plan. Something that would get you to the place I needed. You see, I figured out where most of your hidey-holes are. I built a program to scour the web for any signs of you, your face, signature, any known aliases. It took me a while, but I found a little map of all the places you stayed at during your years on the run. I thought I would come and get you in Dallas and then I was going to suggest we hide out here. You fucked that strategy up when you ran for the Brit. So I came up with the 'Save Al' plan. I wasn't particularly happy when you hung up on me."

"I didn't want to." Simon had made her do it because he was

smart.

Al's lips curled up. "I should have known."

"What's in the package? Is it really at the post office?"

"Of course. I also have two men in the back of the post office. You know that the best illusion is something real. I needed to send you something so the receipt would make it to your apartment. I needed something real for you to find. This didn't have to be so hard. If you had called me when you should have, your friend wouldn't be involved at all and we could have been perfectly civilized."

"You sent bombs to my house. I hadn't talked to you in weeks, and even then it was casual. I ran to Simon because I knew he would protect me."

His jaw tightened, and she knew he didn't like her explanation. "You never mentioned you had taken a lover. And I wasn't ever going to actually blow you up. You're far too valuable to me. You're The Broker. Do you know how long I looked for you?"

"Is this the part where I put my arms up?" Simon's voice was perfectly calm as he lifted his arms but not before he thumbed the device in his ear.

Chelsea gasped and forced herself to stumble a little so Al's eyes would be on her and not Simon. He held her firmly.

Simon had touched the earpiece that connected him to Jesse. Jesse would know something was wrong.

"Get your arms down," the man named Bill said. "Unless you want me to force you."

Simon moved his arms back to his side. "I don't particularly think it's fair for you to force a man to leave a perfectly good espresso behind. I was just assaulted by pigeons, man. I need something fortifying."

He was trying to give Jesse clues about where to start the search. The piazza was known for pigeons and there was only one espresso café overlooking it. Maybe she should try to make it even clearer. She hoped Jesse could hear her because she couldn't exactly shout. "What are you going to try to do, Al? Are you going to shoot us right here in Piazza San Marco? You might be able to pay off the officials and the mob, but I doubt you can keep all those tourists quiet."

Simon's hair curled slightly, covering the small device. Adam had been smart to select flesh-colored material because now she couldn't see it at all.

"Gentlemen, if you wouldn't mind escorting Mr. Weston to my boat, I would appreciate it. We're going to take a little ride. I have a lovely place here, very quiet and private. I bought it after our time together. I think you'll like it. I had it redone."

He was acting like they were going on a romantic trip. So he wasn't just a criminal, he was crazy, too. Lucky, lucky her. "I would really like to know where you're taking my friend."

Simon was being escorted from the shops. She watched, utterly helpless as the two thugs with him turned right toward the lagoon and what she expected was a dock with a boat. Boats were really the only way to get around Venice with prisoners in tow. Her stomach turned at the thought of being separated from him. Please let Jesse hear what was going on.

"Hold my hand like a good girl and know that I have more than one person watching us," Al explained. "If you try anything, they'll give the signal to my men to drop the pretty boy. British? Again, not what I expected."

"What did you expect?" She did as he asked, threading her fingers through his. His hand was oddly soft, so unlike Simon's callused, masculine one.

"I expected you to behave the same way you have for years. I counted on it. My initial plan was to try to hire you quietly. I sent out a few feelers, but you never replied."

She'd had three requests for contact on old Deep Web addresses she'd used when she was The Broker. She'd ignored them. They'd only been slightly tempting and then Ian had asked her to do the European op and she'd shoved all thoughts aside. At the time she'd thought it was because she was trying to stay out of trouble, but now she knew she'd wanted to be with Simon, wanted to prove to him that she could do good. Those little requests had been like shots for an alcoholic, but Simon was her wagon and she was fully on.

"I went legit, Al."

He chuckled as he started to lead her out of the café, the

same path Simon had been taken down. "You're incapable of going legit, baby. That would be like Jeter quitting baseball at the height of his career because he wanted to teach poor children how to read. It's ridiculous. You're a singular talent."

There was no point in arguing with him. "What do you want with me, Al? Is that really your name? See? How good could I possibly be if I don't know your real name?"

"My real name is Albert Nieland."

"You own Nieland Affiliates." The very firm involved in the lawsuits that led to the deaths of lawyers and judges.

"So you put that together. I am the top one percent of the one percent. I have more money than God, but you know what I've never found?"

A soul? Some humanity? "What?"

"A woman interesting enough to be my queen. You see, I get bored easily. I have a genius-level IQ. There are very rarely problems I can't solve. For fuck's sake, I'm about to change the world by bringing quantum computing to the people. Well, the people with heaping scads of cash anyway. I'm the smartest man of my generation, but you're better than me."

"What are you talking about?"

"Three years ago my company ran into trouble. We were negotiating a mineral deal with an African dictator."

Oh, god. She remembered that deal. "You came to me for leverage. I sold you information that proved he was keeping pay from his army."

He smiled. "And I used that information to fund a coup, and I got my mineral deal from the man I put in his place. They executed him, you know. I have the videotape. Took off his head in the middle of the street. Quite invigorating to know I'd done that, but I couldn't have without you. I'd tried three other information brokers and several mercenary units. You were the only one with the magic touch. I knew then and there that I had to meet the man behind the mask. And then I became obsessed when I discovered the man was a woman. That was when I decided I wanted to meet you, but to do that I had to be in your world. I was already a brilliant programmer. I decided to become a hacker."

Her stomach took a deep dive. This had been a long game, and she hadn't even known she was playing. "And you called yourself Al Krum."

"I was smart enough to put a construct in place. If you had checked up on me, you would have seen what I wanted you to see. I was a mild mannered but brilliant hacker, the type of man you could feel comfortable around, depend on. We had some fun times. I have to tell you Chelsea, it was freeing. I liked being Al Krum. Some of the work we did together was amazing."

"I don't do work like that anymore."

He stopped, his eyes narrowing. "Why? Is it the pretty boy?"

"I only did it because we needed the money. My sister and I needed cash."

"To run from your father's syndicate. I know your story. You and your sister had your father killed. You know if you'd been men, you could have taken over. Your cousin did when his father was murdered. According to my information, you had a hand in that as well."

That had been Ian, but she wasn't about to point that out. She was kind of hoping he didn't know much about Ian so when he came rushing in at some point, Al would be surprised to have his ass handed to him by Satan. "I'm not on the run from the syndicate anymore. My cousin called off the hit on me."

"Yes, he's very likely a good connection. The Brit is not. I checked him out. He's got ties to Malone Oil. I don't like David Malone. He and that son of his are very unreasonable."

"Meaning you can't buy them?"

"Meaning they work against their own best interests. I don't understand them and I believe it's best to destroy the things we don't understand. It doesn't matter. Eventually my group will weed them out and they'll be replaced with more logical partners. My point is Simon Weston is a problem for me."

And that was a definite problem for her. "No. He's not going to cause trouble. He's just my friend. He's a lawyer. I got scared by the bombs and I didn't know where else to go, so I ended up at his place."

His hand tightened on hers. "Oh, Chelsea, I'll teach you not to lie to me. I can't prove it but I would bet he's former MI6. Ian

Taggart doesn't hire lawyers. He hires ex-agents. And I figured out who took out my men at that rattrap motel he took you to. That was easy though. Even CIA agents can be bought. Actually, they can be bought for quite cheap."

Her heart nearly stopped at the thought. "Ten?"

He chuckled. "Wouldn't you like to know? We could make it a game. I think I've done a good job of making it impossible to prove, but you are the best. I would love to watch it. We can even bet on who the mole is." He stopped as they reached the dock. "Were you serious about going legit?"

Chelsea could see a very lovely boat moored to the dock. All around her tourists were snapping pictures. The lagoon was full of sightseers enjoying the beauty of the Italian sky. A light breeze cooled her skin. A perfect day and Chelsea finally understood that Al was going to kill her if he didn't get what he wanted. He would likely do it quickly or he would kill Simon in order to gain her compliance. He wouldn't have mentioned the possibility that Ten could have turned if he meant to release her at some point.

He wanted a playmate. A deranged and criminal playmate to match his own personality, but a playmate.

And she had to give it to him.

She rolled her eyes a little. "Do you really think I would give everything up? I've had to play the game because big sister fell for an overgrown Boy Scout. You've checked out Taggart. You have to know he watches my every move. He threatened to turn me in to the Agency if I don't play it straight. I'm biding my time until I can walk away. Once they get settled in and start having kids, they won't give a shit about me anymore."

She could see Simon's head. He was turned away from her, but at least he was upright.

Al brought her hand to his lips. "Well then, I think I can help. I can make it look like you died. We'll build a whole new identity for you and we can rule the world together. Like it should be. I just need you to do one tiny job for me."

She followed him to the boat, praying all the while for the strength to do what she needed to do—to save Simon. He was all that mattered now. She just hoped he could forgive her for what she would have to do to make sure he was alive at the end of the day.

* * * *

Simon sat in between his captors, staring straight ahead, his arms cuffed in front of him. That had been a mistake because he could still work with his hands, but he supposed he looked more normal like this.

Of course, he couldn't do a thing until he knew where Chelsea was. If the boat took off without her, he would risk it. He could see exactly how he would do it. He would get the one to his left with a quick header and then strangle the one to his right. They'd taken his SIG, but he could easily get one of their pieces. He would drop them both and then he would go after Chelsea.

The only reason he hadn't was the very real possibility that there were eyes on them. He believed the little bugger. He'd planned this out, and Simon couldn't risk getting Chelsea killed. Not when he had backup.

"Simon, it's Jesse. I've gotten some weird feedback from your unit. I need you to tell me what's going on."

It could be difficult to hear outside conversations. The comm unit worked best in direct speech. Unfortunately, he couldn't exactly explain the situation.

He kept silent and prayed Jesse figured it out. It was possible he would just think the unit had gone bad.

"Simon, I need you to cough if you've been compromised."

Thank god. Simon coughed discreetly.

"Understood. Can you give me an idea of how many?"

He coughed again. Three times. There were three of them for now. The two guarding him and the man driving the boat. "Does anyone want to tell me where we're going?"

Jesse should be able to hear his side of the conversation easily.

The biggest of the two stared his way as the boat swayed. "That is not for you to know."

Italian. His English was good, but thickly accented. Al was

American. He had to wonder if this was a hired thug. The smaller of the men was American, likely working security in some form for Al's company. Where the hell was Chelsea?

"Seems a bit rude, if you ask me. Can you tell me if the girl is coming with us?" He couldn't be too overt or he might tip his hand. He needed Jesse to know that he was on the move and Chelsea wasn't necessarily with him. It also wouldn't hurt for him to know who'd taken them. "Will Mr. Krum be joining us?"

"Are you kidding me?" Jesse's voice came in low. "The little fucker. We can make his death real. I'm on this, Si. Keep the comm line open as long as possible. I'm calling Ian to let him know and then I've got Adam on this. He'll tie in to the security cams. Keep your face up so we can find you."

Simon looked to his left and sure enough, there were cameras on the docks. He stared directly at one, giving Adam's facial recognition software the best shot at identifying him. Even a starting place to look would help.

All the while, that one question was beating against his skull. *Where is Chelsea? Where is Chelsea? Where is Chelsea?*

What was that bastard planning on doing with her?

He hadn't intended to kill her. That was obvious from the earlier information the DPD had sent. The bombs hadn't been real. They'd likely been meant to send her on the run and away from her normal protection. When he had her alone and vulnerable, he would have taken her easily. Physically, Chelsea would be easy prey.

But then he didn't really want Chelsea. This had been an elaborate setup to gain control of The Broker.

If they got out of this, he was going to make everyone understand that The Broker was gone. He was getting bloody tired of people trying to take advantage of his wife.

Damn. If he got out of this, he was going to marry that insane woman and he would just have to deal with the fact that she was never going to be a quiet little sub. She was fierce, like her sister, and always would be, and it was why he loved her. For everything she'd been through, she'd kept walking, kept living until she found a reason to change.

Him.

It was time to stop questioning, to stop letting his past inform his future. It was time to place some faith in her.

The boat dipped and he looked back, breathing a sigh of relief. There she was. Her face the tiniest bit pale, Chelsea followed her captor. She seemed almost placid, but he saw the tightness of her jaw, the way her eyes didn't quite meet his.

Oh, she was upset. Something was happening and she thought he wouldn't like it.

She better throw him under any bus she possibly could. He would have her ass if she didn't.

Al Krum stood in front of him. Simon was fairly certain at this point that wasn't his real name. Obviously he had something to do with the very companies he'd accused of kidnapping and killing him. So he was some sort of computer guy. It only made sense. He'd managed to find Chelsea, or rather The Broker. He'd found her and gotten close to her.

The question at this point was what he wanted from her.

Simon couldn't miss the way Al's hand was tangled with hers.

So he knew part of what the bastard wanted. Simon couldn't wait to wrap his hands around the man's throat and squeeze.

Al nodded and the ship's motor began.

"So we're heading out, then?" He needed Jesse to know they were on the move. "I don't suppose we're staying here in Venice?"

Al settled Chelsea into a seat opposite Simon's. "I don't think you need to know exactly where we're going. I think you only need to know that you're a pawn here. If you want to stay alive, you should probably be honest with me. I want to know where Ian Taggart is. We can't find him. Is he staking out Chelsea's apartment? I know he's here from the description of my man at the airport."

But he hadn't been able to track Ian. That was good to know. Ian had actually been into Chelsea's flat. The fact that Al didn't know where he was meant that not only had the distraction he'd planned worked, but that Ian had checked Charlotte into hospital under an assumed name, so she was safe.

The boat hummed beneath him, and Simon wondered briefly

if he should take the chance. The trouble was how close Chelsea was. The boat, for all its opulence, was very small. All it would take was a stray bullet to take her out. He could throw himself over the side as a distraction, but he couldn't swim with his hands bound.

"Simon, we have you." Jesse's voice was quiet in his ear. "You're leaving the docks. We caught it on security cam and we have the name of the boat. We're checking records right now. We will find you. Sit tight unless the situation changes. We'll find you, man."

Sit tight. He really didn't have a choice.

The boat picked up speed and Simon looked over at Chelsea, who was wearing that infamous mask of hers again. Aloof. Slightly disdainful. She turned away and started asking Al a question.

Thank god. She was going to play it safe.

He looked out over the lagoon as they turned back into the canals and hoped safe was the way they stayed.

Chapter Twenty-Three

Chelsea walked into the magnificent townhome. She had to give it to Al's decorator. He'd done a fabulous job. Or she. Whoever it was, the whole place was done in modern tones belying the historical architecture of the façade. Al walked in front of her, showing her into the parlor.

"I like to work here." There was an elaborate setup complete with three computers and a massive screen that connected to each.

"You can't do the quantum work here." So far, from what she understood, all quantum work still had to be done in very cold rooms. Super cold. The systems couldn't handle heat.

"No. This is more of a vacation spot. I prefer to do fun things here. Not that the quantum work isn't fun. It's just that's more like my day job, and I like to concentrate on hobbies here." He gestured to a spot behind her. "Bring him in here, please. He'll find this interesting, too."

She didn't actually like the sound of that, but she also didn't want to get separated. Somehow she thought not knowing what was happening to him was much worse than knowing. She pretended to be deeply interested in his computer setup when all the while she just wanted to look at Simon, to let him know how sorry she was for bringing him into all this.

It appeared everything was top of the line, including his Internet setup.

"I feed it through the company so it has use of our satellites as well as our fiber optic lines. My father left me a fortune, but his real gift was the technology company. He viewed it as mere speculation, a blip on his radar, so to speak. He was more interested in his real estate companies. He thought I was an idiot for paying more attention to tech. I hope the old fucker's watching me from Hell."

Where Al would no doubt join his dear old dad one day. "So I take it the woman on the video wasn't your mother."

She'd only seen a few seconds of the video they'd found while she was at the ranch before they'd whisked it away from her, but it had made her believe they were serious.

Al sighed a little. "No, my mother is alive and well and shopping somewhere. Useless thing. I did need to make you believe they really would kill me so I picked up a prostitute. No one will miss her and my guard got to screw her before he killed her. It was a good deal, really. You will note that I didn't touch her myself. I have a thing against germ-infested hookers. I'm a bit more picky than my friend."

Excellent. She would note his standards in the very sarcastic eulogy she was planning for him. "So what is this job you want me to do?"

He stared at her for a moment as though deciding what he should do. She could almost see that big brain of his working. So smart. He was brilliant, really, but that didn't mean a thing because there wasn't a lick of humanity behind his eyes. "I suppose since you know about Nieland Affiliates that you've figured out this is all about a court case."

How much should she tell him? She worried if he picked up on another lie, someone was going to get hurt. "Yes, this is about the patent case."

"Very good, sweetheart. I've used this approach before and it's worked for me, but this particular case is the most important of all. You see, I'm a little behind. Some dumbass professor in Seattle has been working in a private lab and they are just the teeny tiniest bit ahead of me. I found out and made the decision to move ahead with applying for the patent. Patents are a little like races—you really want to be at the finish line first even if you have to cheat to get there."

Billions of dollars were on the line. Whoever got credit would be owed big bucks every time a company used the technology. It would apparently go to Nieland or the man who actually made the breakthrough. Al was determined to make sure it was his company.

"Why don't you just money whip them?" Chelsea tried to make her tone as bored as possible.

Lawsuits like this one happened every day. Big companies could easily get the little guys to give up by burying them in legal fees. Nieland could keep a lawsuit going for decades. It would potentially give them time to catch up and overrun the little guy.

"I did try. This suit has been ongoing for three years. I expected him to give up by now. I even offered the little fucker a fifty million dollar deal to pull out." He shook his head. "Do you know what he's planning on doing with it? He wants to put it out there for free. Like it's a fucking app of the day or some shit. He's a do-gooder and he's funded by some organization with deep pockets that wants to save the fucking world through technology. He's not going away so I needed to do something about it."

"That's when you started killing the people in your way," Simon said.

She looked at him. He was so beautiful but she hated the way his suit had wrinkled. He was always perfectly polished. He needed that control and they'd taken it from him.

Al nodded. "Yes. I did. It was fun actually. I thought about hiring assassins, but that's a bit clichéd, don't you think? I wanted to be the one who pulled the trigger, so to speak. I made a little game out of it. Could I find ways to kill them with a stroke of my keyboard?"

"Pacemakers?" Simon asked as though he wasn't talking about murder, just another socially acceptable topic of conversation like the weather.

Al gestured to his thugs and one of them moved away.

"Absolutely. That was easy. Medical devices aren't truly well protected. Who would think to fry a man's heart through the very device that's supposed to save him? Besides, it hurt a competitor. Now they're being sued for faulty products. I love a twofer."

"You changed the DA's prescription," Chelsea surmised.

"Again, a very simple thing to do. I exchanged it for something she was brutally allergic to. So sad. I actually had to pay for that one. The pharmacy chain is part of my organization."

The Collective couldn't have been happy about that. It must have made it uncomfortable at their yearly evil picnic. "So you killed the people who would be troublesome and replaced them with friendlier judges and lawyers. I don't see what the problem is."

"The problem is the judge I selected to take over the case decided to fucking retire. The new judge is very antibusiness and extremely young and healthy. I haven't figured out a way to kill him yet. I need it to look like an accident. What he does have is a very nice sports car with technical assistance. You know what I'm talking about."

She did. Many luxury vehicle makers offered services that aided the driver in everything from giving directions when lost to calling emergency services when they detected an accident. Cars had gone high tech years ago, and that made the very technology that enabled numerous services vulnerable to hackers like herself.

She drove a car that didn't have a computer chip in it.

"You want to cause an accident."

"Oh, no." He strode to stand right in front of her. "I need you to cause an accident. A bad one. Judge Gold is on a family vacation for the next few weeks. He and his family are at their cabin in Colorado. In order to get to the cabin, they have to go over several mountain passes, but one in particular the judge tends to drive on a daily basis. Wolf Creek Pass. It's quite dangerous if a driver is distracted."

"Why me? Why couldn't you do it?"

"I'm having trouble with the system. Believe it or not, the freaking car company has better firewalls than the medical companies. And this is a small manufacturer. They aren't a part of my group so I can't find a way to get access. It's been troubling. The judge is only going to be in Colorado a few more days. I need to get this done now. I need the best."

So he needed her. Shit. "So this is the job you tried to hire me for?"

"I thought it would be the kind of thing that could bring us together. I intended to pay you handsomely. And then I was going to show up as our hacker friend Al again and get close to you. But then I realized you'd been compromised. You stopped running and settled in with a company with known Agency contacts. Why did you go with your sister? You didn't need her."

The Broker might not have needed Charlotte, but Chelsea certainly did. She was fairly certain Albert Nieland wouldn't get the whole "family love" thing. "I was bored and I wanted to see how the other side lives."

So well. She loved being in an odd family. The McKay-Taggart team watched out for each other, and that was why she had to stall.

Because no matter what he thought of her, Ian would be here and not just to retrieve Simon. She might have told herself that at one point in time. Ian would come to save her because she was his pain in the ass sister-in-law.

Yes, Satan was getting another hug from her.

She had to give him time to get here. He would come with Jesse and no matter how many men Al had, they wouldn't hold Ian Taggart back.

She had faith. It was weird since for so many years she'd had absolutely none, and now she realized that she had faith in her giant ass of a brother-in-law, and she definitely had faith in the man she loved.

Simon would come around. She just needed to keep him alive long enough to give Ian time. Then she would do whatever it took to stay close to him. She would wear him down, get past his hurt, and convince him that she was the right woman for him.

"Has it been terribly boring for you?" Al asked.

Boring? It had been the best months of her life. Nothing was boring with Simon. The man could turn afternoon tea into the sexiest twenty minutes of her day. Everything about the man called to her. She just wished she'd heeded the call from the beginning because even a few wasted months were too much.

She wanted every minute she could have with him.

"So boring." She had to keep her tone bland. "They watched me every damn minute of the day. The only times I was allowed on the net was when the big guy needed help. But I didn't have anywhere else to go. Maybe now I do."

"Oh, I'll give you a place, sweetheart. Like I said, I've always wanted you. Do you understand how hard it was for me to keep my hands off you while we were here?"

"Why did you?"

"Like I said, I didn't want to scare you away. You were more comfortable with me because you thought I was gay. And also, your sister is a little intimidating. She was a roadblock between us. I thought about taking her out, but you seem to care about her and no one else."

She fought hard not to shudder at the thought. "Well, she's moved on."

"Yes, I can see that. And so have you. When did you decide to give sex a try?"

"I thought it was time." It had been time the minute she'd met Simon.

"And he was the right guy?" His eyes trailed toward where Simon stood in between his thugs.

"He was there and he was single. Don't try to make it more than it was. He's attractive and I was curious." God, please let him understand.

"So he's meaningless to you?"

"To me, yes, but he means the world to Ian Taggart. Big Tag doesn't leave his men behind. You should let him live and then Tag probably won't come after you."

"I doubt that." His voice went low and seductive. "But then I also doubt that he's meaningless to you. You forget, dear, that I had a man watching you at the Malone Ranch. Gentlemen?"

The bigger of the two men reared back a fist and planted it firmly in Simon's stomach. There was a dull thud and then Simon was sucking in air.

"Don't hurt him!" She couldn't stop the shout that came from her mouth.

The smaller of the two took a swipe at Simon's jaw, the sound cracking through the room. Simon's body crumpled and they started to kick him hard.

"Please!" She turned to Al, utterly unable to watch her big handsome Brit get his ass kicked.

He gripped her arms. "Yes, I rather thought you were lying to me about your feelings for that idiot."

Simon's head came up, his eyes laser focusing on Al and the place where his hands were on her body. "I swear I'm going to kill you for touching her."

Al hauled her close. "I'll do more than touch her." He put his arm around her throat, the other hand sliding possessively over her belly. He leaned in, whispering in her ear. "If you want him to live, you're going to do everything I tell you."

Slowly, her eyes on Simon, she nodded.

She shivered as Al spoke into her ear, softly, like a lover would. "I knew you would say yes to me. Why don't you sit down and we can get started. I bet you can get into that system before they can kill your boyfriend."

Her hands shaking, she took a seat at the desk.

She let her fingers start to fly as she began to test the system for weaknesses. As Al began to talk to his men, she found his weakness.

He wasn't watching her. As quickly as she could, she slipped onto the web and pinged a certain site. It wasn't much, but a smart man would see that little tiny open door and push his way through.

She prayed Adam Miles was as smart as she thought he was. Simon's life depended on it.

* * * *

He wasn't sure how much time had passed, but it seemed endless. Pain was a constant companion, but he couldn't let it stop him.

No more than an hour, he estimated. An hour of being

brutalized. Sixty minutes of pure hell. Three thousand six hundred seconds of holding on to life and breath because he knew all he had to do was keep going. All he had to do was wait until they turned around because he had an ace up his sleeve.

In his hand, really.

They'd made a mistake when they'd hauled him out. A mistake that might save him and Chelsea, but he had to wait to take advantage.

While they'd hit and kicked him the first time in the parlor, the key to the cuffs had fallen out of the big thug's pocket. He'd failed to reattach it to his larger ring and the tiny silver thing hit the carpet. Simon had quickly turned, almost certain that he'd be discovered, but they were far too busy kicking him in the gut and then the back. He was sure the move looked like he was trying to protect himself when all he was doing was getting to that key.

He'd been able to palm the key in his fist, but then they'd dragged him through the house, their hands so close to the place where he was hiding his prize that he'd been certain he would lose it.

They'd carried him up a flight of stairs, tied him to a chair, and then shoved a filthy rag in his mouth. He would have explained that he wouldn't scream, would deeply prefer to not come down with whatever new form of syphilis was obviously on the gag. He had a perfectly nice gag in his kit and he knew it was clean, but they didn't give him that option. His jaw ached because the rag was improperly placed and forced his muscles into positions they shouldn't be in. He had to concentrate to get enough oxygen.

But all his focus was on that little piece of metal in his left hand. He forced himself to squeeze so he could feel it, know it was real and there. If he didn't, he sometimes thought he'd made the whole thing up. A dream to help him get through the nightmare.

Pain exploded along his chest as he was hit again. He could feel his skin open, blood beginning to flow.

"Don't kill him. The boss wants him alive so he can kill him," a voice said. It was hard to see at this point. "I guess this shows you what happens when you fuck the boss's girl."

His girl. Chelsea was his. Only his. She'd never been anyone else's, and if he died here, she would still be his. Al had no idea who he was dealing with if he thought taking Chelsea Dennis would make her his. Chelsea couldn't be taken. She had to be earned.

"I'm just playing. I won't kill him. Brits are sturdier than you think." One of the two had brass knuckles on his punching hand. He was the taller one. Gio. He didn't remember the smaller one's name. Probably because Gio was attempting to knock him into next week.

He had one thought in his head. Holding on to that key.

He would get his chance. He had to stay alive long enough to use it.

There was the dull thud of a fist hitting his gut and then he felt it. It had gotten bad, he acknowledged. It took his brain longer to process the pain.

It was taking all he had to remain upright. The ropes didn't help all that much. He had to waste some of his concentration on those, too. When they'd started to tie him to the chair, he'd puffed up, making himself as big and wide as possible so when he needed to, the ropes would be loose. All he needed to do was release his breath, pull his arms in, make himself smaller so he had wiggle room.

"Partner, are you still there? Give me a cough if you're conscious." Jesse's voice had grounded him. The whole time, the entire beating, he'd had Jesse talking in his ear. He'd given him updates. They'd lost him in the canals, but they were trying their hardest to figure out who Al Krum really was. After they'd worked over his face in a particularly brutal fashion, Jesse had come up with a name.

Now they were looking for property owned by Albert Nieland or any of Nieland Affiliates subsidiaries.

It was just a matter of time. His team would be here.

And Chelsea would be working her hardest to make sure she bought them some time. At least he hoped that was true. She hadn't quite managed to be the crazy, cold-hearted bitch she'd used to be. No.

Another hard punch and he had to keep his fist closed. It was hard, but he thought about how her whole face had changed when she'd realized he was in danger.

She wasn't a good field operative. She was horrible because she couldn't hide her caring for him.

Her love.

Damn it all. She loved him. She couldn't hide it. She'd looked like her whole world was falling apart. It wasn't something she could fake.

He was a believer. He'd been stupid to think she would lie. He could find a way to deal with her need to work. He would do anything to stay by her side.

Including stay alive.

Another blow. The sound. The pain. Fire licking along his flesh. His vision started to fade, but he held strong. He couldn't lose that key.

If they would just stop, just take a break, he could handle the situation. Didn't torturers take long lunches in Europe?

"Simon? I need a cough to know you're still there."

Damn it. He'd forgotten. He coughed, the very act making his body ache. His bones rattled in his body as though they weren't attached to his muscles, as though they were floating around under his skin, battering against one another.

He forced himself to cough.

"Good. Stay with me. Say something only you would say so I know it's you. If you could only say one word, what would it be, man?"

Only one word mattered at this point. Only one thing in the world could keep him holding on when it would be so much nicer to let go. "Chelsea."

"All right. It's you." A sigh came over the line.

Gio stared down at him. "You won't see her again, you fool. Do you really think you're going to survive?"

It was a good opening to let Jesse know how he was doing. "No. I think I just felt my left kidney go. The situation is actually quite dire. I can barely see anymore." His left eye had completely swollen shut. His right was getting there. His lungs ached. He was fairly certain he would lose consciousness soon. "I don't think I'll last much longer. Don't you need me alive in order to keep Chelsea working? She will ask to make certain I'm still alive rather soon. She won't just take Nieland's word for it."

"Adam thinks he's on to something." The words were quiet in his ear, solid. "Chelsea's working the system. She pinged the McKay-Taggart site, and Adam thinks he can follow it back. He's almost there. Please hang on. We'll get to you."

The line went quiet.

Close, but no cigar. He was still on his own.

There was a chiming sound and Gio stepped back. Simon could hear him talking softly in Italian. He forced his head to turn so he could see where the other one was. He'd turned, pouring himself a drink. It looked like he was on tormentor break time.

How long did he have?

Could he make it work?

His hands were in his lap. They hadn't switched them behind his back as they should have. He rather thought they'd been afraid to. They would regret it.

He slipped the key forward and twisted his hands so he could see the lock. The key was right there. He twisted again so he could fit the bottom of the key into the lock. He struggled with it. It didn't want to go in.

Frustration cracked through him, but he held firm. He nearly lost the key twice, his fingers fumbling when they should have been graceful. He touched the key to the lock and it finally slid in.

"The girl is taking her time," Gio said in his thick accent as he rolled a smoke in his hand. He strode to the window and opened it. "You're right. He can't handle much more. I thought he would last longer. That Russian certainly did."

The American joined him. "I suppose the Russian was used to getting his ass kicked. Brits and Americans have gone soft. Too much good living. Not that I'll be immigrating any time soon. I think he's out. We'll have to wake him up for the coup de grace."

Simon kept his head down. Best if they thought he really was unconscious. He could see the little key in the lock, but his fingers were numb. He had to make them work the way he wanted.

He lifted his head to see where they were. The American was smoking, too. Their backs were toward him as they looked out the window.

"Do you think he'll kill the girl or give her to us?" Gio asked.

The American stared out the window. "Don't know. Don't care. All I care about is that she does her job. If she can figure out a way to take the do-gooder judge out of the picture, then I say give her a quick and painless death. She won't get that from you."

Breathe in. Move. Just his index finger at first and then his thumb. In position. *Breathe out. Slow. Patient.*

As the Italian laughed—an ugly sound—he forced his fingers to turn the key. "No, she won't get a quick death from me. You know I like to make it last."

There was more laughter, which was good because it covered his tiny groan as the cuff eased and blood flow started back into his hand.

Bloody fucking hell that hurt.

"Simon, how many people are in the room with you?"

Two quick coughs.

Gio sighed. "See, he's still alive. Maybe I should get the Taser. See if his balls can fry. That should pass the time."

Jesse's voice again. "Upstairs?"

He kept his hands in his lap. They were still across the room. They shouldn't be able to see one side had come undone. "Yes. My balls can fry, I'm sure. Go get Al. I'm ready to talk."

The American laughed. "You don't have any information we need."

"Of course I do. I worked for British Intelligence for years. I work for McKay-Taggart now. Trust me, I have valuable intel. I can help. Just go and get your boss. He won't be happy you killed me without giving me a chance to talk." If he could get rid of one of them, his job would be easier. Already he was prepping. He took a long breath that made his chest ache, preparing to let it out, to loosen the ropes.

Gio took a puff off his cigarette and slapped his friend on

the arm. "Go. Tell Nieland. I'm sure he'll find it amusing."

The American sighed and started for the door. "Don't kill him while I'm gone."

Someone was going to die. It just wasn't going to be him.

"Now, let's have some real fun," Gio said, tossing his cigarette out the window and walking to the closet. He opened it, likely to get out that little Taser that would most definitely fry his balls if Simon had any intention of allowing it close to his body.

Simon hunched his shoulders and let the ropes slip past them. He was still tied up, but he got his right arm free.

With a powerful thrust that could only come from pure adrenaline, he stood, the chair cracking around him.

Gio cursed and turned, but it was far too late. Simon wasn't allowing the pain to stop him. He wanted one thing and one thing only. Revenge on the man who'd made him briefly feel small.

He gripped the cuffs in the hand that was still manacled and used it to punch out. Gio's nose immediately broke, the crunching sound satisfying to his ears.

Simon had him on the floor before he could shout out. He brought his knee right down on the bastard's cock and let his weight sink in while he hit him over and over again. The world was seen through a hazy film of red and he wondered briefly if his vision was clouded with blood.

It didn't matter. All that mattered was this was the man who'd planned on raping Chelsea. His brain twisted him into the man who had tried, who'd taken something precious from her. And her so called father. He beat on the man who'd broken her bones and sent her into hiding for decades.

Vengeance was his right. She belonged to him. It was his responsibility to make sure she was safe and happy and that her nightmares couldn't come back.

"Tag, I'll take this one." A familiar voice penetrated his rage. "I know a little something about this."

Jesse? He could hear him in his ear, but it was echoed.

"Hey, partner. That dude's totally dead. You did a good job but now it's time to come back from crazyville. I know. Crazyville's a fun place, but we have a job to do. Chelsea's still in danger so we need to stop beating a dead horse and get out of here. I'll try to find you someone else to kill." There was a short pause. "I always think about killing something else when I'm in this state. Just trying to refocus his attention."

"You should write a book," Tag said. "Let's try this my way. Simon, get your ass up. It's time to save your girl and get the flying fuck out of here. I'm tired and cranky and I need to get back to the fucking hospital because my wife is there alone."

Simon sat up, taking a deep breath. That was a mistake because his lungs weren't functioning properly. "There are at least two more downstairs."

Tag winced as he looked at Simon. "There were a couple outside, too. We took care of them before we scaled the wall. If you hadn't killed that fucker I would have for hitting me with a lit cigarette. Asshole. Dude, you are twelve kinds of fucked up. I'll call and get you a bed next to Charlie's."

He must look a mess if Ian was wincing.

Jesse looked worried as well. "Maybe you should lie down. We can get Chelsea out of here."

Simon stood, every muscle in his body aching, and he was fairly certain he had a couple of cracked ribs, one of which might or might not have punctured vital organs. He reached up and straightened his tie. It was soaked in blood, but it didn't matter. It was a motion that settled him, let his mind concentrate on something other than the fact that his body didn't want to move.

He did leave his ruined jacket behind though.

A gentleman didn't leave a lady waiting. "Let's go and get my girl."

Chapter Twenty-Four

Chelsea stared at the screen in front of her. Damn it. How had she found it so fucking fast and why had she bothered trying to find it at all?

Simon. Because Simon was somewhere in this house and he was being tortured.

Tears blurred the screen. She couldn't allow them to fall. She'd already given up far too much. She was supposed to be tough, to be able to make the big decisions. Yeah, some tough girl she was. She'd folded the minute they'd touched him.

He was her weakness and her strength. The fact that Simon's life was at stake had made her focus harder than ever before.

Unfortunately, it also made her more creative. She'd found the tiny little hole in the company's defenses.

"Are you in?" Al breathed the words behind her, crowding her. His hand was on her shoulder as he leaned in. "Holy shit. I've been trying to find a way in for days and you do it in an hour. I always said you were the best."

She wished she wasn't at this point. "I used a backdoor. They're updating the system. They're fine-tuning the way they deliver their own personal satellite radio. It looks like it's low security, but it provided a back door into the high-level area. Everything is connected. No one thinks about that. This is a full system. If you can get into one area, you have the keys to the kingdom."

"That is amazing. I'm going to print out everything you did. I want to read it. I want to see the way your mind works."

And then he would also see that she'd pinged McKay-Taggart with her location, but it really didn't matter. She'd either be dead by then or a prisoner who wished she was dead, so it didn't matter. It was a lot of code. If he wanted to read through it like a juicy thriller, who was she to stop him? "Okay, but it'll take a while to print."

"Not now, sweetheart," he said, his eyes wide as he took in the screen. "We still have a job to do. Have you gotten into Gold's account?"

She'd been delaying that moment. She needed more time. "I can get into the system. But the accounts have individual passwords. It could take a while."

"Get up. Let me try. I've got some highly specialized code breaking software on here." He tugged on her hand until she got up.

Well, of course he did. The minute he got what he wanted, Simon was likely dead. She had to think of something. Anything. Distractions. He seemed to like to talk about himself. A lot. "What are you going to do with all that code breaking software when you don't need it anymore?"

He turned to her, a quizzical look on his face. "What do you mean?"

"The quantum computer. It's the ultimate code breaker. It processes so quickly that what would take a regular computer years to go through, it can do in seconds." Normal computers functioned by processing commands one at a time. They did calculations quickly, but breaking a code took enormous amounts of time if the code was properly formulated. There could be infinite combinations of numbers, letters, and symbols. The modern computer would have to test each of them individually.

Theoretically, the quantum computer could run them all at once.

Al frowned. "Only a few people are going to be able to

afford the technology, Chelsea. This is another win for the people who truly shape this world. It's not like Average Joe is going to buy a quantum computer."

"But you aren't really worried about the average man, are you? Rival companies will definitely be able to buy the tech and they'll use it." She needed to play to his obvious paranoia. "Business is war, right? This is like mutually assured destruction. Everyone will be able to hack everyone else's systems. I guess that's not so bad. If everyone can do it, then no one can have complete power."

His face had gone a nice shade of red, and now he wasn't thinking about the judge or trying to blow his airbags as he went over a dangerous curve. She wasn't foolish. The GPS would show where the car was every second. Al would know exactly when the judge was vulnerable, and that was when he would strike. Even a moment's distraction on a mountain pass could lead to an accident. If the airbag blew, it wouldn't be a momentary distraction. It would be a disaster.

And the minute that judge was dead, so was her lover.

"I have to figure out a way to keep it out of my rival's hands."

She shrugged, happy to have given that big evil brain of his a problem to chew on. "If it's publically for sale, you really can't."

His eyes narrowed and she realized she'd made a mistake. "I can. I can do anything. Don't underestimate me, Chelsea. If I want to delay the rollout until I find a way around the obvious problems, then I'll kill everyone who gets in my way."

"What about all the other companies who are in some stage of production? You're not the only one working on this."

He went silent for a moment, and Chelsea was a little worried she'd pushed him too far. Finally he took a long breath and leaned forward. "I told you I'll take care of it. I will deal with the problems in a way that I see fit. Tell me something. Are you going to get in my way? Are you one of the people I'll have to take out? Because I would hate to do that. I think after we deal with the problem of the Brit, we'll get along nicely, but I can terminate any experiment I have to."

She shook her head, but she was lying. She would do anything she could to stop him. Anything. And if he killed Simon, then she would make it her life's mission to take him down. She'd done it before, but she would enjoy it this time. She would enjoy making him hurt on every level.

The door opened suddenly and Al stood. "I thought I told you to give us some privacy, Bill."

Bill, who seemed to be Al's second in command, strode in with the confidence of a man who didn't think he was about to die. Chelsea hoped he was wrong.

She was going to kill Adam if he was playing Candy Crush or something when he was supposed to be calling in the troops.

Al turned to her. "I expect you to find his account code and quickly, or else I'll bring your boyfriend in here and you and I can watch as I let Giovanni cut his balls off his body. I don't suspect he's quite as pretty as he was before, but so far he's still in one piece. You're the only one who can keep him that way."

She really hated him. Loathed him. Wanted him dead in the worst way, but she sat down and looked at the computer screen again.

How long until Adam found them?

She glanced back and saw Al and Bill talking quietly. Al had taken to wearing a holster with a nasty looking pistol under his arm. He hadn't threatened her with it. It simply hung there, a reminder that he was in power. Bill had a weapon as well. Two big guns and she couldn't even run properly.

If she got out of this, she was working out. Life required too much damn running. She needed to join the cardio club or she wouldn't survive the next time someone tried to kill her.

Or her man. She had to fix herself so she could defend that amazing piece of British hotness she'd somehow snagged.

She turned to the computer. She was afraid if she didn't make some progress, he would do exactly what he said.

"He says he's got information for you." Though Bill's voice was low, she could still hear him.

"I don't need information from him," Al shot back.

Bill seemed determined to play the voice of reason for his boss. "He's former MI6. You know he worked with one of the agents we turned."

Baz. Basil Champion. MI6 agent turned Collective butt munch. He'd shot Damon Knight and sold out for cash.

Someone in the Agency was a mole for The Collective. She had to get that information to Ian somehow. Even if she and Simon died, Ian needed to know that he couldn't trust Ten until he found the mole.

So much was riding on her. This was actual real power and it kind of sucked because she was worried about letting down the people she loved. The games she'd played as The Broker had been for tyrannical children like Al who had no conscience. She was past that now.

Now power was used to protect her family.

She let her hands fly across the keyboard. He would eventually see what she'd done and she would be punished, but she had to get the information out there. She shot an e-mail to the only address she knew by heart. The main e-mail for McKay-Taggart. It was something Grace would check and she would be able to send it on. She hit send just as she felt a presence behind her.

"What the fuck was that?"

Her whole body went tense. "I'm just trying to get into the system like you asked. I don't know how much I'll be able to control though. I should be able to lock and unlock the doors. I don't know how hard it will be to manipulate the airbags. I'll have to see if there's a way to screw with the sensors remotely."

His hand wound in her hair, and he lifted her out of the chair. "That's not what I'm talking about, bitch. That was a fucking e-mail. Do you think I don't know what a fucking e-mail looks like?"

Damn it. She had to try to calm him down. He was on the edge. She went on her tiptoes to keep her balance. Her scalp flared where he pulled on her hair. "I don't know what you're talking about."

He used his free hand and slapped her right across the face. Pure shock. She heard the crack and felt heat and pain. If he hadn't been holding her so tightly, her head would have snapped around from the force of it. "Do you think I'm stupid? Do you think I can't tell what you're doing?"

She struggled but he was too strong. "Fine. I told my brother-in-law where we are. He'll be here soon. You might kill me, asshole, but you will not like what Satan does to you."

"You think I'm afraid of him? Bring him on, sweetheart. And I won't kill you. Like I said, I have plans for you and they don't include death. Not yet." He forced her back into her chair. "Now you get into that system. You've already cost your boyfriend. Let's bring him down and see what he looks like and then for every minute you don't get into that system, I'll take a toe. Then we'll move on to fingers and more interesting body parts. How does that sound?"

Pure fear sparked through her and she turned back to the computer. She flew through the initial security.

"Bill, bring that fucker down here. I want her to see what happens when someone defies me."

Tears dripped from her eyes as she struggled. She started the software. It worked with encryptions. It started up but she had zero idea how long it would take. How much of Simon would be taken from him before she managed to figure it all out?

Her brain worked overtime. She couldn't let this happen. She couldn't let them hurt Simon.

She would have to get the gun.

She could feel Al behind her, watching her every move. His hand came down on her shoulder.

"If you try anything, I'll just kill him and then I'll find that sister of yours and I'll take her, too. I don't want it to be like this between us. I want you to be my partner."

Slowly, she stood, turning. "I'm scared. You're scaring me. Can't you prove you can be tender, too?"

It was a risky move, but she couldn't think of another way to get close to him. She didn't meet his eyes, but allowed her body to soften. She used the advice Charlotte had given her. It made her sick to her stomach, but she did it.

"You want me to kiss you? You know they're dragging him in here any minute now. You want him to look up and see me kissing you?" He leaned in, his mouth close to hers. "I like the way you think. That's a bit of torture I hadn't expected."

He pressed his lips to hers and she went for it. She reached for the gun. She flicked the snap off and as he started to press his body to hers, she could feel the metal against her palm.

"Get your bloody hands off her," a voice roared.

One minute he was all over her and the next he was being tossed across the room like he weighed nothing.

She looked up and Simon was there. Bloody and brutalized and alive.

And her hand was empty.

"He's got a gun," she breathed, trying to get in front of him.

Simon was already moving and another body held her fast. A mountain of muscle was in her way. Ian looked down at her. "Stay where you are, sister."

She struggled to get to Simon. "He's got a gun."

Simon was on top of Al while Jesse held a gun on Bill. There was no sign of Gio.

A loud bang cracked through the air and Chelsea held her breath. Another shot exploded through the room.

Finally Simon rolled off Al, who was left with a hole in his belly and dead eyes staring up at her.

Ian let her go and she fell to Simon's side.

"Baby?" She was almost afraid to touch him. There was blood everywhere. He slumped over in her arms.

His eyes were swollen shut. She had no idea how he'd seen anything. "He kissed you."

Oh, god. He'd seen enough. "I was going for his gun."

His lips curved up. "Next time, kick him in the balls and then go for his gun. Chelsea?"

She could hear Ian on the phone, calling for an ambulance. She looked down at Simon. "Yes?"

"I do love you." And then he was gone, his hand falling. That was when she saw it—the blood pouring from his side.

Al had gotten a shot in and she might lose Simon.

She put her hand to the wound, praying she could stop the bleeding.

* * * *

Simon came awake in a bit of a haze. He was fairly certain he was dreaming since he could hear his mother talking.

"I blame all the boarding schools, you see. Such very formal places. By the time he was ten, he preferred his school clothes. Now he's always in a suit. I suspect the reason he never took to football or polo was the fact that he would have to dress so casually. I made my sister-in-law send me photos of him in western clothes. I loved my little Si in his cowboy hat."

A masculine voice groaned. "She would decorate my hospital rooms with pictures of Simon. I swear, I thought my younger brother was a cowboy most of my life. Then he would show up and he was so stuffy."

No, he was definitely in Hell. He'd died and gone to Hell because he was suddenly fairly certain he was surrounded by family.

"And that Knight fellow was telling the truth?" His father's voice was quiet but steady.

"Yes. He served his country in both the military and in MI6," Chelsea said. "Now he works for one of the premier security firms in the world."

"My brother, the spy. I'm trying to wrap my brain around that. And you," Clive's voice went low. "What's a lovely girl like you doing with a player like my brother? You should really come to England sometime. I have a lovely hunting lodge."

It wasn't exactly a lodge. It was more like a bloody mansion in the middle of the woods, and it was where his brother and his brother's two friends went to share their women. Simon forced his eyes open. "I killed the last man who tried to touch her, you know."

"Simon!" Chelsea was suddenly at his side. "Oh, babe, you're awake. Someone go and get the doctor."

His brother looked down at him from the other side of his hospital bed. Yes, he was in hospital hell. Clive looked perfect, an older, probably much less damaged version of himself. "I'll do it. Good to see you, brother, though you look worse for the wear. We have a lot to talk about. Be back in a minute."

His mother and father were next. It was odd to have them so close. Certainly odd to have them looking down at him.

"Good to have you back, son," his father said.

"We flew down immediately when your friend called us," his mum explained. "Ava is on her way with your cousins."

He tentatively tried to sit up. Pain flashed through him. "I don't need a family reunion."

Chelsea had done this to him. He glared a bit her way, but she merely grinned at him and he had to smile back. That hurt, too, but he did it.

She was here. With him. She was exactly where she belonged. He stared at her in her rumpled clothes, her eyes puffy as though she'd been crying and not sleeping. She'd likely not left his side.

"Could you give me a moment with Chelsea?"

His mum and dad agreed, leaving the room after squeezing his hand and giving him a flurry of statements about how proud they were and how they'd almost lost him.

He turned to Chelsea. "What have you done?"

Her lovely face shined down at him. Even lacking sleep, she was the most beautiful woman in the world to him. "I realized something. When I was sitting there and you were in surgery, I realized that sometimes our perceptions aren't real. I thought I wasn't capable of being loved, but you proved me wrong. You thought your parents didn't love you, but I happen to know that you're the easiest man in the world to love. So I called them and told them everything. I made Damon back me up. Apparently everything is more believable when it's said with a British accent. They came down as fast as they could. They love you. Things just got away from them. You can have your family, Simon. You can have them back."

He hadn't known about the photographs. Hadn't suspected it at all. Hearing his parents talk about him gave him a perspective he hadn't imagined. Had they really done what they thought was best? Had they really talked about him around Clive so much it was annoying? "Do they all have to descend on my death bed?"

She wrinkled her nose at him. "You're not dying and don't even talk that way. I swear, you're never allowed to be tortured again. And you are definitely never allowed to be shot. I forbid it, Simon."

Such a fierce little thing. "I shall endeavor to follow your instructions. Come here."

He tugged her hand, trying to pull her up on the bed with him.

She settled in gingerly, careful of his body. Her head came down on his shoulder and he felt her sigh. "You scared me. I'm so sorry. I thought you were going to die and the last thing you would see was me kissing that animal."

He'd known what was going on the minute he walked in. Somewhere along the way, a deep trust had settled in where she was concerned. "That wasn't going to work, love. It's harder than you think to get a gun out of a holster. How about I simply forbid you to ever be kidnapped again."

She turned her face up to his. "Deal."

The door was opening. "If only we could write that into our contracts," Ian said as he strode in followed by Charlotte and Jesse.

Charlotte winked at her sister. "But after-kidnapping sex is so much fun."

Simon turned her way. "Charlotte, are you…."

"I am perfectly normal, thank you. And so is baby." She patted her belly. "It seems like this child takes after her father and she's going to give her mother hell for nine months. It was just some spotting. As long as I rest, I should be fine."

"Charlie, it's a boy. You should just deal with that. Taggart sperm only makes boys. Obviously, since I have two more brothers to deal with now." Ian frowned at the thought.

"What about Carys?" Chelsea asked.

Ian waved that off. "Sean's spent too much time in kitchens. I'm sure microwaves affected his sperm. Trust me. That is a boy."

Jesse stood by his bed. "They've been arguing about it for hours. How are you feeling? You know you had a punctured lung and a bullet hole in your gut."

But he could still hold on to his girl. That was what mattered. "I've had worse. Now tell me what's been happening besides my parents telling tales."

Jesse grinned. "Do you still sleep with your Pooh Bear?"

Families could be hell on a man. Still. It would be nice to sit and talk with his brother. As long as Clive kept his hands off his future sister-in-law. "I'm ignoring all questions about my childhood. I want to know about The Collective."

Ian nodded. "Chelsea's decoded a ton of proof that Nieland was behind the deaths of the judges and attorneys. Their stock is in free fall. I think we can safely say we've cut off the head."

"But like a hydra, I think we cut off one head and two will grow back," Chelsea explained. "Even if Nieland was the head of The Collective, there are others waiting in the background. There's going to be a power vacuum, but I promise you that someone will fill it. We have bigger problems than just The Collective."

Ian frowned as he stood at the end of the bed. "Ten's unit has been compromised, and I can't trust him enough to tell him. I honestly don't think I could be in the same room with him right now without shooting the fucker."

Simon's not fully functional stomach took a nose dive. "You think someone's gotten to Ten?"

Ian's eyes were somber as he looked at Simon. "I think we need to find out and that means sending Chelsea in. She's the only one who can get the access we need."

He didn't want this. He didn't want it at all, but she needed it. She needed to be important and it seemed like they all needed her. "Promise me you'll be careful."

Chelsea ran her fingers gently through his hair. "I will. I'm not going to DC. I already worked it out with Ten. He was a little late to the party. He was in the air headed here when I called him. I'm pretty sure I convinced him to turn around, but hey, if he shows up at least Ian will have a punching bag."

"Don't joke. What did he say?" He would follow her wherever she needed to go.

"I laid down the law with the new boss, so to speak. I'm going to work from home. As far as anyone knows, I'm on the McKay-Taggart team, but I'm getting clearance from the Agency. I'm strictly behind the scenes, and what Ten doesn't know is that my first job is to find the mole. If it's Ten then Ian will take him down. If it's not, then we'll give him the information. But we have to know. His team is too important to the country to leave it to chance."

"You can watch over her," Ian said. Their eyes met and it really hit Simon that this man was going to be his brother-in-law. They were family, but then they had been since the day Ian had offered him a job. Ian didn't really want coworkers. He wanted brothers. He wanted family.

And now the little boy who'd had none found himself with a wealth of riches.

"Don't worry about Chelsea. I will watch over her." He could see the worry in Ian's eyes though his face was blank. "We'll find the mole. But, Ian, how do we handle it if it's a worse case scenario? If it's Ten himself or…"

Ian's jaw tightened. "We'll take him down. Whoever it is."

Even if they happened to be named Taggart. His boss was in a horrible position. His mentor and two brothers were potential suspects.

And so was Michael Malone, though Simon doubted it. More than likely he would have to find a way to protect Michael. As Michael had always protected him.

It's what family did.

The door opened again and the doctor strode in waving his hands and speaking in rapid-fire Italian.

Simon settled in as the chaos erupted around him. Far too many people were in his room. His parents and brother were back, and Clive started telling stories about Simon's military years while Charlotte and his mum talked about what a good baby he'd been.

The doctor said something about clearing everyone out so he could examine Simon, but he played dumb and held on to his almost wife.

Chelsea looked up at him. "I love you."

He kissed her forehead. "I love you, too. What do you say we make this family a bit bigger? Marry me. You know that was in our contract. At the end of the contract, you have to marry me."

A brilliant smile lit her face. "I'm just going to have to take your word on that since I didn't read the thing. But I'm going to have to find you a suit because you are not getting married in that hospital gown."

He cuddled her close, ignoring the doctor who clearly thought all Americans and Brits were insane.

If this was insanity, he would take it.

And he was definitely going to have to find a proper suit.

Epilogue

Dallas, TX
Four months later

Something was going on at the club. Phoebe was sure of it. It had something to do with the new guy. He was some sort of doctor, but she would bet her life he wasn't a medical doctor.

Of course, she bet her life every single day she walked into McKay-Taggart.

There was a knock on her door and she carefully schooled her expression as she did for all interactions with the staff. Doe eyed, non-threatening, docile.

They should never once suspect that she could kill a man with her bare hands in about a dozen different ways. They should never find out that she'd done it more than once.

Jesse could never, ever know.

God, every day she saw him made it harder and harder to play the role she'd been given.

"Phoebe?" Grace opened the door and stuck her head in. "We're almost ready. I've got the cupcakes. Did you get the punch?"

She gave Grace her best smile. Punch and cupcakes and baby showers. It was so normal. At first she'd hated everything about this place and the stupid assignment she'd been given to babysit these people, and slowly she'd come to care about them. And she'd come to like cupcakes and punch and baby showers. "I did. And the ice cream is in the freezer."

Grace's eyes went wide. "Are you sure? Charlotte's here."

Phoebe didn't need to fake this grin. Charlotte Taggart was just starting to show and everyone knew she was adept at stealing ice cream. "I hid it behind the box of frozen broccoli that's really ice cream sandwiches."

"Smart girl. See you in half an hour." The door closed again.

How long were they going to leave her here? How long would she keep fooling these people she'd grown to like? The baby shower was for Eve and Alex, who had just adopted a little boy they'd named Cooper. It wouldn't be too long before there would be another shower for Charlotte, and if Chelsea Weston wasn't pregnant in a year, Phoebe would eat her socks.

A buzzing sound caught her attention.

She picked up her phone and her blood pressure shot straight up.

Time to play. The Joule Hotel. Room 512.

Oh, shit. She stood up, straightened her skirt, picked up her purse and walked out the door.

Time to play. Code for *do your job*. The trouble was she didn't know what the job was yet and she wouldn't know until she got to the hotel.

She walked through the lobby and got on the elevator. Luckily, everyone else was busy setting up for the party. Everyone except Jesse, who hadn't come back from lunch. She always knew when he was in a room because her temperature went up. She was dangerously close to falling for the man, and that would be a horrible mistake.

If she hurried, she might make it back without anyone noticing she was gone. There was a card in her purse. She could use it as an excuse.

Two blocks up and one over. She found a fast food place, jammed with people. The best kind for what she needed to do. She slipped into the restroom and locked herself in a stall, pulled the travel mirror out of her big bag. Everyone joked about it, but it suited her purposes. She stuck the mirror to the back of the stall door and brought out the makeup kit. Two shades darker and she looked a bit exotic. With the bob-cut black wig, she looked different enough that most people wouldn't pick her out of a lineup. She exchanged her flats for five-inch Choos and worked her arms into a light Chanel cardigan.

All of this was performed within three minutes of entering the bathroom. A short pale brunette had entered, but a tall tan woman with chic black hair exited.

She quickly made her way to The Joule and asked for the keys left by her husband. She was given the card and made her way through the boutique hotel, adrenaline starting to pump through her system.

Room 512 was a suite, but Phoebe didn't care about the clean lines or the lovely modern styles. She cared about the suitcase on the bed.

Sniper rifle. M4 carbine with a red dot scope.

She let her blood go cold. It wasn't the first time she'd been given this duty and it wouldn't be the last.

With steady hands, she put the rifle together and picked up the phone that had been left beside the case on the bed. She opened the door to the balcony. It was easy to see why the big boss had chosen this spot. It had a great view of the street below and she could stay inside the room. She pulled the table from its place and set up. The light of day would work to shield her from anyone trying to look in. She was cocooned in an elegant nest, waiting to sign her name on the target's chest.

She typed the words in and hit send. *In position.*

Through the window, she could see the street below and the giant weird eyeball someone had decided to place in a green space. Who put an eyeball in the middle of downtown?

Who was her target? In the end it didn't matter, but she was always curious. Her boss ran a tight ship. If he told her to kill someone, she did it because it was the right thing to do.

The phone pinged.

Kill order. Coming up the street in front of you. Picture attached.

She flipped her finger over the screen and her heart dropped.

Right there was a picture of a man. Blond and smiling, though his smile often didn't reach his eyes.

Jesse.

Oh, god, she had a kill order on Jesse Murdoch.

Her hands no longer steady, she lined up her shot…

Jesse and Phoebe and the entire McKay-Taggart team will return February 17, 2015 in *You Only Love Twice.*

Author's Note

I'm often asked by generous readers how they can help get the word out about a book they enjoyed. There are so many ways to help an author you like. Leave a review. If your e-reader allows you to lend a book to a friend, please share it. Go to Goodreads and connect with others. Recommend the books you love because stories are meant to be shared. Thank you so much for reading this book and for supporting all the authors you love!

Cherished: A Masters and Mercenaries Novella

Masters and Mercenaries 7.5
By Lexi Blake
Coming October 28, 2014
For more information, visit www.lexiblake.net.

A doctor living a double life

By day, Dr. Will Daley is one of Dallas's most eligible bachelors, but every night he dons his leathers as one of Sanctum's most desired Doms. He's sworn off looking for a long-term relationship but is captivated by the club's newest member, Bridget Slaten, even though they couldn't be more different. She comes from a world of privilege and he was raised in poverty. When he discovers she needs a date to her sister's wedding, he makes certain he's literally the only man for the job.

A woman no longer willing to live in the shadows

For most of her life, Bridget hid herself behind her laptop. She can write romantic, sensuous lives for her characters but not herself. Having Master Will as her date to the wedding is a thrilling prospect but he has a special request. He wants her to accept two weeks of his services as a Dom, a lover, and expert in BDSM, and that is an offer she can't refuse. Their sexual chemistry is undeniable, but it's in the tender moments that Bridget realizes she's falling for a man who might never trust her with his heart.

A love strong enough to cherish

Together in paradise for a week, Will realizes he can't imagine his life without Bridget. As the wedding approaches, ghosts from their past come back to haunt them and threaten to ruin the peace they've found. With everything exposed, they will have to risk it all to claim the love that can set them both free.

You Only Love Twice

Masters and Mercenaries 8
By Lexi Blake
Coming February 17, 2015
For more information, visit www.lexiblake.net.

A woman on a mission

Phoebe Graham is a specialist in deep cover espionage, infiltrating the enemy, observing their practices, and when necessary eliminating the threat. Her latest assignment is McKay-Taggart Security Services, staffed with former military and intelligence operatives. They routinely perform clandestine operations all over the world but it isn't until Jesse Murdoch joins the team that her radar starts spinning. Unfortunately so does her head. He's gorgeous and sweet and her instincts tell her to trust him but she's been burned before, so he'll stay where he belongs—squarely in her sights.

A man on the run

Since the moment his Army unit was captured by jihadists, Jesse's life has been a nightmare. Forced to watch as those monsters tortured and killed his friends and the woman he loved, something inside him snapped. When he's finally rescued, everyone has the same question—why did he alone survive? Clouded in accusations and haunted by the faces of those he failed, Jesse struggles in civilian life until McKay-Taggart takes him in. Spending time with Phoebe, the shy and beautiful accountant, makes him feel human for the first time in forever. If someone so innocent and sweet could accept him, maybe he could truly be redeemed.

A love they never expected

When Phoebe receives the order to eliminate Jesse, she must choose between the job she's dedicated her life to and the man who's stolen her heart. Choosing Jesse would mean abandoning everything she believes in, and it might mean sharing his fate because a shadowy killer is dedicated to finishing the job started in Iraq.

Their Virgin Mistress

Masters of Ménage 7

By Shayla Black and Lexi Blake

Coming April 14, 2015

For more information, visit www.lexiblake.net.

One wild night leads to heartache…

Tori Glen loves her new job as an image consultant for Thurston-Hughes Inc. The trouble is, she's also in love with the three brothers who own it, Oliver, Rory, and Callum. They're handsome, successful, aristocratic, and way out of this small-town Texas girl's league. So she remains a loyal professional—until the night she finds a heartbroken Oliver desperate for someone to love. Tori knows she should resist…but it's so tempting to give in.

And a desperate plan…

Callum and Rory have denied their desire for Tori, hoping she'll heal their older brother, who was so brutalized by his late wife's betrayal. But when Oliver cruelly turns Tori away in the harsh light of day, she tenders her resignation. Rory and Callum realize that to save their brother, they must embrace the unconventional sort of family they've always wanted—with Tori at its center. And it all starts with seducing her…

That could lead to happily ever after—or murder.

Isolated with the brothers at an elegant English country manor, they begin awakening Tori to the most sensual of pleasures. But consumed with regret, Oliver won't be denied the chance to embrace the only woman worth the risk of loving again. What begins as a rivalry veers toward the future they've only dared to dream of. But a stranger is watching and waiting for a chance at revenge. Can the brothers come together to embrace the woman they love and defeat a killer?

Dear Readers,

I was asked earlier this year to beta read a novella by Christopher Rice. I was familiar with his earlier work in thrillers and horror, but this was his first foray into my world—erotic romance. Better than that, I was told this story was a ménage. I kind of love ménage. So I agreed because we're in the same project and I love his other work.

What I discovered was quite frankly my favorite work of erotic fiction I've read in a long time. *The Flame* is unique and beautiful and stunningly sensual. I hope you'll all give this new series a chance. I'm honored to give you your first glimpse at Christopher Rice's *The Flame*.

Much love,

Lexi

* * * *

The Flame
By Christopher Rice
Coming November 11, 2014
For more information, visit www.1001DarkNights.com.

New York Times bestselling author Christopher Rice presents his first work of erotic romance.

It only takes a moment…

Cassidy Burke has the best of both worlds, a driven and successful husband and a wild, impulsive best friend. But after a decadent Mardi Gras party, Cassidy finds both men pulling away from her. Did the three of them awaken secret desires during a split-second of alcohol-fueled passion? Or is Mardi Gras a time when rules are meant to be broken without consequence?

Only one thing is for certain—the chill that's descended over her marriage, and her most important friendship, will soon turn into a deep freeze if she doesn't do something. And soon.

Light this flame at the scene of your greatest passion and all your desires will be yours.

The invitation stares out at her from the window of a French Quarter boutique. The store's owner claims to have no knowledge of the strange candle. But Cassidy can't resist its intoxicating scent or the challenge written across its label in elegant cursive. With the strike of a match and one tiny flame, she will call forth a supernatural being with the ultimate power—the power to unchain the heart, the power to remove the fear that stands between a person and their truest desires.

* * * *

From *THE FLAME* by Christopher Rice ...

The house is dark, save for the sparkling footprints dotting the foyer's hardwood floor. Gold flecks swim in each one, waterborne siblings of the luminescent particles that swirled through the candle's halo as soon as she lit the wick. They have to be Andrew's footprints, but she's shouted his name several times and he hasn't answered.

For the second time that day, Cassidy is soaked from head to toe and questioning the nature of reality. The rain roused her after she lost consciousness. By then, the candle's glass container was completely empty, as if someone had wiped it clean of every last drop of wax while she'd drifted between sleep and waking, utterly drained by the most powerful orgasm she'd ever experienced.

LSD. Acid. Or maybe that Datura stuff Native Americans use for vision quests. Whatever it is, I'm still feeling it.

"Cassidy!"

She cries out. The front door is still open. Shane stands on the porch, soaked from head to toe. When she sees the tiny gold flakes dripping from his earlobes and the tip of his nose, pooling slightly in the hollows of his eyes, her breath leaves her.

Wide-eyed, his jaw tense, he closes the distance between them. He runs an index finger along her forearm and turns up a fingertip glistening with the same gold particles that highlight his face, that swim in the footprints all around them.

"What's going on?" Shane whispers.

"I don't know…" she says. It feels like a lie.

It *is* a lie. She accepted the invitation written on that note; that's what's happening. She lit Bastian Drake's candle at the scene of her greatest desire and now…and now…

Shane's lips are inches from hers. Rain swirls through the open door behind him. Flashes of lightning turn the branches outside into giant claws. But they don't frighten her. They do, however, seem to send a word of warning: *Stay inside. It's not safe to run. The answer, if there is one, is inside this house.*

"Andrew…." she whispers. "We have to find Andrew."

Shane follows her upstairs with bounding strides.

The master bedroom is empty. When she sees the alarm clock's blank screen, she realizes the power's out. She's about to scream her husband's name again when she sees him in the doorway. He is naked and dripping wet. Streaks of gold outline his nipples. They travel the hard ridges of his obliques and fringe the heft of his cock, which jerks from his sudden arousal. The sight of Cassidy and Shane standing together in the shadowed bedroom makes her husband instantly and powerfully hard. While it's too dark to see his face, she can see his muscular chest rising and falling with deep, sustained breaths. He always breathes like that when he's getting ready to pounce. To lick. To taste. To ravish.

"Get on the bed, Cassidy," he says, his voice low and deep.

Yes. Please. Now. If it's a mistake, I'll blame the candle. I'll blame Bastian Drake. But I want it now. Both of them. Here. Now.

In a flash of lightning, she sees Shane's expression. It's a portrait of astonishment and desire as he looks back and forth between the two of them. An expression just like the one he wore when he kissed her for the first time. Not fear, but a kind of dazed wonder over the fact that life could suddenly deliver something so unexpected and all consuming.

When Andrew grips the back of Shane's neck, this visual reminder of their moment at The Roquelaure House enflames her desire. Then her husband says, "Take your panties off, Cassidy," and it feels as if her skin has become a thin layer of radiant heat can no longer contain the desire coursing through her veins.

Hands shaking, Cassidy unbuttons her skirt, kicks her way out of it. It turns into a brief struggle because she can't look away from what's happening in front of her. Bent at the waist, Shane runs his tongue up the side of Andrew's body, following a slender thread of gold all the way up to her husband's pecs. When he reaches Andrew's nipple, Shane sucks it briefly, loud enough to make a pop.

Her husband's low throaty laugh is gentle. Shane's desire for Andrew is a feeling on Cassidy's skin, a tingly blanket, as if invisible hands have just lightly slapped her thighs, squeezed her breasts. As if she is being tweaked and teased and tested by the newness of what they're about to do, by the delicious danger of it. And while everything about Shane's posture says he wants to suck her husband's tongue from in between his lips, Andrew teases him, gripping the back of his neck, holding their mouths inches apart.

"You're afraid, aren't you?" Andrew asks. "Both of you. You've always been afraid of how much you want each other. Afraid of how it doesn't fit into a neat little box." Their lips inches apart now, the two men she loves the most seem connected by a current of fearless desire, a current fueled by her exposed sex, by her wild passion for them both. "Well… *enough*! Both of you. Enough already. I've had enough of watching the two of you together – "

His voice is a low growl and his wording makes her tense. If Andrew is about to punish them, why is he still stroking the back of Shane's neck? Why is he unbuckling Shane's belt with his other hand?

" – All that hunger between you two, and it's got nowhere to go. Well, not anymore. I'm going to give it somewhere to go. I'm going to fuck both of you into loving each other the way you need to. And I don't give a damn if there isn't a name for what I'm about to do. We have *our* names. And that's good enough. Now get on your knees, Shane. It's time for you to taste my wife."

Forbidden Legacy

***Trinity Masters*, Book 4**

By Mari Carr and Lila Dubois

Now Available!

For more information, visit maricarr.com.

An enigmatic leader…

Harrison Adams has served as leader of the Trinity Masters for a decade. He's always placed the group above his own needs—even when it comes to the one woman who calls to him. When a dangerous threat to the secret society surfaces, Harrison sets a plan in motion that could save the organization, but it comes with a price.

A steadfast woman…

Alexis turned down an invitation to join the Trinity Masters, afraid to relinquish control over her life, her future…her heart. That rejection means night after night of unrequited lust as she and Harrison are forced to ignore their desires. Her heart aching, she throws herself into her job and her difficult working relationship with her boss, Michael. He's attractive and maddening, but Alexis has zero plans to give in to the crazy chemistry between them.

An improper proposal…

Harrison asks Alexis to experiment in a ménage relationship with him and she agrees unable to take another moment of longing for him. Perhaps with a third around she'll be able to keep her heart intact. She is completely unaware their third will be her infuriating boss, Michael. She couldn't have known how giving herself to them would inflame her desires. Or how much she would enjoy submitting to them.

But when an evil man looking for revenge sets his sights on Harrison, time is the one thing none of them have. And it soon becomes apparent Harrison's forbidden legacy could destroy them all…

* * * *

He'd waited too damn long for her. Now that he had her in his arms, he wasn't holding back, wasn't denying himself this taste. He deepened the kiss, pulling her closer. Alexis accepted the embrace, put her own spin on it as she nipped at his lower lip, demanding access to his mouth. Her tongue stroked his, betraying her hunger.

Harrison grasped her hair, tugging at her long auburn tresses. She moaned when he increased the pressure. Then he twisted their bodies—careful not to break the connection of their mouths—as he pushed her against the desk.

Alexis placed her hands on his shoulders, shoving him away. "What are you saying, Harry?"

"I want you."

She shook her head, clearly confused. "Is this a proposal?"

His patience was in tatters. Now that he'd opened the gate, the time for conversation was over. There was nothing more to say. At this moment, action took precedence to words. He unbuttoned her blouse.

"Harry." She insisted on an answer.

"What if it is, Lex?" He kissed her before she could respond. He didn't want her answer. Couldn't stand to hear her refuse or deny this. He wouldn't let her lie to him. Not now. Not ever. He moved his hands, pushing them beneath her skirt.

"Damn you," she muttered against his lips. "I didn't lock the door."

He grinned. "Don't move." He crossed the room and engaged the lock. Upon his return, he lifted her and urged her to sit on the desk as he pushed her skirt higher.

She worked the knot of his tie loose and then started to unbutton his shirt. Three buttons down, she got fed up and simply ripped the last few free, dragged the cotton away and dropped it to the floor.

Harrison kissed her once more, pressed his lips hard against hers, demanding, unyielding. He reached beneath her skirt and pushed her panties aside so he could draw his fingers along the slit between her legs. She was hot, wet, ready.

Alexis leaned away from him, gasping for breath. “Stop. Wait. We can’t do this.”

He tugged her blouse open, slid it off and found the clasp of her bra. “We’re not stopping.”

“Harry.” She half-heartedly tried to push his hands away, but they soon fell to her sides when he freed her breasts. Bending forward, he sucked one turgid nipple into his mouth roughly.

“God.” She gripped his hair, attempting to hold him to her. Harrison had never been called a gentle lover. He’d always been careful to choose bedmates who liked their pleasure laced with pain.

Alexis threw her head back, digging her fingers into his scalp. “Harder, Harry. God, suck it harder. Need to feel…”

He gave her what she wanted. And more. He cupped the flesh of her breasts, kneading firmly as he continued to draw on her nipples, increasing the suction until she cried out so loudly there was no way his secretary wouldn’t know what was happening in his office.

He tried to make himself give a damn, but he didn’t. Instead, he doubled his efforts until she moaned again.

Once more, he reached beneath her skirt and found the elastic waistband of her thong and garter belt. His actions jerked her back to reality.

“We can’t do this, Harry.”

“Of course we can. This is long overdue. Stop pretending you don’t understand that.”

His To Take

A Wicked Lovers Novel
By Shayla Black
Coming March 3, 2015
For more information, visit www.ShaylaBlack.com.

Racing against time, NSA Agent Joaquin Muñoz is searching for a little girl who vanished twenty years ago with a dangerous secret. Since Bailey Benson fits the profile, Joaquin abducts the beauty and whisks her to the safety of Club Dominion—before anyone can silence her for good.

At first, Bailey is terrified, but when her captor demands information about her past, she's stunned. Are her horrific visions actually distant memories that imperil all she holds dear? Confined with Joaquin in a place that echoes with moans and breathes passion, he proves himself a fierce protector, as well as a sensual Master who's slowly crawling deeper in her head…and heart. But giving in to him might be the most delicious danger of all.

Because Bailey soon learns that her past isn't the only mystery. Joaquin has a secret of his own—a burning vengeance in his soul. The exposed truth leaves her vulnerable and wondering how much about the man she loves is a lie, how much more is at risk than her heart. And if she can trust him to protect her long enough to learn the truth.

* * * *

"…What about you? You're with another government agency, so you're here to . . . what? Be my lover? Does Uncle Sam think you need to crawl between my legs in order to watch over me?"

Joaquin ground his jaw. She was hitting low, and the logical part of him understood that she was hurt, so she was lashing out at the messenger because she didn't have anyone else. But that didn't stop his temper from getting swept up in her cyclone of emotion. "I'm not here on anyone's orders. In fact, I'll probably be fired for pursuing this case because Tatiana Aslanov isn't on my boss's radar. When it became obvious the agency intended to do nothing, I couldn't leave you to that horrific death. So here we are. But let me clue you in, baby girl. Uncle Sam doesn't tell me who to fuck. I can't fake an erection, even for the sake of God and country. That kiss we almost shared? That was me wanting you because just being in the same room with you makes me want to strip off everything you're wearing and impale you with every inch I've got."

When he eased closer to Bailey, she squared her shoulders and raised her chin. "Don't come near me."

That defiance made him wish again that he was a spanking kind of guy. He'd really like to melt that starch in her spine. If she wasn't going to let him comfort her, he'd be more than happy to adjust her attitude with a good smack or ten on her ass, then follow it up with a thorough fucking. A nice handful of orgasms would do them both a world of good.

"I am so done with people lying to me," she ground out.

That pissed him off. "You think I'm lying to you? About which part? Your parents being agents? That I'm sorry? Or that my cock is aching to fill your sweet little pussy until you dig your nails into my back and wail out in pleasure?"

Her face turned pink. "You're not sorry about any of this. I'm also not buying your sudden desire bullshit."

"I will be more than happy to prove you wrong right now." He reached for the button of his jeans. "I'm ready if you are."

In some distant corner of his brain, Joaquin realized that combating her hurt with challenge wasn't going over well. On the other hand, something about arguing with her while he'd been imagining her underneath him hadn't just gotten his blood flowing, but boiling. If fucking her would, in any way, prove to her that he wasn't lying, he was beyond down with getting busy. If she let him, he'd give it to her hard and wicked—and repeatedly.

"No!" She managed to look indignant, but her cheeks had gone rosy. The pulse at her neck was pounding. Her nipples poked at her borrowed shirt angrily.

He put his hands on his hips. If she looked down, she'd see

his straining zipper. "Do you still think I'm lying?"

"I'm done with this conversation."

"If you're telling yourself you don't want me at all, then you're the one lying."

"Pfft. You might know facts about me on paper, but you don't know me."

"So if I touched your pussy right now, you wouldn't be wet?"

He'd always liked a good challenge. It was probably one of the reasons he loved his job. But facing off with her this way made his blood sing, too.

"No." She shook her head a bit too emphatically. "And you're not touching me to find out. Leave me alone." "You're worried that I'd find you juicy.

You're afraid to admit that I turn you on." He stalked closer, his footfalls heavy, his eyes narrowing in on her.

"Stay back," she warned—but her eyes said something else entirely.

"Tell me you're not attracted to me." He reached out, his strike fast as a snake's, and gripped her arms. He dragged her closer, fitting her lithe little body against him and holding in a groan when she brushed over his cock. "Tell me you want me to stop. Remember, you don't like liars. I don't, either."

She didn't say a word, struggled a bit for show. Mostly, she parted her lips and panted. Her cheeks heated an even deeper rose. Her chest heaved. Never once did she look away from him. "I'm involved with someone else."

"If you think whatever you've got going with Blane is going to stop me . . ." He didn't bother to finish his sentence; he just laughed.

"So you're not listening to me say 'no'? You're not respecting my feelings for another guy?"

"Let's just say I'm proving my sincerity to you." He tightened his grip. When she gasped and her stare fell to his lips, triumph raced through his veins. "I'm also testing you. That pretty mouth of yours might lie to me, but your kisses won't."

Joaquin didn't give her a chance to protest again. Normally, he would have. Women 101 was never to proceed without express consent, but this thick air of tension electrifying his blood and seizing his lungs was something entirely new and intoxicating. Their fight seemed to be helping Bailey forget her shock and sadness, not to mention the fact that it revved her, too. She wasn't immune to him—not by a long shot. Thank fuck.

Thrusting a fist in her hair, he pinned her in place and lowered his head.

About Lexi Blake

Lexi Blake lives in North Texas with her husband, three kids, and the laziest rescue dog in the world. She began writing at a young age, concentrating on plays and journalism. It wasn't until she started writing romance that she found success. She likes to find humor in the strangest places. Lexi believes in happy endings no matter how odd the couple, threesome or foursome may seem. She also writes contemporary Western ménage as Sophie Oak.

Connect with Lexi online:

Facebook: Lexi Blake
Twitter: https://twitter.com/authorlexiblake
Website: www.LexiBlake.net

Sign up for Lexi's newsletter at www.lexiblake.net.

Made in the USA
Middletown, DE
13 August 2015